MW01153779

Complementary Colors

Complementary Colors

Copyright 2014 by Adrienne Wilder

Cover design by Adrienne Wilder

Photo by Dan Skinner

Publisher: Adrienne Wilder

Other books by Adrienne Wilder

www.AdrienneWilder.com

Urban Fantasy

City of Dragons

Blood Bonds

And of Flesh and Blood

Lesser Bred

Stained

Marked

The God Code

The Nephilim Prophecy

The Gray Zone

To Adam With Love

Worth

Skin Deep

Darwin's Theory

Pain

Secrets

Promises

Lost

Found

He Speaks Dead

Urban Sci-Fi

The Others Project

Seven

Contemporary

JACK

Due out 2014

In The Absence Of Light-Contemporary

The Others Project-Urban Sci-Fi

Thirteen

The God Code-Urban Fantasy

Forever Darkling

City of Dragons-Urban Fantasy

The Oracle

Currently in the works

The Sicario-Contemporary

An Accountant, A Red Neck,

And A Unicorn Walk Into A Bar-Fantasy

The Others Project-Urban Sci-Fi

Nine

Four

The list of upcoming books may change without notice.

This book is dedicated to you

There are no silly dreams
Chase them
Catch them
Live them
Believe in yourself because I do

Be Extraordinary

Acknowledgements:

Thank you to Adriana Ruud for your help with the English to Spanish translations, Varian Krylov, Louis Stevens, and Annabel Joseph for beta reading this MS.

Thank you Sharon Stogner for your content edits and Jason Bradly for your final edits.

Larry and Rachel Howell for putting up with me. James Tuck Jr. for always being tough when I couldn't and never doubting me, when it was all I could do.

Also a very special thank you to all the reviewers who review my stories. Know that even when a rating isn't favorable, I still appreciate you giving your time and talent to writing up a review. Your insight has on more than one occasion, taught me something about my writing. Thank you for that.

To the reader:

There are too many of you to name, but I want you to know I have read all your emails, responded, and appreciate every word you send. I could never give you the appreciation you deserve. All I can try and do to show how much you mean is to keep writing books you will enjoy. I will do my best not to let you down.

And last, but definitely not least in my line of "thank yous" is, Edie Marshal who has endured great suffering for the sake of saving others. I owe you my life.
Thank you.

While the story within these pages is 100% fiction, the mental illnesses represented are not. Millions of Americans suffer from mental illness. What's more upsetting is the stigma surrounding mental illness keeps so many of them from seeking out treatment and the lack of resources keeps those who do look for help, from being able to afford it.

Mental illness affects people of all ages, races, religions, and financial status. And millions of those people will die because the only way they think they can escape the pain is to take their own life. Many victims of suicide are Veterans and those in the LGBT community.

Because so many people can benefit from having resources in a time of crisis, a minimum of 10% of sales from each book will go to the American Foundation for Suicide Prevention. With every thousand copies sold I will add an additional 1% until I reach 25% of all monies made.

This donation will be done in the memory of all those who have been lost to suicide.
Friends.
Family.
Total strangers.

For more information about the American Foundations for Suicide Prevention please visit, http://www.afsp.org

And no matter what you think, someone out there cares.

Chapter One

I knew he didn't belong the moment I saw him.

He wasn't cut by money or shaped by political interests, and the rental he wore was a bad joke in the ocean of Versace suits and Chanel ball gowns, fitting him tight across the shoulders and short in the arms. A belt held up his pants, and the waves of extra fabric did nothing to accentuate the ass I knew was just as perfect as the rest of him.

I drank my champagne while the stranger picked his way through the clumps of people gathered in front of the hideous paintings I had on display.

"Paris darling, Mr. Darcy was asking you about one of your works." Julia put her hand on my arm. I ignored my sister and Mr. Darcy. Whatever it was he wanted say to me, I'd heard it before; *Mind blowing, so unique, see the passion, the fire*, and my favorite, *it speaks to me*.

Bullshit.

Only one person could see the dirty secret hidden within the lines, the color, the violence.

Me.

I handed Julia my empty glass.

She tightened her grip on my arm. "These people came a long way to meet you."

They always came a long way to meet me. Even if it was a block away.

"Bathroom," I said. Julia frowned. I think she knew I was lying but didn't want to call me out on it in front of her friends. I peeled away her fingers. "If you don't mind, of course." I slipped into the crowd.

Julia would give Mr. Darcy and his flavor-of-the-year wife some excuse on my behalf. Then she'd slay them with her silver tongue, and by the end of the night, they'd write a check for some ungodly amount and buy a piece of hell I'd spewed out into the world.

They'd hang it in their country home or put it in their yacht. They'd smile and laugh and remain deaf to the confession screaming to be told.

Heat from the track lighting pressed down on my shoulders. Greetings cast out by guests floated in shades of black and gray.

I followed the stranger's trail of color all the way to the back of the gallery. He disappeared around a partition and through a door. I checked to see if anyone was watching before I went in.

Cold fluorescents replaced track lighting, and the hum of the ventilation system snuffed out a burst of laughter. There were only two doors in the maintenance hall, besides the one that shut behind me.

A deep mechanical sound chugged from behind the one left open. I slipped inside and turned the knob so I could control the catch.

The man crouched beside an opening in one of the large metal units. Even on his knees, I could tell he was about my height, but his shoulders were wide and his limbs were thick.

I hoped that trait didn't stop at his legs and arms.

After a few minutes, he seemed satisfied and replaced the panel. When he stood, I had a brief glimpse of the curve of his ass when his slacks tightened.

He turned and dropped the tools he held. His hip hit the metal hull of the unit, and it boomed.

"Jesus Christ. You scared the shit out of me."

A five o'clock shadow dusted his jaw, hardening his features enough to make him look dangerous. And there was already no doubt left in my mind that he could kill me if he wanted to.

He wiped his hands with a rag from his pocket. Scars crossed the knuckles of his callused fingers. The thought of his rough grip on my body left me hard.

"I replaced the coil." The sound of his voice wrapped me in red, and tied me up with gold. "That should relieve some of the strain on the unit. It's pretty old, though." He put his tools into a toolbox. "You might want to consider replacing it."

I engaged the lock on the door.

He followed me with his eyes as I made a half circle around him. His physical appearance didn't make him alluring. It was how he carried himself. Like a man who was one with the world and not above it. I grazed a look up and down his body.

"I'll send you a bill." He reached for his toolbox.

I got in the way, trapping him against air conditioning unit.

"Is there something else you ne—" He cleared his throat. "Need?"

"Are you afraid of me?"

He pulled himself to his full height. "Do I have a reason to be?"

"That depends."

"On what?"

"On how much the idea of fucking me appeals to you." I tilted my head in a way that made my bangs slide over one eye. Like the smile I gave him, it was something I'd perfected.

I massaged his cock through the material of his slacks. The heavy bulge swelled beyond my palm and fingers.

"So," I said. "Are you afraid?"

The black of his pupils swallowed the pale green of his eyes.

"I take that as a no." I undid his belt, the button on his pants, and pulled down the zipper.

His boxer briefs trapped the thick length of his dick against his thigh. I set it free and kneeled. The faint scent of cologne mixed with the headier flavor of musk made my mouth water.

The man watched me with a cautious gaze.

"I'm not going to bite you. Unless, of course, you want me to." I swiped my tongue across the plum-sized head, collecting a bitter tear from the tip.

His nostrils flared.

I did it again, taking the time to tease the slit.

He parted his lips, and his eyelids fluttered closed.

I traced the glans, then chased the movement with a light scrape of teeth.

A shudder ran up his body, and he dropped his head back.

I took him as deep as I could. He grabbed the back of my head and thrust his hips. Just as quickly, he jerked his hands away.

I put them back. When he didn't close his grip, I squeezed his wrists. The man wound his fingers in my bangs, and I tugged on his thighs.

There was only a moment of hesitation before his body took over and he fucked my mouth, stretching my jaw so wide it threatened to lock. Tears ran down my cheeks, and black spots danced before my eyes. The impact to the back of my throat ached. I welcomed the sense of suffocation because it made things real for me.

"Fucking hell." He huffed out desperate breath after desperate breath. "Don't stop, whatever you do, please…" I rolled his balls with my fingers. He rewarded me with a string of incoherent words. His grip tightened, and a rush of bitter fluid filled my mouth. I couldn't swallow fast enough.

When he stepped back, cum poured over my lips and dripped down my chin.

There were shadows in his pale green eyes. "Why?"

I stood. "Do I need a reason?" I wiped the cum from my chin and sucked my fingers clean one at a time. Then I pulled him down until our lips met and plunged my tongue into his mouth. His attempt to keep up with my hunger was ill coordinated, and the kiss turned sloppy and wet.

"Come home with me." With the way he watched me, I knew he would. "Is there a back way out?"

I wasn't in the mood to deal with Julia's drama. I was in the mood to be fucked.

"Yeah." He fixed his clothes. "The other room has an exit to the alley in the back."

Outside, the sickly scent of rotting garbage and wet asphalt clung to the damp air. I dragged the stranger to the line of cabs parked along the curb. If I took the limo, the driver would tattle on me to Julia. She wrote the checks so she was the only one he was loyal to.

I opened the door, and he yanked me around. The handle pulled out of my grip, and the door was slammed shut by the weight of my body. The kiss he delivered was just as sloppy as before, but there was determination now. He was infected with my madness. It infected every man I took to my bed. The fever always disappeared by morning, but until then, I made the best of it.

I hooked a leg around his thigh and ground against his body. His cock hardened. Well hung and fast recovery. I'd hit the jackpot.

He attacked my neck, grazing my skin with his teeth. I had to get him home. "In the cab."

He clawed at the door handle. As soon as he opened it, I shoved him inside and straddled his thighs.

"Hey." The cabby turned. "This isn't the hourly motel."

12

I threw a wad of cash over the seat.

"The Royaute Building." I caressed the stranger's jaw. The shadow of his beard rasped against my fingertips. "Now where were we?"

With a few pulls, I had his tie off and the front of his shirt open. Dark hair dusted his chest, thickening in the center of his pecs and forming a line down his stomach before disappearing under the waist of his slacks.

I pinched his nipples hard enough to make him whimper.

The man sank his fingers into my long bangs and pawed at the shorter hair on the back of my head.

I rocked against him. "Touch me."

His hands followed his gaze down my body. He stopped at the juncture of my legs and rubbed my cock through my pants.

I hissed. "Yeah, like that. Just like that."

He fumbled with the button, and my cock spilled out into his trembling hand.

I pumped my hips, and he chased the head of my dick with his thumb through the tunnel of his fist.

Halogen lights beat against the interior, etching out the details of his parted lips, his wanting stare, the lines of his nose and jaw.

The clumsy kisses we started with vanished. He worked his mouth against mine, meeting the tilt of my head with his own.

"Mmmm—feels good."

He tightened his grip.

"Even better." I sucked on a tender spot near his ear. He responded by dragging his nail across my slit. "Oh, fuck." A prickling rush spread through my limbs. "Harder, squeeze harder."

His eyebrows came together, and reluctance shadowed his eyes.

"Please." I wrapped my arms around his neck. "I need this. I need you."

He did, and every beat of my heart was followed by an ache in my cock. I moved up on my knees so I could slam into his fist. The squeak of the vinyl seat accented my breathing.

"I want you inside me." I nipped his earlobe. The movements of his hand stuttered. "I want you to fuck me until I can't walk, can't see, can't breathe."

13

He huffed against my neck.

A few more thrusts and the pain I begged from him ignited the wildfire inside me. I didn't even try to be quiet. I yelled, I shouted, I keened, and shot all over the front of his cheap suit. The euphoria withdrew, leaving me limp in his arms. He stroked my hair, and every so often, he brushed a kiss against my temple.

It was then I realized the cab had parked at the curb in front of my building. The rearview mirror reflected the cabby's pale face and sweaty brow. There was a crease in his bottom lip from chewing on it.

I caught his gaze, and his eyes widened.

"Did you like the show?"

The rush of red to his cheeks was instant. I laughed and threw another hundred dollars at him.

The stranger and I fled from the cab.

My unbuttoned shirt fluttered around me as we ran across the lobby. No one was there but the doorman. Unlike the chauffeur, I could trust Bill. The thousand dollar Christmas bonus I gave him every year ensured his silence. Considering the things he'd seen me do, he earned every penny. This year, I would double it.

I pushed the stranger inside the elevator, and his shoulders hit the wall. I seized his mouth, worked his lips, and raped him of his breath. In return, he cradled my face and fed from my mouth with long gentle strokes of his tongue. His green eyes burned with something unfamiliar to me. Or maybe it was just the lighting and it was nothing at all.

That's what I wanted to believe. Maybe I could have believed. But then he traced a finger down my cheek, and I found myself struggling to hold his gaze.

The doors opened.

"I take it this is your floor?"

Was it? Behind me, the dimly lit foyer with its cream-colored marble.

I nodded.

He moved, and whatever spell he'd woven shattered. We were barely inside the studio before I shed my jacket, threw my shirt over a chair, and kicked off my shoes.

He stood in the doorway. His eyes followed the movement of my hands as I traced the thin line of hair running down the middle of my stomach.

My pants slid down my hips. I massaged my cock through my boxers. "Don't make me wait."

The width of his shoulders, his height, it expanded in front of me. He stalked me in long powerful strides, wearing the expression of a man about to fight for the last drop of water. Along the way, he worked the remaining buttons on his shirt.

One day when I did this, when I brought a stranger home with me, he was going to be a serial killer or just some maniac who would beat me and leave me for dead. The thought that this might be that day sent a shiver through my body.

I shed my boxers. "You don't talk much, do you?"

He seized me, one hand on my throat, the other smashed against my ear. Fear ran in cold rivulets over my skin.

"I thought you wanted me to fuck you."

"Yeah."

"We don't need to talk to do that."

I grinned because he was so goddamned right.

We tumbled into my workbench. A palette and tubes of oil paint hit the floor. He bent me over the wide slat of wood, and my elbow caught a jar full of brushes, ejecting the contents. Wooden handles ticked off their landing.

He trapped me with his thighs and brushed his hands over the globes of my ass. The buckle on his belt clanked against the tile floor and the length of his cock slid down the crack of my ass. He moved his powerful hands up my back and over my shoulders.

I widened my legs, offering myself. The deep breath he took was exhaled on a growl.

Heated flesh pressed against my hole. Slick with precum, he only needed to push.

He hesitated so I grabbed a jar of vegetable oil I used to thin the paints. "Here."

The metal lid scraped against the glass. "How much?"

Was he serious? "As much as you think it will take."

A stream of oil ran down my crack. "That doesn't mean the whole damn jar." I think he apologized, but I was too drunk on the need for release to be sure.

He put the jar out of firing range of my elbows. Then returned the thick head of his cock to my opening. He rubbed the puckered flesh but didn't push hard enough to enter.

"Goddamn it, will you fuck me already?"

He increased the pressure enough to make the ring of muscle give, but once again, not enough to breech my hole.

I slammed back, forcing my body to take his cock in one stroke. My insides clenched, and my ass burned. I'd forgotten how big he was.

His weight pressed against my back, and he made small hesitant thrusts. I writhed, trying to take control, but he pinned my wrists above my shoulders.

"More."

He peppered the back of my neck with small kisses.

I bucked. "Damn you, fuck me or get off."

He froze. Would he walk away?

The weight on my back disappeared. I was about to tell him to wait. Then he dug his fingers into my hips and thrust so hard the bench moved.

Over and over, he slammed into me, knocking the air from my lungs.

I think I said faster, or harder, or maybe nothing but some sort of animalistic howl. Whatever it was, he understood.

He pulled me by my shoulder. The change in angle allowed his long thick cock to reach parts of me that were never meant to be touched. My vision darkened, and every beat of my heart fought the constriction in my chest.

I went beyond pleasure, into some realm where sensations worked like a creature eating me alive. All I could do was suck in air through my gaping mouth and pray I wouldn't pass out.

Droplets of sweat rained down on my back with every violent surge of his hips. He readjusted his grip, lowering his body, tilting me farther over. Then he pummeled my ass so hard I was lifted to my toes.

16

His thigh muscles rippled down the back of my legs. Some of his weight returned, pushing me forward. Every hot, ragged breath that escaped him blew against the skin between my shoulders.

Static wove around my bones, and the cool air in the studio burned away.

"Almost," I said. "Almost there."

The edge of the bench kept me from reaching down and finishing myself off. I needed him; harder, faster, relentless.

He gave me everything.

His rhythm broke, and he buried a cry into the back of my neck. At the same time I buried my shout against the table. A second later, the pulse of his cock echoed through me.

Then the quiet of the studio blanketed us, and he cradled me against his body.

I don't know why, but I put my hand over his. And I didn't fight it when our fingers entwined.

After a long moment he said, "Do you have a shower?"

No one ever asked me that before, but then no one ever stayed beyond a quick fuck and the time it took to button their pants.

"Sure." I led tall, dark, and silent up the stairs.

He hesitated at the bathroom doorway, and his soft gaze wandered over me. Modesty was something I'd never had, but I found myself looking at anything but him.

"I thought you wanted a shower?"

"Yeah." He trailed a finger along the edge of the counter, touched the brass towel holders, then cast a look over the stone alcove where six shower heads pumped hot water into the air.

"I take it you like my bathroom."

"They still call something this fancy a bathroom?"

I pulled him into the shower, and water rolled over his shoulders, following the valleys of the muscle on his arms and chest.

"Tell me about yourself." Once again, the sound of his voice went right to my dick.

"What do you want to know?"

"You could start with your name."

"Paris Duvoe. And you?"

"Roy Callahan." Soaking wet and surrounded by steam, we shook hands.

17

He grinned. "I guess we forgot the formalities."

I picked up a bottle of body wash and a cloth. "What do you mean?"

"People normally exchange salutations before..." He jabbed his thumb over his shoulder. "You know."

"Before fucking?"

He winced. "Yeah."

"Maybe where you come from." I smiled, but he didn't.

Roy took the bottle and washcloth from my hands.

He loaded up the rag with some sort of earthy smelling soap Alice bought. She picked out all the lotions, colognes, and aftershave. My other sister was all about making me look nice. Not the formal kind of nice, that was Julia's job, but the daily kind of presentation.

"Here," Roy said. "Turn around."

"You plan on fucking me against the wall?" Sex in the shower wasn't my favorite, but I never turned down sex in any location.

"No, I want to wash your back."

He ran the soap-swollen cloth over my skin. "You were serious."

"You sound surprised." His touch traveled down my body to the cleft of my ass. There was nothing sexual in the way he cleaned me.

I didn't know what to make of his actions so I faced the wall. His presence surrounded me in the hush of spraying water. A weight formed in my chest.

He said something.

"Huh?" I glanced back.

"Do you go to those art gatherings a lot?"

"You mean a showing?"

"Is that what they call them?"

"Yeah," I laughed. "But I like to refer to them as a communing of the socially constipated."

Roy swept the washcloth over my hip. He knelt and placed a searing kiss on my left ass cheek. Then he washed me all the way down to my toes.

"If you don't like them why do you go?"

I asked myself the same question every time Julia announced the schedule for my next showing. "The boss doesn't give me a choice."

18

"You work for the artist?"

"Sorta." I hid my grin against my arm.

He stood and turned me around. "Is he as much of a jerk as the curator says?"

I raised an eyebrow. "Hiram says he's a jerk?"

"The words he used were more colorful, but I'm pretty sure that's what he meant." Roy's eyebrows came together. "How did these happen?" He traced the line of fading bruises on my shoulder with his thumb.

"I probably ran into something."

He caressed a spot near my hip. "And here?"

What would he say if I told him? "Do you fix air conditioners full time?"

"I'm kind of a jack of all trades." Roy washed himself with a distracted efficiency.

"Are you married?" A lot of the men I took home were. They came with me because I would give them the kind of sex they couldn't get from their spouse. None of them had ever worried about the bruises. Why should they? I was nothing but a couple of holes waiting to be filled.

"No."

It didn't sound like the complete truth. "You sure?"

He finished rinsing and shut the water off. "I'm divorced."

"Kids?"

"God no."

"You don't like them?"

"They're okay. I just hate the idea of anyone being forced to live with…her."

The towels were folded on the counter. I handed one to Roy, but before I could grab another, he was drying me off.

"Boyfriend?"

His gaze flicked up and was gone again.

"It's not like I care." It was his problem if he got caught.

"No." He stood. "I haven't had the opportunity."

I threw my arms around his neck and toyed with the thick dark curls of his hair. "You make it sound like I'm the first man you've been with."

A dark flush spread up his face.

"Roy?"

He dried himself.

"You've never been with a man?"

He shrugged.

"Never?"

"Is it a requirement?" He folded the towel and looked around.

"Just toss it on the floor. The maid will get it. Or Alice."

"Are you married?"

I barked a laugh. "You've got to be kidding."

"Then who's Alice?"

"Why, are you jealous?" I walked into my bedroom. The bed was covered with black on red. Not silk or satin. I hated both. The rest of the room was occupied by a few pieces of furniture, a thick rug on the floor, and two of my personal paintings on the wall. They didn't harbor the terrible things that lived in the ones I sold. That's why Julia hated them.

"Alice is my other sister." I tossed myself on the bed. The first thing he saw when he walked out was me leaning back on my elbows, legs spread for him to admire or claim.

I watched his reflection in the mirrored ceiling for a moment. He stopped at the door still holding the towel.

His Adam's apple bobbed.

"I'm always up for more." I rubbed my cock and hiked up a heel on the edge of the mattress.

"Are you hungry?" Roy looked away.

"You mean food?"

"Yeah."

"There's probably something in the kitchen."

"You don't know?"

I sat up. "Alice does the shopping." I opened the bedside drawer. The pill bottles inside rattled.

I picked out the funny shaped pink ones. "You want some?" I held out the bottle.

"What is that?"

"Hell if I know." The pills tried to stick in my throat. I drank water from the bottle next to the clock.

"Then why are you taking them?"

"Because they make my mind bleed." Filtering out the thought-numbing guilt that accompanied the worst of the hallucinations let the colors flow. I didn't expect him to understand. Especially since I didn't.

I nodded at the pictures on the wall. "Bleed."

He turned, and I took the chance to admire the tight globes of his ass. There was a dimple above each cheek.

"Did you paint these?"

My grin was wasted on the back of his head. "Yep."

"They kind of remind me of the ones at the gallery."

"What makes them different?"

"They're better."

The room shrank around me. "Why are they better?"

"I was never much of an art student." He turned back around. "But I like the lines. The color. The white voids left on the canvas."

"And you didn't take art classes?"

"Not after the ninth grade."

"But you know they're better." Not just better. They were some of my best.

"Sure. The pictures are clearer."

I rolled to the end of the bed. "What pictures?"

Roy shook his head. "I'm probably imagining it. You know, like one of those ink blots."

I stood. "Tell me what you see?"

He glanced back at the canvas. "I see a woman cradling a child."

If he could see the beauty of these works, it meant he'd seen the sins carved in oil at the gallery. How could he stand to be in the same room with me, let alone touch me?

"Are you okay?"

My heart skipped against my ribs. Maybe he wasn't even real? "I'm fine."

"You're shaking." He touched my cheek. The warmth of his caress assured me he was made of flesh. "You shouldn't have taken those pills."

"No, no, that's not..." I gripped his forearms. My hands looked paper white against the golden brown of his skin. "Maybe food is a good idea. I haven't eaten today."

21

"All day?"

"I'm not going to starve."

Roy picked up my hand and petted the outline of my wrist bone under my skin.

I pulled away. "C'mon, I'll show you around."

He wrapped the towel around his waist and followed me back to the studio. Moonlight traced canvases and easels in silver lines. Pigment mixed with the headier scent of sex saturated the air. Everything that had been on the table where Roy fucked me, lay on the floor.

We reached the bottom of the stairs. "Wow."

"You've already seen this room."

"I wasn't really..." He took a few steps. "You're pretty serious about your art."

"You have no idea."

Roy scanned the room, touched a few things on the table, got something on his thumb and wiped it off on the towel. "If you're this serious, why don't you do one of those..." He snapped his fingers.

"Showings?"

"Yeah, that's the word."

"Who says I haven't?"

He stopped in front of a couple of pieces drying on their easels. "Can you turn on a light?"

I flipped the switch.

The darkness winked out, revealing half assembled frames, tubes of paint, and some of my finest brushes cluttering worktables. Rows of canvas filled the room with offensive color.

Roy clenched his eyes shut. "Those paintings at the gallery were yours, weren't they?"

I leaned back on one of the tables. Like the smile, how I stared, and used my bangs, it was well practiced.

"Those things I said about..."

"Being a jerk?"

"Yeah, that. I'm sorry."

"But you didn't say them, the curator did."

"I know, but—" Roy raked his gaze over me. I don't think he realized he licked his lips.

"You sure you only want a sandwich? You might be hungrier than you think."

The bulge in the front of his towel jumped.

"I think your cock agrees with me."

Roy gripped the edge of the terry cloth like it might run off. His cheeks reddened, and the sight made me ache. Who could have guessed embarrassment was such a turn-on?

Hell, maybe it was just the drugs.

I held out my hand. Roy took the offering, and I pulled him off balance. His weight pushed me into the edge of the workbench.

"You really weren't joking." I nipped his bottom lip.

"About what?"

"About ever being with another man."

"Why would I tell you that if it wasn't true?"

"No. I mean *never* being with another man."

"Is there any other kind of never?"

"Most guys at least experiment. Mutual masturbation, sucking each other off." I shrugged. "But you haven't."

"No." He brushed his fingertips up my arm, shoulder, neck, to my face. I sucked his thumb into my mouth.

The hard line of flesh hidden behind the towel pushed against my stomach.

"It's getting late," Roy said. "You should eat."

I released his thumb. "You'd rather have a meal than me on your cock?" I pinched one of his nipples. "I could use my mouth, or if you want, I could ride you." I traced the shell of his ear. "You know…there are so many places that feel good to be licked."

I would have paid Roy to let me rim him just to see his expression.

"Right now, you need to eat." The kindness in his eyes left me wishing for something to cover myself with. I slipped from his grasp.

Fancy pots hung from the ceiling in the green marble and chrome kitchen. A fridge as large as a walk-in closet occupied the niche in the counter to my left. I opened the door. Tupperware containers filled the middle shelf.

"Find anything?" Roy wrapped his arms around me and rested his chin on my shoulder.

At that point, I couldn't even be sure what it was I'd been looking for.

"You okay?" His words vibrated through my bones.

"Yeah, why?"

"You tensed."

I tried to find that flippant persona I was comfortable with, but he was gone. "It's the cold. I'm not exactly dressed for it."

"Do you want me to go back upstairs and find a robe?"

I coughed to have an excuse to pull away.

He patted me on the back.

"Sorry, swallowed wrong." The double meaning struck me, and I laughed so hard I had to grab the door to keep from falling. He reached into the fridge and took out a carton of eggs, block of cheese, and a few other items that were familiar but my addled brain was unable to give me the names at the moment.

He put the stuff on the counter and led me to the table. "Here, sit."

I was too high and too busy watching the colors surrounding him to argue. It was either that or his rugged features, wide shoulders, or…I ran my fingers along his collarbone. "I'm not really hungry."

"You need to eat."

He went back to the kitchen.

Like the living room, the dining room had a glass wall facing the heart of downtown. The lights on, the neighboring buildings were concealed behind the reflection of a dark haired man with lost eyes. The bones in his shoulders cut sharp lines to his thin arms. Men desired him, pined for him. With one look or pose, he could have them at his feet.

How could anyone want a creature so hideous? The kind of ugly that sank into the soul and birthed terrible things. The coward. The liar.

After a few minutes, Roy appeared with plates full of food. I stuck on my smile and melted into my chair. His cheeks reddened, and the bulge behind his towel thickened.

I loved men with quick recovery. Nothing worse than a limp noodle when you're wanting seconds, thirds, or whatever.

He glanced at the window. "Maybe we should put something on."

24

"We're twenty floors up. And if anyone wants to look, let them. I have nothing to hide, and you most certainly don't."

I picked up the fork on the edge of the plate. "Omelets?"

"They're easy, plus I'm pretty good at them."

"Wow, a man who's hung like a horse and can fix breakfast. I'm impressed."

Roy fumbled with his silverware.

"Fuck, you're actually embarrassed."

His smile waned.

"How the hell can you be embarrassed by having a huge dick? Do you know how many men would kill to have a piece of meat like that between their legs? All of them." I poked at the air between us with my fork. "I've been with a lot of men, few could compare."

A bite of omelet dangled from his fork. "Why so many?"

I tortured my food. "Because I like the feel of a cock in my ass or one in my mouth." I gave him a sly smile. "Even at the same time."

I'd never seen someone concentrate so hard on what they were eating. He cleared half his omelet in just a few bites.

I pushed the table back and straddled his lap before he could protest.

"You should be eating." His gaze said something different.

"Food is boring." I licked his lips. Salt, pepper, olive oil, and crisp eggs. My stomach growled.

He pulled the table back, speared a bite of food and held it up. "Here."

I stared.

"Eat, Paris."

Was this a trick?

"Please."

I accepted the gift. The mix of spices and cheese replaced the memory of his cum. "What did you put in this?" I sucked the oil from my bottom lip.

Roy fed me another bite. "Onions, peppers, mushrooms, cheese."

I started to say something. He took advantage of my parted lips and shoved in another bite.

I talked with my mouth full. "There was all that in the fridge?"

"Yep." He cut another piece.

25

"It's not food I'm hungry for." I ran my hand through his hair. "Please eat."

I kissed his chin, his cheek, then brushed our lips together. I fed him my sigh and devoured his gasp. I undid his towel before he had a chance to stop me. His cock was a rigid bar of fire in my hand. "I could suck you off."

His eyes widened.

"I think you like that idea." I ran my thumb over the thick head. "Or maybe you'd rather fuck me on the table."

He swallowed so hard his throat clicked.

"Yeah, I think you like that idea too." I twisted my grip. Precum smeared on my wrist. "I think your cock really likes that idea."

Roy ran his knuckles lightly down my cheek.

What I wanted was for him to hold me down and fuck me until I couldn't walk.

He cupped my face. "You are so beautiful."

"Roy," I stroked him, and he fluttered his eyes. "I'm horny as hell, and I need you to do something about it." I lined up our cocks. "Here. Your hands are bigger." I showed him how to hold us together. "That's it." I rolled my hips, sliding my dick against his. "Not quite as fun as having you in my ass, but I figured you could use the variety."

Roy gripped the back of my head and plundered my mouth with his tongue. Gone the unsure man who hesitated. He moved his fist, adding to the friction. I wondered, if I asked him, if he would bend me over the chair. I wanted him inside me again. I wanted the heat of his body against my back. I pinched his nipples. His hold faltered only to return tighter and more determined.

"What the hell are you doing?" Julia's angry voice sent Roy toppling backward off the chair.

My ass hit the floor.

He grabbed a towel and covered himself.

I rolled a look up at Julia. "In case you haven't noticed, I'm a little busy right now."

"I've been looking all over for you. I was beginning to think you were dead in a ditch somewhere."

"Oh, if you could only be so lucky." I stood.

She gave me a disgusted look and averted her gaze. "You walked out on some very important people."

"They were no more important than anyone else who buys my work. And did they buy one?"

"That's not the point." She tossed her chin up. "People like to see you and talk to you."

"They like to fuck me too, so what's your point?" I fondled my cock.

Julia glared at me, then Roy. "You're disgusting, Paris. Absolutely disgusting."

"My apartment. I can do what I want."

She grabbed the plates off the table and stormed into the kitchen. The clatter of porcelain hitting the sink was so loud something had to have broken.

Julia returned. "So this is why you left the showing? To get your rocks off?"

"Rocks had nothing to do with it. I wanted a good fuck, and I found it."

"So..." She raked her gaze over Roy. "Is he one of the wait staff, or did you grab the first piece of ass on your way here?"

"Don't be so jealous. He swings both ways. I'm sure if you ask nicely he'll give you a ride." I winked at Roy.

If he turned any redder, he was going to pass out from the lack of blood.

"Not only does he have a quick recovery," I held my hands up. "He's got a really big—"

"Shut up, Paris." She jabbed at me with one of her ruby painted nails. "Just shut up. You're nothing but a sick bastard."

"Hold on." Roy held up a hand. "Don't talk to him that way."

Julia sneered. "Why don't you crawl back to whatever alley Paris dragged you out of?"

Roy clenched his jaw hard enough to make the muscles in his face jump. I was about to apologize to him when his shadowed gaze met mine. He wasn't upset for himself, he was upset for me.

But Roy was the one who didn't deserve Julia's abuse. I don't think he could have aimed a harsh thought in her direction.

No such inhibitions existed for me. I propped my hand on the table behind me and leaned back, displaying all my assets.

"Put some clothes on, Paris, before you embarrass yourself more than you already have."

"I'm not the least bit embarrassed."

"Go get dressed."

"Why? Last time I checked this was still my apartment. It's late. I plan on going to bed. The only way I sleep is nude."

She hissed. "Don't you have a shred of decency?"

"Nope. Now if you don't mind, I think you should go. Roy's going to throw me over the table and stick his cock in my ass." I grinned at her. "Or maybe you'd like to watch?"

The rage in her blue eyes glowed. Only one thing could happen now, and I didn't want Roy to see it. To him, I said, "You should probably get dressed." He flicked a look at Julia. "It's okay. She's like this all the time. I keep telling her she should get laid."

I walked Roy into the studio. He dressed so fast he didn't have time to button his shirt. A streak of dried cum stained the thigh of his slacks.

"Send me the cleaning bill," I said.

"A friend who owns a rental store gave it to me."

"Tell the store to send me the replacement cost. I'll get them something nicer."

Julia's stare beat against my back from across the room. Roy went to the elevator, jacket in hand. I stopped him as he stepped inside and claimed his mouth. A surprised sound bubbled from his chest. He pushed his tongue against mine and fought me for dominance.

How did he learn to kiss me so well in a short amount of time?

I let him go, and he stopped the doors from closing. "I want to see you again." Roy felt his pockets and came up with a business card made from cheap paper. "That's my cell. If I don't answer, leave a message and I'll call you back." People said things like that all the time but never meant it. "If you don't feel comfortable being alone with me, I'll take you to dinner."

I fingered the collar of his shirt. "I think we're way past being uncomfortable together."

He dropped his gaze and ran a hand over his head. "Yeah, I guess we are."

"Go home, Roy." I pecked him on the cheek. "Back to your world where you'll be safe from me."

A V appeared on his forehead. "I don't understand."

"There's a limo downstairs. The driver's name is Jerry. Tell him I said to drive you home."

"Thank you." Roy kissed my palm, then the elevator doors closed between us.

Over the years, a few men wanted to see me again for another quicky, but not because they wanted to take me to dinner. And I'm pretty sure "thank you" never crossed their minds.

I picked up my wallet from the floor and slid his card inside. I don't know why because I'd never see him again.

I left it on the workbench while I gathered up my clothes. As I stood, I caught Julia in my periphery. The section canvas frame she wielded struck me across the shoulder and a blast of pain numbed my arm. She aimed the second swing at my head, but I turned and my shoulder took the brunt of the impact. Sharp colored agony ripped across my chest. A crack echoed through the studio, and I fell on my side. She tossed aside the broken stretcher bar.

"Get up." Julia grabbed a jar off my workbench and threw it. I shielded my face from the explosion of glass and mineral spirits. "I said get up, Paris."

I knew better. It only took once for me to learn the consequences of any action Julia could interpret as aggression. And thanks to a stack of papers and my medical history, no one would ever believe I'd acted in self-defense.

A trickle of mineral spirits burned a line down my cheek. I wipe it away. Splinters of glass stuck to my skin, but there wasn't much blood.

"Fine. Stay there. Being on your knees is about all you're good for anyhow." She picked up her purse from the couch. "You have a dinner party tomorrow evening so get your shit together. Here." She tossed a bottle of pills at me. They bounced off the floor and rolled to a stop near my head. "Make sure to take them. I need you presentable. Your next showing will be in two weeks at the Avalon. Andrew Davis is going to be there. He's interested in the Blue Madonna, and you will do whatever it takes to make him happy. I swear to you, Paris, if you bail and cost me this sale, I will break your leg." Bits of glass crunched to dust under Julia's high heels. The elevator doors closed, and I was alone.

Chapter Two

The light from the neighboring buildings drew outlines around the curtains and left highlights across my body, creating a ghostly image in the mirror above my bed.

"I want to see you again." The echo of Roy's voice created ripples of color across the static of black. Normally nightmares kept me awake, not the memory of man's touch, the scent of his flesh, or how he looked at me.

The weight those thoughts created in my chest wasn't unfamiliar only forgotten. Then in that moment, there in the solitude, a sliver of happiness rose through years of darkness and neared the surface. A precious memory from a time before the screaming inside my head spilled out into the world. Sometimes it was like that, and those rare pieces of my past were treasures that gave me a reason to live.

I had to have it.

Every thump of my foot on the stairs fed the tide of yellows, reds, and oranges. Green followed me across the studio while ribbons of gold connected everything. The need for the brush in my hand burned hotter than carnal desires.

There were a half dozen canvases lined up on a shelf, most of them as wide as I was tall. Nothing I pulled from my thoughts could be contained on a smaller field.

I grabbed a clean palette and filled it with the rainbow droppings of brutalized tubes of paint. A clump of orange went directly on the canvas.

The fight to capture the moment began with blocks of color and lines of movement stitched together by negative space. Dark pushed the light. Colors hummed at the edges. Gradient shades took blistering hues into the background and shoved the rest to the edge.

I carved through the layers of oils until I gasped for air, dimples formed in the calluses on my fingers, my shoulders burned, and cramps twisted the muscles in my back. My sweat fell like tears, mixing with the paint.

The image emerged from the mass of color. A boy. A smile. Kind eyes. I searched for more of him, but there was only the sunlight through broken leaves. It covered him in glorious fragments of golden light.

I'd held his hand. I'd cherished his laugh. His lips had been so soft against mine.

What was his name?

I didn't deserve him after what I'd done, but maybe on some deep level, I hoped by honoring the moment before the darkness he'd forgiven me and I'd be granted peace.

It wasn't unusual for me to pass out after completing a work. Tearing off pieces of my soul was not only painful but exhausting. At least when I fell asleep, I didn't dream.

****

"Paris? Paris, wake up."

Grit concreted my eyelids, and I shivered from the bone-deep chill courtesy of the tile floor.

Alice wrapped a robe around my shoulders. "You need to get up before Julia gets here."

Because she wouldn't show me the same kindness Alice did.

"At least she wouldn't have to exert the effort to knock me down." I tied the robe closed.

"You shouldn't provoke her." Alice picked up the bottle of pills from the bench. "Did you take your medicine?"

No. "Of course I did." I staggered to my feet. Pain went from my hand to my arm. I rubbed the bruise near my elbow.

Alice cocked her mouth to the side. Even when she scowled, her smile seeped through. "Are you sure?"

"Cross my heart, hope to die." I made an X over the left side of my chest.

She put the bottle back on the bench and turned her attention to the canvas. "It's very pretty."

Alice never gave empty compliments. She also didn't pretend to understand what I created. To her, my works were just pretty colors on canvas.

"Thank you."

"What are you going to name it?"

The Kiss. "Why don't you name it?"

Her eyes widened. "Me?"

31

The scent of wet earth was followed by the whisper of a tarp over dead leaves. Dread rose up in my throat with a burn. "I need a drink."

Alice followed me into the kitchen. "I don't know anything about naming a painting."

I leaned against the counter and pressed my palm against my eye in a sad attempt to hold back the pounding in my skull. "Where's the vodka?" I got a glass out of the cabinet.

Alice brought me the bottle from the freezer and a carton of orange juice from the fridge.
I splashed enough juice in the glass to give the vodka some color.

"I think you're supposed to use more juice than that."

"I'm being efficient." I drank too much too fast, and the alcohol threatened to ride up my nasal passages. "Well?" The word came out on a squeak.

"Well what?" She put the juice and vodka away.

"What are you going to name the painting?"

Alice worried the hem of her blouse. "You know I don't know anything about art."

I waved the glass around. "Just name it something biblical or sexual."

She rolled her eyes. "Now you're making fun of me."

"I'm not. I swear." I saluted her confused expression with my drink. "The only rule you need to know about art is that religion and sex sells." I shrugged. "When all else fails, people get kinky or find God."

"Paris…"

I pecked her on the cheek. "Have I told you how much I love you?"

She pulled the glass out of my hand and herded me to the stairs. "You need to go get cleaned up. It's already after three o'clock, and Julia will be here soon to take you to the Bransfords."

"Who are they?"

"They're the people hosting the party for you this evening."
"Why?"

"Because they bought three of your paintings and want to meet you."

32

Great. Three paintings. No telling what extras Julia promised them. "Do you know how long this dinner party will last?" That was usually a clue.

"Not really, but Julia told me not to wait up."

That meant she'd promised them more than I'd want to give. "I think I'm coming down with something."

"No, you're not."

"Would be a shame to puke all over their fancy floors."

"Stop it, Paris. You're not sick, and this is important. These people love you. They want to meet you."

If only that was all they expected. Granted, it was just sex, but I hated that Julia decided who that sex would be with.

"Go, Paris." She pushed me toward the stairs. "I'll make some coffee, then come up there and help you with the makeup."

"We've talked about this, Alice. Just because I like to bottom doesn't mean I'm a girl."

She aimed a finger at me. "Your cheek."

I touched my face. Several cuts patterned a trail to my temple.

"Yeah." I nodded. "Okay. Makeup. Bring me another drink, but make sure it's in a plastic cup in case Julia decides to hit me with it."

Just my luck, the subject of our conversation came through the elevator door. She took one look at me and said, "Why aren't you dressed?"

"Why don't you stay out of my apartment? Or are you hoping to catch me fucking the doorman?"

She drew back her lips. "It wouldn't surprise me."

"Don't worry, he doesn't have enough dick to make it worth the effort."

"I'm not in the mood for your shit." Julia jerked away. "Go upstairs and get ready. We have to leave soon."

I leaned against the railing. "Who says I'm going?"

Her hands became fists.

I often wondered why I felt the need to poke a stick in the hornets' nest, but there was no answer except maybe I enjoyed getting stung.

Alice stepped between us. I didn't bother to tell her nothing short of a brick wall could stop our sister.

33

"He's on his way." Alice turned her pleading gaze on me.

"Fine, I'll get dressed."

"And shower," Julia said.

"What, and miss the chance to look like a palette of paint shit all over me?"

Alice flicked a look to me, then the top of the stairs.

Julia's voice chased me to my bedroom. "You better wash."

I threw a bird over my shoulder and slammed my door closed. The thunder in my chest echoed with a sharp stab in my skull. When Julia didn't come crashing in, I figured it was safe for me to bathe.

The oil paint didn't want to come off so I was forced to scrub my hands and arms raw. When I finished skinning myself, I began the other menial tasks that were required to make myself presentable.

"Paris?" Alice's voice was nothing like Julia's, but she still startled me. "Can I come in?"

"Yeah." I tapped the razor on the side of the sink to clear the blade.

Alice ran a look over me. "Don't you ever cover yourself?" She picked up a towel and handed it to me.

"Only when I have to." I wrapped the towel around my waist because it made her happy.

Alice put a small carry bag on the counter, then led me to the toilet. I closed the lid and sat. She took a straight razor out of the bag.

"I thought you were going to make me up, not slit my throat."

"Don't be silly. I'd never hurt you." No, she wouldn't. "You missed some spots."

Alice angled my head and cleared away the stray hairs with measured strokes. When she finished, she wiped my face with a warm cloth.

"Now what?" I said.

She took out a jar of cream. "Turn your head." Alice caught my chin. "The other way."

"How long will this take?"

"Be quiet." She dabbed my cheek with a wet finger. The cream made the cuts sting.

"Why do you do this?" Alice said.

"What?"

"Torment her."

34

I petted the towel.

Alice smoothed out the dabs of foundation. "With the stress of organizing these shows, Julia's temper is short enough without you aggravating her."

"That's easy for you to say. She never hits you."

"She only hits you because you purposely make her angry. I know things get mixed up in your head and sometimes you get confused and think things have happened that didn't, but you still have to take responsibility for what you do." She applied another drop. "You know, if you'd just apologize, she might forgive you."

An apology was no cure for rabies.

Alice examined her work. "It's not perfect, but it's better than nothing."

"Thank you."

"Well, it's important that you look nice. Especially if they take pictures."

"I still appreciate it."

She began packing everything away. "Oh, I thought of a name for the painting."

"Tell me."

"The Hand of God." Her smile wilted. "You don't like it?" Alice flicked her bangs out of her eyes. "I told you I wasn't very good at this."

"No, no. It's fine. It's a very good name."

"Really?"

"Yes."

Her smile returned. "Then you're going to call it that? I mean, when they put it up at the gallery or in the paper?"

"Sure." I had no intentions of letting anyone see The Kiss. I would protect it. The boy, whose name I couldn't remember, deserved more. But the canvas was all I had to give.

Alice knocked her hand into the makeup bag, and the contents spilled out over the counter. A few things fell off onto the floor.

"Dang it. I'm such a butterfingers."

I laughed.

"It's not funny."

"No, it's just hearing you say that. I didn't think anyone under the age of sixty used that term anymore."

She rolled her eyes at me.

I picked up a lipstick, a compact, and…

A locket.

The heart was woven out of strands of cheap silver. It was the kind of jewelry found in discount stores, not the high-dollar fashion boutiques my sisters shopped at.

I opened it. The picture of me was barely more than a ghost. I must have been seven or eight? There was just enough color to give my cheeks a pink glow, and the dark suit a shadow of blue.

"When was this taken?"

Alice sorted the eye shadows that had broken out of their containers. "What?"

"This? I don't remember it."

"What are you…" Alice's eyes widened. Her gaze went from the locket in my hand to me. "That's mine." She snatched it away and stuffed it in her pocket. Then she scraped the makeup she'd been sorting off the counter and into the bag.

"What did I say?"

"Nothing." She fought with the zipper.

"Alice?"

"Nothing Paris, just drop it." She slammed the door shut behind her.

****

The Bransford estate, also known as the Killigans, Marshals, Potts, and located on the state border, on the coast, near downtown, or in a picturesque mountain setting, was a bloated brick monolith on a painted green lawn.

Hedges were blocks, and rose bushes were beach balls. There was a pool—there was always a pool at houses like this—and a fountain or a pond.

The Bransfords had both.

The water garden crammed into the landscape was as natural looking as a temporary tattoo and the fountain a blight in the center of the driveway.

Limos, Beamers, Mercedes, and Jaguars made a line in front of the house. There were more than I expected.

Julia plucked a mirror from her purse, checked her makeup and fluffed her bangs. "You'd think for three hundred dollars, they could get my hair right."

"There's nothing wrong with your hair." Herds of people shuffled up the steps.

"Why Paris." She tossed me a smile. "Was that a compliment?"

A woman in a fur coat and a man only as tall as her shoulder walked by the window. Julia pinched my arm. "Did you hear me?"

"Yes. It was a compliment."

"Not that, what I said about Greg Bransford, our host."

"What about him?"

"You'll be staying the night."

I dug my fingers into my thigh.

"And you will do what he says."

I went back to staring out the window. "What about his wife?"

"He's not married."

"Girlfriend?"

"He didn't mention one."

"What did he mention?"

"He might have a colleague with him."

"Is that what they're calling fuck buddies now?"

"Don't be a jerk."

Why? Obviously, I didn't mean anything to her. To anyone.

"If you impress him, he might buy more of your paintings."

"Is that how you rationalize this?"

Julia pursed her lips. "What are you talking about?"

"Whoring me out."

"I do not whore you out."

"Really? You take money for sex. I say that's whoring me out. Which makes you my pimp."

She slapped me. The contact left a stinging pulse in my lip. "Be careful or you might screw up my makeup, and then all the bruises and cuts will show when they take my picture."

"If you don't get your attitude in check, smeared makeup will be the least of your worries."

The driver pulled up to the curb, and the valet opened the door. Julia followed me out. The doorman's muddy brown greeting floated off into the light. Inside the mansion, against the ivory walls and shining marble floors, the colors were much brighter, filling the vaulted ceiling in layers.

Around me, conversations stuttered to a halt. Anywhere else I was no one, but among these socialites, like my paintings, I was something to be coveted.

A man walked up. His deep skin tones, dark eyes, and hair suggested Italian descent, but when he spoke, his accent was something out of the Deep South. "Julia, Paris, how wonderful to see you." He kissed Julia's hand and shook mine. His touch lingered. At that point, no introductions were needed.

"Paris, this is Paul Bransford, our host for the evening."

I gave him my best smile. "Pleasure."

"All mine, I assure you." He swept an arm in the direction of a room in the back. "I have all three of your paintings up. They've been a hit." He led the way into a windowless library.

A Van Gogh, a Monet, and a Seurat separated my three paintings, making them all the more a boil among perfection.

Julia beamed. "You have an impressive collection."
There were more. Some paintings, some sculptures. I wandered over to the bookshelf, pretending to be interested in the mass of disjointed shapes and stray wires.

The scent of sandalwood cologne drifted around me. "What do you think?" Paul rested his hand against my lower back.

"It's interesting."

"Don't lie, it's horrific. Worst piece of art I ever bought."

"Then why did you buy it?"

"I was drunk."

"At least it wasn't a tattoo."

He chuckled. "Oh, I have one of those, but it's by a far greater artist." His touch drifted south, and his words left on a heated breath close to my ear. "You'll have to tell me what you think."

"Tattoos are hardly my expertise."

"But you're an artist." Closer and his chest framed my back. "I'm sure you'll know talent when you see it."

I rubbed my ass against the line of a hardening cock.

He hissed. "Be careful or you'll miss dinner."

"I'm not particularly hungry."

"But we have guests."

"Guests or voyeurs?"

Paul growled against the back of my neck. "You are going to be very entertaining, Mr. Duvoe."

He stepped away, and I let go of the breath I'd been holding. A passing waiter offered me a drink. I took two, drank one in two swallows and left the empty on the tray. The other, I sipped while wading through waves of conversation.

"...did you hear about..."

"...pregnant?"

"My broker said I should invest..."

"...a new boat. Can you believe that? He bought another new boat."

I wandered from the library to the dining room.

"Greg thinks we should buy..."

"...Yale turned down their eldest..."

"Mr. Duvoe?"

A woman I didn't know put her hand on my arm.

"You're Paris Duvoe, the artist." Almost innocent wonder filled her eyes. She had a sweet face, minimal makeup, and a splash of freckles on her cheeks. There was nothing artificial about her full lips or flawless skin.

I pulled out of her grasp and smoothed the wrinkles on my jacket. "Yes."

She fumbled with her wine glass, exchanging it from one hand to the next before setting it on one of the trays floating by on the hand of a waiter. The right shoulder strap of her dress slid down. She pushed it back, but it wouldn't stay.

Not that it mattered. Clothing could never enhance someone as pretty as her. "My name is Christine Kline." She offered me her free hand.

"I'm sorry." We shook. "Have we met?"

"No, sir, this is my first time at one of these..." She glanced around. "Events? I've only read about you in Modern Art. The feature they did on you a couple of months ago was wonderful." She leaned closer. There was only the natural clean scent of her skin. Like the rest of her, it was very pleasing. "Is it true? Do you really paint naked?"

I shielded my smile with a sip of champagne. "More often than not."

She grinned, and I wondered if I might be able to steal her away to somewhere quiet. Not because I wanted her, but because she was real and we could talk about real things.

Roy had been real too. A wrinkle in the silk. A glorious imperfection.

A man pushed his way through the crowd with the efficiency of a dull razor. "Sweetheart," he took Christine by the arm. "We agreed that you wouldn't wander off."

"I know, but I saw—"

He stretched his Botoxed face into a sad example of a smile. "Please forgive us. Christine has never been to a dinner party before." He tightened his grip enough to dimple her flesh.

"Yes, she told me."

"She didn't mean to intrude."

"She wasn't."

His vise grip loosened. I drained my glass and held it out to the man. He gave me a surprised look but took it.

"Now, if you'll excuse me," I put Christine's hand on my arm. "I promised your lovely date a private tour around the art room."

Christine's cheeks reddened. So did the man's, but his wasn't flattering. I tugged her into the crowd. On the other side of the room, I took a left into an empty hallway. I checked the first door I came to. It was locked.

"Where are we going?" she said.

"No clue." The third door down led to a study. I slipped inside, taking her with me. There was a flask and tumblers on the desk in the back. I left her hovering at the door and went to pour myself a drink.

"Why are we in here?" She pushed at the shoulder strap of her dress some more, then hugged herself.

I drank down the first glass without even sniffing the stuff to see what it was. The acrid burn pushed tears from my eyes. "I didn't bring you in here to accost you if that's what you're thinking." I poured a second.

Muffled laughter drifted through the crack left in the door.

"If you really want to leave, you can. I won't be offended. I just thought someone like you might want to get away from…" I gestured with the glass. "All that."

"Am I that out of place?" Her smile was sad.

"Absolutely."

She hunched her shoulders. "I told Tom this wasn't a good idea."

"Tom? He looked more like a *Dick* to me."

She put her fingers over her lips, but her smile still showed.

"Why are you here?" I said.

She shrugged.

"You have to have a reason. Better yet, why is someone like you with someone like him?"

Christine fumbled with the bracelet on her wrist. "I should probably—"

"I didn't say that to insult you." I cleared the space in three strides. "I said it because you deserve better."

"Better, where I come from, would be a double-wide instead of a single and cable TV." She dropped her gaze. "I'm sorry, that was rude."

"No. It was honest." I kissed the back of her hand. "And in these circles, that is a gift in short supply."

"You're not like I expected."

"And what did you expect?" She glanced back at the door, and I laughed. "No. I'm not like them. But I promise you I'm not any better."

"I don't believe that."

I held up the tumbler. "Would you care for a drink?"

"No, I uh, the champagne was almost too much." She followed me to the desk. "Should you be drinking that? I mean, it's not yours."

"Probably not. But then we probably aren't supposed to be in this room." I poured myself a glass full and used a random piece of paper to soak up what sloshed over the edge. "So Ms. Christine Kline, where are you from, what brought you here, and what are your dreams?"

"Kansas, desperation, and silly dreams don't put food on the table."

41

I raised my glass. "A toast to silly dreams." Then drank until it was empty. "And what is it you wish for at night when you're snuggled in your bed, hiding in the darkness?" I pulled her closer, and she stumbled into my arms. "Is it Money? Fame? Love?" I swept a thumb over her cheek and tucked a lock of mousey brown hair behind her ear.

"I dream about being a writer." Her eyes lit up.

"And what would you write?"

"Children's books. I'd also illustrate them."

"You're an artist."

"Not like you."

"No one sane wants to be like me."

"But you're—"

I placed a finger over her mouth. "This isn't about me." I traced her lips. "Tell me, what would your stories be about?"

She smiled. "About people who are different and how it's more important to be you, not who people want you to be. I would write about good people who do good things. And I would give every story a happy ending."

"But not all stories have happy endings."

"No, they don't." She smoothed her hand across my shoulder. "But my stories would. Even when you think a character doesn't deserve one."

I helped her regain her balance but continued holding her hand. "Then you should do it."

She laughed in a way only women who are beautiful from the soul can laugh. A sound that comes from the heart to play on the ears in a wash of pristine light. "Do you have any idea how hard it is to get published? Let alone publish a children's book?"

"Is it impossible?"

"Almost."

"But almost still means it can be done."

"Sure, but…" She chewed her lip. "What if I'm not any good?"

"You won't know until you try."

"Tom thinks it's a waste of time."

"Like I said, Dick is a much better name."

She took her hand out of mine and sat beside me. "I have a few books already done."

"Really?"

She nodded. "I hide them under the bed in a portfolio."

"You should submit them."

"I wouldn't even know where to start."

I looked around on the desk for a pen and paper. There was plenty to choose from. "Here." I scribbled out a name and number. "Call this woman. Serena Haus."

"Who is she?"

"She's an agent."

"The article in Modern Art said your sister was your agent."

Unfortunately for me, she was. "True, but Serena has been trying for the last three years to get Julia to sign me up with her. And Serena has a lot of powerful contacts."

"Then why doesn't your sister use her?"

"Greed."

Christine's dark brows came down over her large blue eyes.

"It would mean giving up some of her money," I said. "Julia isn't about to give up her money unless it will make her more money. It would also have to get her more media attention. With Serena in the front seat, Julia would disappear from the spotlight."

"You don't sound like you like your sister very much."

"Call Serena."

"What do I say?"

"Tell her I sent you to her, and if she does this, I'll owe her a favor."

"What kind of favor?"

"I'm sure she'll think of something." I know she'd been to several of my showings. I was willing to bet there was a painting she was interested in. I could probably sweet-talk Julia into lowering the price on one. If not, I could always do something for Serena in private and smuggle it out of the apartment.

Christine slipped the note inside her bra. "Sorry, no pockets."

"I want to hear more about stories. You said they were about people who are different and they all have happy endings."

"Yes." She leaned against me. "My favorite one is about a boy and his stuffed rabbit."

I draped an arm over her shoulder. "I thought little boys had dogs?" We wound up with our fingers woven together and our hands resting where our legs touched.

"Well, that's what makes this boy different. Other children make fun of him. They tell him he's too old for toys, but the rabbit is his friend. Of course, there are other things too."

"Like what?"

"He sometimes wears pretty hats."

"Ah, a drag queen in the making."

"But he's not. That's the thing. He's just an ordinary boy who does extraordinary things."

"What else?"

"He builds incredible machines out of things people throw away, and he takes his rabbit on crazy adventures."

"Far off worlds?"

"Sorta. He doesn't go into outer space or anything. Although that might be fun to write about."

"You'll have to give me credit for that one."

She laughed. Then we were quiet.

"My favorite is the one about the bully."

"Doesn't sound very happy."

"It's not at first. The bully makes fun of the boy, but the boy doesn't care because he has his rabbit. But the bully steals the rabbit and runs away with it. This makes the boy very unhappy, and he chases the bully."

"Does he catch him?"

"Of course."

"How?"

"Well, the bully is so busy running that he doesn't watch where he's going, and he falls into a hole."

"A well." The words fell flat.

Christine made a thinking sound. "I guess. That might make more sense than a random hole, wouldn't it? Anyhow, he drops the rabbit, and the boy is able to get it back."

"A happy ending for the boy but not the bully."

"Oh, the bully has a happy ending too. The boy and the rabbit use one of the fantastical machines to rescue the bully. Then bully and the boy become friends."

"Hola. Cómo estás?" The rich smell of earth replaced her subtle scent.

I licked my lips and tasted copper.

"Paris?"

"The boy, what's his name?"

"You're shaking."

I tried to smile while my insides attempted to crawl up my throat. "He has to have a name, right?"

"He doesn't have one."

"Why not?"

"Because I wanted to make it so any child reading the book could be the boy. Are you sure you're all right? You look—"

The door to the study flew open, and Julia stormed in. "There you are." Tom and Paul followed. Julia's gaze flicked to Christine. "What are you doing in here?"

I composed my face into a mask of innocence. "Talking."

Tom walked around Julia. "I told you to stay with me." He jerked Christine to her feet so hard that she almost fell.

"I insisted she join me." I nodded at the empty tumbler. "I don't like to drink alone."

His grip loosened enough for Christine to pull free. She rubbed the red fingerprints left on her skin.

"You have guests waiting," Julia said.

Paul tipped his head at me. "I'm sure he was just taking a breather."

"Absolutely," I said. "The noise got to be a bit much. I didn't feel well. Christine escorted me in here to make sure I was okay."

"I'm sorry she bothered you." The look Tom cast her was cold.

"And I already told you she wasn't bothering me. I asked for her company. Thanks to her kindness and concern, I feel better. She is an incredible woman, *Dick*. You're lucky to have her."

"My name is Tom. Tom Howard."

"Really? You look so much more like a Dick to me."

Christine hid her smile with a cough. Tom was too busy staring at me with a confused expression to notice.

"Thank you, Ms. Kline, for the wonderful conversation and a happy ending to my day." I kissed the back of Christine's hand. "I hope you will take the chance to find yours." She nodded at me so I knew she understood. "Now if you'll excuse me I must mingle." I ignored Julia and spoke to Paul. "Shall we?"

"Can you give us a minute?" he said.

Tom led Christine out the door, but Julia hesitated.

"Just a minute," Paul said. She narrowed her eyes at me before walking out.

The weight of Paul's gaze hit me full force. "That's a two grand a bottle brandy you made yourself comfortable with."

"You can afford it."

"That's not the point."

I leaned back on the desk and spread my legs just enough to tighten my slacks so the bulge of my cock showed. "I'll make it up to you."

"I'm sure you will." He stepped between my knees, forcing them wider.

"I'd offer to do that right now, but Julia is waiting in the hall." I fondled his tie. "And she'd be pissed if I wrinkle my suit."

"Your sister would get over it."

"Perhaps, but your guests might not appreciate you stealing me away."

"They'd get over it, too." Paul squeezed my crotch. "Oh, the things I am going to do to you, Paris Duvoe."

A hard tug on his tie brought us cheek to cheek. "Are you going to put me on my knees, Mr. Bransford? Choke me with your cock? Fuck me? I'd like that." And I would.

"All of those things and so much more."

"I can't wait."

He was about to say something else when Julia knocked on the door. "Everyone is in the dining room waiting."

Paul grinned at me. "You'd better make sure you save room for dessert."

Chapter Three

There isn't a lot that can make a man more nervous than being responsible for transporting millions of dollars in artwork—even if it's only from the van to the inside of the building—except maybe deactivating a bomb.

At least a bomb would be a quick death. Julia, however, took great pleasure in the slow evisceration of her victims.

And she would look for any reason to do it. Even when it came to acts of God.

Another clap of thunder echoed through the back room. Two of the transport men carried in one of my larger works. Water beaded the plastic it was wrapped in and cut channels down the folds, leaving small lakes all over the concrete floor.

There were towels in front of the door, but under the foot traffic, they'd turned into just another obstacle the frantic workers had to avoid.

"You'd better not get any of that water on the main floor."

I'd lost count of how many times she'd said that, but the threat still made everyone jump. A couple of gallery employees rushed over with paper towels to mop up the mess before they even attempted to unwrap the painting.

Julia walked over to me. "You'd think with what I paid these people, they'd do a better job."

"Maybe the problem is you don't pay them enough."

She tossed her hair back. "I pay them what they're worth."

"Then you underestimate the value of their contribution."

Julia flagged down a young woman carrying an armful of drapes. "I want the red in the front and the white dividing each section."

"You said you wanted just the white."

"I changed my mind."

"But we only brought the white."

"Then I suggest you drive back to the storehouse and get the red ones."

The young woman gave me a worried expression, and I gave back an apologetic smile.

"Well?" Julia said.

"Yes, ma'am." The woman hugged the fabric to her chest. "I'll go as soon as the rain lets up."

"You'll go in the next ten minutes, or you won't have a job."

"But the weather."

"Ten minutes."

The woman hurried off.

"It's raining buckets," I said.

"It's water. She's not going to melt." Julia scrolled through her records on her smart phone. "Do you think ten will be enough?"

"I'm sure it will be fine."

"I don't know. You sold three at the last showing."

"Three?"

"Yes." The men cast a wary eye in Julia's direction. She didn't look up so they proceeded to unwrap the canvas.

"Then ten is all we have."

"I know."

"Then you'll have to make do."

"But we won't have one for the interview."

"What interview?"

"I told you that you have a Q and A on the Allen Rock Show."

"Why would I need a painting for an interview?"

"As a backdrop. This is huge, Paris. Millions of people watch that show."

Millions. I pinched the bridge of my nose.

"Are you okay?"

"Headache."

"Take some aspirin."

"I think I should go eat."

Julia glared at me.

"I haven't eaten all day." I wasn't hungry, but I needed to get away.

"Fine." She gave me her back. "Just don't eat junk, or you'll get fat."

Rain soaked my clothes in droplets of ice blues and frigid whites. I could have taken the limo. That's what Julia would have wanted. Which is why I didn't.

I followed the sidewalk to a stretch of buildings. Neon signs advertising beer and wine glowed in the windows above paper menus of upscale restaurants. The wind shifted, and the scent of grilling meats and sweet pastries was replaced by burned petrol and rot from the dumpsters up the street. People passed me huddled under umbrellas. Fragments of their conversation left vibrant confetti in the air while the passing cars dragged out streaks of gray.

I stopped under an awning. The pounding in my skull eased, and the ringing sound left behind mixed with wet soles sticking to the pavement.

It rained the same way that terrible, terrible day in the woods when the mud caked my clothes, packed under my nails, clung to my cheeks.

My hands trembled.

My heart skipped.

The space around me expanded until I was lost in years past.

Wet earth. Fresh leaves. The tap, tap, tap of rain passing through the canopy of leaves overhead. I flexed my hands, and my knuckles ached like I'd been carrying something heavy.

"Paris?" I knew that voice. Roy stepped out a café.

I hoped my smile didn't look as fake as it felt. "Are you following me, Mr. Callahan?"

"Uh, no, I just stopped to—" He frowned at me. "You okay?"

I ran a look over him, from his flannel shirt to his dirt-stained jeans. He had a tool belt around his waist. "I am now."

He nodded in the direction of the café. "Do you want to go in and get some coffee?"

I stepped closer. "What I want is for you to take me home with you."

Roy glanced over his shoulder.

"Yes, I'm talking to you. Do you have a car?"

"No. I walked." He held up the raincoat draped over his arm.

"Then what are you waiting for?" He didn't move so I brushed my lips against his ear. "I thought you wanted me?"

His exhale shuddered. "I do."

"Then take me home with you, Roy, and fuck me."

He swallowed several times and then nodded. "Okay. Yeah, yeah, okay."

I grinned.

"Wait." He wrapped his raincoat around my shoulders.

49

"I'm already soaked."

"I know, but you're chilled."

"What about you?"

"I'll be fine."

"How about we take a cab?" He dropped his gaze for a moment. I added, "I'll pay."

"You don't…"

I put a finger over his mouth, pushed it between his lips, slid it along the edge of his teeth and brushed the tip of his tongue. "The quicker we get to your apartment, the sooner I can get out of these wet clothes." I pulled him to the line of cabs.

"It's not far," Roy said as he sat down beside me. He gave the address to the cabby, and the car jostled for a spot in traffic. A horn honked, and someone yelled. Through the sheets of rain, two little boys holding hands ran down the sidewalk. They both wore shorts and t-shirts.

Neither one of them could have been more than ten.

They looked so happy. Smiling, laughing, so full of joy they glowed against the world around them.

"Me llamo…" They darted behind a small crowd of people huddling under their umbrellas and didn't reappear. "I can't remember his name."

"Did you say something?"

"I think it's getting colder." I curled under the raincoat as the last bit of warmth seeped out of my bones.

"We're almost there," Roy said.

The cab turned onto a street crowded with old apartments that hadn't seen a face-lift since the seventies. Water from trash clogged gutters flooded the sidewalks. The cars parked on the side of the road came in two varieties, rusted and pimped out.

"Tough neighborhood for a Southern boy, don't you think?" I said.

The cabby stopped. "Twelve fifty."

I dug out my wallet and handed him a twenty. Roy took me with him out of the cab.

We jogged up the sidewalk to an ugly brick building. A crack of thunder was followed by a wash of rain so heavy it erased the outside world.

"Jesus," Roy said. "I don't think I've ever seen weather like this." We dripped water up a flight of steps. "Sorry, there's no elevator."

"I'm surprised there's electricity." I ran a hand along the pitted railing. Missing rungs left gaping holes and very little support.

A blaring TV from inside one of the units was drowned out by the angry yell of a woman. She didn't speak English so I had no idea what she said, but going by her tone, it couldn't have been good.

"I'm down here."

We made our way through discarded toys, forgotten drink cups, and the occasional article of clothing to a door close to the end of the hall.

Roy fumbled for his keys. A man wearing a pair of boxers stumbled out of another apartment. He held up his beer can like he could shield himself from the items hurled at him.

The woman who didn't speak English finished her assault by pegging him in the head with a Bible.

She slammed the door, and the man screamed, "Bitch."

"C'mon." Roy pulled me inside. More yelling was followed by a crying infant. "Sorry about that." He flipped on a light.

Roy's apartment consisted of a cramped kitchen in one corner separated from the rest of the space by a length of countertop. There was less than two yards between the sofa and the bed. A table and set of chairs ate up the blank spot on the other side of the room, and a bookshelf crowded the wall.

Everything was old, worn out, and rumpled.

Roy stared at his feet while he rubbed the back of his neck. "I know it's not what you're used to."

Which was exactly why I loved it. "It's perfect."

He gave me a questioning look. I dropped the raincoat on the floor and wandered over to the bed. A patchwork quilt covered thin cotton sheets. Everything had been carefully folded down. I touched the head-shaped dimple in the pillow.

"Let me make you some coffee." Roy squeezed by me. There was a clink and scrape from the kitchen. "Do you drink coffee? Or would you rather have tea? It's nothing fancy, just those little store packets."

51

"Coffee is fine." I kicked off my shoes and unbuttoned my shirt. There was no place to put it so I left it on the floor at the foot of the bed.

"Are you hungry? I can throw on a can of soup." A cabinet door opened and shut.

My pants wound up with the shirt.

It was warmer inside Roy's apartment, but not much. Definitely not enough to convince my testicles to quit burrowing into my stomach.

I stretched out on Roy's lumpy mattress. His pillow smelled just like him: rich, earthy, with a slight spice. It wasn't strong enough to be cologne, and it mixed too well with the smell of clean sheets. I knew then that wonderful scent was all him.

"The coffee will take a couple of min—" Roy stood on the edge of the linoleum staring at me. The coffeepot percolated behind him on the counter.

I propped my head on my hand. "I think I'm cold, Roy."

"I'll turn up the heat."

"Why don't you come over here and join me instead?"

"The coffee."

"It will keep."

"You need to eat."

"No, what I need is your cock in my ass." I bent my knees and spread my legs.

Roy closed his eyes for a moment. The microwave beeped, and he returned to the kitchen. When he came back out, he carried a bowl of soup and set it on the bedside table. His gaze stayed on the ground.

"Here." He stirred it with a spoon. "It's just canned, but it will help you get warm."

"Look at me, Roy." He stopped moving. "Quit playing innocent and look at me." The hunger in his eyes turned them black. I sat up enough to pull his shirt out of his pants and slide my hands up his stomach. His skin burned my fingertips.

Roy clasped one of my hands between his. "You're freezing." He tugged the comforter around my shoulders. I grabbed him by his face and slammed our mouths together.

The surprised sound Roy made vibrated across my tongue. I forced him to open wider, to take me deeper. He resisted only for a moment, then he wrapped his arms around me, cupping the back of my head as he pushed me into the mattress.

I locked my legs around Roy's hips and rolled us over. He didn't even have time to look surprised before I'd yanked his jeans open, freeing his cock. The thick length of flesh curved toward his stomach.

"Tell me what you want," I said.

Roy watched me with wide eyes.

"C'mon, Roy, you gotta have some idea."

His chest heaved with every breath.

"Alright, then I'll decide for you." His jeans abraded my cock and balls on my way down his legs. I closed my lips over his dick and took him to the back of my throat.

"Oh, God." Roy put his hand on the back of my head. "God, Paris, that's…" A tremor ran down his legs.

I hummed around him as I pulled to the tip. Another down stroke made him tighten his grip on my hair. Every slide of my lips milked another bitter drop of precum.

Roy pumped his hips, pulled my hair, and forced me to take him so deep it became a choice between obeying and breathing. I struggled to time my inhales with the pulls on his cock.

I was sure I was close to passing out when he pulled me up and under him. Roy kicked off his boots, shoved his jeans down his legs, and yanked his shirt over his head so fast a couple of the buttons popped off. Then he covered me with the scorching mass of his body.

"I want to fuck you." A primal growl followed his words.

I yanked his hair. "Then do it." He attacked my neck with violent kisses. "That's it…more." He pinned my wrists above my head with one hand. "Yesss—"

Roy fumbled with the drawer on the bedside table. He pulled away from me long enough to pour lubricant over his cock. It dripped in silky rivulets down the length.

He dropped the bottle and collected the excess on his fingertips.

"Now," I said.

"Just let me…"

I twisted free and flipped over on my stomach. "Fuck me." I drew my knees up and put my ass in his face.

"Goddamn you." He pushed the head of his cock into my opening, then his powerful legs pummeled me with every thrust.

I managed to pull myself up on the headboard. The change in angle tightened my body until every pump he gave me skimmed across my prostate. Electric bursts rode up my spine.

"Harder." I had to lock my arms to keep from being smashed against the wall.

Flesh slapped against flesh. Sweat sprinkled my back. An inferno seared away the chill in my bones.

"Good, so gooood—" I clenched.

To keep his rhythm, he had to grip my hips with enough force to bruise. The glorious assault added pain to the pleasure.

The hum growing in my balls spread until all I could feel was his cock sliding in and out, striking sparks of pleasure that threatened to burn me to ash.

A groan ticked out of Roy's chest, becoming a guttural roar, but he somehow kept from coming until I barked out a cry and shot all over his pillow.

His breath on the back of my neck was almost as hot as his lips when he brushed small kisses against my skin. It bothered me how the gentle touch felt better than his cock in my ass, his hands bruising my flesh, or being pinned and made helpless.

****

My ass hurt when I perched on the barstool Roy had pulled up to the counter. I wondered why we sat there instead of the table until I saw the duct tape on the rungs of the chairs.

Roy caught me looking. "It came with the apartment. Otherwise, I'd get rid of it."

"Their version of furnished?"

"Yeah. At least the bookshelf was usable."

"I hope the sofa and bed are yours."

"Salvation Army but yeah, they're mine. Believe it or not, the mattress set still had the tags on it."

"I believe you." I'd sent enough unworn shirts with Alice when she changed out my wardrobe.

Roy took a bowl of soup from the microwave. "Here." He sat it on the counter in front of me.

"So why were you out in the rain?" He finished assembling two sandwiches. He put the one with the extra meat in front of me. I switched it with his. He frowned.

"It was either the rain or my sister. I chose the rain. If I'd known you were wandering out there, I would have bolted a lot sooner."

The blush in his cheeks was dark under his caramel skin. He ate part of his sandwich, and I chased the letter-shaped pasta around the bowl with my spoon.

"If you dislike her so much, why not make her leave?"

"I can't."

"Why not?"

"Do as I say, Paris, or I'll make sure you spend the rest of your life in this hellhole." I traced the vein in the back of his hand. There was a scar between his first two fingers, at the base of his thumb, another near his wrist. I touched each of them.

"I do construction in the summer and get cut up a lot."

"What about this one?" There was an inch long, raised bit of flesh just under his middle knuckle. Roy flexed his hand and put it in his lap.

I propped my chin on my fist while he concentrated on finishing his sandwich.

"So tell me, what does the great Roy Callahan do on his days off?"

He caught a piece of tomato trying to escape. "Not much time off." He ate it. "But when there is, I usually sleep or watch a little TV."

Was the relic sitting on the opposite counter even color? "It works?"

"Mostly."

"A few more years and it will be an antique."

He chuckled.

"How much do you pay for this place?"

"Seven hundred dollars too much." He shrugged. "But it's dry and people leave me alone."

55

I had a hard time believing someone as imposing as him ever had to worry about being bothered. But he did stick out like a sore thumb in his blue jeans and flannel shirts.

"Where are you from, originally? Not from here, I know." While he talked with a Southern accent, it didn't have the same twang as the natives.

"Arkansas." He nodded at the bowl of soup. "That's going to get cold."

"Why did you leave?"

"There was nothing left to make me stay." He finished off his sandwich.

I pushed mine over to him. "I ate lunch before I ran into you."

He gave me a look that said he suspected I was lying.

"Promise." I gave him a slow smile.

He took a bite of the sandwich. Chewed. Swallowed. "Where are you from?"

"Here."

"You don't have an accent."

"My family was transplanted from a few states up north. But I was born here."

He nodded. "Have you always done art for a living?"

I took a bite of the soup. It was still warm, but barely. "Not always."

"How old were you when you started?"

"You realize you can get answers to all these question with a quick search on the internet or any number of art magazines."

"I'd rather talk to you than read about you."

"Reading about me would be safer."

For me. For him. For my heart.

"How do you figure that?"

I petted his hand. "Because you're a good person and I would ruin you."

"Why would you ruin me?"

"I ruin everyone, Roy. I'm a disease."

"Don't say that."

I shrugged. "Why not? It's true."

"According to who? Your sister?"

"Por favor, señor, ¿ha visto a mi hijo?"

I pressed my fingers against the pain stabbing my temple.

"Are you okay?"

"Fine."

"Me llamo…"

Roy made me look at him. "What's wrong?"

"Nothing?"

"You're pale."

I laughed and pulled away. "Lots of time indoors will do that." The spoon tumbled from my hand.

Roy went to turn up the heat.

"I said I'm fine."

"You're shivering."

"A drink would be far more effective than heat."

"Please eat." He sat.

I ate a few bites of soup, hoping he'd quit staring at me. He didn't until half the bowl was empty.

Roy went to the kitchen and came back with a glass of orange juice.

"You forgot the vodka."

"I'm all out."

The juice tasted weird without the alcohol. "See, you're so wholesome you don't even keep booze in the place."

He finished pouring himself a glass. Roy capped the jug and stood there rubbing the scar on the back of his hand. "My cellmate tried to get a little too friendly and didn't want to take no for an answer. Neither did the guy in the shower. Or the meal hall. After that, I wasn't very popular. I learned really fast it was better when people were afraid of you."

"You went to jail?"

"Prison." He took the OJ back to the fridge.

"There's a difference?"

"County and Federal. So yeah, here's a big difference."

People like Roy didn't do things bad enough to wind up behind bars. It was impossible.

"Why were you in prison?"

He stayed on the other side of the counter. "I killed a man." For a moment, I thought I saw tears in his eyes, but it disappeared behind the glass he drank from.

"What happened?"

"Does it matter?"

"Yes." Because there had to be a very good reason for someone like him to hurt anyone.

He put the empty glass in the sink. "I was in a bar fight, and a man died."

"And the reason for the fight?"

"It was just a fight."

"I don't believe that."

"Then we're even."

"Even? How."

"You lied about eating."

So he did know. "Big difference. Tell me. Please."

Roy scrubbed his hands over his face, then folded his arms over his chest. He stared with no expression on his face but somehow looked destroyed.

He cleared his throat. "The crowds were really bad on Fridays. Construction workers, truck drivers, guys from the college. It was pretty normal for things to get rowdy. I was in the back by the pool tables with a bunch of other men on my crew." The tick returned to his jaw.

"Keep going."

"I really don't..." He sighed. "Like I said, it was crowded. Some of the other guys got too friendly with this girl, a waitress. At some point, one of them made a pass. She turned him down, and he didn't want to take no for an answer. By the time I saw what they were doing, they already had her shirt off. There had to be fifteen other men standing around, and none of them did a damn thing to stop it."

"So you did."

"What else was I supposed to do?"

"Could have turned your back like everyone else in the bar."

He dropped his gaze. "I went to break it up, and they came after me."

"How many were there?"

"Why?"

I shrugged. "Just wanted to know the odds."

"Five to one."

"Not a very fair fight." I sipped my juice while Roy scuffed his feet against the faded linoleum. "And what happened next?"

"After I broke a few noses, they backed off. Except for one. He pulled a knife. He lunged. I grabbed him and snapped his neck. It just happened."

"Self defense," I said.

"Yes and no."

"It was five on one. Not to mention they were trying to rape a woman. Tell me how a jury could possibly find you guilty of anything else?"

"I pled out."

"Why?"

"Because seven years was better than twenty."

"No one would have convicted you."

"It was a small town. I killed someone's son, husband, brother. He'd grown up there, I didn't. He had friends, I was an out of towner just running a construction job. The lawyer said there was a good chance they'd find me guilty on principle alone."

"Should have fired him and gotten a different attorney."

"Public defender. I didn't have any money to hire one in the first place."

So Roy went to prison when he should have been given a medal. "Seven years for saving a woman from being raped and maybe even killed?"

"I got out on parole after three for good behavior."

"Doesn't make it all right." My spoon clanked against the bottom of the bowl.

"Want some more?"

"No thanks."

"I don't mind."

If only he would. "Is that why you left Arkansas?"

"That was the divorce." I have no idea what he saw on my face to make him add, "I didn't always live in a rat hole and work for money under the table. I used to have a really good business."

"Building houses?"

"Sometimes. Mostly commercial buildings."

"And you didn't have money for a lawyer?"

"The ex got the business, the house, plus alimony. There wasn't much left to live on, let alone hire a lawyer. I took the out-of-state jobs to pay the bills."

"If you ran a building company, why are you fixing air conditioners?"

"Construction companies don't hire felons."

"But you still get work."

"Because I'm willing to work for less than anyone else and there are always folks looking to cut corners."

I didn't know whether to be worried or grateful.

Roy watched me with a kind of longing seen on the faces of people who are about to say good-bye for the last time.

"I guess I was wrong about you," I said.

His smile was tight. I hated the fact he wouldn't even try to defend himself.

"Do you want me to call you a cab?"

"Why? Do you want me to leave?"

"I figured…"

"I'd be scared of you?"

"Like you said, you were wrong about me."

"Yeah, I was. You're far more than just a good person. Someone should nominate you for sainthood."

Somehow his expression became even more broken.

"That was a compliment."

"One I don't deserve."

"Why not?"

He went to the cabinet. "I'm out of vegetable, but I have some chicken noodle."

I slid off my stool and cornered him near the stove. Surviving prison with his virtue intact was the proof his wide shoulders, thick arms, powerful body were capable of delivering everything his presence led me to believe.

Yet there he was, crushed against the counter in an attempt to get away, his pulse jumping in his neck, eyes wide, lips parted, sucking in short, panicked breaths, just because I stood close to him.

"Are you still scared of me?" I rubbed the crotch of his blue jeans. The hard length of his cock rode across his thigh in search of escape. "Nope. Definitely not scared."

Roy's incredible green eyes searched my face. He touched my cheek, ran his fingers to my jaw, followed my chin to my lips. I waited for him to kiss me. But he only stared, and touched, and stared some more. The weight of it all became too much, and I stepped away. He followed me until I was the one pinned against the counter.

Roy slid his hands over my shoulders, down my arms, then back up to hold my face. "Stay here tonight."

"Why?"

"Do I need a reason?" His chest and his thighs pressed against mine.

"Will you fuck me again if I do?" The smile I tried to pull fell flat. Roy leaned closer. Instead of hungering for his mouth on mine, I feared it. I turned my head, and he brushed his lips against my jaw.

"Stay the night with me, Paris." I trembled. "Shhh—" His heated touch danced over the back of my neck.

"Why?"

"I want to feel you next to me. I want to know your body."

"You already know the important parts." I hated that my voice cracked.

"No, I don't." He put his hand on my left pectoral.

"Julia will have a fit if I don't come home." And that wasn't a lie.

He made some space between us, and I was able to regain my composure. "Why do you do what she wants?"

"It's difficult to explain." How did you tell someone you had no rights? You'd been made into property? You'd long ago had the fight stripped from your core?

And there was no such thing as parole from Julia's prison.

"Try." Close again, his exhale warmed the shell of my ear.

I found myself leaning into him, searching for the warmth of his body, inhaling the scent of sweat and sex from his skin. What would it be like to be held as I fell asleep and to wake up in those same arms? I wanted to know. I needed to know.

No matter the price.

"I'll stay, but under one condition."

"What?"

I scraped my teeth down his neck to his shoulder. "You make sure to fuck me hard enough there's no way I could even think of walking out."

****

"Where have you been?" Julia cut me off at the bottom of the steps.

"Can you yell at me later? I'm tired." Tired, sore, completely melted. I was going to have to sit on a pillow for a week. God, I hoped she hadn't promised me to anyone.

"Not until you tell me where you were."

"Out. With a friend."

"Please tell me you used a condom."

"I didn't know you cared."

She slapped me. "I work too fucking hard to have you destroy it all just because you can't keep it in your pants."

"Then I would suggest you cancel any further dates you have scheduled me for."

"The clients who have earned your company have to prove they are clean. And they know the rules."

Condoms.

She gripped my chin and turned my head to the side. "Do you have any idea how hard those are going to be to cover up?"

And no visible marks. Especially no hickies.

"Now I'll have to take you to get tested." She pulled out her cell phone. "Have you showered yet?"

"Take a sniff. What do you think?"

"I do not need this, Paris. Not now. You have the biggest interview of your life in three days. I cannot believe you would risk everything for…" Her face reddened.

"Sex?"

She slapped me again.

"Well, what else did you want me to call it?"

She quick-keyed the number. "How dare you do this to me?"

"You can calm down. He's clean."

"Really? He tell you, or did he show you his paperwork? I'm sure he just conveniently had it lying around."

62

"No, he's never had sex with any other man."

"There are more than a few ways to catch something."

"You're right, there are. And those ways won't be stopped by a condom."

"I mean, drugs. Specifically needles."

"He doesn't even smoke cigarettes, let alone shoot up."

"Drug users lie."

"I had my tongue in every crack and crevice of his body. If he had track marks, I would have found them."

She curled her hand into a fist. I braced myself, but the strike never came.

"Look, sex helps me paint. That's what you want me to do, isn't it?"

"Then maybe I should take more applicants?"

"Sex with people I want to have sex with."

"And obviously, that's not a choice you can be trusted with."

"He's the only one I've slacked on in years."

"It only takes one."

"Even without tests, there's less of a chance with him than the people you hook me up with who wear condoms. Now, can I go get a shower?"

A child laughed.

I turned. "Who did you bring in here?"

"What are you talking about?"

With only a dividing wall between the kitchen and open floor plan, there was nowhere for anyone to hide. "Nothing." The beginning of a headache throbbed behind my eyes.

"Here, I have some pills in my purse." She walked over to the dining room table.

"I'm fine."

"If your head hurts, you need to take something for it."

"It doesn't hurt."

"Then why are you rubbing your temple?" Julia dug around in her handbag and came back with a fat white pill. "Here."

"What is it?"

"Does it matter?"

"Yes."

"Take the pill, Paris."

"Fine." I turned to go up the stairs.

"Now."

"I need water."

"Then go to the kitchen."

"My room is closer."

"You have no trouble fitting far bigger things down your throat, so swallow it dry."

"Sucking cock is a lot different than trying to swallow pill the size of an egg. If you'd ever done it, you'd know that."

Another slap.

"Covering up a busted lip is going to be a lot harder than hickies." I pressed my tongue to my lip.

"Take the pill, or a busted lip will be the least of your worries."

I put it in my mouth.

"Swallow."

The chalky rock scraped my throat. I worked my mouth for every drop of saliva I could get.

"Swallow it."

"I'm trying." It got stuck on the way down.

Julia held my face and squeezed my cheeks. "Open." I even remembered to lift my tongue. When she was satisfied, she let me go. "Go bathe. You're stinking up the place."

Cut free, I climbed up the steps.

"Paris."

I stopped at the top. What the hell could she want now? "Yes?"

"I only do this because I care about you."

I always wondered if she actually believed her lies or if she thought I did. "I'll be in my room."

By the time I'd washed, the pill lodged somewhere in my chest had begun to burn a bitter chemical taste back up to my tongue. I drank two glasses of water, but the lingering pain made it impossible for me to tell whether or not it had gone down. Then the room tipped.

The mystery pills Julia pushed on me could either give me the best highs or the worst hangovers.

I staggered over uneven ground and into my bedroom. A blinding mass struck me from above, but the light switch had moved so I had no way to turn it off.

The walls fell, kicking up waves, and my bed rocked in the center of my room. I grabbed the comforter but was swept away by the undertow before I could climb on.

My shoulder knocked against the frame, and somehow I wound up on the ceiling with all the furniture dancing around me. I reached for the bed, but it drifted off the edge of the world.

Then the ants ate all my strength, and all I could do was float.

Chapter Four

Sunlight cast broken pieces of red and gold across the ripples. Fat orange fish made circles, and we watched them for a while before he spoke. I didn't know where he'd come from, but I don't think I cared.

Summer was always so lonely for me.

The boy put his hand on my chest. "¿Cómo te llamas?"

I looked down because I thought I had something on my shirt. "I don't understand."

His entire face lit up when he laughed. "No. Name. You name."

"Paris. My name is Paris." I put my hand on his chest. "Me llamo…"

"Your dinner is getting cold," Julia said.

The salmon and asparagus on my plate had been arranged with bits of lemon and decorated with lacy sauce. Too bad making a pretty food sculpture didn't make it taste like a cheap can of alphabet soup.

I poked the fish with my fork.

The murmur of conversation flowing through the restaurant was chorused by the occasional clink of silverware on porcelain. The contrast spit out shards of lime greens over reds and purples.

With every new chip, the pain behind my eyes swelled. It might have been tolerable if the people at our table would have stopped talking to me.

65

"So tell me, Paris, what are you working on right now?" I think his name was Crayson. "It's going to be difficult for you to top the Trinity you unveiled at that last showing. It was definitely your best so far."

My best. A corpse was my best. A corpse being torn apart by ravaging dogs while onlookers did nothing.

That…That was my best.

"Thank you," I said.

He smiled and so did his wife. There were two other couples at our table. I'd never seen them before, but they must have been serious about purchasing one of my works. Julia only invited out the ones who'd practically given her a blank check.

"Paris is always working on amazing new pieces. I'm sure whatever it is, you will be pleasantly surprised."

"Are you a religious man, Paris?" I didn't know the man sitting across from me at the other end of the table either, but he looked vaguely familiar.

"No."

He arched an eyebrow and sipped his wine. "Then why do all your works have a religious theme?"

"I—"

"Paris respects the need for religion," Julia said. "While we don't belong to a particular church, it doesn't mean we can't recognize intelligent design."

The man folded his hands and leaned forward. His eyes were so dark they were black. I'd never seen a man with eyes like that.

Exactly like mine.

"Is that what you believe, Paris?"

Julia paused mid-bite. The gleam in her gaze dared me to refute her. Would she stab me with her steak knife if I did? Wouldn't that be a wonderful front-page story? At least she would get the fame she'd always dreamed of.

The tension screamed between us.

"What she said."

Julia went back to eating and talking with everyone except for the unnamed man. He stared at me while he plucked cherry tomatoes from the end of his fork. There was no ring on his finger, but he wore an expensive watch and sapphire cufflinks.

I cut a piece of salmon and dragged it through the sauce. It dripped on the way to my mouth. I collected the smear of sauce from my lip and sucked it off my finger.

"Use your napkin." Julia pushed it closer. She resumed her conversation, and I did it again.

The man tilted his head ever so slightly in the direction of the men's room. I flicked a look at Julia. His smile widened as he drank the last of his wine.

"Ladies, gentlemen, if you would excuse me, I'm going to step out on the veranda for a smoke." The man made his way through the crowd of tables.

Off to my right, a woman laughed. Her blonde hair fell in a curtain over her shoulders. A minuscule table separated her from an equally lovely young man. Their hands made love to each other between their glasses of wine.

Every so often, they would share a bite of food, and he would lean close enough to whisper in her ear.

An elderly couple sat behind them. Their table was also small, but they'd moved their chairs to one side. The subtle smiles they shared were twice as powerful.

I drank some wine to soothe the dryness in my throat. After another excruciating minute, I pushed back my chair. "Would you excuse me, please, while I make use of the facilities?"

Julia's hand locked onto my wrist. "You have guests."

"I'm aware of that."

"It's rude to leave the table." She squeezed five burning points into my skin.

"I'm just going to the bathroom."

She did not let go.

"I promise."

She still didn't let go.

"It's right across the room. You can see the door from here."

Her grip loosened. "Don't take too long."

"I'll do my best."

Her heated stare pressed against my back all the way to the men's room. The man with no name stood at the sink washing his hands.

There was no one at the urinals, and all the stall doors were slightly open. As luck would have it, the closet-like design offered maximum privacy.

I entered the one at the end. The man with no name joined me. He locked the door and shoved me into the corner.

"Took you long enough." He attacked my mouth.

"Julia doesn't trust me."

"Really? Does she have a reason not to trust you, Mr. Duvoe?" He bit my ear, and I hissed.

"Absolutely."

"Good."

Our tongues returned to battle. I pulled his hair, and he twisted one of my nipples through my shirt.

"I wanted to fuck you as soon as I saw you." The man worked his belt with one hand.

"Allow me." I knelt and set him free. He grabbed the back of my head and forced me to take his cock to the back of my throat. I swallowed, massaging his length.

"I'm going to fuck your mouth, Paris, like no one ever has. You're going to choke on me. You're going to beg me to stop." He rolled his hips. "And maybe if you're good enough, I will." He yanked me back only to slam himself down my throat again. "That's it. God, yes, just like that." He pumped his hips. "Suck harder." I did. "Yes. Yes. Just like that."

I fought to keep pace and unbuckle my pants.

"Don't you dare touch yourself." He drew out until only the tip of him was between my lips, but before I could catch my breath, he forced his cock to the back of my throat. "Goddamn, you've got a good mouth."

The scent of male musk overpowered his expensive cologne, flavoring every breath he allowed me to take.

Then he held me. Filling my throat until there was no room for air.

I rolled a look up at him, but his features were lost under the tears pooling in my eyes.

"Aw, Paris. Why are you crying?" He wiped my cheek a with manicured fingers. I breathed through my nose, and he pinched it shut. "No cheating."

I glared at him.

"Is something wrong? Is there something you need maybe?"

Black stars burst in front of my eyes.

"It's easy to take breathing for granted until you can't do it."

I groaned.

"Didn't your mother ever teach you not to talk with your mouth full?"

He pulled out, and I gasped for breath.

"Now what were you trying to say?" He petted my face. "Maybe 'stop, I can't take it, it's too much'?"

I met his gaze and smiled. "Is that the best you can do?"

He laughed. "You are something, aren't you?"

"You have no idea."

"Stand up." I did, and he spun me around. "Hands on the wall." He worked my pants open.

"There's a condom in my wallet."

"That's nice."

"Use it."

"No, thank you."

"Julia's rules."

There was a second where he paused. Then he dug a hand through my pants pocket.

"Other side."

He dropped my wallet on the floor. "I hate these fucking things."

"Yeah, and I hate my sister."

"You sound like you're scared of her." He flicked the wrapper, and it landed next to my shoe. "Are you?"

"Do you plan on sticking your dick in my ass or not?"

"Patience. Damn thing is slick as…there." He painted the lubricant left on his fingers over my opening.

The man pushed just enough to work the fat head beyond the ring of muscle of my hole, then took me in one hard shove. "God…I bet you feel ten times as good without the condom."

"Too bad you'll never find out."

"Don't worry," He thrust. "I'll find a way"—he grunted—"for you to make it up to me." I tilted my hips to change the angle and had to bury a cry into my arm.

"One day, I'll have you somewhere you won't get to hide those sounds. I'll make you sing, Paris. Just like a little bird."

I clenched my ass, and he barked in surprise. I laughed.

"Fuck. Definitely going to have you again." He pulled me back while he went forward, slamming our bodies together.

My gut knotted up, sharpening the pleasure. He might have only been average in size, but he obviously knew how to make the best of it.

"Still think that's funny?" He did it again, and the shock picked me up on my toes so far he almost slid out.

"You won't have me again."

"Who says?"

"I say."

"From what I've heard, this ass I'm fucking has a price tag, and here I am using it without paying a cent."

"Free"—Another sharp jab yanked the breath right out of me.—"sample."

"Really now?"

"You have no idea what I can do." I looked at him over my shoulder. "No idea."

"Maybe I'll just have to find out."

"From what I've seen so far, you don't stand a chance."

The flush in his cheeks darkened. "What's the price?"

"Fifty, sometimes sixty. Negotiate with Julia."

The man reached around and grabbed my balls. "She's not the one I'm fucking."

"Not my call."

He squeezed.

I gritted my teeth. "Fucking hell."

"That's right, cry like a little bitch."

I pushed back against him, cutting his thrusts short. The sound of our bodies slapping together echoed off the walls. He grunted with every thrust. "Gonna come."

The bathroom door whispered on its hinges. Laughter floated in, and voices followed. He froze with his cock buried in my ass.

"Might want to hold that thought." I smirked.

"Shh—"

The hazy image of two men moved behind the slats in the door. They met at the urinals.

I leaned my head back until my lips almost brushed his cheek. "Maybe they'll blow each other."

My fuck buddy slapped his hand over my mouth. "I said shut up."

I clenched my ass and rolled my hips. He glared at me. I laughed at him with my eyes.

Next to my ear, he whispered. "If you get me caught, I will do worse than fuck you raw."

I did it again.

He all but crushed my face with his hand.

The two men unzipped and urinated.

"Are you up for a game this weekend?" the man on the left said.

Right guy shifted his weight. "Wedding anniversary."

"See, I warned you not to get married. Ruins your life."

"She's a good woman."

"Ruins the sex too."

Righty laughed. "That's why you keep friends with benefits."

"So no golf?" Lefty finished. The sliced image of his gray slacks moved to the sink. There was a squeak, then the hiss of water.

I used the cover to gyrate my hips. This time when I tightened my muscles, I gave it everything I had. The scowl on my fuck buddy's face turned hungry. I licked his palm.

Righty joined his friend. "I'll see what I can do." Whatever they said next was covered up by the dryer. It cut off, and their voices faded away as they left the bathroom.

My new friend rested his forehead between my shoulders and groaned.

I shook free of his hand. "Don't tell me you're ready to quit. I'm just getting started."

He lifted his gaze. Anger seethed from his black, black eyes. "Better cram your fist in your mouth." His hips shot forward.

I was able to grab the toilet paper dispenser to keep from falling, but I still wound up off balance with my head bent to the side until my ear was pressed to my shoulder.

Every thrust slammed my cheek into the wall until my jawbone throbbed. I pushed myself upright, but he gripped the back of my head and shoved me back into the corner. The man whose name I didn't know fucked me so hard I couldn't even inhale a full breath before it was knocked out of me again.

It wasn't long before his body tensed. The jump of his cock was nearly lost to the thump of my heart in my ears.

"Turn around."

I thought my muscles couldn't scream any louder, but as I stood, the pain chomping at the nerves crescendoed in my spine. No matter how hard I tried I couldn't keep from trembling.

"I said turn around." He grabbed me by my shoulder and pinned me to the wall. "Do you want to come?"

"Is that a trick question?"

He ran a finger down my aching cock. I bit back a plea.

"I'm definitely going to have to do something about that smart mouth." He squeezed my cock. When I clenched my teeth, he laughed. "Hurt much?"

"Yeah."

"But you like it."

"Had better."

His strokes quickened. Precum leaked from the tip of my cock until the foreskin rubbed the head with a wet sound.

The smug look on his face made me want to hold back just to see how long he could jack me before his hand gave out. I knew I could outlast him, but the last thing I needed was Julia hunting me down.

He twisted his wrist and at the same time did something with his thumb. A bolt shot up my cock, making me cry out, and I came. He continued to stroke me until the orgasm turned ugly and all I could do was writhe against the wall, pawing at his chest while every nerve in the head of my dick was set on fire.

Then he stopped, and my knees gave out.

"Right where you belong." He tilted my head up and pushed his cum-coated fingers into my mouth. "That's it. Every drop."

I even licked his palm. When he was clean, he leaned down and kissed me.

"Better get back to dinner before we're missed," he said.

"Way past that already, I'm sure."

He fixed his clothes, and left me to struggle to my feet. We stood side by side at the sink like strangers. I fully expected to look worse than I did. I washed my hands and ran my hand through my bangs.

"You first." He nodded at the door.

The violence playing in Julia's eyes was bright even from across the room. She'd long ago surpassed anger and shot into psychotic.

The man fell in behind me. He clapped me on the back of my shoulder and grinned. "Laugh like I've just told you the best joke in the world."

I did. Julia's gaze went from him to me. We stopped at the table.

"Sorry to keep you waiting, but Paris and I got to talking."

"About what?" Julia looked at me when said it.

"His paintings," the man said.

"Really?"

"Don't worry, Julia, I didn't reveal any of my trade secrets." I sat.

"Your little brother is quite the salesman."

Now she looked at him. "Excuse me?"

He drank from his wine glass. "Oh yes, he's convinced me to commission him to do a mural in my summer home."

"I didn't know you did murals?" That from the balding guy.

"It would be my first."

"How big a mural?" Julia said.

The man propped an elbow on the table and held his chin. "I don't know the exact dimensions, but I am sure it will take a while. He would have to come stay with me. A week…maybe two."

Julia coughed into her napkin. "I don't know, Gregory, he's very busy."

"I'll make sure to pay him a fair price. I figured we could start the bidding at three million."

Mrs. Crayson dropped her fork. While everyone at the table stared at Gregory, Julia stared at me.

"Of course if it takes longer, I'll be sure to compensate him."

"Why, that's very…uh…"

73

I leaned closer to Julia. "I think the word you're looking for is generous."

"Yes." Julia plastered on a shiny happy expression. "Yes, thank you."

"So then I'll have my secretary call you to make the arrangements?" Gregory said.

"Yes. Please."

"You've been holding out on us, Julia." The older gentlemen on her left said. "We had no idea Paris could be commissioned for murals."

"Would he be willing to fly to France?" His wife patted him on the hand. "He could paint on that enormous blank wall at the cottage." She turned her attention back to us. "The interior designer has yet to come up with something acceptable."

"I don't know, Paris and I will have to…"

"We'll pay for the flight, of course," she said. "And the lodging."

"You know." Mrs. Crayson nodded at her husband. "Robert's brother owns a charter company. A private jet would be much nicer than a commercial flight."

While the two couples discussed the possibilities, Gregory stalked me from across the table.

"Please tell me you can paint murals," Julia said.

"A wall is just a bigger canvas."

Julia smiled. "I'm so proud of you." She picked at the corner of my mouth. "Hold still." She licked her thumb.

"What are you doing?"

"You have something on your face." She scrubbed the spot. "Really, Paris, you need to work on your manners and use your napkin once in a while." She wet her thumb again and made a few more swipes before she was satisfied. "There, that's better."

I sipped my wine. "What would I ever do without you?"

****

Layers of paint stained my hands, marking the hours I'd suffered under the brush and bleeding on the canvas.

All I had to do was look at it, give it a name, then I could shove it on the drying rack and forget it ever existed. My hands

74

trembled. My throat tightened. The bones in my neck creaked with the effort it took to raise my head.

The writhing forms reached for me with skeletal hands covered in paper flesh. They had worn their fingertips away on their climb from the pit. Pleading cries turned into angry accusations.

"Everything was fine until you were born." The tone of Julia's voice promised pain.

"You made me do this. Fucking little whore." I shrank away from my father.

A woman knelt down. Her cheeks were wet from crying. *"Por favor, dime dónde está."*

I threw myself back and collided with one of the workbenches. The studio was empty.

Leftovers from a dream. It had to be. I'd painted. I'd put everything there just like I was supposed to. Somewhere in the shadows, a twig snapped.

I stuffed my wallet in my pocket and carried my shoes with me to the elevator. If Bill saw me leave the building, he didn't say anything. And if he said anything, I didn't hear.

At two o'clock in the morning, even the cabs became endangered animals.

After a few misses, I was finally able to get my feet into my shoes. At least my toes were safe from frostbite. I couldn't say the same for the rest of me. I wrapped my arms around my chest. It was useless. My thin shirt offered no protection.

I went from shadows to halogen puddles until I reached the end of the block. The only sign of life was a twenty-four hour liquor store. I told myself it would be warm, but the truth was I planned on getting so smashed I wouldn't be able to tell if it wasn't.

The man at the counter didn't look up from his magazine. "If you're looking for something particular, let me know." He flipped the page.

If I'd known what I wanted, I would have asked. Just to save myself the time.

I headed to the back.

Row after row of cheap wine, liquor, vodka. None of the names looked familiar. I grabbed the most expensive brand of...the letters on the label wouldn't be still long enough for me to read them.

I carried the bottle to the front.

The man put his magazine on the counter and casually unsnapped the holster on his belt. I got out my wallet.

He flicked a look from my hand to my face and nodded, then rang me up. "Sixty-five eighty."

I took out two fifties.

"Forget your coat?"

"Yeah, I was in a hurry."

"Supposed to get colder. They say it might even snow."

No wonder the streets were empty. The threat of snowflakes in the South might as well have been a promise of alien invasion.

"Maybe you'd like to borrow the phone and call yourself a cab?"

The thought of being trapped inside a metal box made my insides crawl.

"No, no. I'm good."

He gave me my change. The dimes leapt from my hand and ticked against the wooden counter.

Leaves clung to my legs. Everything smelled of wet earth.

I dropped the tarp, and Julia screamed at me. "Pick up his feet." The rain mashed the curls to her head and smeared her makeup. "This is your mess, and now you have to help clean it up."

"Son?"

"Por favor, ¿ha visto ami hijo?"

I pressed the heel of my hand against my temple.

The man moved his hand close to his gun.

"I'm okay. Just a migraine."

He nodded, but his hand remained near his holster.

I stuffed the bills back into my wallet. When I closed it, Roy's card stuck up from the folds. I pulled it out. The cheap paper was smooth between my fingers.

"You said you had a phone I could borrow?"

"It's local, right?" I nodded. He set the phone in front of me.

The time didn't even dawn on me until after the third ring, not that I had a right to call him to begin with.

"Hello?" Rough from sleep, his deep voice slid under my skin. The trembling in my hands stopped. "Hello?"

"It's Paris."

Sheet rustled. A mattress squeaked. I was very familiar with that sound as well as the thump of the headboard against the wall.

"Are you okay?" Some of the grit left his tone.

"I'm not sure."

"Where are you?"

"A liquor store near my apartment. Well, about two blocks from my apartment."

"What's the address?"

I asked the clerk and relayed it to Roy.

"I'll be there in a few minutes."

He hung up, and I cradled the phone against my chest.

"You done with that, son?"

I handed the receiver back to the man. "Thank you."

"No problem."

I put my wallet away and gathered up my merchandise. The night pressed against the glass door. I stood with my hand on the bar.

"You can wait inside, if you want."

"Are you sure?"

"Yeah." He picked up his magazine and resumed reading.

****

Roy wrapped his coat around my shoulders, and I stuffed the bottle of liquor in the pocket while he zipped it.

There were dark circles under his eyes, and his flannel shirt was buttoned crooked. The jeans he wore had a hole in the knee, but any skin was hidden behind the long johns underneath.

"I'm sorry I bothered you."

"Don't be."

"I shouldn't have called."

"You did the right thing."

I never did the right thing. I did what was selfish and shortsighted. I did the things that got me what I wanted. And yes, I admit, I wanted him.

I wanted the warmth of his body against mine. His arms holding me together. That voice, that wonderful voice, promising me safety.

Roy thanked the liquor storeowner and led me outside. "I think there's a cab parked up the way."

"I don't want a cab."

"You don't have any socks on. Your feet are going to freeze before you can get home."

They were already freezing. "I don't want to go home."

"Do you want to go to my place?"

"No."

"Is there somewhere else?"

"No."

He stopped. "Paris, what's wrong?"

I pressed myself to him. "Just hold me for a moment." The heat radiating from his skin, the hardness of his body, the strength in his arms erased all the bad things.

The spicy scent I'd come to know as his seemed stronger than usual. I buried my face against his neck. He exhaled, and I inhaled. His heart beat and so did mine.

Roy kissed my temple. "Talk to me, please. I want to help you."

"Why?"

"Do I need a reason?"

"Yes."

He ran a hand over my head. "Then it's because I want to."

"Why? Why do you want to?"

His sigh was warm against my ear. "Because maybe if I can help you, then the world will be a better place."

I huffed. "You sound like a Greenpeace commercial."

His laugh vibrated through to my core and wrapped me in layers of orange and yellow.

"I'll take that as a compliment."

The tires on a passing car made a wet sound against the asphalt. After another long moment, I said, "You're wrong, you know. Helping me won't make the world a better place."

He cupped my chin. The shadows made the lines around his eyes deeper. Instead of looking older, he looked more rugged. "Why not?"

"Because the world will only be a better place when people like me are no longer in it."

He cradled me. "That's not true, and whoever told you that is a liar."

I stepped back. But I don't think he wanted to let me go. "Do you think there's a coffee shop open?"

"There's a Waffle House about a half mile from here."

"Sounds greasy."

"It is. But the coffee is good."

I loved it already. "C'mon. My feet are cold."

He put his arm over my shoulders. "I see a cab."

The yellow car pulled up under a streetlight.

"I don't want to get in a cab."

"Why not?"

"Can we please walk?"

He cast a look at the car, then me. "Are you sure?"

"Yes."

Five blocks up, the street split into a tangle of asphalt. Highway traffic hissed from behind a line of carefully arranged shrubbery. Amber running lights outlined semis and RVs parked beside a gas station. The rumble of their engines pumped into the night.

Fluorescent light spilled out the windows of the Waffle House, illuminating the parking lot. The scent of toast and bacon replaced the oily smell of exhaust.

My stomach growled.

"Hungry much?" Roy held open the door.

"Maybe." I was hungry, and I was never hungry.

There were more people than I'd expected. The short-order cook yelled out a hello, and the waitresses echoed him.

"Do they know you?" I said.

"No. They just do that."

"Why?"

"I guess to make you feel welcome." Roy found us a booth for two in the corner.

One of the waitresses walked over. "Coffee?"

"Yes, ma'am," Roy said.

"Sugar and cream?"

"Paris?"

I nodded.

"Please." Roy smiled at her, and she left.

"Aren't you a Boy Scout?"

He handed me a menu. "Why do you say that?"

"Please, ma'am, thank you."

"That's just being polite."

I turned the laminated rectangle over. Nothing in the pictures looked edible. I couldn't even be sure if it was real food. I squinted at what was supposed to be a T-bone steak. "So what's good to eat here?"

"I guess that depends on what you like."

"What's the greasiest?"

"Greasiest?"

"Yeah. I want heartburn and indigestion."

"Why would you want that?"

"I don't have a clue."

The waitress dropped off our coffee along with a bowl full of cream packets. I could only imagine the shit fit Julia would have if she'd been expected to get her cream from plastic containers.

I poured several into the coffee. The empties left smears of white on the tabletop. Roy wiped up the mess with a napkin, then collected the plastic containers. He put everything off to the side.

"See, you are a Boy Scout."

"I'm just like anyone else."

I drank my coffee. It was still hot enough to burn my tongue. "Really?"

"Yeah."

"Roy, I have news for you. Not everyone is like you. They don't even come close to you."

"They are where I come from."

"And what planet is that?"

"A town called Arrington."

"Never heard of it."

"That doesn't surprise me. The most exciting thing to ever come out of there was soy beans and cotton."

"Sounds riveting."

He humpfed. "In the summer, they have a fair where they race bull frogs and wiener dogs."

My mouthful of coffee went up my nose. I grabbed some napkins.

"You okay?"

My eyes burned almost as bad as my sinuses. "Fine." I blew, clearing out the coffee. "Next time, warn me when you say things like that."

"I had no idea I said anything needing a warning."

I wiped my face. "So what was it like growing up in Arrington, besides the frogs and dog races?"

"It was—"

"You gentlemen ready to order?" Our waitress took out a ticket book from her apron.

"Sure." To me, Roy said, "You ready?"

"Yeah."

"Hamburger, fries, chocolate shake."

She looked at me. "And you, dear?"

I pointed to a random item on the menu. "That."

"Do you want anything on it?"

"Uh, sure."

She held her pen over her note pad.

"Tell her what you want," Roy said.

"All of it."

"Fully loaded?"

"Yeah."

"Sure thing, sweetie." She headed off to give one of the truckers a refill.

"You didn't even look at the menu." Roy put it away.

"I know."

"Do you even know what you ordered?"

"No clue."

He shook his head.

I added more sugar to my coffee. "So finish telling me about Arrington, Arkansas."

"Not much to tell."

"There has to be something."

"Like what?"

"I don't know."

"There isn't. Arrington's just a speck on the map. Population less than ten thousand. Most people who live there don't even graduate high school."

"How come?"

81

He shrugged. "Not much need for an education when all you're going to do is pick cotton, farm beans, or work in a carpet mill."

"Did you finish high school?"

"I did."

"And let me guess, the star player on your football team."

Roy rubbed the back of his neck.

I leaned over the table. "I'm willing to bet half your team would have bent over and spread their cheeks for you."

His elbow caught his cup and coffee sloshed all over the table. Roy ripped out a handful of napkins from the dispenser to soak it up.

"Did you marry your high school sweetheart?"

He wouldn't look at me.

"Were you King and Queen at your prom?" His silence was all the confirmation I needed.

He waved the waitress down for a refill. She topped mine off as well.

Roy finished mopping up the mess. She carried it away.

"Wow, you were right after all."

"About what?"

"You're not a Boy Scout, you're a goddamned hometown hero." The coffee was bitter again so I added more cream. "So with a fairy tale beginning, how come you didn't get your happily ever after?"

"I wasn't happy."

"How come?"

"Because I should have never married her."

"Then why did you?"

"It's what you were expected to do." He picked up my empties again. "Get married, have kids. Being gay was a city folk problem, rooted in a godless life."

"Pray the gay away, huh?" A shadow passed behind Roy's eyes. "Is that why you got married? Because you thought it would just go away?"

"I don't know." He turned his coffee cup around and around. "Maybe I just didn't realize I had a choice."

"And then you did?"

"Yeah. Only it was ten years too late."

"How could it be too late?"

"Carla had fallen in love, and I didn't do anything to stop her. I took ten years of her life where she could have been building a family. Ten years where she could have had someone who loved her back. I loved her, just not the way she wanted me to."

"According to you, she wasn't exactly fit for parenthood."

"I made her that way."

"Yeah right."

"No. I did. I ruined her. I didn't mean to, but I did."

"How?"

"Like I said, small town. A lot of people blamed her for me being gay."

"Why?"

"Same reason people blame the wife when the husband cheats." Roy shrugged. "She had to be doing something wrong, or it wouldn't have happened."

"You could have blamed the divorce on her cooking, and she could have blamed it on you snoring." I waved a hand. "Or something like that."

"I tried. I sat her down, and I told her the truth. Only it didn't go very well. She was really upset and confided in a friend about what I'd said."

"And that friend told a friend?"

He nodded. "Her family found out. Next thing I knew, I was getting divorce papers for infidelity. She had cops who were brothers, cousins who were attorneys, an uncle who was the magistrate judge. I screwed up so I let her have everything and left."

"You didn't screw up. Trust me. A lot of people find out too late they can't change who they are." Most of the men I took to my bed were married.

"And that's why I screwed up. I knew it in my gut, but I thought I could ignore it."

"But she accused you of cheating, and you didn't...did you?"

"Of course not. She was my first and...." I was sure he was going to say 'only'. He shook his head. "It was just her way of trying to save face. Instead, it only made things worse. I broke all the good things in her and what was left..."

"Maybe you didn't break her. Maybe she just didn't have to pretend who she really was anymore."

I think Roy was about to argue, but our waitress reappeared with a fresh pot of coffee and Roy's hamburger. To me, she said, "Jacky is bringing yours."

Jacky—at least I presume it was her since that's what her name tag read—lowered a large bowl of steaming substance, topped with more substance. I think it was onions, or maybe cheese. There were a few green things that could have been jalapeños, but it all ran together in a way only liquefied foods should.

Whatever was in the bowl reeked so strong of hot sauce and black pepper I wasn't a bit surprised when our waitress retreated.

Roy made a sad, sad attempt to hide his smile. I'm not even sure if you could call half coughing, half covering your mouth with your fist, a real attempt in the first place.

"People eat this?" I stuck a spoon in and waited for it to dissolve.

"They must, or they wouldn't have it on the menu."

"Do I even want to know what it is?"

"Sorta looks like chili." Roy snorted another laugh.

The spoon remained intact so I scooped up a bite.

"Are you sure you want to eat that?"

"Like you said, it's on the menu." An oily burn ignited across my lips before I could get any chili into my mouth. I'd eaten plenty of hot food in my life, but at least there'd been flavor beyond bitter, burnt, and slightly salty.

"How is it?"

I blinked back the tears. "I'm not sure. I think my taste buds have melted." I bit down, and something crunched.

"Was that your tooth?"

I ran my tongue over my molars, but everything felt intact. "Must have been a rock." I chewed and swallowed.

"Good?" The smirk on Roy's face told me he knew damn well just how good it was.

"If you like sucking on cheap paint thinner."

He raised an eyebrow. "Why were you drinking paint thinner?"

I jabbed my spoon at him. "If you knew me better, I'd be insulted. I didn't drink it. I have a bad habit of putting the wrong end of my paint brush in my mouth when I'm thinking." I stirred the chili. Peppercorns floated to the top. "I think I found what—"

"Then let me." Roy watched me with a soft expression.

"What?"

"Let me know you better."

All the creamers were empty, and our waitress was nowhere to be found.

"Please."

I propped my elbow on the table and stirred my chili. Beans traded places with chunks of meat only to be taken down by gobs of cheese.

"Look at me, Paris."

I scraped my spoon along the edge.

"Look at me."

I did.

"Give me a chance."

If he'd been any other man, I could have turned on my smile, flashed him bedroom eyes, and promised him his heart's desire. But Roy was not any man. He was special, pure, kind. He deserved so much better.

"I can't do that."

"Why?"

"I don't want to hurt you."

"You won't."

"Yes, I will."

"How do you know?"

"Because I hurt everyone. It's what I do, Roy. It's all I am."

He put his hand over mine. A long time ago, someone else had held my hand, but I couldn't remember his name. "What if I'm willing to take the risk?"

I shook my head.

Roy pleaded with his eyes.

I'd spoken the truth. I would hurt him. It was fact. As firm and absolute as the sunrise.

Because blood had already been spilled.

****

By the time we left the Waffle House, there were more cars on the road and several of the big rigs were pulling onto the highway. A man came out of the RV with a little white dog under one arm. Where did he plan on walking it?

Humidity replaced the bite in the air, creating a fine mist that somehow reached deeper than the cold.

Roy drew me to him. It was an awkward way to walk, but the contact was just too addictive to give up. Some of the early risers we passed gave us funny looks until they sized up Roy, then they tried really hard not to look at all.

If he noticed, I was glad he didn't care. I needed this. A fleeting moment of comfort might be enough to get me through the year, the month, or at least the week.

Or at worst, the day.

I took the bottle of liquor out of my pocket.

"You shouldn't drink that."

"Why not?" I guzzled a few mouthfuls. The burn of cheap alcohol was nothing compared to the nuclear chili.

"It's not good for you."

I drank some more. "Life isn't good for me, Roy."

He took the bottle away.

"Hey."

He took a drink.

"I thought you said it wasn't good for you."

His face twisted up. "It's not."

"Then why are you drinking it?"

His smile made the answer irrelevant. I reclaimed my bottle and stuck it back in his coat pocket.

After a few more swallows, of course.

I pressed my face against him. "I love the way you smell."

"I think that chili burned out more than your taste buds. You've practically got your nose in my arm pit."

"Yeah. I know."

It always amazed me how quick scenery could change inside the city. A few blocks could mean the difference between truckers, restaurants, shops, and ghettos. How taking a right or left could cause the real estate values to triple or plummet.

The people changed just as drastically.

"I want to see you again," Roy said.

"We had this discussion over that bowl of nuclear waste and a heart attack on a bun. Let's not have it again."

"All right, but I just want to say one thing."

"I'm going to hold you to that." I tripped on a crack in the sidewalk, and he kept me from falling. "Someone should fix that."

He kissed me on the top of my head. "Call me. If you need anything. A ride. Someone to talk to."

I closed my eyes and let him guide me.

"I'm not asking you to call me every night. Or even once a week. Unless you want to. But if you need someone, someplace to go, someplace that's…"

I think he was going to say safe.

He sighed. "Please. Just tell me you will so I won't worry."

"You shouldn't worry."

"But I will."

"There are so many more deserving things to worry about."

"But none of them are as important to me." We stopped in front of my building. Small white flecks plummeted to their death on the sidewalk.

"I should have bought stock in bread, milk, and eggs." I held out a hand. The snow became tears on my skin.

"Promise me."

"Maybe it won't stick."

"Please."

"It never sticks in the city. Why is that? How come we never get a white Christmas?"

He held my face.

"I don't want to lie to you." And I didn't.

"If you call me when you need someone, you can't be a liar."

But I would need him. I already needed him.

"Come upstairs with me." I pulled him by the front of his flannel shirt into the alcove near the door where it was still the dead of night in the corners. With an overcast sky, it would stay that way.

Roy's exhale shuddered. He was already hard when I squeezed us into the niche.

"Come upstairs and fuck me." I bit his earlobe. Roy slid his hands under my coat. He dug at my shirt until he found my skin. Somehow his touch was warm, or maybe I was just that cold.

"Paris." My name sounded more like a growl. I rocked against him. "God, Paris…"

I licked his throat, his chin, then found his mouth. His lips were salty from the french fries, his tongue sweet from dessert.

"You want that, don't you?" I said.

"Yes." He tightened his grip.

"You want my mouth on your dick."

"Yes."

"Your cock in my ass."

Roy buried a groan into my shoulder.

"Then come upstairs with me." I pushed my thigh between his legs.

He rolled his hips.

"Unless you want to do it right here. Is that what you want, Roy? To fuck me out here in front of everyone?" I fumbled with his pants. "They could catch us. No telling what would happen."

A man walked out of the building. The shadows of the alcove were so thick, even from a few yards away, he didn't see us.

I freed Roy's cock. "Better hang onto the wall."

He gripped the edges of the brick, and I dropped to my knees. The spices from the food and liquor gave way to his flavor. And it was so much better.

I hummed as I took him as deep as I could. Roy didn't need any encouragement to pump his hips. I pushed my fingers between his legs to the soft spot behind his balls. I stroked the base of his cock with my other hand and worked my mouth over the head. In the darkness with only the slice of light escaping from inside the building, he was nothing more than a dark shape with shiny black eyes.

His pulse beat against my tongue, accenting his gasps. Roy threaded his fingers into my bangs and pulled. Not hard. Oh no, Roy would never pull hard, but I took him down my throat so fast he might as well have.

Roy buried a cry into his shoulder. I wish there had been more light. I wanted to see the bliss-filled anguish on his face.

A shudder ran up his legs, pulling him to his toes. He slammed his hand against the brick. Bitter heat filled my mouth. I tried to swallow, but it was impossible around the girth of his cock. I could only hope I wouldn't drown. Or maybe I should have hoped I would.

Cum trickled down my throat, and I fought the urge to cough. Only when his cock began to soften was I able to swallow. I still didn't want to release him, and I used the excuse of licking him clean to keep him in my mouth. Would he get hard again if I kept going?

Roy pulled me to my feet and pinned me in the corner. He fought with the button on my pants. The calluses on his hand scraped over the weeping head of my cock, sending shockwaves up my spine. Cold fought with heat as I pumped into the tunnel of his fist.

I raked my teeth against Roy's ear. "That's it. Just like that." He squeezed, and I growled. "God, you're getting good at this. Or maybe you've just been getting a lot of practice. Is that it? Are you fucking your hand and imagining it's me?"

He moved faster.

"Oh, yeah. I bet you are. I bet you dream of your dick in my ass every night." I laughed against his cheek. Roy turned his head and caught my mouth. The kiss was brutal, deep, fast. More people were on the street now, more cars, more noise. But none of it could touch us. We'd slipped beyond the real world and hovered where darkness and light made love to create the colors of the universe.

Shivers crawled through my muscles and seized my body. I hissed Roy's name. "Harder, God, harder. Close. So close." I clawed at his shoulders then bit his neck. "Need more."

"Tell me."

"Fingers. I need…"

Roy dipped his fingers into his mouth and then found his way inside my jeans. I hooked a leg around his thigh, spreading myself as best as I could. The burn of those thick digits invading me was almost enough…almost.

"I've got you." Roy huffed against my neck. I wanted him to turn me around and fuck me against the wall. But the spiraling rush reduced my words into pitiful cries.

Roy shifted his weight, changing the angle, giving him more room to move, pushing deeper, hitting just the right spot. Made helpless, all I could do was fall. He swallowed my shout just in time.

Our exchange of breaths became the only sound. Then slowly the rest of the world spilled back into focus, and the refuge we'd found in the corner was simply a dark place occupied by two bodies.

He held me for the longest time.

"You should go." I didn't want him to, but he was dangerous because he made me weak.

"Remember what I told you." He fixed my clothes, then his. "Remember, okay?"

I gave him his jacket. He used the hem of his shirt to wipe his hands before he took it.

"Tell me you'll call if you need me."

I took the liquor bottle out of his pocket.

He caressed my cheek. "Any reason. Any time." Concern shone in his eyes. "Please."

I left and didn't look back.

Chapter Five

Julia waited for me in the limo.

"You took long enough." She dropped a compact in her purse and attacked the top button of my shirt. "At least you dressed decent."

"It's too tight like that."

She slapped my hands away. "Too bad."

Would she feel that way if I suffocated live on TV?

Julia tapped the tinted partition, and the driver pulled into the street. High-end apartment buildings gave way to skyscrapers and traffic. A group of homeless men sat on a street corner picking guitars.

I bet no one made them wear their shirts buttoned up so they would choke.

Julia kicked me in the shin.

"What?"

"Did you hear anything I just said?"

"Obviously not."

"This interview is important. Allen Rock only invites a select few on his show. Millions will be watching. With international attention, the value of your works could double. But you're only going to get one chance, so don't fuck this up."

"I don't need more attention."

"More attention means more money for your work."

"I don't need any more money either."

She glared. "I'm serious."

"Christ, Julia, you're rich. Alice is rich. Why do you need more? You buy everything you want, and it's not like you can take it with you."

"It's not just about the money."

"Well then, I don't want the fame."

Her gaze slid away, and she shifted in her seat.

"I see. Are you hoping you'll get your face in Time Magazine or People?"

Julia flicked her hair off her shoulder. "Just remember to keep quiet."

"I thought this was an interview."

"It is."

"Then I can't keep quiet."

"Then don't say anything without my okay."

I flopped back against the seat. "How about I go back to the apartment and help Alice do laundry and you do the interview?"

"The housekeeper does the laundry."

"Okay, I'll help Alice alphabetize all those Tupperware containers in the fridge."

Julia flashed her teeth. "You're doing the interview."

Of course, I was. I was a puppet, and Julia held my strings.

"Don't pout." Julia put her hand my knee. I wanted to shove it off, but she'd probably bust my lip, then we wouldn't be able to go on the air. I didn't even want to imagine the extent of her wrath that would unleash.

"I'm not pouting. I'm angry."

"And what on earth do you have to be angry about?"

I rolled my eyes.

"Is this about that homeless man you brought to the apartment?"

"Homeless? What the hell are you talking about?"

"Him…that guy."

"Roy?"

"Whatever his name is."

"What does Roy have to do with any of this?"

"I thought you might be mad that I don't approve of you seeing him. It's for your own good, you know."

"I'm not…Roy has nothing to do with this."

"Then why are you upset?"

"Isn't it obvious?" No, of course it wasn't. Not to her. I took a breath. "What will it take to make you quit punishing me?"

"There's nothing you can give me to make up for what you did."

"Why is it my fault?" I didn't ask to be born. "Just tell me that."

"I have."

"No, you haven't."

"We're not having this discussion right now." She smoothed out her skirt.

"Then when will we have it? When will you tell me what I did wrong?"

Her glare cut right through me. "You teased him, Paris. You taunted him. You knew he was weak, and you all but threw yourself at him. He was fine till you came along."

"I was a kid." I rested my head against the window.

"That doesn't excuse your actions. You practically put the gun to Daddy's head and pulled the trigger."

She had remorse for Harrison, but never for the boy. "What if I sign everything over to you and just walk away."

"That won't work, and you know it."

"Then how about I just walk away. You can keep the money, I don't want it." I just want to be free. I massaged my forehead.

"Headache?"

"No."

She dug around in her purse. "I think I have some aspirin."

"I don't want any aspirin. I'm fine."

"You don't act fine." She pulled out a bottle.

I slapped it away. "I told you I don't want any."

"What is your problem today?"

"You." I growled out my frustrations behind clenched teeth. "You're my problem, Julia. You're always my problem. Every day. Every hour." I slammed my hand against the seat. "You. You. You."

Her expression hardened. "I'm concerned about you, Paris. Perhaps I should call Dr. Mason and make you an appointment?"

Ice-cold nausea gripped my insides. "I don't need to see Dr. Mason. And you know it."

"I don't know. You sound awfully distressed. And since I am your legal guardian, it is my responsibility to make sure you're not a danger to yourself...or others." She smirked.

"If you dope me up and lock me away, I won't be able to paint."

"I can request he try alternative treatments so we could forgo the medications. And you can paint in any sized room. With or without windows."

"Yeah, and what if I decide not to paint? Put me in a hole, and I'll have no reason to."

She huffed. "I'd think you'd be more grateful."

"For what?"

93

"For everything I've done for you. Everything I've sacrificed."

"Done for me? You haven't done anything for me."

"Really? If it wasn't for me, you would've been living in a state facility for juvenile delinquents. But instead of letting the police lock you up, I made sure they could never touch you."

It wasn't kindness; she was just afraid I'd tell. And I would have. I tried. But Dr. Mason convinced them the shock of finding my father with his brains splattered all over my bedroom damaged me in a way that skewed my perception of reality.

I wish I could have disputed the claim. He was just wrong about the reason.

I slid deeper into the seat. My next inhale tasted of dust and ammonia. The sensation of spider webs caressed my cheek. Nothing was there.

Julia dug around in her purse. She took out a small clear bag of white powder. "Here."

I took it. "Coke?"

"The last thing you need is to be hyped up. It's X." She handed me a glass straw.

"You want me to snort it out of the bag?"

"No. I want you to put it in your pocket. Then when we get to the studio, discreetly excuse yourself to the bathroom. You can do it in there. And don't you dare do more than one line."

"I don't want to." I tried to hand it back to her.

She sank her nails into my wrist. "You will take it."

"Why?"

"Because the public doesn't want to watch the nervous ramblings of a crazy person."

"Don't worry. I have no intentions of carrying on a conversation with Jesus."

Her grip tightened. I refused to acknowledge it.

"This is important."

"You already said that ten times."

"Then act like it."

I put the baggy in my pocket.

Julia smiled at me. "Thank you."

"You're not welcome."

"Are we going to play this game all day?"

"Try for the rest of my life."

"You are such a child."

I was. And I didn't care.

"I'll tell you what," Julia said. "To make things up to you, I'll treat to lunch after the interview."

"Yay."

"I'll even take you to that restaurant you like. The one with the green-striped awning. What's it called?"

"I don't remember." Cold seeped from behind the window, giving me some relief from the throbbing in my head.

"Maybe Mr. Rock will be so impressed he'll insist on joining us." She smoothed out her skirt again. "If he does, we'll have to eat somewhere else."

"Of course, we will."

"It's important we make a good impression."

"Absolutely."

"When we get there, don't hurry to get inside, or you'll seem desperate."

"Wouldn't want that."

"I hope Richard remembered to wrap the painting."

I looked at her. "What painting?"

"The one I brought for the interview."

"But everything I have finished is at the gallery."

"It's the one you had on the drying rack."

The one on the drying rack? I didn't have any on the...

The Kiss.

"That piece is mine."

She shrugged. "I didn't know."

"That's exactly why you're not supposed to go rifling through my studio."

"I told you I needed one for the interview. And it wasn't like I could have taken one out of the gallery. It would have unbalanced the entire display. What do you want it for anyhow? You're not going to do anything with it."

"That's not the point. Some paintings are mine and mine alone."

"Why? All you do is stuff them in that storage room where no one can see them."

"I don't want anyone to see them." I plucked at the hairs on the back of my head.

"Quit that, or you'll make bald spots." Julia checked for damage. Satisfied, she combed through my bangs until they swept down my forehead and across my cheek. "Besides, a piece like that would never sell in the gallery."

"Doesn't matter because it's not for sale."

"Of course, it's for sale. All your work is for sale."

I dug my fingers into my thighs. "No. They're not."

"Don't be so obstinate. You can make another one."

"I can't just *make* another one."

"Well then, don't get so attached. Selling art is your livelihood, remember? If you don't sell your works, then you can't pay the bills." She licked her thumb and wiped something off my chin. "This is how the world works, Paris. I know that's hard for you to understand so you'll just have to trust me."

The thought of that painting—my painting—in front of the world made me tremble.

"Are you cold? Do you want Larry to turn the heat up?"

"I'm fine."

"Turn the heat up, Larry, Paris is cold."

Dry warmth sucked the moisture from my skin.

"There." Julia fiddled with my hair some more. "You should have said something sooner."

"I didn't say anything because I was fine."

The limo pulled into the parking deck, and the world disappeared behind concrete walls and rows of cars. Several floors down, the driver stopped in front of a set of elevator doors.

"This so exciting." Julia primped in the mirror of her compact before tucking it away again. "We're going to be in the same studio where two vice presidents and five Oscar winners have been interviewed. Just think of all the people who will see us."

"Julia, please." Surely she could spare just one grain of empathy.

"What?"

"I'll talk to the people at the next showing. I'll go home with whoever you want me to so they'll buy a piece. Whatever you want. But please don't take that painting inside. Don't sell it. I'm begging you."

Julia's hard blue eyes met mine. The smile she gave me was a line cut in ice. "Don't be silly. Of course, I'll sell it." She opened the door. "Now get out."

****

The elevator opened at the fifth floor, and an intern welcomed us. She was cute, petite, with wild red hair. I wanted to lay her out, expose her small breasts, and spread her legs. The only thing she would wear was a euphoric expression. Then I'd transform her from the flesh and bones in front of us, chatting and waving her arms, into lines and negative space where she could exist for eternity.

Unlike *The Kiss*, a painting of this woman would be nothing more than pretty colors on a stretch of gesso-covered fabric.

Julia nudged me with her elbow. "Didn't you say something about needing to use the facilities?"

I stared at all the broken fragments of color that were once me, lying scattered around my feet.

"Paris?"

If only I could retrieve a shard and slit my throat.

"Paris."

I nodded. "Yeah. Will you excuse me?" I tried to smile at the intern, but my lips were full of lead. "Which way?"

She pointed.

I escaped into the men's room. There was only one stall and a urinal. I turned the lock on the door. I laid out some of the powder and used one of my business cards to cut a line. The business cards were Julia's idea. Fuck, everything was Julia's idea. What I wore to what I snorted up my nose. She called the shots. She gave the commands. And I was the dog at the end of the leash.

It was temping to throw the bag into the toilet, but I was going to have to go out there in front of all those people who were going to ask me questions, and I would have to answer them. As if they ever understood my answers. Sure, they smiled and nodded, but their eyes stayed blank. It was an act. One big lie.

"Please. Le ruego. Dime dónde está. My son. Where is my son?"

The lights in the bathroom brightened, and a buzz of colors filled the air until they flowed down the walls. Reds and golds. Small chips of orange.

Green made up the negative space.

They were the colors of my painting. Warm and soft just like the kiss. I touched my lips. Why couldn't I remember his name when I could remember every small groove and curve of his mouth pressed to mine?

The line of X was almost invisible against the white enamel of the sink. I stuck the end of the straw in my nose and inhaled. Fire cut through my face to the back of my throat. My nose attempted to extinguish the burn with a wash of snot so I pressed my thumb against one nostril and inhaled.

The tension in my shoulders eased, and the ache in my head floated away. I sniffled a few times and every inhale pushed me farther away from the things that worried me.

The plastic bag stuck to my palm.

"One line, Paris."

So I wouldn't be nervous. Fuck nervous. I didn't want to care.

I stuck the end of the straw inside the bag and followed the line of X in the crease at the bottom all the way to the fat corner.

Once.

Twice.

My sinuses burst into flames, and my head threatened to explode.

The room tipped.

I clung to the sink to keep from sliding into the urinal. Saliva filled my mouth. After a few seconds, everything leveled out and I was able to walk without falling over. There was a crunch from under my shoe. The pulverized glass straw made sparkling crumbles on the black and white tile.

A knock at the door punched me in the side of the head.

"Paris?"

I strangled on my reply. "Yes?"

"You need to hurry up. They're ready for us."

I nodded.

"Paris?"

"Just a minute."

"You need to hurry."

"I heard you the first time." Couldn't she see I was having some technical issues?

"Then get out here."

I used a paper towel to wipe the crusty residue off my nostrils. I checked my shirt, my hands. I used a little water to clean a spot off my lip.

What a joke. Nothing about me would ever be clean.

I giggled.

"Goddamn it, Paris."

"I'm coming." I pulled the handle, but it wouldn't move.

She knocked again.

"I'm coming just..." The lock. I needed to turn the lock. But which way? I leaned against the wall.

Right? Left? Up? Down?

I rubbed my face.

"Paris, open this door right now."

The dead bolt wouldn't turn to the left, so I tried right. It disengaged, and I stepped into the hall.

Nothing in Julia's expression suggested I looked as yellow and pink as I felt. Either I was doing a really good job of holding all my pigments together or she was too worried about the interview to notice.

"Come on." She led me to the studio.

Cameras surrounded an elevated stage back dropped in dark blues. Fat chairs with thick arms hugged the cushions in their center.

A woman fussed over a man with white hair and a spray-on tan. She patted his cheek with a sponge, dabbing away excess makeup.

Did mine need touching up? I figured if it did Julia would say something.

I was guided to one of the chairs by a slim blond-haired man. He caught my gaze under half-lidded eyes, and his plump lips curved up.

"I wouldn't do that if I were you." I sat.

"Why?" He dropped the mic he was trying to attach to my shirt. It landed in my lap.

"Oops, clumsy me." The cute blond reached between my legs to retrieve it. Along the way, he brushed his fingers over my cock.

"I wouldn't do that either."

He tipped his head. "And what do you plan on doing about it?"

I leaned closer, and he gave me his ear. "How about I put you on your knees and fuck your mouth until you can't see straight?"

He turned his head. Specks of brown broke up the gray of his eyes. His mint-flavored exhale warmed my cheek. "I'll look forward to it."

The overhead lights changed angle, and the glare stabbed me in the temple. Static filled up the room, drowning out the voices.

Microphone boy ran a soft brush over my face. "You okay?"

What was he talking about? "Fine."

"So about that threat?"

What threat? Knees, face fucking, blond guy with tight lips. I took a business card out of my wallet. "Here. Call me."

Julia sat in the chair next to me. Glowing red streamers danced around her head.

"What are you looking at?"

"Ribbons."

"Excuse me?"

"Do I have any?"

"Any what?"

"Ribbons."

She leaned over. "What's wrong with you?"

"Nothing." I bit back a laugh.

"Get your head screwed on straight, Paris."

"I'm sorry. I didn't know it was crooked."

"Don't you dare embarrass me."

The ribbons tumbled onto the arm of the chair, and I brushed them off. A rich tone sang against my fingertips. I rubbed the fabric to see if I could make it louder.

Julia grabbed my wrist. "Stop that."

I sank into my chair.

"Sit up, you'll wrinkle your clothes."

I sat up.

"How much did you take?"

"You said one line."

"That doesn't—"

Two men stepped onto the stage with a covered canvas. They adjusted a couple of hangers on the backdrop. The taller man removed the sheet. Everyone stopped talking, or maybe my heartbeat drowned them out.

Under the stage lights, the colors flowing over the canvas turned garish. The men lifted it up.

"Turn around," Julia said.

But the only thing I could do was stare while two brutes manhandled a sliver of my soul. A woman wearing headphones directed the men on how to hang the painting.

"You need to tell them it's upside down," I said.

Julia shot a smile to someone as they walked by. "Don't be so melodramatic. No one cares."

"I care."

"Turn around, Paris."

I did.

The staff dropped colored bits all over the floor as they danced between the darkness behind the cameras and the offensive light coating the set.

Our host joined us on the stage. He sat in a chair on the other side of the coffee table positioned between us.

"Paris, this is Mr. Allen Rock."

His rubber mouth stretched into a toothy smile. "Are you two ready for your interview?"

"Yes, thank you." Julia flipped her hair back. "I just have to tell you what an honor it is to be on your show."

I snorted. She probably never even watched it.

"The pleasure is all mine, I assure you."

I sat forward in my chair, then back.

"Be still." To Allen, Julia said. "Sorry. Paris has never been on TV before."

"Well, there's absolutely no need to be nervous. Just pretend we're sitting in a coffee shop discussing art over your favorite cappuccino."

"Vanilla," I said.

Allen gave me a questioning look.

"My favorite is the vanilla cream mixed with the house blend."

There was a second of absolute silence, then Allen laughed. "I did say your favorite, didn't I?"

Julia turned her smile on me. Her mask of civility was perfect, but hell churned behind her eyes.

"We're about to go on," Allen said.

"So dear sister, what's your favorite flavor of coffee?"

A crack appeared in Julia's expression, and for the first time, fear radiated from her gaze.

I grinned at her.

A faceless voice in the darkness counted down from ten.

"Paris…"

I kept grinning. "Julia…"

Everything went quiet, and we were welcomed to the distinguished program by a theme song and canned applause.

Allen smiled at the camera. "Good morning, America. Today on the Allen Rock Show, we have a very special guest. Hailed as a revolutionary abstract artist, he has become one of the fastest growing names among collectors across the globe. And we at the Allen Rock Show have the privilege of hosting his first televised interview. Will you please join me in welcoming Paris Duvoe and his sister and agent, Julia Duvoe?"

The applause rose and fell on cue. Allen gestured to us with a wave of his hands. "I want you to know how wonderful it is to have you with us today."

The smile Julia wore turned excruciating. "Thank you."

"Last month, I was invited to do an opening at the prestigious Killian Gallery." Allen crossed his legs and tugged on his jacket. "Although it wasn't my first time attending an art exhibit, I am by no means a connoisseur. But standing in that gallery, between those works, I was completely overcome by the powerful presence radiating from them. " He addressed the camera again. "Now, those who know me will tell you I have never been a fan of abstract art. I guess, like a lot of people, I don't understand what the artist hopes to accomplish by turning a still life into bizarre shapes.

"But that day in the gallery when I walked by those paintings?" If his smile got any bigger, it was going to run off and leave him. "I didn't have to understand the picture. I felt it. After that, I had to meet the man who created those works."

Julia beamed.

I stared at my feet. Still attached. So all was well.

"And now I get the opportunity to introduce him and his genius to the world." There was another round of fake applause complete with whistles. "Mr. Duvoe—"

"Just Paris."

Julia patted me on the knee. "Paris isn't very big on formalities. He wants his people to feel comfortable with approaching him."

Allen nodded at me. "That's very thoughtful of you. I'm sure fans appreciate that."

"Oh, they do. They do." Julia gave me another pat on my knee, then a short squeeze that might as well have been a verbal threat.

To me, Allen said, "Over the past several years, you have gained popularity as a contemporary abstract artist. Your paintings have earned remarkable bids at auction that are usually reserved for legendary artists long gone, and yet, very little is known about you."

I picked at a seam in the arm of the chair.

Julia cleared her throat. "Yes, well, Paris is a very private person."

"And I bet that's the secret to his success."

Allen and Julia shared a laugh.

"So, Mr. Duvoe."

"Paris."

"Ah, yes, forgive me, Paris. Tell us about yourself."

I raked my fingernails over the velvety fabric. Happy tones played through the air, and the millions of fibers caressed my fingertips one strand at a time. "What would you like to know?"

"Anything you like."

"Could you narrow it down please?"

"All right. Why not start by telling our viewers when you began painting."

"I don't remember." I think his shoes were a size or so too big. They looked more like spit-shined barges than expensive leather footwear.

Julia patted my arm. "What he means is, he was too young to remember. You see, Paris has always been the artist in the family. Always painting. Always drawing."

"Makes sense."

More sense than Allen did. I'm pretty sure his socks didn't match. Of course it could have been the light. It was everywhere, running down the chairs, the walls, flowing across the floor.

"Then tell us when you decided to pursue it as a career."

"I didn't."

"You didn't decide to do this professionally?"

"No." I rubbed my knees. The fabric of my slacks wasn't nearly as colorful as the bumpy texture of the chair.

"What changed your mind?"

"Noth—"

"About twelve years ago an art collector saw one of his paintings," Julia said.

Mr. Rock sat forward in his chair. "So someone discovered you?"

I rubbed my forehead. "Yes."

"And who was that?"

Julia squeezed my arm. "Richard Nix. He's passed away now, but he was the first to recognize the genius in Paris's work."

I only had faint memories of the man. I'd been so high on Thorazine I'm surprised I could even hold a brush. I think he was at the hospital to visit his brother. Or maybe it was his wife. Could have even been his dog.

I giggled.

Julia tried to laugh, but it fell flat.

Allen swooped in. "How old were you when this happened?"

"Sixteen," Julia said. "A prominent business man had purchased the painting and put it in his gourmet restaurant in New York." Julia tossed me a quick glance, dared me to say otherwise. "That's where Mr. Nix saw Paris's work."

"Then would you say that was your beginning?"

"No, that was after," I said.

"After what?"

The dirt turned black with his blood, and I huddled in the shadows, too afraid to come out.

"After his first showing," Julia said. "It was small, but there were some known artists there. Both of the works he had on display sold for the highest amount."

"And how did it make you feel when someone recognized your talent among the ocean of other struggling artists?"

Blues and oranges picked at my brain. A hint of bronze muddied the hue.

"Privileged," Julia said. "It's an honor and privilege to have so many esteemed individuals recognize Paris's talent."

I rubbed the arms of the chair with both hands and then my slacks. The music from the chair went even better with the light.

"Such humble beginnings for a man the art community has titled as the next step in artistic evolution."

Is that what they thought of me when they looked at those terrible paintings? If it was, how did something beautiful make them feel? Like the boy who kissed me. The boy whose name I couldn't remember.

"Mi nombre es…" The space behind me was empty.

"Paris." Julia's grip tightened. "Mr. Rock has a question for you."

I turned back around. Allen waved a hand at my painting.

"Tell me about the painting you brought with you today?"

"I didn't bring it."

Allen tossed Julia a perfect smile, but his eyes were confused.

"Julia brought it. I didn't want it here, but she never listens to me."

Rage burned through the ten layers of foundation on Julia's cheeks.

I shrugged. "But that's okay. I'm used to it."

"Well, in my experience, most older sisters are like that." He laughed. Julia tried, but I don't think it could get past her gritted teeth. "Will this particular work be available at your next showing?"

"No."

"Why not?"

"It isn't for sale."

"What Paris means is it's a very special work that would need a collector who could understand and appreciate its sentimental value."

"No, I mean it isn't for sale."

Allen came alive in his seat. "Really. Now why is that?"

"It's private." I sank in my chair.

"So you would never sell it?"

"No."

"No matter the price?"

"That's what 'not for sale' means." I traced the ridges of the fabric on the arm of the chair. "What's this made of?"

"Pardon?"

I tapped the arm. "This. This chair."

"I'm not sure. Picking out chairs is the job of the prop director."

To Julia, I said, "We should get a few of these. Our furniture never makes this kind of music."

Allen laughed, and people behind the cameras joined in.

I laughed too.

Julia didn't.

Would she kill me now?

"So, your painting."

"What about it?"

"Would you tell us what you call it and why it's so special to you?"

He had a better chance of getting me to cut off my dick.

"Paris, tell Mr. Rock the name of the painting." The darkness in Julia's glare promised terrible things if I didn't.

But thanks to the X I'd snorted, I was too full of colored bits to care anymore.

I stared right into the camera and said, "My Vagina."

Allen's spray-on tan darkened to a shade close to magenta. He exchanged a look with Julia who'd turned into a marble statue.

I held up a hand. "I know what you're thinking. How can a man have a vagina? Well, I don't, which is why I painted one."

The stage manager made a rolling motion with her hand. Allen cleared his throat. "I'm sure now everyone can appreciate why you were reluctant to display this—" He cleared his throat again. "—highly provocative piece. I admire your courage to risk scrutiny."

"Courage had nothing to do with it." The colors bubbled up inside me, and I bounced in my seat. "In all honesty, it's not even original. I simply took an underappreciated piece of human anatomy and presented it in a way it couldn't be ignored. For example." I motioned for the redheaded intern standing just beyond the camera, to join us.

Allen nodded, and she walked out.

I patted the arm of the chair. "Sit, sweetheart. I won't bite."

She perched her hip on the edge. Her posture so rigid it surprised me when it didn't split her skin.

To Allen, I said, "Take this young woman. She is a prime example of someone who is underappreciated. She has a great smile and a warm presence. She's so beautiful, she glows."

Allen raised his chin. "That's why she's one of our most promising interns."

"That look on your face." I pointed. "That look right there, is exactly what this is all about."

"I'm sorry, but I don't…"

"Of course not. You're a man. And millions of men just like you will never understand what it means to truly appreciate women." I indicated the intern with a flip of my hand. "Young and beautiful, doors will open. The world is at her fingertips. But she only gets that chance because she meets society's standards of beauty. When she reaches your age, you'll toss her to that five minute segment where they talk about exotic foods and popular vacation spots. But as she is now, beautiful and perfect, she is led to believe she is appreciated, when ultimately it is her vagina men want to possess."

Any minute now, Julia was going to catch fire.

And I couldn't wait.

"Let me show you exactly what I mean." I stood. The intern didn't resist when I tugged her to her feet. "Here, sweetheart, take off your clothes and spread—"

Someone yelled for a cut to commercial. Julia had me by the arm and shoved into the hall before Allen could turn in his fat musical chair.

"What the hell was that?"

I snorted a laugh. "Careful or you'll smear your makeup."

"Goddamn it. Are you trying to ruin me?"

"I thought I was the artist? Or maybe it's just the X. I love this stuff by the way." I wiggled my fingers in the air. "Everything you touch sings. I was serious about those chairs. We really should get some."

Julia dragged me in the direction of the elevator. "Go home. And you better pray I can salvage this disaster."

The doors opened, and she stuffed me inside. "Oh," I said. "You know when you asked me how many lines I did?" The doors started to close. "Just so you know. I snorted the whole fuuuucking bag."

Anything Julia said was cut off.

I slid to the floor and drowned in the gold walls swirling with the recessed lights.

My painting. My beautiful moment. The boy whose hand I'd held, lips I'd kissed, trust I'd betrayed.

If only I could remember his name.

The doors opened to a bustling office, and a man in a suit with a woman in a wheelchair.

A flash of white moved in my periphery. I scurried to my feet. The corner was empty.

"Hey," the man said. "You mind? You're blocking the door."

There was nothing in the elevator except garish walls and equally ugly paisley carpet.

"Excuse me," the woman said. "Hey, excuse me." They both glared.

I pushed past them and dove into the maze of cubicles. People filled the gaps between work stations. I swam through their black and red words. The roar of voices and the ringing phones filled up my skull with sharp points of yellow.

It should have been impossible to hear the two little boys laugh.

The wet smell of old dirt breathed across my skin.

"*¿Ha visto a mi hijo?*"

"Shut up."

The hall I took had doors on one side and windows on the other.

"*You know. I know you know. Dime. Le ruego.*"

I pressed my palm against my eye. The pounding in my head beat louder.

"I don't. I don't know where he is. Now stop asking me."

I hadn't realized I'd shouted until a ripple of silence moved through the room. People turned to look at me. I dropped my head and picked a random direction.

At the bottom of a flight of stairs, gray light poured through the foyer of the lobby. I shielded my eyes as I shoved open the doors. An icy wind cut through the columns edging the walkway of the building and slapped my shirt. Invisible leaves crunched under my feet, and a twig snapped. My walk turned into a run.

I crossed the street on a green light. A car screamed to a halt, and someone yelled. The air seared my lungs, my ribs ached, and my feet throbbed from pounding against the sidewalk. But it took the muscles cramping in my legs to make me stop. Even then, I hobbled like some wounded bird trying to keep from being eaten.

"This is your fault." Julia's voice left a ringing in my ears that grew into a scream.

"Where is mi hijo?"

"Tell her you don't know."

"Por favor, I'm begging you."

"Keep your mouth shut, Paris, or I'll break every bone in your pathetic body."

"I know you know. Dime dónde está."

"I can't. I'm sorry." I beat my fist against my temple. "Please, please, stop." I collapsed against a brick wall.

"Hey," a male voice said.

Silence. Then the hum of cars and bustling people led the way back to the here and now.

An elderly man leaned on his cane. "Are you okay, son?"

Was I? I wiped my cheeks. "Yeah."

"Are you sure?"

"Yes." I nodded. "Yes. Yes. I'm…" My teeth chattered.

"You might ought to go inside. You'll catch your death out here." He offered me a hand up.

"I'm okay. I'm fine." I struggled to my feet. "Thank you."

"If you like, I can buy you a cup of coffee. They probably have a phone inside, and you could call someone."

"No, really. Thank you. I'm okay." The fever in my skin banked, leaving my fingers numb. He was right. I did need to get out of the cold. I did need to call someone.

I wedged myself into the doorway of a vacant shop and fumbled with my cellphone. I took out Roy's card and dialed the number.

The phone rang.

It picked up, and Roy's voice bled across space courtesy of voice mail.

I faced the corner to shield my face from a blast of wind. "I'm sorry. I don't mean to bother you. But I need…" I needed somewhere safe. "You said to call so I'm calling." I held the phone with both hands to keep it steady. "I'm going to go to your apartment. I hope that's—" The voice mail cut off with a beep. An electronic voice offered me the chance to replay my message.

I hung up.

There was a line of cabs at the end of the block. I picked one and got in. "Trip Drive."

The cabby didn't start the meter.

"Did you hear me?"

"I heard you."

"Then what's the hold up?"

"You got money?"

I must have looked worse than I felt. "Yeah. I got money." I pulled out a couple of twenties from my wallet and showed him. He nodded, and we merged into traffic.

Traffic was light so it didn't take long for the office buildings to transform into high-rise apartments that quickly shrank into storefronts. A few more blocks and abandoned factories and worn-out apartments replaced well-kept buildings.

Young black men crowded at the corner of Roy's street. Their skeptical gazes followed the cab as it made the turn.

"Are you sure this is the right place?" the cabby said.

"Yeah." I searched for Roy's building. But it had been raining so hard. What if I couldn't recognize it?

"You want me to double check the address? I gotta GPS I can plug it into."

"I don't remember the address, just the street."

We passed a pretty Asian girl talking with a man sitting in a rusted out Impala.

A familiar stretch of ugly brick came into view. "Pull in there." I handed the cabby his money.

"Are you sure, mister? This don't look like the kind of place someone like you should be."

Where was that? A place drowning in desperation, filled with people trapped by circumstances so long they'd given up trying to find a way out. "I have a lot more in common with these people than you know."

I made my way to the building and up the stairs. It wasn't until I reached the top that I knew for sure I had the right place. Toys and trash littered the hall, the TV was too loud, and the people in the unit at the end argued. Nothing had changed.

Exhaustion rode over me on a wave of shivers. The artificial warmth created by the X receded, leaving me chilled.

I staggered down the hall moving from door to door until I found the right one. I knocked, but no one answered.

My knees gave out, and I fell in a heap. I made a sad attempt to knock again, but my arms were too heavy. Everything was too heavy.

"Pick it up, Paris."

"I can't."

"Pick it up now."

"Please don't make me."

"Stop your whining, and do what I tell you. This is your mess. Now help me clean it up."

Julia grabbed my arm and shook me.

"Paris? Paris, wake up."

I pushed at the hands cradling my face. "I'm sorry…please don't…" It was a brush of rough fingers on my cheek that drove away the last of the dream. Worried green eyes looked down at me.

"Roy."

"Yeah."

"I called you."

"I know."

"You didn't answer."

"I'm sorry. I was on a job, I came as soon as I heard your message."

"I knocked. I knocked, and you weren't here."

"I'm here now." Roy put my arm over his shoulder and helped me inside.

I stubbed my toe on the doorjamb. "My shoes." I felt my pockets. "Fuck."

"Wallet?"

"Yeah. And my phone."

"Just be glad that's all they took."

Roy locked the door and slid his toolbox under the edge of the bed. I pulled away, took the two steps toward the sofa and fell.

"Wait, and I'll help you." He led me to the bed.

"If you want to fuck me, you only have to ask."

Roy took a penlight out of his shirt pocket. A beam of light seared through my eyes with the sound of nails on a chalkboard.

"Ow. That hurts." I batted his hand away.

"What are you on?" He tried to shine it in my eyes again, but I buried my face into the covers.

"For God's sake, you're blinding me."

"Fine, I'll call an ambulance."

"No." I grabbed his arm. "No...no...I'm fine. It's just X. I've taken it before. I'll be all right."

He pushed my bangs back. "How much have you taken?"

"I don't know. Julia said a line, I think I snorted half the bag, all the bag, fuck, I can't remember." I laughed. "My Vagina."

"What?"

"They asked me what my painting was called, but I couldn't tell them. My Vagina was the first thing that came to me. A vagina. Can you believe that? You'd think it would have been my dick, but nope." I squeezed Roy's cheeks with my thumb and finger. "So do you think that makes me straight?" Once I touched him, I didn't want to stop.

He caught my wrist.

"But I liked the music the stubble on your chin makes."

Roy got out his cell. I made a grab for it but wound up with only a handful of his shirt. "No. Please. God. If they take me to the hospital, she'll find out where I am."

112

"Who?" He all but growled the question.

The effort to hold his gaze made me tremble.

"Who are you afraid of, Paris?"

The name wouldn't form on my lips.

"Julia?"

I nodded. "I screwed up."

"How?"

"The interview. Some big stupid interview. I must have forgotten my lines. I screwed up, and she kicked me out. She told me to go home, but I couldn't." I lay down and rubbed my face against the blankets. They smelled just like him. Every inch. Right to the tip of his cock. I nuzzled the folds and cradled the fabric in my arms. "I love this bed." I inhaled so hard I snorted, and that sent me into a fit of laughter.

Roy put his phone back in his pocket and pulled me to my feet.

"Do you want me to blow you first or get right to main course?"

"I'm not going to have sex with you."

"Aww—but why not?"

He pried the sheets from my hands.

"Where are we going?"

"To sober you up."

"I'm not drunk, I'm high."

"Well, I need to do something to bring you to your senses. Besides, you're cold."

"Am not."

"Trust me, you're cold."

"You could make me warm in your bed." He shuffled me through a door to the bathroom.

"This will be faster."

"But I like your bed. Best fucking bed ever. And it smells like your cock. I love your cock. Best goddamned cock I've ever had."

"Here. Step in."

"But I need to take my clothes off." Roy tossed my shirt on the floor with my slacks. "How did you do that?" I was naked. "Do you do those little balloon animals too? Can you make me a tiger? The repairman magician."

"Just repairman."

"But you made my clothes disappear."

"No. You're just out of your gourd and don't remember me undressing you." He turned on the water. "Sit."

"A bath?"

"I think it's the best choice. I'm afraid you'll fall."

"You could hold me up." Warm water rose around me, washing away the tension in strings of pink. I flicked the ripples to make them turn violet.

Roy knelt beside the tub.

"You really don't want to join me?"

"Not right now."

"You said for me to call you."

"I know. And I'm glad you did."

"If you didn't want to fuck me, why did you tell me to call you?" Roy smiled. His lips were two strong masculine lines. "You have the best mouth."

"I'll take that as a compliment."

"You should. I don't say that often, and when I do, it's because the mouth I'm referring to is wrapped around my dick." I slumped to the left, and he pulled me upright. Water cascaded over my head and down my face. "What…" I wiped my eyes. Roy had a small pot in his hand. He scooped up water and poured it over me. "Where the—" I snorted to keep my nose clear. "—hell did that come from?"

"What?"

"The pot."

"I got it out of the kitchen."

"No, you didn't."

"Then where do you think it came from?" Roy watched me with a worried expression.

I rubbed my face. "I must be blacking out."

"You haven't quit talking."

"Doesn't mean anything."

"You sure you don't want to go to the hospital?"

"For a black out?"

He nodded.

"I'm used to it. I do some of my best work when I don't even know what planet I'm on."

Roy dumped another scoop over my head. "Finish telling me about the painting."

My ears popped under the cascade. "The what?"

"You were telling me about the painting Julia stole."

"When?"

"Just now." His frown deepened.

I didn't want to, but I had to ask. "What did I say?"

Roy handed me a washcloth from a stack on the back of the toilet. "You said you begged her not to take your painting. You didn't want anyone to see him. It was your moment and the only thing you had to give him."

I rubbed my face. "Did I say his name?"

"No."

"I can't remember his name."

"Who was he?"

"The boy I kissed. I think I was ten." I hugged my knees with one arm and held the washcloth to my chest. "He looked at me like you do. Like I mean something. Like…"

Roy stroked my head and massaged my temple with his thumbs. Light purples and scarlets burst behind my eyelids, filling my consciousness with a soft music.

The ghost of a boy long gone brushed his lips against mine. I drank down his sigh, and he devoured my surprise.

"Are you afraid he'll see the painting? Is that why you don't want it on TV?"

"No one *sees* what I paint. For the world, it's all about pretty colors and abstract lines."

"I do."

Yes, he did. And for some reason, it terrified me. "Even if I wanted him to, he can't." *The piece of plywood covering the well made a sucking sound as we lifted it.* "There's not enough light."

Roy held my face. "What do you mean?"

I leaned closer to Roy. "I'm not allowed to talk about it."

"Why not?"

"Bad things happen. Terrible things."

"What kind of things."

"Please Julia, don't leave me."

"Maybe a few weeks in here and you'll learn to keep your mouth shut."

"Paris?"

A heavy weight I hadn't felt in years shifted inside my chest. I put my finger on my lips. "Shhh—you'll wake it up."

"What?"

It was right there. All I had to do was open my mouth. I looked for something to grab hold of. "I'd like to get out now."

He searched my face.

"Please. I'm tired."

"All right." Roy helped me stand.

As I stepped from the tub, my foot caught the edge and I slammed into his chest. Water from my body soaked his shirt. His muscular arms turned to concrete under my hands. Trapped in his embrace, the beat of his heart thumped against my ear. I longed for the studio so I could paint the moment.

"You okay?"

"I'm fine. Just slipped." I tilted my chin up, and it put my mouth close to his.

The tendons along Roy's neck strained with the effort to swallow.

I ran a finger down one of the tight cords. "You want me."

He clenched his eyes shut.

"I can see it." I inhaled. "I can smell it." I molded my body to his. His breathing hitched, and his grip tightened. In the depths of his green eyes boiled feral lust. I draped an arm over his shoulder and licked a line along his jaw to the soft spot under his ear. I exhaled against his skin.

"Don't be ashamed." I brushed my lips against the shell of his ear. "Whatever you're thinking. Whatever fantasy is playing in that head of yours. Let it go. Play it out." He gave me the smallest gasp when I dropped a kiss on his neck.

Roy ran a hand down my back to the crack of my ass.

I raised up on my toes, encouraging him to go lower. "Touch me, anywhere you want. Inside. Outside."

For a man with such heavy hands, his caress was feather light. And how he cradled me didn't match the desire in his gaze. I stood there in the safety of Roy's arms with no idea what to do.

"You should get some rest." He took down the towel hanging from the shower rod and wrapped it around me. "After you take a nap, I'll make you something to eat." He patted my skin dry.

"Why do you always want to feed me?"

"Because you're too thin, and it worries me."

No one worried about me. I curled under the towel, wishing I could disappear inside the folds.

Roy put me in his bed and covered me up. The way he looked at me made me feel so small. He ran his knuckles down my cheek. "If you get cold, just tell me, and I'll turn up the heat."

Then he left me there, and I slept.

****

Outside the cab, the street lamps cut out swaths of orange in the black. Streamers of light broke apart on the vehicles passing by and made stars on the windshields of the ones parked by the curb.

"Are you going to be all right?" Roy said.

To tell the truth, I wasn't sure. "Yeah."

"Do you need me to go up there with you?"

I chuckled. "Just because I like it up the ass, Roy, that doesn't make me a girl."

His face reddened. "That's not...I didn't mean..."

"It's okay." It was my turn to be nervous. "I appreciate you letting me stay so late."

"I don't mind if you stay the night."

"Really?"

"I told you to stay."

"If I do, are you going to sleep on the couch?" His silence pushed me out of the cab.

"Wait." Roy ran after me. "Paris, wait. Please."

He caught up to me next to the doorway. The alcove we'd hidden in just a week before begged me to enter. I would have. Hell, I would have gladly blown him right here in front of everyone, but something had changed since then, and I didn't understand what.

I crossed my arms. The few people out this time of night wore the current club fashions in the form of glittering dresses and skinny jeans.

"I meant it when I said I wanted to get to know you."

117

"And I meant it when I said it wasn't a good idea."

"At least let me take you out to dinner. One time. A real place to sit down and eat and—"

"No."

He frowned.

"Now if you excuse me, I have a bottle of alcohol and some little pink pills calling my name." I went to push past him, and he grabbed my arm. Before I could protest, Roy captured me next to the wall. The sudden closeness, his breath against my ear, the heat of his body radiating through the flannel shirt he'd wrapped me in, made my balls ache and my dick hard.

"There's a nice dark corner right over there." I grazed my teeth over his earlobe. "I could lean against the glass, and you could fuck me. No one would ever even see us. But of course, you already know that."

"Paris…"

"Are you hard, Roy? I don't even have to look to know you are. I can smell you."

"Paris…"

"Or maybe you'd rather stuff your cock down my throat until I can't breathe." Roy stepped back. The lust in his eyes disappeared under something resembling hurt.

"I should go," I said. When I tried to duck under his arm, he lowered it, blocking my path.

"I go to the park every Saturday around seven," Roy said. "I sit over by the fountain near all the dogwood trees."

"Why are you telling me this?"

"I think you know why."

"Then you're going to be disappointed."

He tilted my chin up. I thought he was going to kiss me, but he caressed my cheek. I knew what the hell to do with his mouth, but Roy's concern confused me.

"Seven o'clock." He walked back to the cab.

"I'm not coming."

"Over by the fountain."

"I told you I won't be there."

"Under the dogwoods."

"Goddamn it, Roy, I will not be there."

He got in the cab. Mist formed droplets on the window. I thought he turned to look at me, but the cab pulled out into traffic and disappeared before I could be sure.

Water dripped from my bangs and down my cheeks. It wasn't until it soaked the shoulders of the flannel shirt that I went inside.

Bill didn't look up from his newspaper when I passed him on the way to the elevator. Closed inside the small box, Roy's scent thickened. If he'd just taken me to bed, everything would have been all right. But no, he had to go and screw things up by...

I wasn't even sure.

I took off the flannel shirt with every intention of throwing the damn thing into the corner for housekeeping. Instead, I wound up pressing my face into the wad of material and inhaling. Warmth flowed through my body, but it had nothing to do with carnal need.

I missed him. His touch. His voice. The feel of his hand over mine.

The lift doors opened, and I stepped out.

I didn't even see Julia sitting on the couch. She stood. "I've been calling your cell phone for hours."

"It was stolen." I left Roy's shirt on the chair near the elevator.

"Stolen? What do you mean it was stolen?"

"You know, when someone takes something from you that doesn't belong to them? Sound familiar?"

She followed me into the kitchen. "I want you to know your little stunt back there almost ruined your career."

I took out the vodka and orange juice from the fridge. "Well, since you haven't pushed me off the balcony, I can assume you worked your magic and all is well."

She crossed her arms. "No thanks to you."

"You never thank me, Julia." Even when I deserved it. Which I admit, was rare.

I sipped my drink. "Is there a reason why you're in my apartment other than to yell at me?"

"Ms. Amelia Thorn has invited me to attend a private showing at her chalet up north."

The people in Julia's circles never had homes, they had manors, lodges, and...chalets.

"And she is?"

"The President of the American Feminist Society. She organizes a two-week retreat every year that's invitation only. Some very important people will be there."

"Sounds riveting."

Julia sneered. "She's expressed an interest in your painting from the interview."

I knew better than to show weakness. "It has a title, you know."

"A very inappropriate title."

"My Vagina is not inappropriate."

"Mrs. Thorn likes it, so that's all that matters." Julia twisted her fingers together.

"I like it too. In fact, I think it's perfect. My Vagina. It even has a nice ring to it." I swirled my drink in between sips.

A tick jumped in Julia's jaw.

"If she buys it, maybe she'll enter it into the Women's Choice awards." I gave a dramatic sigh. "Just think, Julia. If she did, My Vagina could be seen by people from all over the world." I emptied my glass. "And God, what if it won?"

Greed and revulsion fought a battle in Julia's expression.

"Is there a reason you don't like the title?" I tried not to smile. But not too hard.

"It's vulgar."

"What's vulgar?"

"That word."

"You think the word vagina is vulgar?"

"It's not a word to be thrown around in mixed company."

"Why not? It's a medical term. If I'd named the painting My Pancreas or My Lungs, you wouldn't be offended."

"It's not the same."

"It is."

"No, it's not."

"You really can't say it, can you?"

She narrowed her eyes at me.

"You can't say the word vagina."

"That's irrelevant."

"Now, Julia." I crossed my arms and gave her a long look. "Need I remind you that you actually have one of those?"

She jerked her chin up. "I'll be leaving tomorrow afternoon."

"C'mon, Julia. Say it."

"I'll call you when my plane lands."

"Vagina."

She glared.

"Vagina." I sang it like an injured seagull.

"Stop it, Paris."

"Va-gi-na."

"Paris."

"Say it with me, Julia. Just once." I loved the rage burning in her eyes. I loved the jump of her pulse in her neck.

"I will do no such thing."

"Vagina."

"Last warning, Paris." She clenched her hands.

The smile on my face was slow to form, and it was as satisfying as drawing out a wicked blade.

I met Julia's gaze, and said, "Vagina."

She charged me. I ducked to cover my face, and she landed the blow to my ribs. A kick to my legs took me to the floor. Another shockwave blew through my lower back and was followed by a searing burn in my knee.

Two or three more punches to my shoulders and back and she quit. The deep throbbing left behind guaranteed bruises.

"Get up."

I unwound myself. A sharp jab in my side made me gasp.

Julia hobbled over to the counter. "Just great." She took off her shoe. The heel flopped from the end. "Do you have any idea how much these cost?"

"Maybe you shouldn't kick me. Then they wouldn't break." I stood, and my knee screamed.

"I was going to wear these to the retreat. Now I'll have to go by Raphael's and get another pair. And you'd better hope they still have them." She threw her shoes into the sink. "Now thanks to you, I'll be up all night packing so I can make my flight." She walked out of the kitchen. A few seconds later, the elevator dinged.

I counted to three and then at the top of my lungs yelled, "Vagina."

Chapter Six

As I put on a pair of black jeans and a dark blue cashmere sweater, I told myself I was not going to the park. No matter how many times I said the lie, out loud or in my head, I'd yet to believe it.

I found a pair of ankle boots in the back of the closet. I had no idea where they came from, but they were fur lined, it was cold outside, and I despised wool socks no matter how warm they were.

What if Roy didn't even show up?

Why did I even care?

If he was there, good. If he wasn't, no big loss. Yet the thought of finding an empty bench cinched my throat with a deep, aching sadness.

He would be there. He had to be.

Unlike my lie, my heart was willing to believe that proclamation. I could only hope my heart would hold up in the event I was wrong.

The scent of fresh cookies followed Alice from the kitchen. "Where are you going?"

"Out." I took my coat off the hanger and put it on.

"But I made your favorite. Chocolate chips." She held up a plate.

"Thank you." I kissed her on the cheek. "I appreciate the gesture."

"But you're still leaving."

"I have a date."

Both of her eyebrows went up. "With who?"

"A friend."

"Does Julia know?"

"Yes." Technically.

"Does she know you're going out with him tonight?"

Ah, Alice. She knew me too well. "The cookies look wonderful. I promise to eat one when I get back."

"She doesn't know, does she?"

"Don't wait up."

Alice followed me across the studio. "You know how she is."

"And she's not here."

"Doesn't mean you can go running around. Something could happen to you."

If only. "I'll be fine."

"How well do you know this man?"

I couldn't stop the smile. "Very well."

Alice's cheeks turned pink. "Really, Paris..."

"I'm going."

She set the plate down on one of my workbenches. "Wait. You need a scarf."

I pulled up the collar on the overcoat. "I'll be fine."

"No, you won't. You'll take a cold. If Julia comes home to find you sick, she'll be angry. Worse, you could miss your next showing." She ran to the closet and came back with a thick black scarf. It wasn't wool so I let Alice put it on me.

She buttoned my coat and fiddled with the collar. "Please be careful."

"I will."

"I worry about you."

"I know."

Alice brushed away some invisible lint on my overcoat. "You look very nice."

"I should, you pick out all my clothes."

"Oh." She held up a hand and ran back to the closet. "I almost forgot." She came back with a pair of gloves. "You'll need these."

I put them on.

She clasped her hands. "There, now your fingers won't get cold."

"Thank you."

"It's what I'm here for." She looked so pleased with herself. Not long ago, I thought she would never smile again. The day her father died, all she did was stare at me. When she didn't stare, she cried. I think the only reason she didn't hate me was because Julia did enough for both of them.

"Would you like to take some cookies?"

"They'll keep till I get home."

"Are you sure? I don't mind. I can put them in a container. It will only take a minute."

I caught her arm before she could dash off. "I promise to eat the whole plate when I get home."

"You better not." She gave me an indignant look. "You won't be able to wear those new slacks I bought you."

I laughed. "Okay. I'll eat half."

"Paris."

I kissed her on the cheek again. "Remember, don't wait up."

"Wait…"

I didn't.

"What do I tell Julia if she calls?"

I put out a hand to keep the lift doors from closing. "If I were you, I'd tell her I was asleep, or painting, or anything that doesn't involve me leaving the apartment."

"I can't lie to her."

"Then you'd better not answer the phone." I released the doors.

A gust of frigid air rode up my legs as soon as I stepped outside. Alice was right; I did need the scarf and the gloves. Even then, I had to stick my hands in my pockets to keep my joints from aching.

I huddled in my coat and went in search of a cab.

The wind changed direction, and I caught a familiar rich scent. Clean skin. Male musk. Cheap soap. Then a line of warmth pressed against my back. "Mind if I join you?" Roy fell in step beside me.

"What are you doing here?"

"I'm on my way to the park."

"A mile out of the way?"

"I took the scenic route."

"I'll say."

"What about you? Out for a stroll?" Two women with shopping bags over their arms watched Roy with seductive smiles. He nodded a hello as we passed.

"I'm on my way to meet with someone."

"Really?"

"Yes."

"Who?" There was just enough lilt to Roy's tone to make me wonder if he might actually be concerned.

"Just some guy."

"Does he have a name?"

"I'm sure he does."

"Do you mind if I ask what it is?"

"Yes." I tried to keep my expression blank, but I don't think I did a very good job because laughter glittered in his eyes.

"It must be serious."

I shrugged. "Not sure, but I think he really likes me."

"Why is that?"

"I don't know, just something about him."

Roy leaned closer.

I leaned away. "Better be careful. If he thinks you're making any moves on me, he might get jealous."

"Does he seem like the type?"

"To get jealous?"

"Yeah."

"I don't know, but he's pretty tough looking."

We passed a guy walking four big white poodles. They all wore coats.

"Is there a reason why you're meeting him?" Roy said.

"He wants to get to know me." I gave a dramatic sigh. "Can you believe that?"

"You can't?"

"No."

"Why is that?"

"I don't know. Sounds so old-fashioned."

"Maybe he's an old-fashioned kind of guy."

"God, I hope not."

"Why?"

"Because missionary is boring."

His cheeks turned pink. "Well, I'm sure he's not that old-fashioned." Two cabs were parked at the corner. "Since we're headed in the same direction, do you want to ride together?"

"My mother always told me to never get into a cab with a strange man."

He chuckled. "Wise woman."

I tugged up my coat collar and pulled the scarf higher to cover my ears.

"Are you sure you don't want a cab?"

"I'm sure."

We waded through the light spilling from a line of store windows.

"Do you think he meant it when he said he wanted to get to know me?"

Roy stuffed his hands into the pockets of his coat. Frizzled threads lined the hem and padding showed through a hole in the elbow. He didn't have it zipped up. Was it broken? As cold as it was, it had to be.

"I'm sure he meant it." The humor was gone from Roy's words.

"How does that work exactly?" I glanced at him.

"What?"

"People getting to know each other."

"Talking, hanging out, going to dinner."

"And what happens if he gets to know me and doesn't like me?" Did he notice the waver in my voice?

"I'm sure he'll like you."

"How do you know?"

"Because he'd be a fool not to."

The light turned red, and we stopped at the crosswalk. Roy stared off in the distance. His smile had turned into something soft and almost innocent.

"Well, I think he'd be a fool if he did like me."

"Why would you say that?"

I shrugged.

"You have to have a reason."

"I'm not exactly likable. Fuckable, yes. Likable? Not so much." The light turned green, and we crossed the street.

"That doesn't answer my question."

How did you tell someone you were born hated? Your entire life was built on a series of exclusions from your family's life because you were a forbidden fruit? I didn't know, so I said, "Because no one ever has."

"No one?"

I nodded.

"I don't believe that."

I met his gaze. "No one." The wind kicked up between the buildings, and I picked up my pace.

"I still don't believe you."

"It's true."

"It can't be."

"Why? Because you say so?"

"Because I know so."

I stopped. "Really?"

"Yes."

"So you're psychic?"

"Not at all."

"Tú eres mi mejor amigo. My very best friend."

The smile returned to Roy's face. "Who was it?"

"I have no idea what you're talking about." I walked, and he followed.

"You said no one has ever liked you, but I saw it in your eyes. Someone did. I'm willing to bet a lot of someones do."

"You'd be wrong."

"No, you're just not giving yourself enough credit."

A homeless man waved at us. At the next corner, a guy with a guitar picked out Jingle Bells on five strings. He looked at me and licked his lips. Roy stepped closer to me. .

"We were children," I said.

"The boy in the painting?"

I watched my feet. One foot in front of the other. Just like life.

"Who was he?"

"Just some boy I met one summer. I can't remember his name." Just as we stepped off the sidewalk, the light turned red, and a car honked because we were in the way. Roy held up an apologetic hand.

"Why not?"

Large oak trees beckoned us closer. Even in the winter, the grass in the park stayed green.

"I don't know that either."

"Did something happen to him?"

I rubbed my forehead.

"No te preocupes. I am your friend forever."

The ground was thick with leaves and mud sloshed over the edge of my tennis shoes with every step. Soaked to the bone, I could only shiver.

128

There were briars between the trees and sticks out in the open. It wasn't long before my legs were a mess of bloody scratches.

I waited for the terrible memory to recede. But the woods remained. The tarp in my hands remained. And so did Julia's voice. *"Hurry up. I don't have all day."*

Roy jerked me back to safety. His mouth moved, but whatever he said couldn't reach me.

He cupped my face and pulled up one eyelid, then the other. For some reason, that gave me back my voice.

"What are you doing?" I tried to push him away, but he held me with an arm around my back, my chest against his. Touching him made me helpless.

"What are you on?"

"Nothing."

"Are you sure?" He wouldn't let me look away.

"I promise. I haven't even had a drink today." He loosened his hold, but I pressed closer. The worried expression on his face wavered. "You know that guy I'm supposed to meet?"

"What about him?"

"He could be watching us right now." I pushed my groin against his.

"So?"

"He might get jealous."

"Let him."

"You're not worried he'll hurt you?"

Roy squeezed my ass through my coat. "If he does, it will be worth it."

****

The footpath led us through a tunnel of dogwoods. The blooms were long gone, but the knotted limbs were a sight all their own. Twisting and turning, each one was a natural sculpture made by time and Mother Nature.

"So what brings you out here every Saturday night at seven o'clock?"

"If I tell you, it'll ruin the surprise."

I leaned against Roy. It made me look drunk, but so what? A couple sat on a picnic table sharing a private conversation. Their gazes followed us. I rubbed a hand over the swell of Roy's ass. The male half of the couple looked away while the woman stared and drank her coffee.

"What are you doing?" Roy eyed me.

"Nothing."

"You wouldn't be trying to make those two lovebirds over there uncomfortable, would you?"

"Now why on earth would I do that?" I tried to sound offended. The grin on Roy's face told me I'd failed miserably.

The dogwoods peeled back, and we emerged into an open area with a fountain constructed from natural stone. It looked like something that belonged in a niche cradled by mountains not in the center of a park.

Water rolled from the top and traveled down the grooves and valleys into the pond below. Ivy had been cultivated up the sides and back. Large areas of dirt surrounding the base promised more flowers in the spring.

"It's very pretty," I said.

"You've never seen it?"

"No."

"Have you even been to the park before?"

"No."

"How long have you lived here?"

I laughed. "Long enough to make me think I've outstayed my welcome."

Roy pulled me to a halt and wrapped me in his arms. "That's not true."

"What?" He held me tighter, and suddenly, I was afraid.

"Don't ever think that." He laid his forehead against mine and traced the lines of my face. The raw concern in his eyes made it difficult to breathe. "You will always be welcome."

I was going to tell him he'd read into it something that wasn't there. But I'd meant exactly what those words implied.

"Are you ever going to show me?" I said. He crunched his eyebrows together. "The reason you come here." I just wanted him to quit looking at me like that. Like I'd threatened to take away someone he...

"Yeah." Roy kept his arm around me while we walked.

From deeper in the park, the sad cry of a violin beckoned us. The pitch was perfect, and the open space left nothing to inhibit the powerful notes from floating off toward the sky, trailing oranges, limes, and reds.

Anxious calm followed it, and memories of a highly polished floor coated in melting sunlight was strong enough to rise through decades.

"What are you looking at?"

I hadn't realized I'd stopped until Roy turned.

"Vivaldi." I swayed in time with the swirling music. In another life, fueled by a woman's laughter, I would dance until I was drunk. Then I'd lie on the floor and giggle until she beckoned me to lunch.

Her face. Her beautiful face hovered in the warm sun. But the details were blurred by the passage of time.

"What's Vivaldi?"

The memory winked out, leaving me in the dark, the cold, and a life where no light could reach me through the layers of obscene colors smeared across a canvas.

I started walking again, and so did Roy. "He's a composer. This piece is by him."

"Oh, you mean the song."

I chuckled. "Yeah, the song."

The deeper voice of a cello joined in. Roy hummed.

"I never pegged you as a fan of classical."

"Really?"

"Yes, really."

"What kind of music did you think I liked?"

"I don't know." I put my arm through his. "Something involving cowboy hats."

He laughed. "Just cowboy hats?"

"If the band members only wore the hats, I'd attend the concerts. I've recently learned country boys can have some impressive equipment."

Roy scuffed his feet. "Actually, I like rock. Even some of the grunge bands."

"And yet you come here every Friday at seven."

"I like the music; I just don't know anything about it. But that's not the only reason I come."

The footpath led us around a playground, to a large area paved in brick. Park benches edged the circular space, and picnic tables dotted the grassy areas under the trees.

Out of place among all the perfection was a small group of older men under a popup canopy. They sat on fold-down chairs and wore a mismatched blend of army jackets and tattered sweatshirts. Three of them held violins, and the other two braced cellos between their knees.

Unlike their clothing, the instruments were groomed to perfection.

A few people dropped change into the bucket in front of them as they passed by.

"They collect the money for the food bank," Roy said. "Once a week, they go out and buy nonperishables to hand out to the homeless. The rest they use to help the church with the soup kitchen."

The center man on the violin clearly had more skill than the rest. It wasn't just the way he coaxed the notes from the strings, but how he held himself, how his face glowed, how he pined for the music with every stroke of the bow.

"That guy." I indicated the man with a nod. "Who did he play for?"

"Some big orchestra in New York, I think."

"The Philharmonic?"

Roy nodded. "I think that's what it's called."

A couple stopped to listen. The woman put her head on the man's shoulder.

"What?" Roy said.

"I didn't say anything."

"No, but you have a funny look on your face."

I didn't doubt it. "Not just anyone plays for the New York Philharmonic."

"I don't think Jim was just anyone. He won't talk about himself, but Eddie, the guy on the right with the cello, he'll talk your ear off about the man. Apparently, Jim went to college on a music scholarship and started playing in an orchestra before he graduated."

I was willing to bet if he had a better violin he'd sound twice as good. And he was already better than almost anyone I'd ever heard.

"What made him quit?"

"He went to Vietnam. He had some problems when he came back. By the time he got himself sorted out, they had no interest in him anymore."

"Then they were fools."

The piece ended, and they took a moment to get sips of water and stretch their fingers. The couple watching them left without dropping anything into the bucket.

I didn't miss the disappointment in Roy's eyes.

"Evening, gentlemen." Roy walked over, and the men tossed him hellos. The guy with the cello stood. They shook hands.

All the while, Jim stared into the darkness beyond the trees with a lost expression.

One of the other men suggested a piece, and they prepared to start. The redhead next to Jim tapped him on the arm. On his return from wherever he'd gone, he caught my gaze.

It was then I realized we knew each other, because we walked the road of madness together. Shoulder to shoulder, even hand in hand, but never aware the other existed. Even though we traveled in the same direction, we remained alone.

I found no comfort in the realization he was there, rather confirmation that once the rabbit led you astray, there was no escape.

Jim acknowledged me with a nod. I did the same.

The small group of men struck up another song where the violins dominated even the deepest note from the cellos.

Roy took out his wallet. The worn piece of leather had been carried in his back pocket so long it held the curve of his ass.

He flipped through receipts until he located a bill. Roy pinched his lip between his teeth. His expression was a cross between worry and pain.

"What's wrong?"

Roy removed the bill. "Nothing, why?" Without looking at it, he folded it in thirds and dropped it into the bucket. I think it was a five or maybe a ten, whatever it was, it looked very lonely among coins.

He went back to watching the men with enough intensity to suggest he was trying very hard to avoid any more questions.

I took out my wallet. I used a five dollar bill to conceal three hundreds, folded it in thirds just like Roy, and dropped it next to his.

I was sure he hadn't seen me do it until he held my hand. "How much did you just put in there?"

"Put what where?" I glanced around.

Roy rubbed his thumb against my palm. "You didn't have to do that, you know."

"What?"

"That." He nodded at the bucket.

"I have no idea what you're talking about."

He bumped me with his elbow. "Thanks."

Never in my life had that word felt so sincere. But it seemed every word from Roy's lips had meaning. Just like his smiles, his touches, and the way he looked at me. It was all done with the purest intentions. I don't think Roy even grasped the concept of ulterior motive.

And in a world where it was the driving force of society, he was at a disadvantage.

Roy tugged me over to a bench, and for a very long time, we sat in the darkness of the park surrounded by orange halogen lights making more shadows than they pushed back.

"What happens if I say yes?" I said.

"To what?"

"This." I waved a hand. "All of this. What we're doing." I shook my head. "What are we doing?"

"Sitting in a park listening to Vil…" He scrunched up his face. "Vivaldi."

"That's what we're doing."

"But what about next time? Or the time after that?"

"What do you mean?"

"I'm not sure to tell you the truth. I've never had anybody…" I bounced a knee and tugged at the hairs on the back of my head. The gloves made it impossible to get a hold. At least I was able to make myself stop. "No one has ever wanted to know me. To be honest, I'm not even sure why you want to."

"I told you why."

"But it isn't enough."

"Why not?"

"I don't know."

"Then will you at least trust me enough to believe it's because I think you're intelligent, clever, and very beautiful."

"Beautiful?"

"Yeah."

"I thought we already had the girl discussion." I tried to laugh, but it crumbled.

"Handsome just isn't a big enough word for what you are. Maybe if I knew a better one."

"No, no, beautiful is fine, it's just..." I nodded. "Never mind."

"Tell me."

"I need a drink. Is there somewhere we could go?"

"You don't need a drink." Roy took me by the hand. Touching me made it impossible to move.

All the worry and hope in his eyes should have killed me. "But I'm not. I'm not beau—" I swallowed against the tightness in my throat. "I'm ugly and foul."

"How can you say that?"

"Because I've done terrible things." Laughter broke out. A couple of teenagers walked past with skateboards tucked under their arms.

"Like?"

"I can't tell you. I just can't." If he pushed me too hard, I would. I wouldn't be able to stop myself. I might have not broken right then, but I would have eventually.

"All right."

"Thank you." My smile wouldn't work either.

Roy held me captive with his gaze, and the park, the music, the world vanished. I pressed my lips together to keep them from trembling.

"But," he said. "When you're ready to talk about it, I'm here. Until then, I want you to remember, whatever it is you think you've done, it has not changed the good person I know you are."

****

We sat there sharing the silence long after the rag-tag group of old army vets left. Clouds erased the stars, and snow floated down from the sky.

I couldn't remember a time when I'd felt so at peace. I wasn't even sure I ever had been. But I was now, and it was a moment I didn't want to end. I think I would have stayed there all night if Roy hadn't pulled me to my feet.

There was only the sound of the occasional car on the wet asphalt and the snow as it whispered against the ground. It would be gone by morning. A new day always meant the destruction of so many things.

Roy walked me inside my building.

"Will you come upstairs with me?" I already knew the answer, but I had to ask.

He pushed my bangs back. "Not tonight."

"Then when?"

"I don't know."

"I wish this getting to know each other didn't involve abstinence."

"Why?"

"You still have a few nooks and crannies I haven't taste-tested." I laughed when his face turned red. "You know, you blush really easy."

"One of my downfalls."

"Something tells me you don't have very many." I pulled him closer and put my lips close to his ear. "Please come upstairs with me. I want you, Roy. I ache to feel you inside me."

He made the smallest whimper.

"You want to."

"Yes."

"But you won't."

"No."

"Well, you can't blame me for trying."

Roy tugged on the front of his jacket, but it wasn't nearly enough to cover the impressive bulge behind the zipper of his jeans.

"You better be glad that thing is attached, or it would follow me home. Then I'd have to keep it."

He tried to adjust himself, but there was no rearranging something that large. If anything, shifting it around just let it creep farther down his thigh. He gave up and stood there looking defeated.

"So this is good-bye." I said. "Or at least goodnight."

He pressed his mouth to mine. I parted my lips, wanting his tongue, but he kept that chaste too.

"I'm really beginning to hate this." I sighed and stepped away.

"You haven't even given it a chance."

"I'm not even sure I want to." Roy smiled at me in a way that said he knew I didn't mean it.

"I'd like to see you again," he said.

"Like a date?"

"Sure."

"Okay. What do you want to do?"

"We could go get something to eat."

"Where?"

He stuck his hands in his pockets. "Where do you normally go?"

"Lorna's, Dante's, The Blue Dog, Dumonds." I shrugged. "And a few I can't remember."

"Suit and tie?"

"Yes, why?"

"Just checking. What time do they open?"

"Around five, but you'll need to call in a reservation by twelve."

"Do you have a preference?"

"Not really."

"Then I'll take you to Lorna's." There was something in his tone I couldn't quite place.

"What's wrong?"

"Nothing."

But there was something, and I had no idea how to get him to tell me. I nodded at the elevator. "I guess I better go."

"Yeah."

"Are you sure you—"

He held up a hand. "I'll make the reservations for six tomorrow. Do you want me to pick you up?"

"It's closer to your side of town. I'll meet you there."

"You sure?"

"Yeah." I stepped into the elevator. "I guess I'll see you then." He vanished behind the doors, leaving me alone.

Roy and his stupid 'get to know you' bullshit. Why couldn't he just come upstairs and fuck my brains out like any other man would? But that was just it. He wasn't like any other man. I knew what they wanted, and I knew how to give it to them.

But Roy?

Back in the gallery, in that maintenance room, and again in his apartment, I thought I'd known him. Obviously, I'd been wrong. The thing was, I didn't miss it. I wanted to, because then I could get a handle on the montage of emotions eating away at my insides. But I didn't, and it left me wanting.

And I wasn't even sure what it was I wanted.

I entered the apartment. It wasn't a surprise to see Alice curled on the sofa with her head propped on her arm.

"Alice?" I put a hand on her shoulder. "Alice, wake up."

She squinted at me. "I'm sorry." She sat up. "I didn't mean to fall asleep."

"I told you not to wait up for me."

"I—" She stifled a yawn. "I just wanted to make sure you were all right."

"I was fine."

"But what if you weren't? Something could have happened, and there wouldn't have been anybody to call the police." I helped her stand. "My shoes." I picked them up from beside the chair and handed them to her. "Thanks."

"Next time, don't wait up."

"Are you going out again?"

I laughed. "Did you think this was only a one-time thing?"

"Yes, uh, no...I..." She finished putting on her shoes. "You really like this guy, don't you?"

I shed my coat and took it to the closet.

"Do you?"

It was a good question. "I think so."

"You don't know?"

I shrugged.

"You do like him." Her smile was contagious.

I put the scarf and gloves with the coat.

"When are you going to see him again?"

"I thought you didn't want me to?"

"No, it's not that, it's…"

She didn't have to explain. I rarely saw any man twice, and even then it was never for anything more than sex. Uncomplicated, no commitment, sex. "It's okay."

I left my boots by the door. The chill in the tile didn't waste any time sinking into the soles of my feet.

Alice's face lit up. "Having a boyfriend will be good for you."

"I don't know about that."

She followed me into the kitchen and cut me off at the freezer. "It will. I promise." She took the vodka out the freezer.

"If a boyfriend is such a good thing, then why don't you have one?" I leaned against the counter while she poured me a drink.

"I just don't."

"Why not?"

"I guess I don't want one." She fumbled with the juice box and stuck it back in the fridge. "Here."

I took the glass. "Thank you."

"You're welcome." Alice made herself busy putting the vodka away and rearranging some things in the freezer in the process. "Are you hungry? I could fix you something."

"No. I'm fine."

"You really should eat better." A bag of peas fell out, and she picked it up. "I read this article one time that when you don't eat a balanced diet you're more susceptible to getting sick."

"Alice, why don't you have a boyfriend?"

She gave me her back as she shut the door. "Would you like some ice?"

"No. It's fine." I put my drink on the counter and took her hand. She didn't resist when I turned her around.

She wouldn't look at me. "Daddy didn't understand that all boys weren't bad. I tried to tell him, but he said…I really should get going." She fluttered her hands. "I have shopping to do, and I need to pick up your blue suit."

"Alice?"

Her lip trembled. "Daddy said Andrew didn't love us. That's why he ran away." Alice snapped her mouth shut. "I need to go. I have to get up early…" She fled in the direction of the door.

"Alice, who was Andrew?"

139

"Your suit. If I don't pick it up, they'll charge extra. Or worse, they might lose it again."

"Alice…"

She grabbed up her purse and coat.

"Alice, please tell me…"

She spun around. Tears streaked her crimson cheeks, but she kept her gaze on the floor. "Whore. That's what he called Andrew. A whore. A dirty filthy whore who was nothing but a liar."

"Filthy little whore."

My feet became too heavy for me to pick up.

Alice straightened her shoulders. One quick swipe of her manicured fingers under her eyes removed most of the tears. "If you need me, just call. I have to get up early. There's the shopping and…"

"You need to pick up my suit."

The hammer glistened black in the light of the bare bulb. My father pointed a finger at me.

"I do." She nodded. "If I don't they'll charge—"

"Extra."

"This is your fault. All your fault. You made me do this."

"Yes, exactly." Alice hurried to the lift.

The cold burrowing into my skin was replaced by a familiar dread.

I ran to the kitchen. After I downed one mixed drink, I made another. More vodka than juice. I blamed it on the fact my hands were shaking, and I sloshed half of the juice out of the carton instead of in the glass.

My sinuses burned with every swallow. In order to cool the fire in my face, I lay my cheek against the fridge door. The throbbing in my head backed off.

"Get it together." I rubbed my temple. "Get it together, or you'll wind up in a room wearing a white coat with really long arms." I laughed even though there was nothing funny about what I said. If anything, I should have been more terrified because it had already happened.

The lift dinged.

"Alice?" I walked to the end of the partition. The foyer was empty. I took a few more steps, putting myself near the front of my studio.

The elevator doors were closed.

A flash of white scurried behind the sofa.

Bare feet slapped against the tile. I dropped my glass, and a star-shaped mess of orange juice spread over the floor.

There was nothing but darkness around the stairs, and the door leading into the laundry room was closed. Same with the bathroom.

I backed into the edge of one of my workbenches.

The heavy sigh came from the walls rather from any particular direction. A breath of air colder than ice. It passed through my body. It lapped at my soul. Then a cacophony of screams filled up my head.

"No!" I pressed my hands over my ears, but it didn't muffle the sound. "Shut up. For the love of God, shut up!" The noise would wake it up.

Canvases sat on the easels stacked against the wall. I grabbed one and dropped it on the floor.

Alice had organized my paints in a divider tray. I grabbed a tube, tossed aside the cap and reached for a brush. They were miles away on the table, so I squeezed a glob of paint onto the canvas and used my thumb to move it around.

Poor lighting stripped away the vibrant color. With nothing to hold down the horrible image, it popped from the canvas on a monochrome field.

The dread festered into fear, and the fear into hate. It crawled out of its black pit...

No, not a pit.

A well.

Dust and copper. Sour skin and death.

"I'm painting, goddamn it." Dirt coated the back of my throat. "Please, just give me more time."

I grabbed another tube and lost the cap somewhere between the box and the canvas. The pigment made oily slugs that became angry slashes.

Teeth. I think they were supposed to be teeth.

I dug furrows through rivers of paint with my fingernails. Tears in the flesh. The blur of white moved closer.

I tried to find the tube of red, but my fingerprints covered the labels. I grabbed orange out of the box. If I used it right, it would be toxic enough.

No. I needed the red. I had to have the red.

I wiped the labels clean on my slacks as I dug through the pile of mutilated tubes. I found the red and filled my palm. "It will go back to sleep." It would. It had to. "That was our deal. You leave me alone, and I paint." Crimson turned a shade close to black in the shadow of the workbench.

Figures reached for me from the oils fighting on the canvas, begging for help and pleading with frightened eyes.

"I'm painting, goddamn it." I held out my hands to show them. "I'm doing everything I can. Just let me work. I'll tell them. I'll tell all of them."

"Por favor, why do you lie? Tell me where is mi hijo? You know. I know you do."

"Shut up!" I pointed at the boy's mother. "Just shut up and let me work."

"Tell me."

The demand stabbed me in the temple. "I don't know!"

"Por favor, por favor, le suplico."

"I said I don't know!"

My tears made it impossible to see. But I didn't need my eyes to paint these images because they bled from my fingertips, pulling my hands where they needed to be. Using me to bring the nightmare to life, exposing what I was.

Wet leaves, old dirt, and copper tainted the air.

The boy whose name I couldn't remember stared at me with dead eyes. Dirt turned the right one it into a gritty orb.

"You're nothing but a filthy whore. My father loomed over me. *"You made me do this."*

"No!" I clawed the canvas. "Stop saying that."

"It's the truth, and you know. I see how you look at me. How you walk. How you flaunt."

"I don't." I slapped a glob of blue between two ruddy lines. They might have been red, or orange, or some muted shade of yellow. Whatever hue, it was sick and pockmarked with rot. "I don't do any of that."

"You're a whore, Paris, and that's what whores do."

The boy's mother petted my cheek. *"Help me por favor."*

142

Julia knocked me in the shoulder. *"You better not say a word, or I'll break every bone in your pathetic body".*

I covered my ears.

"...whore..."

"...why do you lie..."

"...keep your mouth shut, Paris..."

"Shut up! Just shut the fuck up!" I threw the plastic tray at them. It caught the edge of the workbench and the remaining tubes of paint scattered all over the floor.

"And you!" I chucked a tube of paint at the pair of black button eyes staring at me from the shadows next to the shelves. "You go back down the hole and leave me the fuck alone."

I wiped my face with the hem of my shirt and returned to the canvas. Swatches of color to close the wounds. Lines to tie it down. Layers upon layers, until the sound of their voices formed a hum.

I painted to silence them.

I painted to tell the truth.

I painted to free the boy whose name I couldn't remember.

Chapter Seven

The lights on the veranda highlighted the veins of water on the street and peppered the hoods of various luxury cars on the backs of melting snowflakes.

A line for the valet filled the front of the parking lot so I had the cabby drop me off at the corner. Lorna's was always busy this time of night no matter the day of the week. Good food, strong drinks, people with money and others looking to spend it.

If you were close to the owner, he'd take you into a back room where the millionaires club gathered to dine on salmon eggs from the endangered species list. If he liked you, he might even invite you into his private office to share a line. If he really liked you, he'd fuck you over his desk.

I pulled up the collar of my coat and dipped my chin behind the fold of my scarf. Even under layers of expensive clothes, the cold found me. I darted between the line of waiting cars, passing two identical Jaguars parked side by side.

Roy was a monolith in the loose crowd of patrons gathered at the front.

He smiled at me when I walked up. "Where's your coat?"

"I left it at home. It didn't exactly go with the suit." He tugged at the sleeves, but they were inches above his wrists.

"Someone needs to have a conversation with your tailor."

"I think that's the problem. These are off the shelf."

"Your suit rental friend?"

"Yeah. He says I'm out of the standard size range."

I grazed a look down to his crotch and back up. "He has no idea."

The ruddy color in Roy's cheeks spread over the rest of his face.

"You're too easy, Roy. Too easy." I closed the distance between us, and his exhale mixed with mine, floating away into the night. "Did you miss me?" His eyes darkened. I brushed my lips against his ear. "Did you think of your dick in my ass when you jacked yourself?" Roy swallowed, and his throat clicked. "How many times did you come? How many times did you cream the palm of your hand with my name on your lips?" The scent of his clean skin mingled with my cologne.

"Three."

"Only three?"

"Five if I count the ones this morning."

I pressed my chest against his. "And to think, we could be at your place right now making every one of those fantasies come true."

Roy collected my hand. The heat of his bare skin saturated the leather of my gloves. "I promised you dinner."

"Break your promise."

He collected my other hand. "I never break my promises."

"Never?"

"Not if I have any control over the situation." A water droplet fell from his bangs, into a gap of my scarf, and trickled down my neck.

"Well then." I flicked away some of the snow trying to gather on his shoulder. "I guess we better go in before they run out of the good wine."

I pushed through the crowd.

"Excuse me." Roy squeezed between two elderly couples exchanging the moth-eaten details of their lives. He bumped into a fat man wearing a toupee. "I'm sorry...I just need to..." Roy caught up to me. "It didn't look crowded standing on the sidewalk."

"It isn't crowded." I took him by the elbow. "You're just the only one with concern for other people's personal space."

A woman in a fur coat tried to cut in front of me. I stopped her with my arm and herded Roy through the gap. He brushed against her. "Sorry about that, ma'am."

"Quit apologizing, no one cares." I found the line and claimed a spot between people. Roy lingered at my shoulder so I pulled him in front of me and behind a blond who wore more jewelry than his girlfriend.

To him, Roy said, "Is this the end of the line?" If it wasn't the end before, it was now.

The man gave Roy a onceover and turned away.

"Told you," I said.

"It didn't hurt to make sure."

"No, but it was a waste of seven words the asshole didn't appreciate." Said asshole glanced back in my direction. I smiled. He didn't.

"Is it always like this?" Roy scanned the crowd.

"Usually."

"The food must be really good."

"It's not the food that brings people here, it's the atmosphere. Rubbing shoulders with some of the wealthiest people this city has to offer."

Roy pressed his lips together.

"You all right?"

"Yeah." He tapped his fingers against his thigh.

"What are you counting?"

"Huh? Oh, nothing."

"Five," I said. Roy gave me a look. "You've only fucked me five times. Eight if you count my mouth. Sorry Roy, hand jobs don't get a place on the score card."

Several couples in front of us glanced back. Roy rubbed the back of his neck and looked away.

"I don't think I've ever seen you so red." I massaged Roy's ass through his slacks.

"You probably shouldn't—"

I moved down until my fingers were between his legs. "I shouldn't what?"

Roy stepped to the side, breaking the contact. "Be good."

"What are you going to do if I'm not?"

The people in front of us moved, and we followed. Inside, the light clogging the air was broken by gaudy crystal chandeliers. Silverware made delicate scrapes against fine china, adding grit to the liquid hum of voices. Somewhere among the crowded tables, a patron tapped their wine glass and made a toast. Closer to the front of the restaurant, a woman laughed.

Roy stopped beside the small desk. I'd seen the host almost every time I came here, but I'd never bothered to learn his name. He skimmed his gaze over Roy's suit. "I'm sorry, sir. To eat here, you have to have a reservation."

"I do."

The host wrinkled his nose. "Name?"

"Callahan."

He flipped a piece of paper. "Sorry, I don't have a Callahan listed."

"I made it this morning."

"Maybe you called the wrong number?" He cocked his mouth to the side. "Happens all the time."

"Will you please check again?"

Our host made more of a show with his search. Flipping papers, checking his black book.

To me, Roy said, "I did make a reservation."

"I believe you."

"No, sorry. I don't have a Callahan listed anywhere. If you like, I could put you down for next week. But I can't promise—" I stepped around Roy. "Mr. Duvoe." And just like that, Roy became invisible. "Would you like your usual table?"

"I would, but unfortunately, it seems you've lost our reservation."

"I'm sorry?"

"*Our* reservation."

He flicked a look at Roy, then me, and then back. "I'm sorry, what was your name again?" His hands shook as he rifled through the pages of his book.

"Callahan."

"Six o'clock?"

"That's what they said."

"You're a bit early. No wonder I missed it." He struggled to smile. "Robert will show you to your seat."

"I'd like a private table," I said. Robert paused mid-step.

"They're all booked up," the host said. "But your usual table is open."

"The private table. Preferably a corner seat."

"Mr. Duvoe…"

"Should I call Shane?"

"Show Mr. Duvoe and his guest to a corner table in the guest hall."

Robert led the way through the maze of tables and into a secondary room divided by a large door. There, the light was more subtle, the conversation barely a whisper, and the space between tables adequate.

"Your table." He laid out two delicate cards next to the empty wine glasses. "Would you like me to bring you a bottle?"

"Yes. Make it my usual." Our waiter left. I laid my coat on the chair next to me and sat. Roy gave his chair a test shake. "I promise it will hold."

He eased down on the seat.

"See?" I picked up the card. "Order the veal or the lamb, it will go better with the wine."

Roy flipped the card over. "Where do you see that?"

"I don't. But they'll cook it."

"Not a very big selection." Roy stared at his card far longer than it took to read five items. "How do you know what everything costs?"

"You don't. It changes according to the market."

He tapped his fingers on the edge of the table.

"Counting again?"

"Uh—"

The waiter returned with our wine. Roy's gaze followed the man's hands as he uncorked the bottle and poured.

"Leave the bottle," I said, and he did. I poured a drinkable amount into my glass. "That's why I tell them to leave the bottle."

Roy read the label. "It's not very old."

"It's a newer wine, and in my opinion, better than some of the older ones."

Roy picked up his glass and sniffed it.

"What are you doing?"

He sloshed the wine around. "Isn't that what you're supposed to do with expensive wine?" He sniffed it again. "What is it I'm supposed to be smelling?"

"Fuck if I know. Just drink it." I showed him. "That's how you appreciate a glass of Tignanello."

"That doesn't sound French."

"Italian."

"Italians make wine?"

"What, you thought the only thing that ever came out of Italy were noodles and tomato sauce?"

"No…I just." He put down the glass and fumbled with his tie. It was crooked. "Who's Shane?"

I emptied my glass. "The owner."

"You know him?"

Sure, I did. I'd probably ruined half a dozen desktop calendars and broken just as many picture frames when I knocked them onto the floor. The words I wanted to say withered. I dropped my gaze. "Not really, why?"

"With the way that guy acted, I thought maybe he was a friend."

"He hovers around my sister when we eat here. That's all." I rubbed a water spot on the base of my wine glass until Roy went back to looking at the menu. "You keep staring at that thing like you're waiting for it to say something."

He put it down. "Sorry."

"If you don't want the veal or lamb or anything they have listed, I'll ask them to cook you something different."

"Why do they have a menu if they'll cook whatever people want?"

"Because they don't cook whatever people want. They'll cook whatever I want."

"Isn't that an inconvenience for them?"

"It's the price they pay if they want my business."

A couple in the center of the room got up and left. Another waiter came in. He took the order of two older women near the window. One of them wore a green dress, the other one yellow. The muted light made pink streaks in their white hair. A diamond bracelet glittered on the wrist of the woman wearing green.

Roy smoothed out his shirt and attempted to fold back the threads hanging from the right cuff of his jacket.

The waiter paused by our table on his way out. "I'll be back in a minute to collect your order."

Roy watched the man leave while he rubbed at the pale strip of skin on his wrist.

"Where's your watch?" I said.

"Oh, the strap broke. I planned on getting a new one but…" Roy took inventory of the room. His lips moved, and his fingers tapped.

149

"But what?"

"Huh?"

"You were planning on getting new watchband, but what?"

"I guess I just haven't had time." He flipped the menu over and then back.

"Are you going to drink your wine?"

He picked up the glass and took a sip.

"What do you think?"

"I guess it's good."

"You don't know?"

"I don't have a lot of experience with what good wine tastes like."

"Well, for three hundred and fifty dollars, it's a very good wine." I drained my glass. "Do you want another?"

He put the glass back on the table without taking another sip. "No, I'm good."

"What's wrong?"

"People actually pay that much for a bottle of wine?"

"People pay a lot more than that for very good wine."

"This doesn't qualify as very good wine?"

"For someone who just likes to drink it, sure. For someone who's a connoisseur, who knows?"

Roy went back to tapping his fingers on the table. One, then two, then back to one. His gaze went from the bottle, to the plate, to the menu.

Three hundred and fifty bucks was half of what Roy rented his apartment for. An apartment he kept cold to save on the electric bill. His sofa was worn down to the springs, and his bed came from The Salvation Army. The rest of his furniture went with the apartment.

And last night, he'd taken the only bill out of his wallet and dropped it into a bucket to help five veterans buy food for the homeless.

"Where's the last place you ate dinner, Roy?"

"Why?"

"Humor me."

A furrow creased his brow. "The Slaughter House."

"The what?"

He laughed. "Yeah, I know it sounds bad, but they specialize in slaughtered hot dogs, dress them up a hundred different ways."

"Are they good?"

"You have no idea. And their cheesecake is to die for."

I stood and put on my coat. "C'mon."

"Where?"

"Let's go eat cheesecake."

His smile was the most beautiful thing I'd seen all day. He started to stand. "Wait, what about dinner?"

"You said the food was good. We'll eat there." I jerked my head at the door.

"What about the wine?"

I grabbed the bottle. "If it goes with veal and lamb, I'm willing to bet it will be even better with hot dogs." Roy followed me to the back of the room, and we slipped through the side door leading into the kitchen.

Men in white jackets and black slacks arranged meats beside vegetables on a canvas of white porcelain. There was a door in the back where the waiters and cooks went to smoke. Sometimes when the meals got too boring with Julia, I'd slip outside and share a cigarette.

Roy stopped me at the end of the hall. "We need to pay for that." He nodded at the wine bottle.

"Are you kidding, it was horrible? Practically vinegar." I pulled him by his hand. "C'mon, before our waiter sees us." We exited the building and half jogged, half walked our escape.

I made it to the corner before I broke out in laughter. Roy held me up while looking over his shoulder.

"Do you think they'll call the police?"

Shifting my weight forced Roy's body flush against mine. "It's not like we robbed a bank." I played with the short hairs on the back of his head.

"No, but that wine is three hundred bucks."

"Three hundred and fifty."

"We should go back and pay for it."

"No, we shouldn't. I told you, it was terrible. Worst wine I've ever had." I took a sip from the bottle and offered it to Roy. He shook his head. "If it makes you feel any better, they would have thrown it out. This way it won't go to waste." I drank some more, and it dribbled down my chin. "Sorry, I usually hold my liquor much better than that."

Roy wiped the droplets away with his thumb. I caught his hand and held it against my cheek. The calluses on his palm scraped against my freshly shaven skin, sending an electric crackle down my spine.

"Paris…" Roy brushed his lips against my temple. I turned my head, hoping to catch his mouth, but he held my face just out of reach.

Under the halogen lights, his green eyes were some shade of black that had no name, clear, dark, and on fire. If he'd been any other man, I would have had him eating out of my palm, but I was the one who'd been tamed.

"I guess we better go get something to eat," I said.

"Yeah." He stroked his fingers along my jaw and down my neck. The pleasant heat collecting in my balls condensed into an ache.

"Roy…"

He traced my pulse back up to the soft place behind my ear. Then he expanded his hand until he cupped the back of my head.

I whimpered. "Roy, please…please…please…" My need for him went deeper than flesh and tugged at something inside me I didn't know existed. Whatever it was crushed my will.

"Please what?"

"Kiss me." He started to pull away, and I clung to him.

Roy sighed. "It's not that I don't want to."

"Then why don't you?"

"You know why."

"It's just a kiss."

"Nothing is just a kiss when it comes to you."

"Please."

Roy put his mouth close to mine. "A kiss."

"Yes," I said. "Just one."

"No more."

"No, no, no more."

Roy took the wine bottle from the fold of my arm and put it on the ground. "So you won't drop it."

"You must be planning on some kiss."

Roy put his arm around me, sealing our bodies together. My erection pressed against his thigh.

"You're blushing," he said.

"It's the cold."

"Are you sure?"

I started to put my hand on his cheek, but he'd barely agreed to the kiss.

"You can touch me. There at least."

His skin burned my fingertips. I searched his face, but I didn't know what I was looking for. Even though I knew it was there, right in front of me, I couldn't see it.

Roy tipped his head, and the ghost of his exhale mixed with mine. "You still haven't told me why you're blushing." He moved just enough to put a pressure against my cock. If he did it again, I would come. "Paris?"

"My kiss." The words scratched my throat. "You promised. One kiss. And you never break your promises." I gripped the lapels of his jacket.

"I'm not going anywhere."

I drank his words on a gasp.

"I promise you, I'll be here as long as you want me to be."

Closer, the snow landing on his skin became tears on my face.

"A day...A week..."

His lips brushed mine.

"Don't close your eyes."

If Roy had ordered my heart to stop, it would have.

"That's better."

"My kiss."

"Your kiss."

He erased the space between us.

I parted my lips, begging Roy to fill me, but there was only the weight of his mouth on mine, the velvet of his skin, the tiniest bit of silk fed to me on the tip of his tongue.

The contact was brief, but it set fire to my insides, dug into my bones, scattered my thoughts, and crushed me.

Broke me.

Then he stepped away, and I returned to my body, standing on that stretch of sidewalk at the corner of a building near two parked cars.

It was snowing.

And it was so very cold.

****

The Slaughter House was a hole-in-the-wall café between a pawnshop and a drug store. Chrome framed the windows, and a red awning hung over the door.

A layer of snow covered the three tables out front.

Roy held the door open, and I stepped into a world where the closest thing to ambience was a flickering fluorescent light in the back. The one empty table was missing chairs.

"There're seats at the counter," Roy said.

I shrugged off my coat, but there was no place to put it so I draped it over the back of the stool. A strip of duct tape covered a crack on the vinyl cushion.

"Well, look at what the cat dragged in." A black woman hugged Roy before he could sit down. "Where you been, stranger?"

"Working."

"You don't come see me as often as you used to." She winked at him, and Roy glanced at me.

"Most of the jobs I've taken have been on the other side of town."

"That's no excuse. You can always visit on the weekends." She offered me one of her plump hands. "And you are?"

"I'm sorry," Roy said. "Louise, this is Paris."

We shook.

"Paris? Uh-huh…now that's a fancy name. Roy knows this side of town like the back of his hand. Make sure he shows you around. 'Cause something tells me a pretty boy like you could get into a whole lot'a trouble."

"I'll be sure to do that. The last thing I want is trouble."

To Roy, she said, "Are you gonna have your usual?"

"Uh, sure." Roy sat beside me.

"What about you, honey?"

"Make mine the same, I guess."

When she spoke to Roy again, it was just above a whisper, and the bright grin she wore turned subtle. "So have you made any plans for Christmas yet?"

"Not really, no, ma'am."

154

"The invitation is still open. And you know, Betty isn't seeing anyone right now."

Roy fumbled with the silverware. "Betty is a real nice girl..." He moved the fork to his right, then added the butter knife. "But I'm seeing someone."

"Oh..." Louise straighten her shoulders. "Do I know her?"

"Uh...actually...actually it's..." He cleared his throat. He took a breath. He fumbled with the silverware some more. He took another breath, and then his hands fell still.

Roy met her gaze.

"Actually you just met *him*."

She glanced at me and then back. "Oh." Her eyes widened. "Ohhh—" Louise took out her ticket book, then patted down her pockets. "I, uh...you said your usual, right?"

"Yes, ma'am."

"I'll go get a pen and write that..." She shook her head at me. "I'll make sure Jonathan puts extra chili on yours. Maybe it will put some meat on your bones." She hurried away.

Roy slumped in his seat.

"Did you just come out for the first time to a waitress?"

"I think so."

Louise went from the cash register to the back counter. She patted down her pockets again and pulled out a pen. Instead of writing anything down, she went over to the man rolling hot dogs around in an iron skillet. He was tall, with black hair, and skin just a shade darker than Roy's. The man glanced over his shoulder at us.

"I think you're about to become talk of the town."

Roy's Adam's apple bobbed when he swallowed.

"You regret telling her?"

"Never."

Right there in front of the world, he kissed me on the forehead.

"Oh my God." A girl with wild curly hair and green eyes appeared from behind a door in the kitchen. She propped her elbows on the counter in front of us. "Momma wasn't lying. You gotta boyfriend." She had her mother's smile.

"This is Shara," Roy said.

She waved at me. "Is your name really Paris?"

155

"Yes."

Shara clicked her tongue and shook her head. Curls stuck to her cheeks, and she pushed them back. "You white people come up with some funny names. Countries, states, and cars. There's this girl in my homeroom, her name is Lexus. Can you believe that? If I was gonna have to be named after a car, it would at least be a cool one."

I propped my chin on my fist. "And what do you consider a cool car name?"

"Lamborghini, or Bugatti, or maybe Aston Martin. That would be a good name for a boy."

"Aston Martin does have a nice ring to it. Maybe I should consider changing my name." I nudged Roy with my elbow. "What do you think?"

"Your name's fine the way it is."

I shrugged. "You heard him. No name change."

"Well, you ain't married to him yet. Means you can do whatever you want. So if you want to change your name, change it. Momma says no man should own a woman. I guess that would go for boys too." She eyed Roy. "You should've told Betty you liked boys. She's gonna be heartbroken." Roy stared at the fork in front of him. "Momma and her been looking at wedding dresses."

I raised my eyebrows at Roy. "Wedding dresses? Sounds serious."

"I only met her once," he said.

"Must have made quite an impression."

"He did." Shara bounced on her toes. "Betty done nothing but talk about Roy since she met him. Roy this, Roy that. She talk about you so much I almost get tired of hearing your name."

I folded my arms and fought the smile trying to crawl across my face. "Well, maybe we need to rethink this dating thing we have going on."

For a second, Roy paled.

"Naw," Shara said. "When you like boys, you like boys. Momma said when that happens, they'd just made that way." She leaned closer, and so did I. "But I know this girl, she likes girls and boys. She really do."

"It happens," I said.

"You think Roy might like both?"

I flicked him a look.

Shara nodded. "If he do, then he could marry Betty and you. Then he could have both."

Roy made a strangled sound.

"No," I said. "I'm pretty sure Roy only likes boys."

She stood back up. "Oh well. Guess that means you're gonna have to adopt, seeing you can't have no babies."

"Shara." Louise popped her head out from behind the door in the back. "Get your butt in here right now."

She rolled her eyes. "I gotta go. Momma will want me to do inventory now that she's all on the phone. See ya." She leaned forward again but stopped. "Since you like boys, do that mean I can't kiss you on the cheek no more?"

Roy turned his head. She gave him a peck and bounced away.

"That was cute," I said. "How old is she? Fourteen?"

"Twelve."

"Isn't she tall for twelve?"

"All of Louise's kids are tall like their father." He nodded at the man hovering over the stove, cutting up hot dogs in buns and drowning them in a myriad of toppings. The teenager helping him looked like a younger version.

"How many does she have?"

"Eight."

"Wow. I hope you're not expecting us to have that many."

Roy opened his mouth. Then shut it. "Not funny."

I poked his stomach. "I bet you'd make a terrific mommy."

"No, I—"

"Butterball stomach."

"I'm not—"

"Your feet would swell, and I'd rub them."

"Paris—"

"You'd get to eat all the ice cream you want."

"Don't—"

"We could go to Lamaze classes together, and afterward, you could go out with all the other mommies and talk about baby shoes and diapers."

He scrubbed his face. "Why are we even talking about this? It's not even possible."

"With the wonders of modern medicine? Never say never."

An older version of Shara stopped by. "Momma said she forgot to get your drinks."

"Coffee and water," Roy said.

I nodded at the wine bottle. "Just a glass. I brought my own."

"It's still a quarter, but the ice is free."

"A quarter is fine and hold the ice."

She cocked her mouth to the side and gave Roy a look. "Why you have'da get some white boy who's gonna blow away in the wind?" The girl tromped away.

"Yeah," I said. "What the hell were you thinking?"

"You're not that skinny."

"Then why are you always trying to feed me?"

"You're not skinny enough to blow away."

"What about the white boy part?"

"Nothing I can do about that."

I laughed. "Maybe I should get a tan."

"You'd burn to a crisp."

The girl delivered our drinks, and her father followed up with two mutilated hot dogs in buns drowning under a tower of chili, cheese, peppers, and other substances I couldn't identify, contained in two metal boat-shaped trays. She left, but he didn't.

"Roy, I hope you're proud of yourself." He took the towel off his shoulder and wiped his hands. "You got Louise stirred up so bad I'll never get her off the phone tonight."

"That wasn't my intention, Jonathan. I'm sorry."

"So when you boys gonna tie the knot?"

Roy almost dropped his coffee cup.

"Don't look at me that way. With the way Louise is talking, you two done bought a house, a dog, and got three kids."

"And you told me you couldn't have children," I said.

Roy glared at me. To Jonathan, he said, "We haven't been together that long."

"Well, you better keep this one." He nodded at me. "'Cause she's probably back there ordering your cake and booking you a place at the church." He slapped Roy on the shoulder. "Enjoy."

"Have we set a date yet?" I said.

Roy rubbed his forehead while poking his food with a fork. "Sorry about that. Louise can get a little exuberant."

"I'll say. You married her daughter and divorced her within a minute, proposed to me, got pregnant, and now we have a dog." I poured some wine into the empty glass. "That's a lot to happen in one night. Even for me. I'm kind of speechless, come to think of it." I held up the bottle. "Want some?"

"No, thanks."

"Might make you feel better."

"It's not...I don't..." He made a frustrated sound.

"So when you propose, will it be on your knees and with a ring?" I held up my hands and wiggled my fingers. "I'm partial to platinum. Plain. Nothing gaudy."

There was something close to sadness in his eyes. "Unfortunately, the best I could ever do is something from the pawn shop."

I pulled over my boat. "That's pretty clever of him to use sundae dishes for the hot dogs." A glob of chili dripped over the side. "I'm having flashbacks of my last chili experience. Strangely enough, I'm not turned off by the similarities, and another evening with heartburn and indigestion has acquired some appeal." I took a bite. Sweet and spicy, tipped with reds and yellows, spread over my tongue. "Damn that's good."

He quit staring at me and ate a few bites of his food. The knots in my back loosened.

"So what's his secret?" I said.

"No clue."

"Do hotdogs taste different cut up?"

"You've never had them before?"

"Maybe when I was little, but I don't think so, because I'd remember this." Another bite made me moan. "I'm going to come here every day and eat these. Maybe twice a day." A slice of yellow pepper slid off the mound of spreading chili. I caught it on my fork.

Roy laughed. "I'm glad you like it."

"Like it? I think my tongue is having orgasms." I held up my glass. "You should really try some of the wine. The hotdog makes it taste like ambrosia." I missed my mouth, and a glob of chili landed on my shirt. "I think it's trying to escape."

159

Roy handed me a couple of napkins.

"Are you kidding? I'm not going to waste a drop of this." I scraped it off with my finger and licked it clean. "Who needs veal and lamb when you have…what do they call this?"

"A slaughtered hotdog."

"Glad it tastes better than it sounds."

He drank his coffee, and I poured myself a second glass of wine.

Between the last few bites of his dinner, Roy said, "Thank you."

"Hey, this was your idea, not mine." I moved the remaining lumps of bread and chili around in my dish. I was too full to eat anymore but not quite ready to surrender.

"I mean for what you did. At the restaurant."

Surely I could get one more bite down. I scooped it up on my fork, and it dripped through the prongs.

"I'm just sorry you had to do it."

I put down my fork. "I'm sorry I didn't stop to think about what a place like that costs. I should have paid for it to begin with."

"I'm the one who wanted to take you to dinner."

"Doesn't matter."

"I would have never let you."

"I know." I pushed my bowl away. "That's why I didn't suggest it."

"I appreciate that. At least this way, I get to save face."

"You were never at risk of losing it to begin with." I guzzled the second glass of wine just to fill the silence. The room tipped, and I almost sat my glass down in the empty boat. Roy took the glass before I dropped it. "Sorry, that hit me harder than I expected."

"Maybe it's because you drank the entire bottle."

"I did not." My temples throbbed. "You had a glass."

"But I didn't drink it. You did."

"I usually hold my wine a lot better than this." I touched my nose. "At least it's not cold anymore."

"Are you ready to go?"

"Sure."

"Wait here, and I'll pay the bill."

"I'll leave a tip."

"No, I'll let them keep the change. This is my treat, remember?" When he walked away, I stuck a twenty under his coffee cup.

While Roy exchanged goodbyes, I pulled on my coat and made my way to the door.

"Hey, wait up."

I teetered to the right, and Roy caught me.

"You running off?"

"No, I just…I thought maybe the cold would clear my head."

"Clearing your head is one thing, freezing to death is something else." Roy buttoned my coat and tightened my scarf. "Where are your gloves?" He patted down my pockets. "Here, put them on."

I did. "Happy?"

"Very."

We stepped out into a new world silenced by a blanket of white. The streets had cooled enough for the snow to gather in the gutters. More covered the cars parked at the curb. There was hardly anyone left on the street, driving or walking.

"I don't think I've ever seen it snow like this before." I pulled my scarf higher to protect my ears.

"Do you want me to hail a cab?"

"I'd rather walk."

"You might slip and fall."

"Then you'll have to catch me."

"And who's going to catch me?"

"The sidewalk is tougher than it looks."

Roy fell into step beside me.

"Besides," I said. "If you hail a cab, then I'll get home quicker."

"And that's a bad thing?"

"Anything meaning less time with you is a very bad thing." I looped my arm in his, partly because I wanted him closer and partly because my knees were rubbery.

We'd gone two blocks when Roy said, "I know I can't afford to take you to fancy places or buy you nice things."

"Roy, I—"

"Let me finish."

161

We stopped under the awning of a clothing store. The lights in the windows turned the mannequins into faceless ghouls.

Roy dusted some of the snow from my bangs and tucked them behind my ear. "I don't have money, but you do, so you can buy yourself everything I can't." He put his finger over my lips, stopping another reply. "But there are some things money can't get you. Things I know you've never had." His touch followed the curve of my mouth, sending a shiver through me. "That's what I have to offer you, if you'll give me the chance."

A boy's laugh echoed off the building and was followed by the crunch of dead leaves.

At the corner, the red light turned green, and a man on a bicycle made an illegal left turn.

"Paris?"

The lost wail of a car siren started and stopped. There was music playing, but I couldn't tell if it was coming from one of the bars a few blocks down or a car I couldn't see.

There was nothing but me, the snow, and the darkness. Sweat cut a line down my back.

Roy made me look at him. "What's wrong?"

I swallowed and tasted dirt.

Roy shook me. "Paris, talk to me. What's wrong?"

I took a step back. Mud caked my shoes and ankles, bits of forest clung to the leg of my pants.

"Hurry up, Paris." Julia stood by the tree. Her dress was stained, and the white stockings she wore had runs all the way to her knees. At some point, she lost her shoes.

She'd blame me later.

"I'm tired." The muscles in my arms refused to pick up the shovel, and the bottom of my foot hurt from trying to push it into the ground.

"Like I care." She pushed her hair back, leaving a streak of dirt on her cheek. Her melting mascara gave her raccoon eyes.

"The ground's too hard."

"Dig, Paris."

"There are too many roots."

"Fine. Fine. We'll put it somewhere else."

"Please, Julia. I don't feel good." I tried to show her the blisters on my hands, but she turned away.

"Quit your whining and help me pick it up."

Snow surrounded me, and Roy searched my face. "What did you take?"

Everything felt so far away, but it was getting closer by the second.

"Answer me."

"No...no. I didn't take anything."

"Don't lie."

"I'm not."

"Then why are you talking about the ground being too hard?"

What else had I said? I gasped for air.

Roy dragged me to the store window and sat me on the ledge. He scanned the street.

I held up a hand. "I'm..." My throat squeezed tight. "...fine..."

"You're not fine."

"...panic..." My inhale whistled in my lungs. "...attack..." It had been years, and I'd taken the gift of air for granted. Black spots danced in front of my eyes. "...happens..." A tingling throb touched my lips and spread to my chin.

I leaned forward, putting my head between my knees. The vise in my chest eased enough for me to draw a mouth full of air. Then my throat relaxed, and I could swallow.

I found myself timing my inhale and exhale to the slow rhythm of the Roy's hand as he rubbed my back.

In.

Out.

In...

The bubble popped, and I sat up, sucking in bouts of cold air. Snowflakes melted on my cheeks, cooling the fever burning inside me.

"Are you sure you're okay?"

I nodded.

"How often does this happen?"

"Often enough, but..." I rested my elbows on my knees. "But it's been awhile since I've had one that bad." I wound up leaning against Roy. He continued to rub my back.

Up.

Down.

Up…

The residual fear drifted away. Freed from its hold, I still didn't want to move.

"Are you seeing a doctor?"

"Hmmm?"

"Are you seeing a doctor?"

"Yeah."

"Do you need me to call them?"

"No." I would've rather had another attack. "No, I'm fine. I am." My legs were still weak so Roy helped me stand.

"There's a bar around the corner so there should be a cab."

"I told you, taking a cab means getting home too fast."

"I don't think walking would be good for you right now."

I nodded. "Okay. We'll get a cab." He put his arm around me. "But let's at least take the long way around."

****

I insisted Roy stay in the cab and let me go up alone. It had nothing to do with my pride and everything to do with the fact he'd never come inside with me. It wouldn't have been a problem if I could refrain from asking.

But I could never refrain from asking.

The cab didn't pull away from the front door until I reached the elevator.

I took off my scarf and unbuttoned my coat. I was going to be lucky if I could make it up the stairs to my room. There was always the sofa, but it was too short to be comfortable. With my muscles dripping off my bones, it probably wouldn't have mattered.

"Well, look what the cat dragged in." Gregory sat draped in one of the lobby chairs with his ankle over his knee. A king on an upholstered throne.

"What are you doing here?"

"Waiting for you."

"Well, now you can leave." I hit the call button on the lift. His reflection grew on the brass plated doors.

"So was your date business or pleasure?"

"Why are you here?"

"I couldn't stand the anticipation of a week with you in my house."

"Until you pay for the work, there will be nothing to anticipate."

"And I'll pay when I get another test drive to make sure you warrant the investment."

The doors opened, and Gregory followed me inside. I pushed the hold button. "Get out."

He met me toe to toe. "So did you fuck him?"

"Get. Out."

"I hope so, it will save me the prep work." He shoved me into the corner, and the doors closed. Gregory swallowed my threat. I yanked my mouth away, but he jerked me back by digging his fingers into my neck.

He forced my mouth open, and I sank my teeth into his lip.

Gregory let me go. "You fucking son-of-a-bitch. You bit me." He spit a glob of red saliva on the floor.

"You shouldn't have tried to stick your tongue in my mouth."

He pressed the back of his hand against his bottom lip. I reached to open the doors, and he got in the way. "I don't think so. Not after this." He dabbed away another trickle of blood. "After this, your ass is mine." Gregory made another grab. I blocked him, but it left me open for a punch. The impact left my head ringing and my face throbbing.

I lost my balance.

He seized my arm and twisted it behind my back. I have no idea how the hell he got his belt off so fast, but it was around my neck before the static quit buzzing in my skull.

"You want rough? I can give you rough."

Everything darkened.

The boy reached out to me while he lay in the dirt, and I crouched behind a wooden crate. He begged me with his eyes to help him. The pig of a man grunted, and the rabbit ran circles in its cage, faster and faster until it shook and its feet were raw.

But like the pig, it wouldn't stop.

Gregory had let go of the belt so he could unbutton his chinos, and a high-pitched tone tolled in my ears as the confines of the elevator came back into focus. I pushed up only to be shoved back down.

Gregory threw my coat up over my shoulders. "I told you I was going to teach you a lesson or two about respect. Bite me? Fucking bitch. You want blood, I'll give you blood." He felt around the front of my pants to unbutton them.

I pulled my knees up just enough to give him a few inches of space. The crook of his arms pressed against my side. When his ragged breathing was close to my ear, I shoved my upper body off the floor. The back of my head connected with his face, and he howled.

Gregory tried to stop me from getting to my feet by grabbing my coat. I shrugged free, and without the tension, he fell back. His bloody face left a red streak on the wall.

He flailed until he got to his feet. "I'm going to fucking kill you for that. I'm going—" Gregory was silenced by the thump in my chest. Rage twisted his features into something inhuman. I wasn't afraid. I wasn't angry. Whatever I'd been had gone away, leaving me empty.

Gregory dove at me, and the cold stillness inside me shattered.

I countered his punch with my forearm, and he went for my throat. A slight turn to my left forced him to overextend, sending him off balance. I grabbed his thumb.

He tried to twist free, but I cranked the digit back until it popped. The flush in his face went white, but before Gregory could scream, I jerked him off balance by his hair. On his way down, I guided him into the wall. But once wasn't enough.

"Please stop." He clawed at my wrists. Whatever he said next was drowned out by the whoosh of air I stomped from his ribs. Gregory wailed, and tears burst from his eyes. He curled up in a feeble attempt to block my next strike.

As quick as the rage had risen, it flickered out. The second kick knocked me to the side, and I slumped against the wall.

I was close enough to the panel to open the doors. A sticky trail of vomit and blood traced Gregory's path as he made an escape out the elevator. He got to his knees about the same time I regained my balance.

I walked behind him as he crossed the threshold and planted my foot in his ass, shoving him into the lobby. He landed facedown. Then he rolled on his side, bawling like an infant.

Bill came from the direction of the men's room. "Mr. Duvoe?"

I held up a hand. "I'm fine."

"You're bleeding."

"It will wash."

He looked at Gregory who slid around in his own piss.

"Do me a favor and throw that bag of shit in the alley."

"I think he needs an ambulance."

"Yeah, well, he's got a cell phone and nine working fingers. If he does, he can call one."

"What about you?"

"I told you, it will wash."

I managed to stay on my feet until I punched in the floor code for my apartment.

Chapter Eight

A terrible hammering noise cracked open the festering wound behind my eyes.

"Paris?" Alice.

I tried to shoo her away by waving my arm.

"Are you in there?"

Another round of banging forced me out from under the covers. A thin stream of sunlight lasered a path across my room, and bright shards of broken color exploded around me.

"Paris."

The doorknob rattled.

I croaked out a "What?"

"It's three o'clock."

"So?"

"Don't you think it's time you got out of bed?"

"What for?"

"Your friend has been calling you all day."

Friend?

"He said his name was Roy? Is that the guy you're dating?" She rattled the doorknob. "It's not polite to ignore his phone calls. Did you two break up? Is that why you're hiding in your room?"

"No...we didn't....goddamn it." I tried to sit up and wound up sliding off the bed and onto the floor. My elbow hit the nightstand. The clock tripped off the edge.

"What was that noise?"

"Nothing."

"Something fell. I heard it. Paris, open this door."

"Not now, Alice. Please. Just...just leave me alone."

"Are you drunk? You sound drunk. If Julia calls, you won't be able to talk to her. You know how ill she gets when you've been drinking."

"Fine. I won't talk to her." I reached for the side table and knocked off the lamp.

"What are you doing in there?"

"Redecorating."

"What?"

"Just go home. The dishes can wait or dinner or whatever."

"Are you sick?" She beat on the door.

"Please stop. Just..." I rolled to my side.

"If you're sick, I need to call Dr. Mason."

"No, no, I'm fine." Anyone but him. "It's just...the flu, I think."

"Are you sure you're not drunk?"

"Does it matter if I am?" I got my arm on the edge of the mattress and was able to pull myself to my feet. "Are you still there?"

"Yes."

"You're not calling Dr. Mason, are you?"

"You said not to."

I nodded.

"Paris?"

"Yeah, yeah. I did. Just... thank you."

"Are you sure you're okay?"

The dark red blotch on my side had turned an ugly purple. "I'm fine." It hurt when I pressed my fingers on it, but not as bad as it did when I crawled up the steps.

"Okay, if you're sure you're all right, I'm going to go home."

"I'm sure."

"I won't be here tomorrow. I'm supposed to go back to the museum and help with that charity event, since Julia isn't here."

"Yeah, yeah. Okay. Charity event."

"So you may have to call the doctor yourself if you can't get me."

"I will." My bladder clenched, and I took several wobbly steps in the direction of the bathroom.

"Paris?"

"Yes?"

"I love you."

"I love you too, Alice. It's okay. I promise. Go to the event. I'll be fine." I stepped over the trail of clothes I'd left on the floor and stumbled into the bathroom. I barely made it. To stay upright, I had to prop my shoulder against the wall.

I left my boxer briefs in front of the toilet and turned on the shower. Even though I made sure to dial down the pressure, the water stung like a blast of superheated needles. I forced myself to stay there until the worst of it eased enough for me to wash.

The aches and stiffness flowed away with the water, and when I finished in the shower, I was able to take care of the basics. By the time I was done brushing and shaving, I was too tired to bother with getting dressed, and put on a robe. Besides, coffee was more important than clothing.

While the coffee percolated, I dug through the containers on the counter looking for the bread. Toast would be safe to eat. I hoped.

"Damn it, Alice. Where did you hide it?"

There was a wooden box on the other side of the kitchen near the stove. It didn't match any of the appliances. The word 'bread' had been carved into the front.

How the hell had I missed that?

It could have been new. Knowing Alice, she probably changed out the food containers on a weekly basis. I stuffed two pieces into the toaster and ate a third slice out of the bag, then went on a search for the aspirin.

There was a half full bottle in the cabinet on the condiment wheel. I kept it there so when I woke up in my studio with a hangover I didn't have to make it all the way to my bedroom to get it. Sometimes Alice would move it. Thank God she hadn't.

I poured a few in my hand. Was two enough? Was six too many? I took four and washed them down with water from the tap.

The toast popped up. It barely had a chance to cool before I crammed a piece in my mouth. I was still chewing when the coffee finished. It was going to take it forever to cool, and I needed to wash down the crusty lump of dough stuck to the roof of my mouth. I got an ice cube from the dispenser and dropped it in my cup.

The intercom in the living room beeped. I drank my coffee. It beeped again. I went over to the elevator and pushed the talk button. "Who is it?"

"Paris?" Roy's voice was even strong over the tinny speaker.

"Yeah?"

"Are you all right?"

"Fine."

"Will you let me come up?"

I laid my forehead against the wall. "Now's not exactly a good time."

"I called you last night on the way home to make sure you got in okay. You didn't answer. You didn't answer this morning either."

"I'm okay."

"You don't sound like you are."

"I'm just…" I sighed.

"Please let me come up."

I punched the send button. "Elevator's on the way down. Top floor." Julia was on the first floor, Alice had the third. Or maybe it was the fourth? I made my way back into the kitchen to drink the rest of my coffee.

The elevator doors opened. "Paris?"

"In here."

Roy walked past the partition. "Are you sure you're… Jesus, what happened to your face?" Then he was right there. Cradling my head, stroking my chin, my cheek, my throat. I closed my eyes until he stopped. "Did Julia do this to you?"

"What? No, no, she's not even in town."

"Then how did this happen?"

"It's not as bad as it looks."

"That's not what I asked."

"I had a disagreement with a client who couldn't take no for an answer." I stepped away.

"Did you call the police?"

A fresh cup of coffee from the pot was still too hot to drink. I got another ice cube. "Do you want some? I just made it."

"Did you call the police?"

"For what?"

"Someone beat the shit out of you, that's for what."

"He was the one who had to crawl out of the elevator." I drank. "Believe it or not, I can take care of myself. Now do you want some coffee?" I took out another cup. "Goddamn it, will you quit looking at me like that? It's just a few bruises."

"If it's just a few bruises, then why didn't you answer the phone?"

"Coffee or not?"

"Why didn't you answer the phone?"

"Is it illegal for me not to answer the phone?" Yelling made my face hurt. Roy touched the back of my neck and made small circles with his fingers. "I think I took a pain pill. I don't really remember. I'm sorry."

"What if you'd had a concussion? You could have died." His voice cracked.

I stared at the coffee cup in my hands.

"You should have called me."

"Why? So you could baby me? Tend to my wounds? Nurse me back to health?" I laughed.

"Is that so bad?"

I narrowed a look at him. "I'm not helpless."

"I never said you were."

"Then quit treating me like I am."

"I'm not."

"You are."

"So you're saying if you showed up at my apartment and I was all bruised up, you wouldn't care?"

I pinched the bridge of my nose. "I'm too tired to argue."

"We're not arguing."

"We're disagreeing, it's the same thing." I poured him a cup of coffee. "You like it black, right?" I nodded for him. "Here."

Roy took the cup and put it down on the counter. "Who did this to you?"

"I told you."

"I want a name."

"Why, so you can warn him to stay away? Trust me. He knows. Fine, if it makes you feel better, Gregory Tims. But if I were you, I'd at least wait until he was out of the hospital. Threatening a guy with his jaw wired shut just doesn't have the same heroic effect."

Roy picked up my hand. I almost pulled away, but he stopped me by rubbing my knuckles. The bruises ran all the way to my wrist. I hadn't even noticed until then. They didn't hurt.

"I'm sorry I yelled at you." I leaned against him. "I didn't exactly sleep very well."

"It's okay."

"You deserved it, though."

"Probably." He petted my head and kissed my temple. I tried not to wince. "Sore spot?"

"Only when you touch it."

He chuckled.

"Can we go somewhere?" Away. Far away.

"Where do you want to go?"

"Anywhere but here. The park?"

"It's cold."

"I don't care."

"You should probably rest."

"I don't want to." I turned my face into his neck. He didn't wear any cologne so there was just the subtle scent of soap and the powerful ambrosia of male. "Please. I just need to…go."

He kissed me again on the other side of my face. "Have you got any boots?"

"Yeah, why?"

"Because there's almost a foot of snow on the ground."

"No, there isn't."

"Yeah. There is."

"And the city didn't shut down?"

"It's got a pretty bad limp."

I pressed closer. My robe parted just enough so there was nothing between him and everything below my waist. "Maybe you should just take me to your place, fuck my brains out, and put me to bed."

Roy held me. "How about I just put you to bed?"

I buried a frustrated groan into his shoulder. "You're killing me."

"I don't mean to."

If he'd been anyone else, I would have called him a liar. "There's really a foot of snow on the ground?"

"Close to it." He petted my back.

"How about we go to the park and build a snowman?"

He laughed. "I don't know. My last few attempts failed big time."

"Too bad we don't have a sled and a hill. We could just go sledding. I've never been sledding. Always wanted to."

Roy tipped my chin up. "Get dressed, and I'll see what I can do."

****

173

The address Roy gave the cab driver took us to the far side of the park where there were no paths or picnic tables.

"I've lived here all my life, and I've never seen snow like this." It obliterated the sidewalks, the bits of trash in the street, turning stone and asphalt into a perfect stretch of white.

A canvas waiting to be filled.

The cold pressed against my cheeks, and a slight breeze carried away my exhale.

"Are you sure you're warm enough?" Roy said.

"I put on two long-sleeve shirts and a sweater like you said."

"Socks?"

"Two pair."

"I'd feel better if you had some long johns."

"Not in fashion."

Roy shook his head.

"What? I can't go around wearing something that would make my ass look like a marshmallow."

He knocked on the driver's window. "Can you pop the trunk?" Roy went to the back and got out a flattened cardboard box. He had to fold it over to keep it from dragging on the ground.

"Are you ever going to tell me why you dug that out of the dumpster?"

"I told you, you'd have to wait and see."

I paid the cabby, and he left.

"C'mon." Snow crunched under Roy's boots as he walked to the trees.

"Where are we going?"

"Wait and see."

"You keep saying that." Within a few steps, snow crusted my boots and clung to the cuff of my jeans. The extra weight caused me to fall behind.

"Hurry up, slow poke."

"Slow poke? People still say that?" I was out of breath when I caught up to him. "How do people walk in that stuff?"

"You should try several feet of it."

"No, thank you."

"This way." He slipped through a gap in the row of Leyland cypress.

"You realize if you want to have your way with me, you don't have to haul me off into the woods. The bed would have been just fine." A branch flicked back, launching a clump of snow into my face.

He laughed. "Having fun yet?"

I tried to brush it off of my scarf before it could drip down my neck. "You didn't say anything about having to fight shrubbery."

A culvert made a sharp drop between the edge of the park and an industrial area. Roy unfolded the piece of cardboard.

"What are you doing?" I said.

"Making you a sled."

"You do origami?"

He rolled his eyes at me. "C'mere."

I walked to the edge of the dip. "That's a long way down."

"Seventy-five, a hundred feet."

"And you expect me to sled down that."

"It's not that steep."

"We should go to the mall and see if they have any parachutes on sale."

Roy laid out the piece of cardboard. Ironically, the extended side flaps gave it an airplane outline. "Here."

"What?"

"Sit down on it."

"You're kidding."

"You said you wanted to go sledding."

"Down a hill, not the Grand Canyon."

"The kids in the neighborhood slide down this thing on cardboard all the time."

"With no snow?"

"Sure. A hill's a hill. You just get something that will slide on the grass and go."

"Why would anyone want to slide down a hill with no snow?"

"Because it's fun." Roy yanked me over. "Now sit."

I did, and he got behind me, framing my body with his.

"Pull the front up and tuck your feet behind it."

My bruised knee protested, but I managed to squeeze myself in. Both of us on the cardboard shrank it down to a shoebox.

"Are you sure this thing is big enough?"

"You only need enough to cover your ass." Roy put his arm around my ribs.

"Kind of like a Speedo."

"A what?"

"Never mind. So how do we make it go?"

Roy extended one of his legs out to the side and did the same with the opposite arm. He rocked his body and the cardboard went a few inches. "Work with me here, Paris."

"What do you want me to do?"

"Scoot the box." He rocked again. I did the same. We moved another handful of inches.

"It might just be me, but I think we're supposed to move faster than this."

"We will, but we just have to get going." Roy shifted his weight and dug his heel into the snow. "Now on the count of three, give it one good scoot."

"There's a good scoot?"

"One…"

"I don't think this is going to work."

"Two…"

"There's a reason they make sleds."

"Three." He pulled with his foot, pushed with his hand, and shoved with his hips. Our makeshift sled went a whole two feet before stopping on the incline.

"Wow," I said. "That was exciting."

"You didn't scoot."

"Oh, so it's my fault."

"You were supposed to scoot." He stood.

"Where are you going?" I started to stand.

"Stay there, I'm going to give you a push."

"What?"

Roy put a hand on my shoulder. "Trust me, I know what I'm doing."

"So you're sending me down alone?"

"No, I'm going to jump on when it gets moving."

"Roy…"

"On three."

"Roy, I don't think—"

"Three." Roy pushed hard enough to tip me forward, and I leaned back to keep from landing on my face. The cardboard began to slide, and Roy dropped down behind me. The angle of his landing shoved us forward.

Then the bottom of the culvert headed right toward us. "Roy?"

"Hang on." Roy got one foot on the box, but his left leg was still cocked out. His heel caught the ground before he could pull it in. The box turned, and the view went from the bottom of the hill to the edge we'd dropped from.

Any minute, I expected to break the sound barrier.

"Roy!"

"I got you."

"Roy!"

"We're okay."

"Roy!" The box made a slow turn. Roy tipped, and I went with him. Then world went head over heels.

My cheek plowed a line in the snow until Roy pulled me back. I tried to grab onto something to slow us down, but there was only powdered ice. It collected on the arms of my coat and rode up the sleeves. Roy hit the ground with the heel of his boot. What promised to be a stop turned into another spin. Any second we were going to smash into the ground, break an arm, a leg. As if it mattered. It would all hurt.

I clenched my eyes shut.

The rapid descent became a gradual slide. Braced against Roy's chest, we made another half turn, then stopped.

"Are we dead?" I cracked an eye. Gray clouds meandered overhead.

"No, of course not."

I tried to sit up, and my elbow caught Roy in the ribs.

"Ugh—"

"Sorry."

"You okay?"

"Yeah." I knocked away the snow turning my bangs into dreadlocks. Another attempt to sit up failed. I rolled over.

Our cardboard sled joined us at the bottom of the culvert. Roy followed it with his eyes as it came to a landing a few yards away.

"I'm no expert," I said. "But I think your sled had a malfunction."

177

"Looks like it."

"What about you? Anything broken?"

"Just snow in unpleasant places."

"At least now I can say I've been sledding." I buried a laugh into his shoulder.

Roy held me. "Sorry that didn't work out like I planned."

I picked at the snow clinging to his hair. He caught my hand and pressed his thumb into my palm. Our gloves kept us from making skin to skin contact, but they couldn't stop the heat radiating from his flesh to mine.

"I think next time, we should stick to something safer," I said. "Like snow angels."

"The ride might have been rough, but you have to admit the landing was worth it."

"So you're saying risking life and limb was only a small price to pay to get me to top."

His smile was subtle. "Just to get you at all." He cupped my chin. I let him pull me closer. My bangs lay across his forehead, and the tips of our noses touched.

All I had to do was steal the hair's breadth between us to touch my lips to his.

"Was it worth it?" he said.

"It happened so fast I didn't even know what was going on."

"But was it worth it?"

The wind kicked up, bringing a fresh snowfall. Somewhere a horn honked.

"Tell me, Paris." He was so close the ghost of his lips brushed my mouth. "Was it worth it?"

Caught in the power of his voice, held by the strength of his gaze. There was only one answer. "Yes."

****

Roy and I walked to a café about a block from the park in search of something warm to drink. The street lights turned on, and the temperature dropped. I huddled in my coat.

"You should have said something." Roy put an arm around me.

"What? That it's cold? I don't know if you've noticed the three feet of snow on the ground."

"Almost a foot."

"One, three, it's all the same." I shivered.

"You should reconsider getting a pair of long johns." We crossed the street.

"I'll freeze before I wear those horrible looking things."

"You're frozen now."

"Point taken." I pulled my scarf up higher. A bitter gust of wind shot up my legs. "How much farther?"

Roy stopped at the door. The lights were out, and the neon sign was off.

"Closed?" I said.

"Looks like it."

"Fuck, it's cold." I scanned the street. "Where's a taxi when you need it?"

"Ice on the road."

"Didn't stop them earlier."

"Okay, more ice on the road, and more snow. C'mon, my apartment is just another block over."

"I don't know if I can make it that far." I tried the door.

"Satisfied?"

"No. I want coffee and someplace warm."

"If we cut down that alley," Roy nodded at the part between the café and a bookstore. "We can be there in ten minutes."

I grinned. "Hot coffee and a warm bed, who can ask for anything more?"

"It's just coffee."

"Sure, it is." I jogged down the alley, and Roy ran to catch up.

The broken-down line of apartments and junk cars had been cleansed by the winter storm. There were only a few trails stamped into the snow, suggesting the drug dealers had closed up shop for the day.

The fight between rap music and heavy metal rolled out of the building into the street. Roy took the steps up to his apartment two at a time. I followed him down the hall. On the way, I tripped over a fire truck.

Roy caught me. "Easy." He nudged the toy to the wall.

"Someone needs to tell them to come pick up their stuff."

"It's just easier to step around it." Roy unlocked the deadbolts on his door. The inside wasn't much warmer than the hall, but at least I couldn't see my breath.

"Hang on, I'll turn up the heat." He adjusted the thermostat.

The sheets on the bed were blue now and the comforter brown. It wasn't quite big enough to cover the white knit blanket under it.

Roy went to the kitchen. "I don't think I have any milk. I do— I doubt it's any good." He shed his coat and left it on a chair at the breakfast bar. His thick arms flexed under his flannel shirt. The layers of clothes ruined the definition, but the fabric strained as he moved. Half-moon wet spots cupped each ass cheek from where he'd sat in the snow.

I left my coat on the couch along with my scarf and gloves.

Roy got something out of the cabinet. The movement raised the back of his shirt and long johns high enough to flash the cleft of his ass over his belt line. I itched to run my fingers down his crack, fondle his balls, and taste his cum.

My cock hardened.

"Are you hungry?"

"You have no idea." I unbuttoned my shirt and kicked off my boots.

"I've got soup. Do you like grilled cheese?"

"Sure." My pants and boxers joined my shirt on the floor.

"Is the heat on? It doesn't feel like it's on." He went back over to the wall and tapped the thermostat. There was a soft rumble from the vents, and a breath of warm air washed over me from the ceiling. "There, that's—" Roy turned around. The rose of winter's kiss in his cheeks darkened.

"What's wrong?"

"I'll get you some sweats."

I got in between him and the dresser. "What? You don't like me naked?" I moved closer, and a tick jumped in his jaw. "Look at me, Roy." Feral heat burned in his eyes. I put my hands under the hem of his shirt and traced the line of hair from his navel to his pecs with my thumbs. I found his nipples and pinched them. His breath quickened. "It's time to quit playing choir boy." I pushed his shirt up, and he pulled it back down. "You want me. You want me, and I want you to

180

have me." He wouldn't let me take off his shirt so I went for his pants. Roy grabbed my wrists.

"I like that." I licked a line up his neck and blew across the shell of his ear. "I like it when you hold me down, when you take me, when you fuck me like you own me."

A small sound ticked from Roy's throat.

"I'm willing to bet you like it too."

"Paris, please…"

"Touch me."

A tremor ran down his arms into me.

"Use me."

His nostrils flared.

"Fuck me with that beautiful cock of yours."

The black of his pupils ate up the green.

"And make it nasty."

Like a freight train, Roy came right at me. I would have fallen if he hadn't grabbed me, one arm around my ribs and his free hand gripping the back of my head.

He slammed his mouth against mine, forced my lips apart, and invaded me with his tongue. The ache in my cock spread through my body, turning into a raging need.

Roy moved to my throat.

"Oh, God, yes…"

He raked his teeth down my neck.

"Like that, Roy, like that."

He squeezed one of my ass cheeks, pressing his thick fingers close to my hole. I clawed at his jeans. Roy pushed me backward, and the weight of his body made it impossible for me to resist.

"Want you," he said.

"Then take me."

On the way across the room, his shin hit the coffee table and shoved it into the couch. "Want my dick in your ass. Want to feel you come."

I got his jeans open, and his delicious cock leaped into my hand. Roy rocked into my fist. "That's it," I said. "Don't hold back. Don't hold anything back."

My hip hit the wall, and he pinned me against the doorjamb of the bathroom.

"I dream about you, Paris. Oh, God, I dream about fucking you over and over, and you beg for more."

"Do it." I attacked his mouth.

A groan rumbled in Roy's chest. I had him. He would never back off now. I went for Roy's shirt again, but he spun me around.

The length of his cock left a wet trail along my crack. He parted my ass cheeks and pushed a finger into my hole. "Yesss—"

"Need something slick." He bit my shoulder. "Need to be inside you."

"Spit..." I gasped. "Just spit."

He pulled me into the bathroom. "Don't want to hurt you." But I wanted to feel the pain as much as the pleasure.

I wound up straddling the toilet with my hands against the wall. Roy grabbed a bottle of lotion off the counter. A cold glob hit me at the cleft of my ass. Another one landed closer to my hole.

"Now."

He dropped the bottle.

"Fuck me, now." I lifted my ass.

Roy slathered lotion over my opening. He pushed in one finger, then two.

"Your cock. I want your cock." I rocked back. "Do it."

He pulled his fingers out.

"You want it. Do it."

He pushed the head of his cock against my hole.

"That's it. More."

It breached my opening.

"Goddamn it. I want all of it." The burn and stretch made me hiss. The first thrust sent a crackle up my spine and across my skin. The second lit me on fire. "Yes, yes, yesss—" The third, oh God, the third. Then the only thing I could think about was the hard length of flesh in my ass.

He pumped his hips.

"More."

He thrust harder.

"Give it to me." And he did. Over and over. From the tip and to the root. Roy shoved his cock so deep the muscles in my lower back tightened, and the impact pushed me up on my toes. "That's it. That's it."

"Paris…"

"Right here. I'm right here."

"God, Paris…" Lust and desperation echoed off the tile, carried on the sound of Roy's grunts.

He leaned back. The change in angle sent shockwaves through my body. I barked out a cry, and there was a hitch in Roy's thrusts.

"Don't stop." I clenched my ass cheeks. "Don't you dare stop."

He put one hand on my shoulder and the other on my hip. One slow withdrawal was the only warning I had.

I didn't think Roy could fuck me any harder, but I was wrong.

The slap of our bodies added another layer to the symphony of sex. Yellows, golds, whites bled through my veins. Blues, violets, and scarlet danced behind my eyelids. And every return of his cock created two dull aches above each hip.

Roy pummeled me until my head bounced between my shoulders, sweat dripped from the tip of my nose, and my bangs clung to my cheeks. My senses blended until I didn't know where I ended and he began. Time was ticked off by my thundering heart. Euphoria crossed the line into pain, making my insides cramp.

But the last thing I wanted was for Roy to stop. I was hungry for this, and I gorged on his offering.

A deep rumble expanded in Roy's chest until it vibrated through me. The sound transformed into a growl, and the growl into an animalistic roar. He covered me with his body, still fucking me even as his cock pulsed.

It only took a few strokes before I was shooting my load all over the back of the toilet. Each slowing rock from Roy's body dragged a spark across my prostate. The sensation echoed with the dying waves of my release.

The muffled beat of rap music leaked through the walls, eating up the newfound silence.

"God, that was good," I said.

Roy stepped back.

"I'm not going to be able to sit straight for a day. Maybe two." I turned around. Roy stared at the bottle of lotion on the floor. "What's wrong?"

His expression pinched. "I'm sorry."

"Sorry?"

"I didn't mean...I didn't mean for that to happen."

"Excuse me?"

"It shouldn't have." He shook his head. "Please forgive me."

"For what? Fucking me?"

He lifted his gaze.

"You're serious?"

The pity—the regret—in his expression was too much. I tore free of his grip and gathered up my clothes.

"Please don't go."

I pulled on my jeans. "Why not? Obviously, my presence disgusts you."

"You don't disgust me."

"Oh, so that 'taste like shit' expression you're wearing is a figment of my imagination." I didn't bother to button my shirt.

"It's not that, I just...please."

"Fuck off."

"Paris..."

He reached for me, and I knocked his hand away. The hurt expression on Roy's face was worse than any punch. I forgot to take out my socks when I crammed my feet into my boots, and they bunched up in the toes.

"Will you let me explain?"

I grabbed my coat and put it on. "You've made yourself perfectly clear. Sorry I ever wasted your time." I went to the door. "I promise you'll never have to worry about me doing it again."

He called after me, but I was already down the steps and back into the cold.

Chapter Nine

I sat on the couch across the room from a clean canvas. After three days of waiting for the colors to bleed through, it remained blank. The more time passed, the less sure I was the colors had ever existed.

The phone rang. I no longer looked at the caller ID. If it wasn't Roy, it was Julia, and if it wasn't Julia, it wasn't anyone else I wanted to talk to.

The phone stopped.

I kept staring at the canvas.

The setting sun broke over the tops of building and left streaks of bronze sunlight across the tile floor. It turned orange, then red, then a pale purple. Night fell, leaving nothing but me and the canvas.

It remained empty.

I remained empty.

The phone rang again.

I picked up my glass from the side table and drank the last bit of orange juice and vodka. There was no sweetness, no bitterness, just nothing.

Like the canvas.

Like me.

I rubbed my face, pushed back my bangs, and found myself tugging at the hairs on the back of my head. They were almost long enough to pull, but not quite.

"I'm sorry..."

"Yeah, you should be." I stood. "You should be, Roy. You should be so fucking sorry." My voice bounced off the walls of the empty studio.

"I shouldn't have..."

"Shouldn't have what? Given me the best fuck of my life? Or maybe it was everything else. Dinner, the wine, your goddamned cardboard sled." I wiped out a tray of brushes sitting on one of the worktables. "Or maybe it was..."

"One kiss..."

I touched my lips.

Brushing my teeth, showering, doing it all over again could only erase Roy from my skin but never my mind. He was gouged so deep that thoughts of him scarred my bones.

185

I leaned against the workbench. The spiraling helplessness inside me promised dark and terrible places I'd sworn I'd never go.

"I don't care."

My breath rattled.

"I don't care if you don't want me."

My heart ached.

"I don't care if I disgust you."

My voice cracked, and my words shattered. I clutched my chest, trying to crush the pain.

"Fuck you." Closing my eyes forced me to relive the sadness in Roy's gaze. "Fuck you."

I didn't need him. I didn't want him.

And I'd prove it.

I grabbed my coat and left the apartment.

Melted snow made streams in the gutters and left gaps on the sidewalk. The city had revived thanks to layers of salt and sand on the streets. I could have taken a cab, but my legs refused to quit moving.

I passed through a crowd lingering at the front of a shop, went around two teens on bikes, and stopped at the corner. Car horns blared as I crossed on the red light.

Three blocks down, I took a left and headed toward a cluster of pimped out cars carrying violent melodies. Fishnet and stiletto heels clashed with faux fur coats and leather jackets outside the entrance of the Diablo. A man with a Mohawk whistled at me as I walked by. I could have picked him, but he wasn't dangerous enough.

The floor wasn't as packed as I remembered, but the young faces and groping hands were all the same. Neon lights edged the twist and turns of the bar. Bodies crowded the space, becoming people under the dance of colored lights.

I waved at the bartender. "Flat-liner." He nodded.

The man I was looking for stood a few yards down, leaning back on his elbows against the bar. Blond hair, nice jacket, he could have been the average joe. I almost dismissed him until he caught my gaze. Eyes like that had tracked me through my home when I was younger. Eyes like that had pooled with sinful thoughts. Eyes like that had not only seen those horrors, they'd led the way.

The bartender brought me my drink. I tossed it back before he could leave. My throat closed, and my sinuses flooded. "Another." I

186

wasn't sure if he heard me so I knocked the bottom of the shot glass against the bar.

"Sure thing."

A chill prickled the back of my neck. The two women beside me moved, and a breath of stout cologne replaced the flowered scent of perfume.

The bartender brought me another drink.

"It's on me." The man squeezed into the space and put a twenty-dollar bill down on the counter.

"I can buy my own."

Those hard eyes of his glittered. Were they blue, gray, or hazel? The strobes bleached out the color, and they alternated between a deathly white and pitch black.

"Not tonight," he said.

The bartender raised an eyebrow at me. I nodded. He disappeared with the twenty.

"What's your name?" The man moved closer.

"I'm not interested in exchanging names."

He grinned, flashing a chipped front tooth. "What are you interested in?"

"...you deserve more..."

I tossed back the second drink. It didn't go down any easier than the first.

"Well?" He was tall enough to put his lips close to my ear. "What are you into?"

The Flat-Liners turned the lull of a day's worth of vodka into a humming static. "Anything that will hurt."

He caressed my cheek with the back of his finger. "I have a hard time believing someone as pretty as you could even comprehend the meaning of that word."

"Really?"

"Really."

"Then perhaps you should teach me."

The hardness in his eyes turned murderous. "Be careful what you wish for."

I put us chest to chest. "My last teacher wasn't strict enough." I pulled down my scarf flashing the bruises on my throat and tipped my head to the side so my bangs would slide off my bruised cheek. His cock hardened against my thigh.

"My car is out back," he said.

I grazed his jaw with my teeth. "The alley is closer."

He put a hand on my throat. His fingers were long, his skin smooth. Was he a banker, an accountant, or just a rich boy who lived off daddy's money? The man stroked my windpipe with his thumb. Each pass increased in pressure until there was a dull ache every time I swallowed.

He searched my face.

"Harder," I said.

A drop of sweat ran from his temple, and his breath hitched. The man tightened his grip enough I had to work for every breath.

"Feels good." I rubbed his cock through his pants.

"I really want to take you to my apartment. I can…take my time."

I brushed my lips across his. The momentary change in lights brought color back into the world. Blue. Death had blue eyes. "Lead the way."

He put his hand on my lower back, and we wove through the crowd, pushing through skinny pants, midriff shirts, fuck-me heels and studded boots.

A woman with spiked pink hair bumped into me. The man caught me by the arm.

"Easy."

In between the gyrating bodies stood a little boy wearing a red shirt and shorts. He was just like I remembered him.

"¿Qué l es tu nombre? You name?"

"Paris."

"What?"

"My name is Paris."

"I thought you didn't care about names." The man glanced over his shoulder. "What are you looking at?"

"Eres mi amigo, Paris. Me very best friend."

The man took me by the wrist. "C'mon."

The boy stepped in my way. I swallowed. "I'm not."

"Sí, you are."

The man yanked me by the collar of my coat. "Paris, right? You and I have a date, remember?"

A wooden door slammed shut, making the bare light hanging from the ceiling sway. The shadows inside the shed grew and shrank under clouds of dust.

"Backing out isn't an option."

And the boy who kissed me lay dead.

The man dragged me toward the door.

Leaves buried my shoes and clung to my ankles.

My hip hit the passenger door of a dark-colored sedan. It was parked somewhere the streetlights couldn't reach. Broken laughter and music drifted down the alley connecting the parking lot to the rest of the world.

"Get in." He grabbed me by the throat.

Twigs snapped.

"I have so many wonderful things planned for you."

Rain soaked my clothes.

"If you impress me, I might even keep you around till tomorrow."

The tarp crackled as it scraped across the concrete edging the well.

"If you really impress me, maybe I'll even let you live."

There was no sound until he hit the bottom.

"You're going to be a shit ton of fun, baby." The man yanked open the door. A pale shape huddled in the backseat of the sedan and stared at me with black button eyes.

"I said get in."

I planted my foot on the frame of the car.

"You're really starting to piss me off," the man said. "And you do not want to do that."

The rabbit sat up.

A terrible cold swelled inside me. It ate its way from my bones into my muscles with sharp teeth and slit my flesh with claws. "No, you promised."

"Yeah, I promise you if you don't get in the car, you're going to bleed."

A pink nose and twitching whiskers broke the line of shadow concealing the rabbit's body.

189

"No." I kicked myself off the doorframe, knocking the man off balance. His heel came down on a patch of ice, and he hit the ground. I tried to crawl away. "You promised if I painted, it would leave me alone!"

"You fucking little bitch."

There was a hammer in my father's hand. The head glistened. "You fucking little bitch…"

"I told you, no backing out." The man lunged, and I hit the door. "You asked for this, remember." He squeezed my throat. "You wanted this."

"I saw how you looked at me. How you wanted me."

"Fucking cunt."

"Fucking whore."

I grabbed the man's wrists, but he was no longer the man from the bar. Blood covered his hand, speckled his cheek, and his blue eyes were now the color of rich earth.

My sleeping monster stirred in its pit of darkness. God help me if it woke up. "Let go of me."

He grinned. "Oh no. No, no, no. You're mine."

"You'll wake it up. Please…" I dug my nails into his wrists. "You have to stop. It's too loud, all of it."

"Loud?" He put his face close to mine. "You haven't seen loud. But don't worry, my house is private and the basement walls are thick."

"Listen to me. I have to paint. It's the only way to put it back to sleep."

His mouth twisted up. "What the fuck are you on?"

Deep inside my chest, the monster opened his eyes.

The man rubbed my cheek with his thumb. "Awww—no need to cry yet."

"Please…" The beast raised its sleepy head.

"Get in the car."

"Please…" A tremor ran down my arms.

"If I ask you again, it's going to hurt."

"Please…" It shifted its weight, and mud sucked at the folds of its skin.

"Now, bitch, get in the fucking car."

"I'm sorry." The massive creature pushed itself up.

190

"I'll make you think sorry…"

The terrible thing inside me opened its jaws and exhaled a breath of old sour ground.

"Last chance. Get…in…the…car."

I'd forgotten what it felt like. It should have been impossible to do that. To forget that level of anger and that kind of thirst for freedom. But I'd kept it placated for so long by telling the world the truth while maintaining the lie.

I knew the moment it came to the surface because the hardness in the man's eyes shattered.

I'm not sure, but I think he tried to run.

It grabbed him, hand on each side of his head, and sank its thumbs into his eyes. His scream was cut short when it landed a knee into his groin. He lost his balance and fell against the backseat of the sedan.

The monster punched the man in the side of the head. He turned away to shield himself from another strike so it sank a hand into his hair and smashed his face against the frame of the door.

Over.

And over.

And over.

Then it was gone, leaving my body chewed up and spit out.

Blood spread in a pool under the man's crooked jaw and a broken tooth stuck to his bottom lip.

A snowflake landed on my arm, then another in my hair. They grew in number until the air was a cascade of white.

The shush of snow floating to the ground seemed impossibly loud. A woman's laugh and the thump and grind of a heavy bass chased me down the alley. A single halogen light at the corner barely kept back the dark. I walked on numb legs in some random direction. With every step, the temperature dropped and the snow thickened.

I came out on a street and followed the line of dark windows to a café. Empty tables huddled around the window. I pulled out a chair and sat.

Bells rang, but I couldn't find the strength to look up.

"Paris, is that you?"

I knew that voice.

"Jonathan? Jonathan. Get out here and help me."

191

The bells on the door rang again. "What's go—"

Louise made me look at her. "What's wrong, honey?"

I spoke, but there was no sound.

"Is he drunk?" Jonathan said.

"I don't know."

"You want me to call the police?"

"Let's get him inside."

Tables with stacked chairs dotted a checkered floor. The sterile odor of bleach mixed with the ghosts of hotdogs and chili. It was quiet inside the café but not the same kind the snow brought. Inside, the silence wrapped around me in comfort.

Louise turned the lock. "C'mon, honey, let's sit right over here." They led me to a table.

"He's got blood on his hands."

I did. Old blood. New blood. "I'm…" My voice cracked.

Louise pushed my hair back from my eyes. "It's gonna be okay, sweetheart."

"We should call the police." Jonathan went over to the counter.

"You pick up that phone, Jonathan Brewer, and so help me God…"

"He's got blood on his hands, Louise."

"Then get me a wet rag so I can clean him up." She held up a finger, cutting off whatever her husband was going to say. "Wet rag. Now. And put a little soap on it." Louise pulled out a chair. "Were you mugged?"

I shook with the effort to push out the words and still got nothing.

"Paris, did someone hurt you?"

I clenched my fists. Blood made my fingers sticky.

Jonathan walked up with a wet rag. "Here."

Louis took it and cleaned my hands.

"We really need to call the police."

"We are not calling the police. And that's final."

He folded his arms and then unfolded them. "He's been in a fight, or hurt , or—"

"And you think the police are going to care? They didn't care when that Bishop boy got knocked over the head."

"That was different."

Louise stood. She didn't even reach the man's chin. "Different how? Because he wore women's clothes or because he wasn't white?" She hit him in the chest with the rag. "Go wash that out and bring it back with a towel."

"Louise..."

"What?"

"If something happened to him..." Jonathan glanced at me and then dropped his gaze to the ground.

"Go, and don't forget the towel." The way she said it suggested she feared the same thing. "And make some coffee."

Jonathan left, and Louise wrapped her arm around my shoulders. "It'll be okay." She petted my back. "Whatever happened, it will be okay."

The fight to speak made me tremble. "I'm sorry."

She pulled out a chair and sat. "What are you sorry for?" Louise held my face and made me look her in the eye.

Everything. The boy who kissed me. The lie. The secrets I couldn't tell. But I didn't have to anymore, because they were spilling out of me. If Julia found out, she'd lock me away in that terrible place.

"Coffee's on." Jonathan returned with a rinsed-out rag and a towel. He grazed a look over me. "Who messed up your face?"

"Probably the same person who bloodied him up."

"Bruises are a few days old, the blood was fresh, and he doesn't have any cuts."

Louise resumed cleaning me up. "It doesn't matter right now. He'll tell us when he's ready, or he won't."

"Fine. You want sugar and cream in your coffee?"

"Yes...please..." I said.

While Jonathan fixed the coffee, Louise dried my hair. "You want to take off your coat?"

"No."

"What about your scarf?" She reached for it, and I stopped her.

"No. Please. No." She touched me below my jaw, and I pulled the scarf higher.

"I know you don't want the police, but if someone did something to you..."

"Noth—" I cleared my throat. "Nothing happened."

"Paris."

"Nothing happened."

"You're all bruised up."

"Fight."

"The bruises on your face might be old, but those fingerprints on your neck aren't."

At least she didn't see the bruise left by the belt. "Just a fight."

"With who?"

I shrugged.

"Please, honey, let me help you."

"I started it." And I'd ended it. Was the guy from the club dead or alive? I didn't want to know, and at the same time, I did.

We sat there, Louise begging me with her eyes to talk to her and me undeserving of her pity. She petted my back and brushed the hair back from my eyes. Every touch was a fist to my heart.

Jonathan came back with a cup in his hands. "I couldn't find the filters, so I made you some hot chocolate."

I took it, grateful to have something warm in my hands.

"There's a brand new box in the cabinet. I put it there this morning."

"I looked, and I didn't see them."

"Jonathan Brewer, I think it's about time to get you some glasses."

He glanced at the door. "If you don't want the hot chocolate, I can go look for the filters again."

I hugged the cup to my chest.

"We don't mind." Louise gave me a cautious smile.

I drank some of the hot chocolate and tasted nothing.

Jonathan glanced at the door again. "I'll go throw you a cup of soup in the microwave."

He left before I could squeak out a no.

"You're cold. The soup will help."

"I should—" My hands shook hard enough to slosh the hot chocolate out of the cup. Louise took it from me and put it on the table. "—go."

She mopped up the mess with some napkins from the dispenser. "What do you mean?"

I nodded at the door.

She stopped me before I could get up. "If you want to go home, I'll take you." Only home wasn't far enough away.

Jonathan came out of the kitchen carrying a bowl. Tendrils of steam followed it all the way to the table. "Careful, it's hot."

I stirred it with the spoon. If I ate it, I'd be sick.

A pair of headlights ran along the window, and Louise stood. "If that's what I think it is..."

Jonathan held up his hands. "I had to call someone."

"You did not have to call anyone."

"Please, honey. It's not what you think."

"Not what I think? Then why did a car just pull up?"

A car door shut. The reflection in the windows made it impossible to see how many cops there were. The door opened, and the bells clanged against the glass. There were black smudges on the right thigh of Roy's jeans, and neither one of his boots were tied.

"I told you," Jonathan said.

"C'mon." Louise pushed her husband toward the back. "Let them talk."

The closer Roy came, the higher my heart crawled up my throat. He went to his knees and pulled me into his arms.

"Roy..."

"Shhh—"

"I..."

"It doesn't matter. Whatever it is, it doesn't matter."

A sob broke out of my chest.

"It will be okay."

I buried my tears in his shoulder.

"Everything will be okay."

But Roy was wrong. So very wrong.

****

I waited in the cab while Roy spoke to the Brewers. Both of them glanced my way several times. Then Louise hugged Roy, and Jonathan shook his hand.

They went back inside the café, and Roy got in the cab. "If it's okay, I want you to come home with me."

How could he want to be near me?

He put a hand under my chin. "Is that okay? Or would you rather go home?"

I just wanted to disappear.

Roy gave the cabby his address.

There was only the sound of tires on wet pavement and occasional slide of the windshield wipers. We turned away from the direction of the club, the parking lot, and the man I might have killed.

The cab fell through the snow until we stopped in front of Roy's apartment. Powdered ice collected on the windshield only to be swept away.

I didn't even realize Roy had gotten out until he opened my door. "C'mon." The barest touch was enough to pull me from the car. He paid the cabby. I should have paid it, but my wallet was lost in my pocket.

Unlike before when I'd been here, the apartment was quiet. Was it early or late?

Roy guided me inside. "Is it okay if I take your coat?"

I didn't know.

He peeled the scarf away with the coat, folded both, and laid them on the sofa. "Your pants are wet." He made me sit on the edge of the bed. There was blood on my shirt. "How about I just throw everything in the wash?"

Roy undressed me. Every brush of his skin against mine forced me away from the edge. He collected all my clothes and wadded them up. If Julia saw my shirts and slacks being manhandled like that, she would have killed him.

"Dry clean," I said.

"The clothes?"

I nodded.

"I'll take them in the morning."

I shook my head.

"You don't want me to take them?"

"I don't want them anymore."

Roy put everything in a trash bag. I glanced at my coat and scarf. He took out my wallet. The coat and scarf joined the rest of my clothes at the bottom of the bag. Then Roy stuffed it in the trash.

"Do you have enough blankets?" Roy said. "I've got a couple more if you need them."

The sheet was soft and the quilt softer.

Roy pulled out a wooden crate from under his bed. He took out two blankets; one he tossed on the couch, the other he wrapped around my shoulders.

I gripped the sleeve of his shirt.

"Aren't you going to ask me?" I said.

"It doesn't matter." He sat beside me, pried my fingers open, and held my hand.

"Why not?"

"Because you're okay."

My stomach rolled. "You wouldn't say that if you knew." All the terrible things I'd done. "You'd hate me. I don't want you to hate me."

"I can't hate you."

Two points of pain blossomed under each ear. It spread down my neck and squeezed my throat. "You need to."

"Why?"

Saliva flooded my mouth. "I'm gonna be sick." Roy had me in the bathroom before the first heave pushed up everything in my stomach. I vomited bile into the toilet. The second heave knocked my legs from under me. Roy lowered me to the floor.

"Please hate me." A dry heave snatched my muscles off my bones.

"Shhh—" Roy held me.

"Hate me."

"Paris..."

"Please, Roy." Tears fractured the world around me. Colors crawled up the walls and bled together. Every convulsion exploded with reds and greens. It was no use. The sickness my body wanted to expel wasn't in my stomach. It was in me. It *was* me.

The sink was close enough for Roy to wet a washcloth. He brought it to my face. The dampness pulled the fire out of my cheeks. At the same time, Roy's body next to mine promised warmth.

"I think I killed him."

"Shh—"

"I went there to the club. I was going to go home with him."

197

"Let's not worry about it right now."

"The man looked like Julia's father."

"Shh—"

"Not on the outside but the inside. I saw it in his eyes. Like the day he held the hammer. The way he looked at me."

Roy wiped my face.

"The man at the club was going to kill me."

Roy stopped.

"I wanted him to kill me."

The faucet in the tub dripped. Roy's heart beat against my ear.

"I wouldn't get in the car. I told him to let me go. I told him. I tried to make him stop. I didn't want to hurt him. He woke it up, and there was nothing I could do."

"It's over."

"But it's not. The blood stains and the terrible secrets it makes fester."

"I'll get rid of the clothes."

"It won't matter. I can't hold it in anymore. I paint, but it doesn't want to go away."

Roy got the mouthwash off the counter and poured me a capful. "Here. That will get the taste out of your mouth."

I sloshed it around and spit in the toilet.

"Better?"

"I should have been the one who died."

He put me in the bed. "Do you want me to stay?"

"She asked me if I knew where he was."

Roy stripped down to his boxers and shifted around next to me until I had my head on his shoulder.

"She begged me to tell her, and I said I didn't know."

He held me, and I cried myself to sleep.

****

Morning turned the kitchen into gold, and dust motes dance and twirled in the sunbeams. A door slammed somewhere, and a woman yelled. An infant cried for his mother. Then someone turned up their radio drowning the sounds of urban poverty under a steady bass thump.

Roy's long lashes rested against his cheeks, and his eyes flicked behind his lids. Sleep had erased decades of worry, leaving behind a youthful innocence.

There was a scar on his chin and a flat round mole near his ear. Silver salted his shadow of a beard, and I itched to run my finger up his jaw just to hear the sound it would make.

What would life be like filled with simple moments like this? For time to be measured in heartbeats and exhales rather than seconds and minutes?

What would it feel like to know I was safe, not because of a lock on the door but because of the line of warmth pressed against me and the weight of an arm around my ribs?

The idea of never knowing cut me with dark blues and pierced me with gray. There were other colors too, but I didn't know the names and had no control over how they mixed and where they flowed.

Roy opened his eyes. They were darker than usual, making him all the more rugged.

"How are you feeling?" He caressed my cheek; a dull ache followed his fingers.

How was I feeling? No anger. No contempt. Just more worry and concern. Words that should have meant nothing to me, but like everything else about Roy, they broke through the layers of color and line I'd wrapped myself in.

He ran a hand down my back. "Do you want me to get another blanket?"

"No."

"You're shaking."

Because I was afraid of waking up another day without the man in front of me, the sound of his voice, and his touch on my skin. Roy had broken me open. If I lost him now, I'd fall into a place far darker than the rabbit hole. I'd never needed anyone to want me.

Part of me hated Roy for that.

He pulled the covers higher. I shoved them away and sat up.

"What's wrong?" Roy propped himself on his elbow.

"Why did you come get me last night?"

Confusion crumpled his features. "Because you needed help."

I stood, and he moved to the edge of the bed. Roy reached for me, and I stepped back.

More colors I didn't know and couldn't name. I pressed the heel of my hand against the side of my head in a sad attempt to stop them from filling up my skull. Like everything else when it came to Roy, I was helpless.

He stepped in front of me. "Paris…"

I stumbled back. "No. Just…just…" I held up a hand to keep him back. "Just tell me why. Explain to me. All of it."

"What's to explain?"

I clenched my hands. Heat ate a path up my face. My throat tightened. Spit flecked my lips. "Everything, Roy! Explain everything! Your stupid park, your stupid slaughtered hotdogs, and your stupid, stupid sled! Goddamn it, just tell me what you want from me, because I can't get away from it. I can't get away from you."

Roy held me prisoner against the wall, not with the strength in his body but the power in his eyes. That look I saw the first time we were together, only it had grown, taken over, come alive.

He cupped my face, and I couldn't turn away. "I came for you because I care about you. I did those things because I wanted to give you something you've never had before. I want to show you that being with you wasn't about sex, it was about you. Just you."

"You weren't a bit put off by sticking your dick in my ass before."

"I know."

"Then what changed? Why don't you want me now?"

He touched his forehead to mine. "I do want you." His sigh brushed my lips. "I want you so bad it hurts."

"Then what's stopping you?" If only he would throw me against the wall and fuck me. That I could understand. Those colors I could name.

"Because you can have sex with anyone but very few would ever want to love you." Roy's touch burned through my skin, my bones, and flowed over my body in a wave of need and lust. It ravaged me with a kind of desire I'd never experienced.

The room blurred.

"Will you let me?"

I swallowed, but my voice still cracked. "What?"

"Love you." Roy rubbed his cheek against mine. "Please, Paris. I know it's not what you're used to, and it might not even be what you want, but it's the most valuable thing I have."

Those colors I didn't know had a name now. I knotted Roy's shirt in my fist. "I don't know how."

"I'll teach you." He kissed my neck.

"What if I fail?"

"You won't." Roy slid his hands down my body.

"It'll hurt."

"Only a little."

No. It would chew me up and spit me out. But not before tearing me apart and breaking every bone in my body.

"Paris. Please let me love you. Even if it's just for a little while. Even if it's just this moment."

I pressed my face into his neck. "I'm scared."

"I know." He pulled me away from the wall. "But I won't hurt you. I would never hurt you."

I believed him, but the precious gift he called love came with a price, and there wasn't enough money in the world to repay the debt I would owe.

He maneuvered me to the bed and pushed me into the sheets. I must have made a sound, cried out or maybe whimpered because Roy shushed me and petted down my side.

Roy brushed his lips across my shoulders as he traced my arms, my fingers, and then my ribs, leaving a tingling outline around my body.

"It's okay."

Only it wasn't okay. I couldn't do anything. I didn't even know what I was supposed to do.

Roy pressed his lips to mine, and with languid strokes of his tongue, he worshiped my mouth.

I was wrong to ever think I knew how to kiss. What I did was a gluttonous feeding. What Roy did, coaxing my tongue to twine with his, caressing my mouth with his lips, sighing into me, and stealing away my breath, was a kiss.

Roy stroked my aching cock once and squeezed my balls. I spread my legs wider, but his touch disappeared and it was like nothing below my waist even existed.

Frustration ticked out of my throat in small desperate cries. I pawed at him wanting more and getting none of it. Roy murmured something against my throat, but I was too ignorant to understand.

I wasn't even sure I was capable of it.

Roy kissed my palm, my wrist, even my goddamned knees. Sometimes he held me close or far enough away to run his gaze over my body. The way he coveted me with his eyes made me burn.

"Please."

Roy drew a hot line with his tongue from my neck to my shoulder. "Please what?"

"I need…"

He teased my lips with a caress from his. "What do you need?"

"Something…anything." His cock in my ass, his mouth on my dick, his lips pressed to mine or his tongue invading me and raging battle.

I dug my fingers into the mattress. The muscles in my back tightened until my spine bowed. My aching cock bled precum on my stomach, but the need for release didn't compare to the violent hunger Roy stirred inside me.

He blanketed my body with his bare skin. "It's okay." He thumbed my right nipple. An electric burst danced through me and settled in my nuts.

There was a hollow scrape from the bedside table followed by the rustle of things being moved around. A soft snick cut through the sound of me panting. Roy put my leg against his hip and slid a cold slick finger into my ass, and the air rushed out of my lungs. The mattress squeaked and dipped, then more fluid ran down the crack of my ass.

"Look at me, Paris."

I'd die if I did. The power he held me with would cut me into pieces.

"That's it. Show me your gorgeous eyes. Let me see how good you feel." Roy added a second finger.

"More." I tried to rock against him, but he braced me with a hand on my stomach while he pumped both of his thick fingers in and out of me, slicking up and stretching my opening to take his cock. I put my other leg on his shoulder.

Roy kissed my ankle. "I'll give you everything, Paris, every part of me." He took away his fingers, and the thick head of his cock pressed against my hole.

In one long stroke, he breached my opening, filling me fuller than any time before. It was forever before the weight of his balls pressed against my ass.

Roy chewed his bottom lip, and the cords stood out on his neck. For a while, he just stayed there, kissing the tears from my cheeks. Then he cradled me against his body—cherishing me, protecting me—and I clung to him. My life raft in the torrid wake of existence.

I realized then I'd been waiting my entire life to find him.

The muscles in Roy's body flexed as he withdrew to the tip and sheathed himself inside me again. Every measured inch he gave me or took away was the more intense than the hardest fucking of my life.

I let myself flow into his touch and submit to his body. I let him command from me each second of pleasure down to the core of my fear.

He filled me, all of me and I hungered for more.

All the while he told me how he saw me. Not with words but with the way he touched me, kissed me, and…made love to me.

Roy raised himself on his arms, changing his angle and increasing the strength of his thrusts. "I won't make you wait long. I promise."

The well of fire building inside me crackled through my bones and danced down my limbs.

"Close, Paris." My name came out on the back of a growl. "So close. I want you to come with me. Can you do that?" He gripped my cock and stroked.

I wasn't sure. I don't even think I cared if I ever found release because I was so wrapped up in the most beautiful experience of my life.

Him.

Roy snapped his hips forward hard enough to bang the bedframe against the wall and shove a cry from my throat.

"Come for me, Paris."

He squeezed my cock and pressed his thumbnail against the slit. The bite of pain freed me. I sank my fingers into Roy's shoulders, and with every ounce of strength I had left, I tightened my legs, forcing him as deep as possible. Roy jerked like he'd been hit. The pulse of his cock was followed by a rush of heat. I screamed because I didn't want this to end, and he drank the sound from my lips.

The chaos faded, leaving the sound of our breathing to fill the space.

What had I done? Somehow I'd let Roy into a place in my heart that I hadn't felt since I was a child. One that I'd forced myself to forget. A dark and sacred corner where there were first kisses and a boy whose name I couldn't remember.

Would I betray Roy too?

"It's okay, Paris. You're safe." Roy rolled to the side, taking me with him. "It's okay." He kissed me on the temple. "I promise it will be okay."

But it wasn't. I'd lost myself to him. Forever.

****

Even with the string pulled tight, the sweatpants I'd borrowed from Roy barely stayed on my hips. I ran the towel over my head one more time before I put on the shirt. The flannel smelled just like him. I would never get tired of that scent. Never.

Would Roy get tired of me?

The rich scent of vanilla filled the rest of the apartment. Roy stood in the kitchen, and the TV on the counter was turned low.

"I'm making french toast." He moved slices of bread around in a frying pan. "I hope that's okay with you?"

I sat at the breakfast bar. "It's fine."

While he got out dishes, I watched the news. It was going to snow or maybe rain, the weatherman couldn't decide.

"Do you want some bacon?" Roy didn't wait for an answer before getting it out of the fridge. "It's sugar cured. Really good." The fabric of his shirt tightened across his shoulders. There was a hole near the neck. There were no frayed edges or holes in the shirt he'd given me.

Why?

The weather went off, and a commercial came on. Roy dropped the bacon into the pan. Grease popped, and he jerked back. "Damn." He sucked his thumb.

"I think it's retaliating."

"Might help if I could remember to turn down the heat. I do this every time. You'd think I'd learn my lesson." He put some paper towels on one of the plates. "So how do you like yours cooked?"

"The same as yours, I guess."

"You sure?"

I nodded.

"Okay, extra crunchy it is."

The news returned. A car wreck flashed up on the screen. I picked at the crack in the bar. Everything Roy owned seemed worn-out or broken. I'd eaten meals that cost more than his rent. Yet sitting there in his decrepit apartment, I'd never felt so at home.

"Roy?"

"Hmmm?" He took a jug of orange juice from the fridge and poured two glasses. He sat one down in front of me. "You ever going to finish that thought?"

"Those things you said." I twisted up my fingers.

"What about them?" He put his hand over mine.

"Did you mean it?"

"Yes."

"Why?"

He went back to the stove, turned it off, made our plates, and got out the silverware.
Just those few minutes felt like a lifetime. He came back with the food and sat beside me.

Scrambled eggs, french toast, and bacon. I couldn't remember if I'd ever eaten the combination; if I had, it was never on a chipped plate and with mismatched silverware.

"Please tell me why." I picked up a piece of bacon but couldn't find the strength to get it to my mouth.

"I have. Many times."

"Tell me again." I need to know it wasn't a figment of my imagination. Or maybe my desperation.

Roy took the piece of bacon, broke off a small piece, and pushed it past my lips. His thumb lingered, and I sucked the tip. "Because you are beautiful and unique."

"I'm not."

"You just can't see inside yourself."

205

He was wrong. I could. And what I saw was terrifying.

"Eat."

Drinking some of the orange juice seemed to pacify him. Roy ate, and I moved the eggs around the slices of french toast. The TV flickered with a nightclub scene and two figures moving through the crowd. It was a bad angle and the film was grainy, but I knew what it was.

Then his face filled up the screen. The blue of his eyes was brighter than I'd originally thought. In the photo, he wore orange and there was a number stamped across the bottom.

I dropped my fork.

"Paris?"

The new ticker passed the anchor, but my ability to read froze up on murder.

"Paris? What's wrong?" Roy tried to make me look at him. I pushed his hand away. Nothing existed but the TV screen.

Roy picked up the remote from the edge of the bar and turned up the volume.

"…person of interest in the murders involving three other young gay men. Authorities are still trying to identify the individual who left with Hensley last night from the Diablo nightclub on Princeton Avenue.

"Hensley was last seen driving a mid-sized sedan either black or blue, with a broken headlight. If you have any information regarding the whereabouts of Thomas Hensley, you are encouraged to call…" I took the remote from Roy and muted the sound.

"He didn't look like a Hensley." I hugged myself. Any moment, I expected to see my breath in the air.

"That was him, wasn't it?" There was no emotion in Roy's voice. But something deadly had replaced the light in his eyes. Did he wear that same expression when he'd snapped the man's neck at the bar?

"Yeah."

"If they're looking for him, you didn't kill him."

"No." I didn't feel any relief. What did that say about me?

Roy pushed his plate away and stood. "C'mon."

"Where?"

"I'm taking you to the police station so you can fill out a report."

"What?" I pulled away from him. "No."

"The police are looking for him, and they need to know that he came after you."

"Why? It's done, it's over."

"But it doesn't change the fact it happened. And it could happen again."

"He's not going to track me down."

"What about someone else?"

The faces of three young men flashed up on the screen. They could have been anyone. But even without reading the subtext, I knew they were the men Hensley had killed. Were they the only ones? I wanted to believe they were, but there was no cure for the kind of hate and evil that drove a man to obliterate a life.

If I went, the police would ask questions that I had no answers for. Then they would contact Julia, and she'd bury me under a rock. "I can't."

"Why?"

"I just can't."

Roy stepped in front of me. "I'll be right there with you."

"I know."

"You didn't do anything wrong."

Only because I'd gotten lucky and picked out a killer rather than some married guy looking to play reindeer games behind his wife's back.

Roy held me by the shoulders. "Whatever you're thinking, it wasn't your fault."

He was wrong. It was my fault. "I can't. I'm sorry."

"You don't have to be afraid."

"I'm not."

"Then why can't you tell the police you saw this man?" He pushed my bangs back. "He could have hurt you."

He wouldn't have hurt me; he would've killed me.

"If I talk to the police, I'll have to tell them how I got away from the man."

"Why is that a problem?"

"Because they'll tell Julia."

Roy's eyebrows came together over his nose. "So what if they do?"

"If they contact her..." The scent of disinfectant and human sorrow was just one of the many facets in my nightmares. "It would be bad."

Roy scraped his hand through his hair. "Then tell them not to contact her."

"They won't have a choice."

"You make it sound like she owns you."

I pulled at the hair on the back of my head. The hairs were still too short so I settled for digging my fingers into the crook of my arm. "Julia controls everything in my life. Even me. If she knew I was here right now, she'd...make me leave."

"Julia can't make you do anything you don't want to do."

"Yes, she can."

"How?"

I had to force out the words. "She's my legal guardian."

Somewhere in the apartment building, a door slammed. Footsteps stampeded down the hall.

"You're a grown man. How can she be your guardian?"

I sat on a stool before my knees could fold. I didn't even have the strength to lift my chin. I counted the whirls in the hardwood floor. "When my mother died, Julia's father got custody of me. When he died, Julia was the oldest so she took over."

"That would have ended when you were eighteen."

"Under normal circumstances." A pain pecked me in the side of the head.

"And your circumstances weren't normal?"

"No. When I was thirteen, I hurt someone. A boy in my school. They sent me to a hospital."

"How bad were you hurt?"

"It wasn't that kind of hospital."

"What other kind is there?" There was a moment of confusion in Roy's expression. "A mental hospital?"

"Yeah. After my father died, the nightmares wouldn't stay in my head anymore."

"Why didn't you tell me?"

My laugh got hung in my throat. "How do you tell someone you're crazy?"

"You're not—"

"Yes. I am. I told you I was a disease. I'm sick, Roy. I'll always be sick." Roy stepped back, and my heart sank.

He picked up his coat off the sofa. "I need to take a walk." He sat on the end of the bed long enough to stomp on his boots. "I'll be back in a little while."

When he left, all the color leached from the world.

****

My mouth watered for vodka; my body ached for the pills. It wasn't the first time I'd stared into the darkness of the rabbit hole, but it was the first time I didn't run from it.

I was so close. Just one step.

"...let me love you..."

The warmth of Roy's touch ghosted my flesh.

"...Please, Paris..."

The memory of his mouth on mine still burned.

"...I'll teach you..."

His scent stained my skin.

Somewhere far away, a door opened and closed. There was a shuffle of fabric followed by two heavy thumps.

Roy's presence invaded the void of space at my side. He sat beside me on the kitchen floor. The cabinet door rattled.

On the back of a sigh, he said, "You should have told me." The disappointment in his voice cut deeper than any scream. Roy held my hand between his. He traced each finger, petted the back of my hand, and kissed my knuckles.

"You don't hate me?"

He smiled a little. "Never."

"You're not angry?"

"I was. At first. It hurt that you didn't trust me enough to tell me." He kissed my hand again. "But then I realized, why should you? You've never been able to trust anyone before."

He was the only person who ever gave me a reason to. He was the only person who'd ever given me a reason to want more than the alcohol, the pills, even the canvas. With Roy, I had nothing to run from.

Nothing to be afraid of.

"Roy?"

"Yeah?"

"I don't want to go home."

"You're welcome to stay as long as you need to."

"Never go home." I gripped his hand.

He tilted his head. "Okay. But the food isn't all that great, and it can get pretty damn cold. I think I get three channels on the TV and that's it."

"I don't care."

"If you change your mind—"

"I won't."

"What about your sisters?"

"I don't care."

"They'll want to know where you are."

"I don't care."

He bit his bottom lip. "Can I ask why?"

"Because when I'm with you, the colors are so beautiful."

"Colors?"

"Yeah."

He chuckled. "I guess a little color could do this place some good."

I leaned against him, and he put an arm around my shoulders.

"I know you don't want to go home." I tensed, and he shushed me. "It's not what you think."

And I could trust him.

"That's better." He rubbed his chin against my temple. "I'd like for you to talk to a friend of mine."

"Who?"

"A doctor."

"You mean a shrink."

"She's not. But I know she has friends who are."

"I already have a doctor."

"The pills?"

"Dr. Mason gives them to me."

"There weren't any labels on those bottles."

I shrugged.

"That's illegal."

210

"I know what they do, based on shape and color."

"That doesn't make it any less illegal."

I tried to sit up, and he held me. "If you don't want me to stay, just say it."

"I'm not trying to get rid of you."

"You're trying to fix me. That's just as bad."

"What if she could help you? Maybe she could even get you away from Julia."

"No one can get me away from Julia."

"Have you ever tried?"

I didn't even want to think of what it would be like to be free of her. It only gave me false hope inside my even bigger lie. "It won't do any good."

He pulled my chin up, and forced to meet his gaze. "Why not?"

"Because I'm broken, Roy. And I'm broken in ways that cannot be fixed."

Chapter Ten

My reflection followed Roy's across the plate-glass window. Dressed in thrift store hand-me-downs and a wool hat, I didn't recognized myself. I hoped no one else would either.

If I learned anything besides how clothes could drastically change a person's appearance, it was that designer wear obviously wasn't meant to be worn outside. In the real world, thick socks, boots, long-johns under jeans, and a sweat shirt was the only way to fight Mother Nature.

For the first time in what felt like forever, I was warm. No more cashmere for me. I was sold on corduroy and fake lamb's wool.

It had stopped snowing three days ago, but the temperature dropped and now everything was covered in ice. Sand and salt crunched under my boots, sprinkling lime green dots into the air.

A cab passed by, and two businessmen got out of their Lexus. The Slaughter House drew in all kinds.

The boy stood in the space between parked cars.

"*¿Cómo te llamas?*" He tilted his head and smiled.

"I know this is hard for you," Roy said. "But I promise Dr. Howell just wants to talk."

A woman passing by blocked my view for a second. Once out of the way, the boy was gone.

"Please trust me." Roy ran his thumb down my cheek.

I leaned into the contact. "I do."

"I know this is scary, but I think it could do some good."

"Nothing good comes from talking to a shrink."

"I told you, she's just a doctor."

"But she works in the same hospital as a shrink."

Roy dropped his gaze for a moment. I wanted to feel bad for snapping at him, but I couldn't get by the winding barbwire of my own fear to care. At least I hadn't bolted when he suggested talking to Dr. Howell in the first place.

I think I would have if there'd been somewhere else to go.

I took him by the arm. "C'mon, before I lose my courage."

Roy opened the door, and the jingle of bells sent bloody red streaks into the air. Almost all the tables were full. I followed him to a booth in the back occupied by a woman. Even dressed in a sweater and jeans, Howell radiated her profession.

She stood. "Long time no see, Roy." They shook hands. "How have you been?"

"Good."

"You must be Paris." Dr. Howell greeted me with a manicured hand. I hoped she couldn't feel me shaking. "Please sit."

I slid in beside Roy.

"Are you two hungry? They're still serving breakfast."

"Paris?"

"No."

"You didn't eat anything this morning."

I picked up the menu. Each item had a cartoon illustration. My stomach rolled. "I guess I'll have whatever you do."

Louise came out of the kitchen. She saw us and walked over. "Hey, you two here for breakfast?" Her eyes said something else. Was I alright? Had I talked? And would I tell her what happened?

"Louise, this is my friend Dr. Kim Howell." Roy tipped his head at Howell.

"You should have told me you knew Roy. Pleased to meet you."

"Likewise. Roy has said a lot of good things about your food. I've been meaning to get here sooner."

"Well, you're here now, and that's all that matters. So, you boys want something to drink?"

"Coffee, please," Roy said.

"Black?"

"Always."

Dr. Howell raised her cup. "And I'll take a refill when you get a chance."

"Paris?"

"Vodka and orange juice."

"I'm all out of vodka, but I can get you the orange juice. I'll bring you boys some silverware when I get back." Louise patted me on the shoulder, then left.

"I've seen your work," Dr. Howell said. "You're very talented."

I picked at the edge of the table.

"You don't think so?"

"Could we just get to the real reason why we're here?"

"Okay, I can do that." Howell ran her thumb over the handle of her cup. "Roy seems to think you might need some help."

I folded my arms across my stomach. Three men dressed in coveralls got up from the table beside us.

Roy squeezed my thigh.

"Like I told Roy, I can't be helped."

"You sound so sure."

"I am."

"Have you ever talked to a doctor?"

I sat forward, then back.

"Paris?" Dr. Howell folded her hands on the table.

"Yes."

"Would you mind sharing their name?"

"Yes."

"Whatever you tell me is between us. I will not break your confidence."

"No." I couldn't risk it. If Howell did call Mason, he'd inform Julia. I'd been gone for over five days. She'd make sure I paid for it.

"Are you seeing him now?"

"Sort of."

"What do you mean by 'sort of'?"

I shrugged. "He gives Julia pills, she gives them to me."

"What are you taking?"

I shrugged again.

Dr. Howell flicked a look up at Roy. To me, she said, "Have you ever thought about seeing someone else?"

"I can't."

"Why not?"

"My sister is good at getting what she wants. And she doesn't want me to see anyone else."

I pulled at the hairs on the back of my head. Tiny sharp stings bit my scalp. If I kept going, I'd be bald by the time I got out of there.

"Paris, why doesn't your sister want you to see anyone else?"

"You tell anyone. I mean anyone, I will have you locked up for the rest of your life."

"I don't know."

"Are you—"

Louise returned with our drinks. She laid out napkins and silverware. "You decide what you want?"

Roy put down his menu. "Do you have any biscuits this morning?"

"Of course, new batch is due out of the oven in five minutes."

"Then two biscuits with gravy please, ma'am."

"What about you, Paris?"

I nodded.

"Any eggs?" Louise said.

"No, thanks." Roy tucked the menu behind the napkin dispenser.

"And you, Dr. Howell, what will you have?"

"One egg, two egg whites…do you have any fruit?"

"Strawberries for the pancakes. Blueberries for the waffles."

"Waffles, huh?"

"Best you'll ever eat."

"Bring me a waffle with blueberries but don't tell my husband."

Louise laughed. "Secret is safe with me. I'll be back in a bit with your food."

Again, we were alone.

Dr. Howell drank some of her coffee and watched me over the rim. "I want to help you, Paris, but that's going to be difficult for me to do with nothing to go on."

"You can trust her," Roy said.

"Please let me help you," Dr. Howell said.

"Why?" The door was just thirty feet away. I mapped a path between the tables. "What reason could you possibly have that makes you want to just 'help' me?"

"Because Roy is a friend, and I owe him so much."

"Really, for what?" A look of pensiveness fractured her neutral expression.

"About six years ago, my daughter got a job waiting tables at a bar. One night, she was assaulted. If it wasn't for Roy, she would have suffered more than a few bruises."

"If you owe him so much, why did you let him sit in prison?"

"Because I didn't know who he was until a few years ago when Roy came into the hospital for some stitches. My daughter was waiting for me so we could go to lunch. She recognized him."

Roy fiddled with his fork. I didn't know whether to be angry at him for not asking for help or in awe because he'd been willing to sacrifice so much for a person he didn't know.

But I wasn't brave like him. "I can't tell you his name. I'm sorry."

"Because of your sister?"

"Yeah."

"She's your legal guardian."

I nodded.

"How would you feel about talking to someone who might be able to change that?"

"Who?"

"A colleague of mine, Dr. Carmichael."

My fingertips turned cold and my palms sweaty. The muted sunlight coming through the windows burned my eyes.

"He has experience with competency evaluations. He's gone to court many times on an individual's behalf."

A throbbing pain beat against my temple.

"Paris?"

I rubbed my eyes.

"Do you think you might be interested in meeting him? He has an appointment open this afternoon. Roy can even go to the hospital with you."

"I told you what would happen if you ran your mouth."

My heart skipped.

"Does that sound like something you might be interested in?"

"You don't have anyone to blame but yourself."

The air thinned.

"Or if you don't feel like going today, he has time tomorrow."

"Cause any more trouble and I'll make sure you never get out."

I clamored out of the booth. My shoulder caught Louise's on her way to our table, and she dropped the plates she carried. The jagged crash tossed up orange shards that chased me out the door.

216

Cold air froze the sweat on my skin and slipped under my coat. People dotted the sidewalk. Cars rolled past on the street. There was no longer a left or right, just the deluge of gritty footsteps and wet rubber sucking slush.

I walked, but I didn't know where.

"Paris." Roy's voice was muted by distance. "Paris, wait."

I couldn't have, even if I wanted to. Fear possessed me, pumping the buttery smell of disease and despair into my lungs.

"Think you can keep your mouth shut?"

My throat tightened.

"Or do I need to leave you here?"

Every swallow I took fought against the urge to vomit.

"I will. I'll leave you in that room to marinate in your own piss."

The buildings swelled, taking up the sidewalk. I slid on the tilting ground.

"You lied, Paris."

People stretched skyward, thinning out and curving upward until I was surrounded.

"And that's what you're going to tell them. You lied. You did this for attention."

I stumbled into the street, and a car horn wailed. A wall of black lunged for me. Roy pulled me out of the way. "Jesus Christ!"

The man driving the truck flipped me off. "Learn to use the crosswalk, asshole!"

Roy pinned me to his chest and cradled my head on his shoulder. "It's okay."

"Let me go." I couldn't lift my arms to make him.

"Never."

"I'll leave. I'll go somewhere, and you'll never have to look at me again." I'd even go back to the apartment and face Julia.

"I don't want you to leave. You know that."

"Then why…" A tremor ran through my body. "Why are you trying to have me locked up?"

"I'm not…I wouldn't. I just wanted to…" He petted my hair. "I'm sorry."

"No more doctors."

"No. No more." He tried to step back, and I clung to him. "Let me fix your coat."

"I'm fine."

"Your teeth are chattering."

"I don't want to let go yet." I didn't ever want to let go, but my muscles began to ache from shivering. Roy reached for the front of my coat. "I can zip my own coat."

His cell phone rang, erasing the embarrassment from his face. He took it out of his pocket. "Hello?" Roy looked at me. "Yeah, I found him. No. No, that's okay. Maybe later."

I zipped up my coat and crammed my frozen hands into the pockets. A couple of people glanced my way. I wrapped my scarf around my neck and pulled it up to my nose.

"Tell Louise I'm sorry about...you know." Roy dug the toe of his boot into a slushy pile of ice. "Right. Sure. That will be fine."

There was a TV on in a pawnshop window. On the screen a crowd of supporters swarmed a two blonde haired women.

Even if I'd never seen their faces, I would have known who they were.

As always, Julia's hair was perfect, her makeup precise, the polish on her nails flawless. Her cheeks were flushed, but it was the cold. I knew her fake tears when I saw them.

Alice was a different story. She looked scared.

A photo of me from the last showing flashed up on the screen. I'd dressed in Julia's favorite Armani. It made me look taller. Was I really that thin? Maybe it was because I'd clasped my hands behind my back. Then the scene with Julia surrounded by a group of reporters returned.

Roy joined me by the window.

My painting replaced the image of my crying sisters, and the world stood still.

Lines of red and violet swarmed the canvas mixed with gold and orange. The moment all those years ago hovered beneath the surface. His lips had been so soft, so warm...

I went inside the pawnshop. There was a man behind the counter reading the paper.

"Give me the remote for that TV." I pointed.

"You interested in buying it?"

"Please, I need to hear what they're saying."

"You even got any money to buy a TV?"

"The remote."

"This ain't no 'try it then buy it' store, buddy."

I grabbed him by his shirt and yanked him over the display case. "Give me the fucking remote." The shop owner waved a hand at the cash register. A TV remote lay next to it.

I went over to the window and pulled the TV around.

Roy walked into the store. "What are you doing?"

I increased the volume. The reporter's voice popped with excitement at the beginning of each word.

"...disappearance sparked a bidding war at Christie's in New York, and Paris Duvoe's controversial painting broke record bids, selling for almost fourteen million dollars."

The room dipped.

"She sold it." The walls bled. "She sold it." The muscles in my legs tightened, and I curled my hands into fists. Heat boiled from my stomach, rising into my throat on the back of bitter flavor. I stumbled back, and Roy tried to catch me. I slapped his hand away. "She sold my painting." I stabbed a finger at the TV. "That fucking bitch sold my painting."

"We'll get it back."

"How, Roy? Tell me how the fuck am I supposed to get it back?"

"I don't know, but we'll figure it out."

Whatever I was about to say dried up in my throat. The white rabbit sat at the base of the TV, regarding me with dark eyes. It ran its paws over its face and flicked an ear.

"No."

It cocked its head.

"No, you promised."

"Paris?"

The rabbit took a small hop toward the edge of the tiered stage filled with TVs.

"Paris, look at me." When I didn't, Roy made me. "What's wrong?"

"It promised."

"What promised?"

"The rabbit, the rabbit…" A blur of white flashed in my periphery. It was closer now and sat with its paws on the edge. Long delicate whiskers danced on each cheek beside its twitching pink nose.

I scurried back. "I'm not going with you." It leaned forward like it was about to jump to the floor. I threw the remote, and it cracked the screen. The rabbit scurried back and disappeared behind the display.

It was not going to take me. I would not let it take me. But it didn't have to. The weight inside me thickened until it crushed my lungs. Leaves clung to my pants, sticks snapped underfoot, and the cold winter air turned sour.

Shelves and display cases. Display cases and shelves. The door was gone, and the ceiling sank. I turned, trying to find some way out.

The ringing in my ears muffled the shop owner's yell.

Roy's lips moved, but there was only the sound of mud-sucking rotting flesh. The monster filled me, overflowed, dulled my senses until there was nothing to feel, nothing to think about, nothing but the fury of its need to be heard.

It roared, and its anger rolled out of me in waves.

I snatched something from the table behind me, a toaster, a skill saw, I had no idea. It hit the TV, causing it to topple back. Roy tried to restrain me, but I slipped out of his arms, grabbed the TV, and hurled it at the window. It struck the metal bars and fractures spider webbed up the glass.

Roy pinned my arms to my side. But he was no match for the monster. If anything, his attempts to stop it only fueled its rage. I thrashed, kicked, and got loose. Items on shelves became missiles, punching holes through display cases, knocking TVs onto the floor. Roy hooked an arm around my ribs. I elbowed him in the side of his face. He went back.

There was a chair off to the right. I had no idea where I threw it. Glass shattered under my fists, and the blood of my sins dripped from my hands. I think Roy tried to stop me again, but the monster was stronger than he would ever be. Other people poured out of the creature's cesspool. They grabbed at me, pulling me toward the pit. I kicked them. I bit them. I clawed at their eyes. They struck me with lightning, and a searing pain rode down from my shoulder.

Then there was nothing.

****

It left me destroyed.

Muck sloshed under my skin, and it took everything I had to stay upright.

Julia shoved past me and stormed into my apartment. "You are an embarrassment, Paris. Do you have any idea what your little temper tantrum could do to your career? You better be glad the storeowner agreed to a check, otherwise you'd be in jail right now. And wouldn't the reporters love that?"

When had the stairs to my room gotten so tall?

"Are you listening to me?" She blocked my path. "I swear to God I will sue the whole department if they hurt you. A Taser. I cannot believe they used a Taser." Julia started to pull my shirt to the side and examine the burn on my shoulder. Instead, she flicked her hands and wiped them on her skirt. "Go change. No telling what's living in those clothes. Make sure you throw them in the trash. Good God, what the hell were you thinking?"

Alice came from somewhere. She hugged me. "We were so scared."

Could I get up the steps, or would I need a ladder?

"Why didn't you call?" Alice petted my cheek.

"I'll tell you why, because he's worthless."

"Don't say that."

"Why not? It's true. He doesn't respect this family. He doesn't even respect himself."

Alice pushed my bangs back. "If you'd called, I would have sent a car."

"He was with that…" Julia made a disgusted sound.

"What happened to your hands?" Alice touched the bandages.

"I cut myself on some broken glass. It's nothing. I didn't even need stitches."

"Quit babying him, Alice." She dropped her gaze and stared at my feet. Julia said, "Go upstairs and make yourself presentable in case I decide to call Dr. Mason."

Everything solidified. "No."

Julia smirked. "I don't think you have a choice."

221

"I'm sorry. I just…"

"What? Wanted to whore yourself out to some bum?"

"Roy isn't…" I rubbed my temple, hoping to stop the coming pain.

"I'll get you some aspirin." Alice went into the kitchen.

"He doesn't need an aspirin; he needs a swift kick in the ass."

"And I bet you're just the person to do it for me."

The tendons in Julia's neck stood out. "Do not test me."

"Don't worry. You've already proven yourself a hundred times over."

She drew back her shoulders. Alice walked into the room. "Here." She handed me a couple of white pills and a glass of water. "Take that. They're extra strength."

I took the pills. If anything, it might delay getting hit by Julia. "Thank you." I handed back the empty glass. Alice smoothed out the front of my shirt.

"Make sure you wash your hands," Julia said. "No telling what kind of filth those rags have on them."

"You should go lay down, you look tired." Alice guided me to the stairs.

I was tired. The exhaustion went beyond my body and into the core of my being. There, everything I had lay broken.

"You better hope that piece of white trash doesn't sue us," Julia said. "He probably will. People like that aren't satisfied by just having their hospital bill paid. When he does, it's going to come out of your allowance."

"Fine." I hoped Roy would sue. I deserved worse. How bad had I hurt him? I climbed the stairs.

"You're still going to the showing at the Vanguard."

"What if I don't feel like going?"

She tossed her hair over her shoulder. "Make sure you wear the Armani."

"I still don't feel like going."

"You'll have to talk to the press. They'll want to know where you were. I'll speak to Bruce to see what he suggests."

"You could always let me tell them the truth rather than some lie thought up by a lawyer."

"Don't be stupid. Depending how we spin this, it may help more than hinder."

"You mean it will sell more paintings."

"I'd think you'd be grateful. That piece of rubbish you painted went for 13.5 million."

"You could kill me, then sell the lot. You'd be richer than God." I leaned against the railing.

Alice joined me on the steps. "Do you need me to get you something else?"

Sweet Alice. Innocent Alice. I kissed her cheek. "I'm fine."

"You're pale."

"He said he's fine."

Alice looked at Julia, then me. I said, "You better go do the shopping." I had no idea if she had any. Alice went over to the couch and picked up her purse. The elevator door slid shut behind her.

"Three days," Julia said. "That's how long you have to get your shit together. And if you know what's good for you, you'd better do just that. Dan Brunswick will be there."

She started to turn, and I said, "How much am I worth now?"

"What?"

"You sold the painting for 13.5 million. How much are you getting from Brunswick for me?"

"Hopefully, he'll buy the Woman in Red. He's been eyeing it for a month. You going home with him is just a courtesy for his patronage."

I headed up the stairs and shut myself in my room.

If I could have tolerated the stench of blood, sweat, and jail grime, I would have skipped the shower just to make it unpleasant for Dr. Mason and to piss off Julia.

When I was done, I left the clean clothes in the drawers and the towel on the rack. Water droplets made puddles on the tile. Goosebumps spread down my arms when the first breath of cool air rolled into the bathroom, and a cloud of steam followed me out.

On my bed, the black comforter on black sheets was smooth and perfect. I wanted rumpled bedclothes, worn thin by the movements of a muscled body, stained with the scent of musk and spicy cologne. The quilt would have small holes in some of the patches and bits of fluff would poke out. But it would be so warm.

I lay on the thick rug next to the bed. It was just me and my reflection in the mirror on the ceiling. Paint concealed my sin on canvas, and flesh concealed the vile creature staring down at me.

As the evening faded, my room transformed into a dark cube divided by the strips of manmade light sliding through the gaps in the curtains. I shivered, and my bones ached, but I couldn't will myself up any more than I could will my body to stop breathing.

There in the quiet, all the good things Roy had given me peeled away. I didn't fight it. It was better they disappear now, or Julia would take them. Even if I never put the moments to canvas, she'd burrow into my skull and dig them out.

"Let me love you..."

Now that I had, I didn't know how to live without him.

When I inhaled, Roy's scent washed through me. A current of air preceded the filling of space. The bedside light clicked on.

My heart jumped.

"Paris?"

Even zipped only halfway, the coveralls he wore were stretched tight across his shoulders. A city ID badge hung from the chest pocket.

Roy knelt beside me. There was a line of butterfly stitches over his right eye and a bruise on his cheek. "What did you take?"

"Are you real?"

"Yes."

"Are you sure?"

He pushed my bangs back. "Tell me what you took and how much."

"If you're real, why are you here?"

"To make sure you're okay. Please tell me what you took."

"How did you get in?"

He thumbed the badge. "Borrowed it from a friend. Now tell me what you took."

"Nothing."

Roy pressed his lips together.

"I didn't take anything."

"Then why are you laying on the floor?"

There was another cut on his ear. I touched it.

"It's just a couple of scrapes and bruises," Roy said.

"I put them there."

"You were upset."

I petted Roy's arm. "You're such a good man." Better than anyone I'd ever known.

"Can you sit up?" He slipped an arm under me.

"I don't want to be here anymore."

"Then we'll leave. Dr. Howell still wants to help you."

I slumped against him, my face in his neck. He was so warm and his scent so calming.

He cupped my chin. "That's not what you meant, is it? About not being here?"

"I'm a rabid dog. I need to be put down."

Roy petted my head. "Don't say that."

"It's true."

"No. It isn't."

"You saw what I am."

"I saw someone who needs help." Roy moved me to the edge of the bed.

"Go home." I meant it, but I couldn't get my hands to let go of him.

"Only if you'll come with me."

"I can't."

Roy sat. "Yes, you can."

I kissed his pulse, and it fluttered against my lips. "Why? So you can save me?" I slid my hand inside his coveralls and found the edge of his shirt. The heat of his skin flowed up my fingers.

"Paris, you need to…"

"Let you love me. That's all I need to do." I found one of his nipples. He growled between clenched teeth. "I like it when you make those sounds." I pinched him again, and he hissed.

"You need to get dressed."

The firmness of his body close to mine made it easy for me to forget what lay ahead of me and impossible for me to care what happened next. It killed the pain like no drug or drink ever had. I did not want to lose Roy, but I also knew I couldn't keep him. But one more time wouldn't hurt. One more chance to overdose on what he had to offer. Maybe it would take me from the world.

If only I could be so lucky.

225

I slid a leg across Roy's thighs.

"Clothes, Paris."

"Yeah, clothes." I yanked on the shoulders of his coveralls. The zipper gave, sliding all the way to his crotch.

Roy caught my wrists. "We need to leave."

I exhaled against his lips. "Love me, Roy." I sucked on his bottom one. "Even if it's just for a little while. That's what you said."

"Paris, we—"

I placed a finger over his mouth. "I'll go, but not today."

He held my hand. "Then when?"

"I have a showing in three days at the Vanguard. There's a coffee shop on the corner. I'll meet you there." Roy searched my face. Even under the light of a forty-watt bulb, the green in his eyes was bright. Somehow I managed to look him in the eye when I said, "I promise."

A tear rolled down his cheek, and I kissed it away. "And you don't break your promises, right?" His voice cracked, and that was how I knew he understood.

"Never, Roy."

"I'll be there."

"I know." I peeled the coveralls off his shoulders. Roy freed his arms.

"I won't leave till you get there."

I pressed my lips to his and fed him the truth with long strokes of my tongue. I was his. I would always be his, even when I wasn't here anymore.

Julia might have owned my body, but I'd freely given Roy my soul.

Ten aching points blossomed on my ass cheeks. One for each finger he gripped me with.

I urged Roy back and was grateful when he didn't resist. As he moved to the center of the bed, I tugged off his boots, then the coveralls. He lifted his hips to help me with his jeans and boxers.

I pinned him down with a knee at each of his hips. His thick cock brushed mine, and a burst of static raced across my skin.

"Your shirt."

He pulled it over his head, and I tugged on his long johns. They joined the shirt on the floor.

I ran my hands down Roy's chest, following the planes of muscle down to the dips above each hip, then back up to his throat.

"I want you." I kissed his chin. "But I don't want to fuck you." I nipped his earlobe. "I want to make love to you, Roy. Will you let me do that?"

Roy smoothed his touch up my body until he cupped my head with one hand and held my back with the other. "You know I will."

I trailed a line of kisses down past his navel and nestled between his knees. I held Roy's gaze and swept my tongue over the thick head of his cock. His nostrils flared. I did it again. The muscles in his legs tensed.

I took the tip into my mouth.

Roy's chest expanded. He knotted his hands up in the comforter.

Deeper, and a low moan ticked out of his throat. I pulled back to the tip, and he whimpered.

"Do you like it when I suck you?" I blew across the tip of his cock. It jumped and tapped my chin.

He lifted his head. "Yeah."

I ran my tongue down the length of his dick. "What else would you like?" His nuts were heavy in my hand. I gave them a slight tug. He grunted.

I pinched the skin below his navel between my teeth. Roy jerked. I soothed the spot with my tongue.

"Tell me."

"You."

I wet two of my fingers, and his eyes widened. I rubbed the wrinkled skin of his opening. Roy clenched his ass cheeks. I applied pressure, and he dug a heel into the mattress. "Breathe, Roy."

He exhaled a breath.

"Now push."

He didn't.

"Aren't you curious to know what it's like?"

His cheeks reddened.

"Ah, so you have thought about it."

Roy nodded.

"Is that what you want? My dick in your ass?" I coaxed the ring of muscle to accept my fingertip. "Push, Roy." His opening

relaxed enough for me to invade him all the way to my knuckle.
"That's it." I kissed his thigh, the base of his cock, then returned my
mouth to the head.

Would he let me fuck him if I asked? Of course, he would. As
tight as Roy held my strings, I held his the same way. But it wouldn't
have been fair for me to take that from him. He needed someone who
would appreciate what he had to offer, savor every moment, and most
of all someone who could give back in equal amounts.

That someone was not me.

The tip of Roy's cock brushed the back of my throat at the
same time I pumped my finger in and out. He clawed at the blankets,
riding up on his elbows, giving me more of his ass. I changed the angle
of my thrusts, and he cried out.

I grazed my teeth over the swollen flesh around his slit. "You
want another?"

He rolled a look down at me. The war between pleasure and
surrender played across his face.

Roy clenched again but, at the same time, lifted his hip, giving
me better access. I nudged his entrance with my other finger, but the
saliva had already dried and I didn't want to hurt him.

It was enough. He knew what it could feel like. It would feed
his curiosity, and one day he'd let a man bury himself balls deep.
Would he call to him? Would he make those deep guttural sounds?
Would Roy bury his face in the man's neck and exhale his desperation
against his skin?

He would, and I already hated the man Roy hadn't even met.

I removed my finger, and Roy settled against the comforter.
He ran his hand through my hair, and I started to suck him again.

He stopped me. "I want you to."

A sharp twinge pulled at my heart. "You're not ready."

"Yes, I am."

I moved high enough to kiss him on his chest. "You need to
wait." Would he argue? Or would he listen to what I wasn't saying?

Roy closed his eyes, and the tension in his body shifted.
Again, I knew he understood.

"The drawer," I said.

He glanced over.

"Inside."

He opened it. There was a rattle of medicine bottles. He found the tube of lubricant and handed it to me.

I kissed him, my mouth to his, not brutal, not soft, but firm enough to make it difficult to breathe. Roy begged me, with a swipe of his tongue and a hand on the back of my head, to come home with him. He offered me hope, freedom, and a lifetime of love.

Even if I thought I deserved that, Julia would hunt me down and Roy would not be safe.

I slicked up my fingers with lubricant and sat back. The gel was cold on my opening. Roy petted me down my body, following the path of my hand to where I plunged my fingers in and out of my hole. He pushed my hand away and replaced my fingers with his.

"God, Paris." He thumbed one of my nipples during a pass down my ribs to my cock. There, he rolled the foreskin over the head, tugging the folds, then pushing back to massage the glans.

I rocked against his hand, pushing him deeper. Roy picked up the tube of lubricant lying next to his hip. He removed his fingers and started to squeeze out more gel.

"It's enough."

"I don't want to hurt you."

"You won't." And if he did, I'd welcome it. I moved over him.

"Paris…"

"Shhh—" I tossed the tube out of reach. "Now where was I?"

Roy pulled me down until my face was close to his. He brushed a line of kisses along my jaw. There was heat in his eyes, but it was tempered by something more powerful than lust.

I feared it.

I wanted it.

Roy guided his cock to my entrance. I rolled back, and he raised up. The pressure turned into an ache, and the ache into a burn. I exhaled a gasp, and he froze.

"More." My thoughts frazzled into an explosion of color. Roy tried to hold me, but I broke free. He dropped his hips in an attempt to stop me, but I followed him down.

The sharp twinge of being stretched crackled up my spine. My stomach tightened, and the air was shoved from my lungs. I grabbed

Roy's thighs and forced my body to take the rest of him. His cock rubbed across my prostate.

"Oh, God." Sound and light shattered. "More." The shards flayed me. "Please, Roy." He raised himself up, pushing me to my knees, giving me the last inch.

I didn't give myself time to adjust before I raised up on my knees only to drop my weight again. The second thrust hit me harder than the initial penetration, and my lower back cramped, feeding my desperation.

Roy met the rhythm I set, and our bodies slapped together with a hollow sound. I braced my hand on his chest and worked my hips, clenching my ass hard enough to make him jerk.

The flush spreading over Roy's shoulders darkened as it crawled up his neck and reached his cheeks. The crimson made his features harder.

"You are so beautiful, Paris." Roy alternated between pinching my nipples and massaging them with his thumb. The tingling threads it created made my cock jump. "You are so perfect."

I closed my eyes.

"Don't."

I rode him harder.

"Look at me." He cupped my face, and I lost my will to disobey. "That's it." Roy traced my lips with a finger. "Let me see how good you feel."

The reverence in his gaze only fueled my self-hate. I gripped my cock.

"No." Roy seized my wrist. "I'm nowhere near done with you yet." I changed hands, and he rolled me over, pinning me to the mattress, each wrist in his hands, his face close to mine. "I told you, I'm not done with you yet."

And his eyes said he never would be.

Roy plucked away my retort with a kiss and, at the same time, rocked forward. The momentum lifted my thighs, and the new angle struck me so deep my insides screamed in protest.

A ringing in my ears vibrated the colors flittering around me. "Oh God…" He backed out, and I gasped for breath.

Roy nuzzled my neck and nipped my ear. Why couldn't he have been a nameless entity? Someone who would never care about me and I could never hurt? Why did he have to infect me with emotions I couldn't begin to understand?

"Tell me what you're thinking about?" He laid his forehead against mine. "I see it in your face, and it scares you."

I swallowed against the tightness in my throat. "I can't."

"Why not?"

"Because I don't know how."

"Try."

"I don't have the words."

"But you have colors."

I did. And they cascaded around me, through Roy, and through me. "Reds, with white." Roy pushed deep again, and I cried out. "Bronze, gold, violet. It makes the edges vibrate and the color sing."

"Sounds beautiful."

"It is."

He gripped my hips, raising my legs and draping them over his arms.

"Oh Roy, Roy, Roy…"

"I'm right here."

I wrapped my arms around his neck and dug my fingers into his hair. Roy sank his cock into my ass.

"Greens and blues." I tightened my hold. "Strips of orange. It's divided by yellow."

"Why yellow?" Roy let his weight come down on me. Fully sheathed inside me, he snapped his hips.

"Please—" I bit his ear. Again Roy withdrew to the tip, but there was no slow entry this time. He shoved his hips forward, knocking the headboard against the wall. The bedside lamp shimmied toward the edge of the table.

"Why yellow, Paris?"

"I don't know."

"There has to be a reason." He ground his hips against my ass.

"It's beautiful. It's warm. It's safe. It gives balance to the extremes." Sweat dripped from Roy's chin onto my lips. "Please, Roy…"

"Tell me what you need." He pulled back in a measured pace, then returned with the same kind of focus. "Anything you want, Paris. Anything."

Him. I wanted him, but it could never happen. "Harder."

The muscles in his back flexed under my palms as Roy gave me what I asked, and the lamp fell onto the floor.

I clawed his back. "More, Roy. I need more." The next thrust was short but powerful. "Yesss—"

Roy pumped his hips, and I hoped the headboard knocked holes in the fucking sheetrock.

A tremor ran through his body, and his breathing hitched. I tightened my arms around his shoulders until he was forced to curl against me. His sweat became my sweat, our breathing one. I could never get enough of him, and from this day forward, no man would ever be able to satisfy me again.

Roy dug his grip into my hips. "Close."

"Yes." I pulled his hair.

"Want to feel you come."

"Almost." The tingling spreading over my skin turned into an electric dance. "Almost. Almost." I raked his ear with my teeth. "Need more, just a little…" He tilted his hips, and a rush of white noise shorted out my senses.

For a few seconds, there was nothing but a void. I existed without pain, guilt, and self-hate. I was free.

Then the colors bled back into my reality, and my soul returned to the prison it had been condemned to. Roy's muscles hardened under my hands as he drove himself one final time. His cock thickened, rekindling the burn, and he buried a guttural scream into the pillow beside my head.

With every pulse of his cock, Roy rocked on his knees. Then he was still, and there was only the rapid pounding of his heart against my chest. It slowed, and his breathing settled.

Roy lowered my legs, and a sharp jolt told me just how unhappy my hips were.

He traced my jaw with his lips, stopping at my mouth. "Leave with me."

"Soon."

The crow's feet around his eyes deepened. "Three days…"

"Yeah."

"You'll meet me at the café?"

It took everything to keep my voice from breaking. "I promise."

I let Roy go. Watched him dress. Then lay there as he walked out of my life forever.

Chapter Eleven

After the banquet and the showing, I walked with Dan Brunswick to his limo waiting by the curb. He held open the door. I got in, and he followed.

The limo pulled into the street.

Dan slid his ring off his finger and slipped it into his pocket. Then he opened the minibar and poured a drink.

It always amazed me how many men could rationalize their infidelity just by removing a bit of metal from their hand. As if taking it off meant it never happened. Or perhaps it was putting it back on that erased the deed.

"Here." He handed me a tumbler half filled with a rich amber bourbon. Champagne was for socialites. Whiskey was for pimps, johns, and whores. The liquor burned my throat on the way down.

Dan watched me over the rim of his glass between sips.

Rain speckled the passenger window, warping reality into swollen points. We passed the café where I'd promised to meet Roy.

How long would he wait before he gave up? I could only hope he'd leave when they closed. If only I'd been strong enough to keep my word.

"You're quiet. Is something wrong?" Dan swirled his glass, and the ice cubes clinked against the sides. The limo took a right, the café disappeared, and the street lamps abandoned me to the dark.

"Everything's fine." I gave him my fake smile, and unlike Roy, Dan did not see through it.

He plucked my empty glass from my hand. "Refill?"

"I'm good."

"You want something stronger?" He produced a small bag of white powder. "It's the best."

"What is it?" White powder could be so many things.

"Heroin."

"I don't do needles."

He took out a palm-sized mirror. "I know. Julia told me." Dan handed me a glass straw and cut a line. I had to practically sit on top of him to reach it.

My eyes teared up as soon as the H hit my nasal passages. I pinched my nostril shut to keep it from being flushed out. Dan handed me a tissue. Wiping my nose was more difficult than I expected. The H had to be top of the line if it could hit me that fast.

"What about you?" I said.

"Not tonight."

I had a feeling it was more like 'not ever.'

"Now." Dan grazed my lip, my neck, then his fumbling hands found their way to my crotch.

While Dan was busy groping me, I cut another line. He gave me some room to lean forward. I snorted the H, and the lights inside the limo shattered. I clung to him so I wouldn't float away.

"Here." He repositioned my legs. "Let's get more comfortable, shall we?" When Dan was done shifting around my body parts, I was in his lap facing the table, the bar, and what was left of the powder. He worked my pants out of the way, and the fabric of his expensive suit caressed my ass.

"You're going to ride me."

I nodded.

He tilted me forward enough to get his belt and zipper undone. "You're going to ride me and I'm going to fuck you until you can't walk."

I poured out more H and inhaled what I could from the pile on the mirror. My limbs detached, and the world blinked in and out.

Dan pressed his cock to my hole. Did he even slick me up? Stretch me?

"Condom." I planted my hand on the door to keep myself from falling forward.

"No. I don't think so."

"Julia…said…"

"Yeah, and I showed her I was clean, and I know you are. I bought that painting at top dollar, and I'm going to enjoy the hospitality gift."

He pulled me back and thrust his hips. A bolt of pain struck me from the moment of penetration, burrowing deeper until he filled me. I yelled, and he laughed.

"God, you're tight." He shifted his weight. Tears blurred my vision. I scrambled for something to hold onto. Streaks of white smeared all over my skin and clothes.

I realized in that moment between Dan pushing deeper and positioning his long legs for leverage, this would never end. The lie I'd told to the boy's mother had condemned me to a life of hell. I would forever paint to make Julia her fortune and I would ride cock to make her customers happy. And my suffering would not end until I drew my last breath.

I snorted the powder left on the mirror. The explosive rush roared through my body, evaporating everything anchoring me to the world. I struggled against the crushing weight twisting my limbs into balloon animals. Streaks of color distorted the space around me, filled my mouth, my throat, my lungs, and the pain of being fucked dry was lost to the static numbness.

I leaned down to snort another line, missed my nose and wound up jabbing myself in the corner of my eye with the straw. Crimson dominated my vision. I gave up.

Dan popped his hips, but the ass he fucked belonged to the man on his lap, bouncing like a rag doll with every thrust. My grip slipped off the door, and I failed to keep my face from smacking the table. The mirror danced near my nose, celebrating the moment.

Dusty air tickled my throat, and I coughed. The bitter taste in my mouth increased with every inhale until I gagged. I closed my mouth and breathed through my nose. It burned, and I sneezed, but it didn't go away.

"Gonna come, Paris. I'm gonna fill you full."

There was a pig in the limo. It grunted and squealed. It fucked me so hard my insides tried to push him out. It wouldn't stop, and I wanted it to. I wanted everything to end.

With the last happy moment in my life sitting abandoned at a café, it just wasn't worth fighting anymore. Shadows crawled from the corners of the limo, followed by the white rabbit wearing a cheap pinstripe suit.

The rabbit could take me some place even Julia couldn't reach. I'd been there once before, and I realized I should have never left. Now that there was no reason—no one—to keep me here, I was ready to let go.

I took the white rabbit's paw, and he led me down the rabbit hole.

****

A monotone bird chirped close to my ear. I tried to push it away but couldn't find it. I reached higher. I yanked on the vines hanging from the weird metal tree over my head, and it came crashing down.

"Whoa, whoa, Paris." Roy grabbed my arms. "Easy. It's okay."

He picked up a white block near my arm. God spoke, "How may I help you?"

"Get Dr. Howell. Paris is awake."

Roy cupped my cheek. Before I could ask him how he'd fallen down the rabbit hole, a big square pig on wheels squeaked by a lighted window. Was it looking for me? The monotone bird chirped a warning.

"Paris." Roy braced my arms. "You're okay. Relax. There aren't any pigs."

"I heard it."

"It's just the food cart."

"A trough. It's called a trough." The bird kept singing. "How did you get here?"

"Dr. Howell called me when she saw you in the ER."

The white rabbit climbed through the window and stopped by my bed. It plugged its ears with a stethoscope. "I didn't know you were a doctor." I tried to sit up, but Roy held me down.

The rabbit took something from the pocket of its coat. A coat, not fur. And the rabbit had the hands of a woman.

A light poked me in the eye.

"Hold still, Mr. Duvoe." She flashed one eye, then the next. "Now I'm going to ask you a few questions."

"Sure, but I didn't study for the test."

She glanced at Roy. "Do you know what day it is?"

"Friday. Went to the showing."

To Roy, the woman said, "It's okay. He's been out for a while. I didn't expect him to know. But he remembers where he was, and that's good." She looked at me. "Do you know your name?"

"Paris Duvoe."

"And what is it you do, Mr. Duvoe?"

"I paint terrible pictures, and people buy them."

"Do you know where you are?"

237

"No." I only knew it wasn't the rabbit hole. There was only darkness down there, no doctors, and no Roy.

"You're in a hospital. Do you remember how you got here?"

"No." I was going to fail this test.

"Do you remember anything before you blacked out?"

"There was a pig." A jumble of memories and tactile sensations made my head spin. "Not a pig. He just sounded like a pig. Julia told me to go home with him." I squinted at the doctor. "I know you. I met you at the café."

Dr. Howell smiled and patted my hand. "It's good you remember."

"Is he going to be okay?" Roy said.

The doctor stepped back. "We're going to run more tests. But I'm hopeful." She squeezed Roy's shoulder. "This was close, Roy. Talk to him. We can't help until he lets us."

She left.

The monotone chirp continued. "Can she take the bird with her?"

"Bird?"

I pointed in the direction of the sound.

"It's a heart monitor," Roy said.

"It's annoying."

He searched the machine and punched a button on the front. The chirping stopped.

"Better?"

"Yes."

"Here." Roy adjusted my pillows and pulled the blankets up to my ribs.

I touched his hand and played my fingertips over his knuckles, to the tip of his nails, and down each digit.

Roy's worried gaze squeezed my heart.

"I didn't mean…I'm sor…"

"It's okay."

"It will never be okay." Saying it made the truth even bigger than before. I tried to turn away, but he wouldn't let me.

"It will be okay, Paris. I promise."

"How?" I didn't expect him to have an answer. I think I even hoped he wouldn't. But I should have learned by then, there was nothing impossible in Roy's book.

He kept his promises.

Unlike me.

"Dr. Howell's colleague, Dr. Carmichael wants to meet with you."

"He's the shrink."

"Yeah."

Roy pushed my bangs back. "Will you talk to him?"

I fondled the sheets. Outside in the hall, another food cart passed by. But it didn't squeak.

"Paris?"

I swallowed against the lump in my throat. "How did I get here?"

"One of the nurses said you were dumped out of a car at the ER entrance. They didn't get a tag."

"Limo." I licked my lips, and they burned. "It was a limo."

Roy pulled over the roll-away table with a pitcher and stack of plastic cups. He poured a cup of water and held it up to me. I drank, washing the grit from my throat and soothing the burn in my stomach.

I didn't stop until it was empty.

"Do you want more?"

I had no idea.

Roy put the cup on the table. "Tell me if you do."

I nodded. For some reason, it was then I noticed the wrinkles in Roy's clothes, the spot of coffee on the edge of his T-shirt barely hidden by the vee of his flannel shirt. There were dark circles under Roy's eyes, and his hair stuck up on one side of his head.

"How long have you been here?"

Roy ran a hand over the bedrail. "It's not important."

"Tell me."

"Two, maybe three days."

"Are you sure it's not five or six?"

A smile pulled at his mouth, but it never formed.

Voices echoed from up the hall, someone laughed, an intercom buzzed, and a lady walked by the door crying. An older gentleman was with her. He draped his arm over her shoulders.

"I waited for you." There was the smallest waver in Roy's voice.

I never doubted he would.

"Why didn't you come?"

"Because I'm not good like you." I plucked at the blankets. "Does Julia know where I am?"

"No. Dr. Howell still has you listed as a John Doe. The police wanted her to call them as soon as you were awake."

"Police? Why did she call the police?"

"She had to turn in the rape kit."

"What?" I sat up, and he put a hand on my shoulder. "Rape kit?"

"It's okay. She pushed the tests through the lab, and everything came up negative. She put you on some drugs as a precaution, but she's sure everything will be okay."

"Of course everything will be okay. Julia requires a clean blood screening and condoms. I'm checked monthly, sometimes more."

"She can't have them all checked."

"She can, and she does."

"I wasn't tested, and we didn't use a condom. Whoever raped you didn't use one either."

I flopped back against the pillows. "I wasn't raped."

"You had injuries."

"He was a little stingy with lubricant. I knew what I was getting into. I did exactly what I was there to do."

"And what about me? What if I wasn't negative?" He rubbed his face and then ran his hand through his hair, making it stick up on that side too. "You'd think at my age I'd know better. It didn't even cross my mind until Dr. Howell said something. I know I'm not, but I had her run the tests anyhow."

"You were practically a virgin, Roy. You've only been with one other person, and you were married to her."

"It was still stupid of me."

I laughed, but the sound broke off, turning into a hissing cough.

Roy poured me another cup of water. "Here."

"I'm fine."

"Drink."

I glared at Roy while I buried another round of coughing into the back of my hand. He tried to put the cup in my free hand, and I slapped it away. Water splatted over the blankets and left dark splotches on his flannel shirt.

"I said I don't...don't want it."

"I'm only trying to help."

Rage shoved me into a sitting position. "I don't want your help, Roy. I don't want anyone's help." I clawed at the IVs in my arm. Roy grabbed me by my wrists. "I'm fucked. I will always be fucked." I kicked the bed rail and it dropped halfway.

"Stop."

"Why, because you say so?" I jerked, but he held on. "Let go of me."

"Never."

"Goddamn it. Let go of me."

"Please..."

I twisted one hand free and got a hold of the IV line again and snatched it out of my arm. A spurt of blood made red freckles on the white sheets. The line got tangled between us, and the pole toppled. Roy yelled to someone over his shoulder.

My strength left me as quick as it came, and all I could do was bash my head against the pillow.

"Don't, you'll hurt yourself."

"Has it ever occurred to you maybe I want to hurt?"

His expression crumpled.

"I'm tired of it, Roy. All of it. I want out. Forever. So for God's sake, please quit trying to save me and let me die." I think the words shocked me more than him. Mostly because it was the truth.

Footsteps slapped against the tile. To whoever it was coming through the door, Roy said, "We're okay."

Tears ran from the corners of my eyes, across my temples, and soaked my hair. I couldn't wipe my nose because Roy wouldn't let go. He kept his promises. He always kept his promises. And he deserved someone who would appreciate that.

I gritted my teeth in an attempt to hold back a sob. It didn't work, and once one was out, I was helpless against the rest.

"Shh—" Roy gathered me in his arms. "Shh—it's okay."

"No."

"It is."

"I can't do this anymore. I'm tired of fighting the monster. I'm tired of singing its lullaby. I'm tired of everything."

"I know, baby. I know."

"But I'm too scared to face it. I'm a coward."

"You're not."

"I am."

"No, Paris."

"It should have been me." I dug my fingers into the softness of his shirt. "But I was scared, and I hid."

"I know you did."

"You can't know. No one does. Julia won't let me tell them." I buried my face into Roy's neck, hoping it would block out the scent of sour earth.

"I know about the boy."

A cold wash of shame started from my head and bled to my toes. I couldn't stop shivering.

"I know you were afraid. I know you hid."

"How?" I lifted my head. There was nothing but kindness in his eyes. "How can you know?"

"Your paintings."

Because unlike anyone else, Roy saw what I hid behind colors and lines.

"I lied," I said.

"To who?"

"His mother."

"Of the boy?"

"Yes."

"Who was the man with the hammer?"

"I'm not supposed to tell."

"Was it your father?"

I shook my head, and then I nodded. Leaves and sticks crackled from somewhere behind me. I never even noticed Roy let me go long enough to lower the bed rail. He was just there, sitting on the bed, holding my hand, and petting my hair back from my eyes.

"Did Julia know what happened?"

I squeezed his hand so hard my fingers hurt.

"Did she?"

I closed my eyes.

"The Judas. That was her, wasn't it? Standing at the door."

"Yes."

"The Red Crucifixion. Who was the woman on the cross?"

"My mother."

"The innocent. That was you?"

"Yes." I wanted to look away, but I was pinned down by Roy's gaze and made helpless by his presence.

"The Crying Prophet?"

"My father."

"How old were you when he shot himself?"

"Nine. Ten. I'm not sure." All these years, I'd wanted people to see the truth hidden in my lie, and no one did. Now I wished Roy couldn't see either.

"You found him?"

"In my room. He shot himself in my room."

"The Love Letter?"

Tears bled out of my eyes. "My confession." Cold. I was so cold. "Because I couldn't tell anyone."

"But you did tell."

"Later. When it didn't matter anymore."

"And you still tell. In every painting you create, you tell the world what happened."

"No one hears me."

"I hear you."

"No one cares."

"I do."

"No one believes."

"I believe you. Every word."

His beautiful green eyes glowed against his toffee-colored skin. Eyes that saw. Eyes that didn't condemn. Eyes that found something inside me worth keeping.

Worth saving.

I put my lips close to Roy's ear. "Thank you."

****

Dressed in paper shoes, a hospital gown, and pushing an IV pole, I was a man taking his final walk to judgment.

243

My trembling and shortness of breath had nothing to do with needing a high and everything to do with fear. Pure fear. Raw fear. A swarm of angry rats working to destroy me.

"Are you sure you don't want me to get a wheelchair?" Roy put his arm around my back.

"No."

"This is crazy, making you walk to this man's office."

"Crazy, huh?" I laughed. "Have you stopped to look around and see where you are?" I told myself I'd die before I ever came back to a place like this. The only reason I hadn't thrown myself out a window was because this was just a detox wing and the windows wouldn't open.

My feet stopped moving a few yards from Dr. Carmichael's office.

"Paris." Roy stroked the back of my head.

"I'm okay."

"Let me take you back. He can just come to your room."

"No. I'm good. I am. I swear. Oh God, please don't let me puke or piss myself." I shook my head. "I did that once. Don't ever piss yourself, Roy. It chafes." I grabbed his arm because I was sure I would faint.

"Breathe. Just breathe."

"Easier said than done." I clung to him. "I think my balls are in the way."

"C'mon." He tried to turn me around.

"No. I have to."

"No, you don't."

"What if it's a test? What if I don't go and they lock me up? I can't get locked up again. I can't. I'll lose what little is left of my fucking mind."

"This isn't a test."

"You don't know how these psychiatrists think. They aren't normal. Hell, I don't even think they're human."

"I hate seeing you like this."

"This is nothing. Wait till the puking and pissing starts. I've already told you about that. Shit. I did. I forgot. Holy Christ on a popsicle stick, I can't shut up. Make me shut up, Roy, before the wrong thing falls out of my mouth."

I didn't expect him to kiss me. Right there in front of doctors, nurses, orderlies, and stoned out druggies sweating ten pounds of toxins a day.

The warmth of Roy's lips, the wet of his tongue, the softness of his touch on my cheeks while he cupped my face, it made everything disappear, if only for a second or two. The whole world ceased to exist.

He pulled away.

"I'm okay," I said.

He kissed me on the forehead.

"The mouth, Roy. The mouth. Kiss me on the forehead, and I'll cry."

He chuckled.

"Right. Twenty feet. I can walk twenty feet." I gripped his arm so tight there was no way I wouldn't leave bruises. "C'mon, Roy. Don't be a chicken shit."

Roy stayed by my side one painful step after another.

Dr. Carmichael's office had three large chairs and a love seat. He sat at a desk facing the wall and clutching a red ball in one hand.

Books lined the shelf in the back, and a variety of colorful trick toys cluttered his workspace. On the end table next to the love seat, there was a top hat with a stuffed white rabbit peeking over the edge.

I laughed, and I kept laughing. Even when I covered my mouth, I couldn't stop. Dr. Carmichael waved us in, and Roy led me to the couch. The rabbit watched me with glass button eyes, and the last of my laughter died out. I turned the hat upside down so I wouldn't have to look at it.

"Mr. Duvoe." Doctor Carmichael held out his hand.

"Just Paris."

"And Roy, good to see you again." Roy shook the doctor's hand, and it was like watching a boa swallow a mouse.

The doctor looked at me. "Would you feel more comfortable talking to me alone, or would you rather your friend stay?"

"Stay." I nodded. "Definitely stay."

Dr. Carmichael motioned for Roy to sit beside me.

"I wanted to thank you for trusting me enough to see me."

I clutched Roy's thigh with my un-IV'd hand. "I don't mean to sound...no. I mean it. I do. The only reason I'm here is because of

245

Roy. Thank him. Not me." I plucked at the hair on the back of my head. Roy made me stop by holding my hand.

Dr. Carmichael tossed the ball from one hand to the next. "I supposed you're feeling better after a few days rest?"

"Yeah. I think." I looked at Roy. "Am I?" He patted my hand. "Yeah, good. Great."

Carmichael stopped throwing the ball and propped his elbows on his knees. "If it's okay with you, I'd like to start with a few questions. Are you up for that?"

"Sure. I mean no." I rubbed my forehead. "I'm sorry. I just…" I rubbed my palm against the arm of the sofa.

"It's normal to be nervous."

I nodded.

"Just take your time."

I nodded again. Doctor Carmichael watched me, Roy watched me, the fucking toys in the room watched me. The rabbit in the hat didn't, but only because I'd turned it upside down.

"Go ahead. Ask your questions."

His chair squeaked as he sat up. "How many times a week would you say you use drugs?"

"I can't count that high."

"Try."

"Sometimes once a day, twice a day, five times. Fuck…"

"Is it just the heroin?"

"What? No. No. I only use that once or twice a year."

"A year?"

"Not my thing."

"Then why did you use it the other night?"

"It was there. I didn't want to be. I figured I might as well not remember it."

He squeezed the ball, and it collapsed in his hand only to spring back out when he relaxed his grip. "Would you like to try it?"

"What?"

He held out the ball. "Helps with stress."

"How?"

"Gives your hands something to do."

I stopped rubbing the arm of the sofa and took the ball. The rubbery foam squished between my fingers. "I'm not sure I'm doing this right." I squeezed it again.

"Why is that?"

"I don't feel any different." I tried to hand it back.

"Hang on to it for a little while."

I didn't know what good it would do.

"You said you didn't want to be there. Where was it you didn't want to be?"

"With him. Dan Brunswick. The guy who bought my painting."

"Why didn't you leave?"

"I couldn't. I mean…" I squeezed the ball hard enough to turn my knuckles bone white, and bits of red rubber pushed between the cracks of my fingers. "Julia told me to go home with him."

"Does she make you go with people a lot?"

"No. I usually take them home with me." I laughed. No one else did. I squeezed the ball. I couldn't stop squeezing it.

"Tell me about Julia."

"She's a bitch. The end."

He picked up a cube with multicolored squares on each side and twisted the sections up and down. There was a soft tick-tick as the mixed colors separated and the like colors gathered on opposing sides.

"Do you have any other family?"

"Alice. She's my other sister."

"What's she like?" Red, blue, green, white, yellow. The colors replaced him, the room, and Roy.

"She's fragile."

"What do you mean by that?"

"I broke her. Now she doesn't work very well."

"Do you care to explain?"

Explain what? How she'd been so destroyed by her father dying she didn't even cry? When she finally did cry, she didn't stop? Then there was the silence. Weeks of silence. She'd stare at me, watch me. Not in the same way her father did but with tremendous sadness. As if I'd torn open her chest and ripped out her soul.

"Next question. I don't like that one."

"How about we talk about your paintings?"

247

"Anything you want to know about those, you can read in an art magazine. Or watch that interview." I snapped my fingers. "What's his name? Rock. Allen Rock. Does he look as much like a Cheeto on TV as he does in real life? Someone should tell him to stop using spray paint and get a tanning bed."

"Sorry, I've never had the pleasure of seeing his program."

"Very prestigious. He's interviewed vice presidents and has the best sounding chairs ever." I slapped a hand over my mouth. "I'm sorry, I'm babbling."

"It's quite all right." Dr. Carmichael continued to twist the cube. "Will you tell me about your paintings?"

"What's to tell?"

"How do they make you feel?"

Round and round, colored squares went.

"Paris?" Carmichael leaned forward. "How does painting make you feel?" Green. Click.

Like the heavens were folding up, the sky was tearing apart, and the blood of every lost life stained my hands. "I hate them." I said.

"Why?" White. Click, click.

"They're terrible."

"The art community seems to think you're quite good." Red. Click, click, click. "I've seen your work myself, and I have to agree with them." Blue. Click, click, click, click, click.

"That's because they can't see." I met his gaze. "You can't see."

"Can't see what?"

"The truth."

Yellow. Carmichael put the cube on his desk, and everything returned. "What do you mean by the truth?"

I opened my mouth. *"You breathe one word, Paris, one word."* I closed it.

"Paris?"

"I'll make sure you rot in there. I'll make sure you never get out."

"Paris?"

"This is all your fault. You did this. If you hadn't been here, none of it would have ever happened. You ruined it. All of it. You're nothing but a filthy boy."

"What are you thinking about right now?"

My arm trembled, and the tendons in my wrist stood out. There was nothing left of the ball in my hand. I forced my fingers open, and it reappeared, whole and unscathed. "Can you ask a different question? I don't think I want to answer that one either."

Every word fell flat.

"Sure." Dr. Carmichael picked up a pen lying next to a set of chattering teeth on his desk and scribbled on a notepad. "Do you ever hear voices?"

"Pick it up, Paris. Now."

"It's too heavy."

"Quit whining and pick up the tarp."

"Sometimes."

"Do you see things?"

A withered leaf tumbled across the floor.

"Paris, do you see things?"

"Yes."

I wasn't sure if he heard me until he said, "What kind of things do you see?"

"Colors."

"What do you mean?"

"Lines of color, sprinkles, streaks, splatters, shapes."

"When do you see them?"

"All the time."

"Is there any particular time you see them more often?"

"When people talk."

"Are colors the only thing you see?"

Three more leaves followed the first.

"Paris?"

"Yes."

A wrinkle appeared over the doctor's eyebrows. "Are you sure?"

"Yes."

He didn't believe me. I could see it in his eyes. I waited for him to keep prying, but instead he said, "Roy said you've spent some time in a hospital before."

"Yeah. I have."

"Do you remember who you saw?"

"Dr. Harold Mason."

"Do you still see him?"

"Sometimes."

"Has he talked with you about medication?"

I pressed the squishy ball against my temple. "Yes."

"Are you taking any now?"

"Yes."

"Can you tell me what and how much?"

"Pink round ones when I'm tired. White ovals when everything is moving too fast."

"You don't remember the names?"

"He never tells me."

"What's written on the labels?"

"There aren't any."

The clock on the wall counted off the seconds.

Dr. Carmichael put the pen down and picked up the cube again. He switched it from one hand to the next like he'd done the ball.

"Dr. Howell thinks you might benefit by staying with me for a while. I want to know what you think."

"I have a doctor."

"Do you think he has your best interests at heart, or your sister's?" His eyes said he already knew the answer.

"Julia will never allow it."

"What if it was no longer her choice to make?" Something must have shown in my face because he smiled. "Would you be open to staying with me then?"

For the first time, I'd been given a door out of the darkness, and I was terrified to look on the other side. Until I remembered Roy held my hand, he would stay with me, and he cared.

"Yes," I said.

Roy gave me a cautious smile.

"But what's the catch?" There always was one.

"You have to stay here with me for a minimum of thirty days. Then, if you're ready, you can leave. After that, you will come to see me twice a week. You must stay on the medication I give you, and there will be no alcohol or drugs. You will be tested every time you step through my door. You fail, and you will wind up back at square one, which means another thirty days."

"I can do that. I can. I think I can do that."

For Roy, I would. Or die trying.

****

"I'm sorry." Roy put the pair of jeans he held in the duffle bag.

"Quit saying that. You have to go home sometime. You have a job, an apartment." *Please God, don't leave me here by myself.* I chewed my thumbnail until the quick bled.

Roy walked over and shielded me in his arms. "I'll come back."

I nodded. "You shouldn't. You're too good. You deserve good things." And I was anything but. "You should find yourself a cute little twink or maybe a bear. You'd go good with a bear." I laughed. "Settle down. Adopt some kids. Buy a dog."

"I'm coming back."

"Thirty days. Thirty days is a long time. Lots could happen. You could meet the twink or a bear."

"Paris."

"You could win the lottery."

"I don't play it."

"You should play it and get rich." I clung to Roy like some scared kid.

"I couldn't forget about you in thirty years, let alone thirty days." He kissed the top of my head.

"I'm a fucking mess, Roy. You don't deserve a fucking mess."

"Paris."

"Don't come back." A punch to the balls would have hurt less than saying that.

"I will."

"Maybe I don't want you to. Maybe I'm done."

Roy pulled my chin up and covered my mouth with his. I welcomed the invasion of his tongue and swallowed the growl he made.

He pressed his lips against mine until it hurt.

I hooked a leg around his hip and climbed up his body. He squeezed my ass with his powerful hands.

I broke the kiss to suck the soft spot near his pulse. Roy pushed my head back and attacked my neck.

With every rock of my hips, my cock ground against his stomach. Roy carried me across the room and pinned me against the wall.

"Paris." His voice, my name, his touch. I should have burst into flames.

"Want you." I clawed at his shirt, but it was trapped between us. "Please."

"I'm here." Roy pushed the hospital gown up and slid his hands over my skin.

"I need you inside me. I need to feel you."

"We can't."

"Yes."

"People."

"Don't care." The door was closed, the room was private, and to be honest, I didn't give a shit who saw us. I bit his ear.

"Fuck."

"That's exactly what I mean."

I latched onto his first two fingers and sucked them down my throat. If he wasn't going to do what I wanted, then I was going to make sure he knew what he was missing out on.

"Jesus Christ."

I teased his thick digits in the same way I had his cock. Roy pulled them out, and they left my swollen lips with a pop.

His weight against my body kept me from getting my hand between us. I scooted higher and used the tightness in an attempt to get some relief.

Roy pressed his wet fingers against my opening.

"Yes...oh God." He pushed in one finger, then two and pumped them in and out. "Like that, just like that." I found his mouth again but didn't so much kiss as taste his exhale. My hunger for him was a wicked viper. Its poison flowed through my veins, twisting my senses and saturating my muscles.

"You're so beautiful." Roy bit my nipple through the hospital gown. I cried out and grabbed his head. Not to push him away, but to hold him. To make him bite me again.

He did.

"Almost, almost there."

He pumped his fingers faster, and I rode against him, not caring his shirt chafed the head of my cock or that I crushed my balls with the force of my thrusts.

"Come for me, Paris."

My grunts became a wail. One more roll of my hips and I unloaded everything I had. It slicked up his shirt, and I kept humping him. The head of my cock became so sensitive it was more pain than pleasure, but I wasn't going to let go of the euphoria until every drop of cum was lost. If it had been possible, I would have stayed in that moment, drowning forever in absolute perfection.

The last electric wave receded, and I slumped in Roy's arms. He lowered me to the floor, and the sticky mess I'd left behind on his shirt smeared on my hospital gown.

Cradled against Roy's chest, I followed the beat of his heart back to the here and now.

"You'll come back?"

"Yes."

"You'll call me?"

"Every week."

"Why?"

He slid his hand down the side of my head and traced the shell of my ear with his thumb. "Haven't you figured it out yet?"

"No."

"Because that's what you do when you love someone."

"No one's ever loved me before."

"I know."

"What if I don't know how to give it back?"

"It's not hard, and you have plenty of time to learn."

I laughed. "I'm not exactly a model student."

"That's okay." He kissed the side of my head. "I'm a patient teacher."

****

Watching the elevator doors shut and Roy disappear had to be one of the most difficult moments of my life. When he was gone, the repercussions of what it meant to stay there crashed into me.

A dull shock traveled from where my knees hit the floor to my hips.

Dr. Carmichael knelt. His hand on my back warmed my frigid skin. "It's time for you to get ready so I can check you into your room."

I nodded, leaving streaks of tears on the tile.

He helped me to my feet. "C'mon, I have you some clean clothes so you can get rid of the gown."

When we reached my room, I said, "He's not coming back."

"Is that what he told you?"

"No."

"Then why would you say he's not coming back?"

"Because no one does."

He patted me on the shoulder. "Trust. It's an easy thing to break and almost impossible to rebuild. Trust him. If Roy told you he would come back, you have to trust he will."

I dressed in the thrift store hand-me-downs Carmichael gave me. The fabric was so worn it barely felt real against my skin. He'd even bought me a skull-cap and coat. I'd worn the best my entire life. Clothes hand-tailored in high priced specialty shops. My jeans never cost less than two hundred bucks, and I got a new Armani suit twice a year.

My shoes were made in Italy and my suits tailored. But out of all the thousands of dollars' worth of clothes in my closet, the simple patchwork garments given to me by Dr. Carmichael instantly became my favorite.

He waited for me in the hall.

"So now what?" I said.

"Now you come with me downstairs so I can get you checked in."

We walked to the elevator, and he pushed the button.

"And after I get checked in?"

"Well, I figured today you could look around. You know, survey the territory and meet some of the other staff."

The door opened. The rich earthy and cinnamon scent of Roy's cologne hung in the air. One inhale left my heart aching and my eyes burning. I started to follow Dr. Carmichael inside. The white rabbit sat beside his left foot. It stared at me with shoe button eyes.

"Paris?"

"Yeah?"

Dr. Carmichael caught the doors before they could close. "Is there a problem?" The rabbit cocked its head as if asking the same question. Carmichael looked down at the space beside his foot.

"I'd like to take the stairs," I said.

"It's four floors down."

"I need the exercise."

"The last thing you need right now is to exert yourself."

"I feel fine."

"Please, step into the elevator with me."

"The stairs would be safer."

The white rabbit cleaned its face.

"Why don't you want to use the elevator?" Carmichael had that "tell me all your woes" tone to his voice. I had enough of my wits to know to keep my mouth shut. Especially about the ball of white fur sitting on the ground staring up at me.

"I just don't like closed-in spaces." I took a breath and stepped inside, making as much room between me and the rabbit as an eight-by-eight box would allow. The doors slid shut, and that space shrank by tenfold.

"Have you always had a fear of small spaces?"

"Huh?" I glanced at him. "Oh. I don't know. Why?"

He dropped his gaze to the space beside his foot again. Carmichael said something, but my heartbeat pounded my eardrums so hard I couldn't hear him. The rabbit hopped closer. I didn't realize I'd thrown myself back until my head smacked the wall.

Carmichael grabbed my arm to keep me from falling. "What's wrong?"

"Nothing. Nothing." I struggled to get away from him because I needed more distance from the rabbit.

Carmichael shook me. "Look at me."

I couldn't take my eyes off the rabbit.

"Look at me, Paris." Carmichael gripped my head and made me. My eyes ached from rolling them down. Carmichael turned my head, and I lost sight of it.

I grabbed his wrists. "Let go." Where was it? I couldn't see it. And I had to see it.

"Not until you tell me what's going on."

I shifted back and forth on my feet. Was it close?

He shook me again. "Talk to me. This is what I'm here for."

The elevator doors opened, and I tore out of his grip and fell flat on my stomach in the hall. Being on the ground put me to close to the rabbit. But the elevator was empty except for a frustrated Carmichael.

"Paint," I said.

His eyebrows crunched together.

"Paint. I need to paint. You have an art room, right? All crazy places have an art room."

"We have a craft studio, sure."

"Take me there."

"Now?"

"Yes, now."

"Sure, we'll go as soon as we do the paperwork."

I slapped my palm against the floor. "No. I need to paint right now."

He held up his hands. "And I need to get you signed in."

"No. Now."

"The studio is inside the hospital ward. In order to go in, you have to be an employee or a patient."

I stood. "Then I'm leaving." I didn't really want to go back in there, but I needed to paint more than I wanted to escape Julia.

He held his arms out, blocking the elevator. "Remember our agreement. You walk out of here, and there is nothing I can do to help you."

"Move, goddamn it." I screamed loud enough to get the attention of an orderly. Carmichael met his gaze and shook his head.

"Think about your sister. You walk out, you give her control. If you want to be free, we need to do this. It's part of the process. I want to help you, but there are protocols we have to follow."

"How…" My voice cracked. "How long will it take?"

"Fifteen minutes tops."

I would make it five. "Fine."

He herded me down the hall with his arm behind my back, but not touching. A door at the end took a key card to open it. He scanned the one dangling from the lanyard around his neck. There was a buzz, and the door to a reinforced glass foyer opened. A nurse in a room on the other side of a second door cleared us for entry.

It closed behind us, and the lock chunked. My body trembled until my teeth chattered.

"It's okay," he said.

We went down another hall into the main ward. I readied myself for the smell of piss and cleaner, the screams, the curses, and patients begging for help or sitting on the floor drooling. Because it had been that way in Mason's facility.

Carmichael used his key card to open another door, and there was only silence. Not void of sound but free of the chaotic symphony I'd expected. Hotel-style rooms, with private bathrooms, were spaced wide from each other.

A couple of the patients waved to us as we passed. They were well groomed and wore regular clothes.

"I take it this wasn't what you expected?"

I shook my head.

"Are you still in a hurry to paint, or do you want to take a look around?"

"Paint."

"Okay. The office is this way."

A simple table and chairs occupied the office. The secretary was sealed inside a side room by a half glass, half steel door. She slid a clipboard full of papers through a slot and onto the small lip sticking out the front.

Carmichael picked it up and led me to the table. I grabbed the clipboard before my ass even hit the chair. "Pen." I snatched at the air.

"We need to talk first, and you need to read that."

I gripped the side of my head.

"Breathe."

I did. Several slow, long breaths.

"Tomorrow, a person from Adult Protective Services will come and see you."

"Why?"

"In order to keep your sister from removing you, there needs to be an investigation by APS of her alleged treatment of you."

That didn't sound so bad. "Okay."

"After they decide it is in your best interest to be removed from her charge, the state will appoint a guardian who will work on your behalf."

"What if she finds me before all that can be done?"

"She won't."

"How do you know?"

He sat back and drummed his fingers on the table. His gaze slid to the secretary's office, then back. "I already started the proceedings when Roy told me what was happening. The hospital took photos of your injuries when they did the rape kit."

"I wasn't raped."

"She told you to go home with him."

"I go home with a lot of men. I enjoy sex. A lot."

"Yes, but because she told you to do it and has control over you medically and financially, that constitutes as abuse. It's ammunition. With the authorities involved, we can keep your location hidden until ordered by the court to tell her where you are."

It sounded good in theory. In reality, I don't think I cared either way. I was done caring a long time ago.

"I need a pen."

"Read the paperwork."

I forced myself to look down at the documents. I read what I could. Some of the words I'd never seen before. Others were probably ordinary, but the spelling prevented me from sounding them out.

"Do you understand what you're reading?"

I gripped the clipboard so hard my knuckles bleached out. "I didn't finish high school. And when I did go, I wasn't a very good student."

"Would you like me to read it to you?"

No. I wanted to paint. But Carmichael was trying to help me. He was on my side. I handed him the clipboard.

So much for five minutes or even fifteen. Between him reading and telling me what the legal words meant, it was almost an hour. When he was done, he handed the clipboard back to me with a pen.

I signed my name so fast I ripped the paper. Carmichael smoothed out the tear and took everything back to the secretary.

The white rabbit sat on the chair beside me. It raised up on his hind legs and sniffed the air. "More time. Need more time." I swallowed against the burn in my throat.

"You ready?" Carmichael said.

It hopped down on the floor and disappeared under the table. I stood so quick my chair went back. The doctor caught it before it hit the floor. "Take me somewhere I can paint."

Carmichael led me to a large room down a different hall. The buttery scent of glue hung in the air, and a variety of crafty disasters decorated the shelves.

Who was I to judge? I tried to build a birdhouse once. It needed to be condemned halfway through the project.

I made a beeline to the row of paint jars in the back. Acrylics. I hated acrylics. The colors never mixed well. but it was either them or nothing.

I looked around. "Canvas?"

Carmichael unwound a sheet from a large roll of paper. I hated paper too. "Bigger." When it reached about six feet long, I nodded. The drawing boards on the easels were too small.

"What about the wall?" he said.

It would work. "Tape," I said. He already had it in hand.

I grabbed the paint and went for a brush from one of the coffee cans. The white rabbit sat on the shelf between them.

Fuck it. I'd use my fingers.

I attacked the paper, working my hand like I did the most expensive brush. The images, the broken swatches of color poured from me in a mad rush to be expelled. Using substandard acrylic paint, I vomited everything in my mind on the crappy newsprint. I didn't have to look to know the rabbit watched. I could feel it. And it wouldn't leave until I'd purged everything boiling inside me the only way I knew how.

By painting.

Sweat plastered my hair to my face. My feet hurt. My back cramped. I was hungry and thirsty. I even had to piss. I knew all these things, and yet I felt none of it. They were inconveniences I could deny myself. *Had* to deny myself. So I did.

Along with the memories and images I trapped in a multicolored collage was my strength. I didn't know where the chair came from, but there it was, so I sat.

Around me, soft voices passed words back and forth. A small crowd of nurses and orderlies stood near the door.

Carmichael put a hand on my shoulder. "Feel better?"

My mouth was so dry I could only nod.

"You ready to get dinner now?"

We hadn't even had lunch.

The sky beyond the mesh-covered window bled purples and blues. I never got used to losing hours. The extent of my exhaustion meant the painting could only hold horrid things.

"It's beautiful work." I didn't see which of the women said it, but compliments were never a good sign either.

Then the picture called to me. I lifted my gaze.

Screaming faces surrounded a naked man held to the floor by a chain around his neck. He couldn't defend himself from the crows picking the flesh from his ribs. His insides gleamed crimson against the white of bone. He didn't need a voice for me to know what he wanted to say. His pain-filled eyes spoke for him.

"Why? Why have you put me here? Why must I suffer on your behalf?"

"Because I'm afraid to do it alone."

Dr. Carmichael leaned down. "Did you say something?"

I shook my head.

"Well, c'mon then. Let's go get you cleaned up and something to eat."

Paint covered the Goodwill clothes, and my hands were wrapped in layers of color all the way to my elbows.

He helped me up. "Eat first." I wasn't sure if he could hear me through the grit clogging my throat.

"Okay, we'll eat."

A woman stopped us on the way out. "What should we do with the painting, Mr. Duvoe?" Her gaze flicked to the horror show on the wall, and her expression transformed into the same kind of hungry mask my sister wore when she saw a profit, but here I was free to decide the fate of the man in the painting. I could choose to condemn him or set him free.

I had to swallow several times to get some of my voice back. To the woman, I said, "Burn it."

Her eyes widened. "Doctor?"

"Do as he says. Dispose of it."

Carmichael led me out.

****

"I'm sorry about the clothes." I truly was. But even covered in paint, I liked them. Maybe even more.

"I have three more pairs of pants and a few shirts in your room." He laughed. "Don't look so surprised. You didn't exactly have time to pack. I know they aren't as nice as what you're used to, but they'll cover you up."

"I like them." He arched an eyebrow. "I do. They're comfortable, soft, and…" They reminded me of Roy because they were the kind of things he would wear.

"And what?"

"Nothing." I picked up my plate. The dining room was empty except for us, and I couldn't find a bin to drop the plate in. "Where do you want this?"

"You only ate half your sandwich."

"I drank the orange juice."

"Sit and eat."

I sat and picked at the bread.

Carmichael folded his hands on the table and watched me.

I rolled up tiny dough balls. Sometimes I ate them, and other times I flicked them around my plate. He kept staring. When I couldn't stand it anymore, I said, "What?"

"Would you mind telling me why it was so important for you to paint?"

I made an attempt to pick at the hair on the back of my head.

"Paris?"

"You've followed me around all day. Don't you need to go see your other patients?"

"There are other doctors, and right now, you're my priority."

I'd decimated the top piece of bread so I started on the meat and cheese. The cheese made better balls than the bread. "Then don't you have to go home?"

"I will."

"When?"

"Tell me about the painting."

I bounced my leg.

"Paris?"

I stuffed the rest of the sandwich in my mouth. But like the white rabbit, Carmichael wasn't going to quit.

I swallowed and said, "Do you think you can show me my room? I'm really tired."

"I'd really like to talk about this first." He sat back.

"And I'd really like to lay down."

"Okay. But tomorrow, I want you to tell me about the painting. Does that sound fair?"

"Sure." It would never happen.

Carmichael took me to room 12 A. Inside, there was a bed, a small TV, a dresser and a lamp. The walls were sandy brown and the floor gray.

"Kind of empty," I said.

"You're welcome to decorate."

"I hope I'm not here long enough to need to."

"Good. I like to hear that." He clapped me on the shoulder. "I just keep amazing you at every turn, don't I?"

"I thought you'd want me to stay."

"Why?"

"It's how you get paid, isn't it?"

"Sure. But if you have to stay, then I'm not doing my job right."

I'd never thought of it like that.

I touched the keyhole in the doorknob.

"You're free to come and go as you want. You're not a prisoner."

"What about all the other doors?"

"That's for your safety as much as anyone else's."

"So you do lock people up."

"Only if I have to."

"When do you have to?"

"If they are a danger to themselves or others."

"Does that happen often?"

"Thankfully, no. I keep the patient numbers here low. I want people to get treatment, not be wheeled in, drugged, and wheeled out." He clapped me on the shoulder again. "Breakfast starts at six and goes till nine. I'd like to see you in my office at twelve. Room 231. Straight down this hall." He pointed. "And take a left. It's the fourth door on the right." He started to leave. "Oh, the nurse will be by later to bring you some meds."

"Why?"

"It's part of the treatment."

"Uppers? Downers? What?"

"I'm going to put you on mood stabilizers."

"What does that mean?"

"Hopefully, it means your extreme mood swings will lessen."

The sheets on the bed were white and the comforter dark brown. I counted the wrinkles in the pillow.

"Are there any questions you'd like to ask me?" he said.

"Do you know what's wrong with me?"

"I have some ideas, but I'll need to talk to you a bit more, run some tests, that sort of thing before I can say for sure."

I nodded at the phone sitting on the bedside table. "Roy said he would call. He doesn't know my room number."

"All calls go through the front desk. The nurses know what room you're in, and they'll transfer the call."

"What if I'm not here?"

"Then she'll page you."

I rubbed the back of my neck, inching closer to my hair. I stopped myself. "Do you think he will?"

"Call you?"

"Yeah."

"Trust, Paris. Trust that he will."

I wasn't sure I knew how.

Chapter Twelve

There were even more outrageous toys and gadgets in
Carmichael's office inside the loony ward. All colors, all sizes, some
old, some new, brightly colored and often annoying to the point of
offensiveness.

Oh, the degree of torment I could inflict on Julia with them.

"What's so funny?" Carmichael said.

"Just thinking."

He gestured to the fat chair in the corner.

"You look like you feel better today?"

I picked up a floppy hippo draped over one arm and sat. The
legs whacked together when I shook it. "I guess I was tired yesterday."

"After painting for six hours straight, I can see why." He
steepled his fingers against his lips and rested his elbows on the arms of
the chair. "Are you—"

"Why toys?" I held up the hippo. I used it to point at the
shelves and his desk. It was about as effective as a wet noodle. "I see
you as more of an antique kind of guy."

"I have an impressive collection of matchbox cars going back
to the fifties. Does that count?"

I strangled the hippo. "Not really."

Carmichael scanned the room as if he'd forgotten what he had.
There was a lot so it was possible. "I'd like to believe we never truly
grow up. That some part of us always remains the happy innocent child
who enjoyed games like cowboys and space invaders."

His gaze came back around, and I waited for him to ask about
the painting.

Instead, he said, "What kind of games did you play as a kid?"

"I don't remember." I put the hippo back on the arm of the
chair.

"There has to be something."

"Not really. I stayed in my room a lot. I painted mostly."

"So your favorite toys were art supplies?"

"Sure." I searched for something else to play with. Carmichael
handed me a Slinky. "Alice had one of these." I tossed it hand to hand.
The spring gave a metallic sigh with each shift.

"You never had one?"

"Nah."

"You didn't want one?"

I did. I was so jealous of Alice I wadded hers up into a springy mess when she wasn't looking. "They're kind of boring." I held it out, and Carmichael slowly took it from my hand as if he was trying to communicate something to me by how he plucked it from my grip. He returned the Slinky to its space on the desk.

"So." I bounced a leg. "What do you want to talk about?"

"What would you like to talk about?"

I dropped my head back. "I hate it when people answer a question with a question."

"Fair enough. When we did your paperwork, I noticed you put deceased for your mother."

I sank in my seat. "Yeah."

"How old were you when she died?"

"Five, I think." I counted off the years. "No, six. I think I was six."

"Would you mind telling me how you lost her?"

"You're a disease, Paris."

"Cancer."

"Was she sick a long time?"

"I'm not sure. I don't think so."

"What was she like?"

For a moment, I was wrapped in warmth. "She was the only person who ever loved me." The pain that came with those words left me gasping.

"Were your sisters close to their mother?"

"I don't know."

Doctor Carmichael tipped his head.

"My father married my mother after Julia and Alice's mother died."

"I see. How old were they when he married your mother?"

"I think Julia was twelve and Alice was about seven or eight. I'm not sure."

"And how long was he married to your mother before you were born?"

I ran a hand over my head. "A year, maybe? Two?"

"Do you have any other family?"

"What do you mean?"

"Grandparents, cousins, aunts, uncles?"

"I…" Did I? "I'm not sure."

"You've never had any extended family come and visit?"

I rubbed my temple. "I…no. No, I don't think so."

"No one at all?"

"He didn't like visitors."

"Who?"

Somewhere a door slammed. Was it now or then?

"Paris?"

"Harrison." Shards of time ticked against the floor. Seconds I'd misplaced. Minutes I'd forgotten. Hours I'd never acknowledged.

Where had they been?

"Your father?"

"He didn't want to be. Harrison was Julia and Alice's father, but never really mine."

"Why do you say that?"

"He hated me."

"Hate is an awfully strong word." Dr. Carmichael pulled at the Slinky, then let it fall back into place. Again. Again. Again.

"Not strong enough." Whatever the man felt toward me had been powerful enough to cause my heart to race. He'd watch me. Follow my movements. He'd loom in the corners as if waiting for something.

"And Harrison didn't like visitors?"

"No."

"So you never had family visit or friends come over?"

"¿Cómo te llamas?"

He came from the small stretch of woods separating us from the neighbors. I stood under a tree hitting the leaves with a stick. The ones weakened by the coming fall fluttered to the ground in flashes of yellow.

He wore a red shirt and brown shorts. His eyes and hair were dark, his skin some shade close to caramel. He smiled, and I'd never seen anything so wondrous.

How many days did we play together in those weeks where summer ended and fall was close to being born? How many times did

266

he hold my hand before that day? That terrible, terrible day when the sun went behind the clouds and never came out again?

The day when the mud soaked my socks and swallowed my shoes. When the blisters burst on my hands and no matter how hard I tried I couldn't dig the hole deep enough.

The dirt stained my skin. Grit clogged my nails. The smell of sour ground saturated the air.

"Paris?"

I blinked, and it was gone.

"Where did you go?"

"I haven't moved."

"Up here." He tapped his temple. "You went somewhere. Where?"

"Nowhere."

"What were you thinking about?"

"Nothing." A bead of sweat ran down my neck.

"Paris." The very sound of my name from his lips plucked at my will.

I picked up the popup book on the end table. "How long have you collected toys?" I opened the book, and a smiling fat bear unfolded from the page.

Dr. Carmichael watched me while I tugged at a tab to make the bear dance.

"Thirty years, give or take."

The next page had a tiger. I looked at the cover. "Day at the Zoo." Made sense.

"Tell me about what happened at the pawn shop."

"What do you want to know?"

"Was it the first time you ever got angry like that?"

"No." Three monkeys were on the next page, then an elephant.

"Do you remember the first episode of anger you experienced?"

I could never forget. I closed the book and petted the front.

"Paris?"

I nodded.

"What happened?"

"The cat."

"What about the cat?"

"There was this cat hanging around the school. Everyone petted it. I used to feed it some of my lunch. We all did."

"How old were you?"

"Thirteen. I think."

"What happened?"

The high-pitched scream of little girls made me jump. But there were no panicked children in Carmichael's office. Just him. Just me. And lots of toys.

"One day at lunch, we were sitting around outside. I was drawing, and some girls were playing with the cat, teasing it with a long piece of hay. Stupid cat would chase it for hours. It would bite your toes too. If you wore sandals. Not to be mean but, you know, just being a cat.

"A guy from a few grades ahead of me walked over." I popped my fingers by forcing them one at a time to my palm with my thumb. "He killed the cat."

"How?"

The crunch was close to my ear. I wiped my cheek, but there was no blood on my fingers.

"Tell me how he killed the cat."

"He stomped it. One minute, the cat was playing, the next...the blood sprayed. All over. And it shit itself." *The group of girls scrambled to their feet. Tears streamed down their faces. Their screams echoed off the side of the building. The boy laughed. He kept laughing.*

When I swallowed, I tasted pennies.

Carmichael snapped his fingers in front of my face. His gaze fell to my arm. Red welts covered my skin and ended where I'd buried my fingernails into the back of my wrist.

I let go. "Sorry."

"It's okay."

I nodded. "What was I saying?"

"The cat."

"Yeah. He killed it. That boy. And I got angry." I flexed my fingers.

"How angry?"

"Angry enough."

"And how angry is 'angry enough'?"

I flexed my hand again. My knuckles ached.

Sounds from outside and the tick of the clock haunted the dead air between us. Doctor Carmichael watched me again, but the expression on his face had changed. I couldn't read it.

"Tell me. How angry is angry enough?"

"They said I stabbed him over twenty times with a colored pencil. I think I would have kept stabbing him if it hadn't broken off." Unlike the screaming girls and the dead cat, the memory of that bleeding kid did not flicker in my mind. The only thing I ever saw was a blank spot. A solid slate of nothing.

"Where do you think all that anger comes from?"

From the well where it lived in the blackness, stinking of rot. Its cold breath left moisture clinging to my skin.

I met his gaze. "I'm sorry, what was the question?"

"When you get angry. Where does it come from?" There was knowledge in his eyes, but there was no way he could know.

I walked to a shelf cluttered with a variety of tin toys. I touched the metal horse, and it rolled an inch. "These look old."

"They're from the twenties."

"Are they hard to find?"

"They used to be. Now there's eBay."

I picked up a circus bear. A key stuck out the side. I turned it, and the bear's spring-loaded legs popped.

"That will work better on the coffee table."

I put it down beside a magazine. The bear flipped a half dozen times before stopping. I put it back on the shelf.

"I'd like for you to answer my question," he said.

"I can't." I found a chicken. When I pressed it down, little plastic eggs shot out of its ass. I laughed.

"Why not?"

"I don't know."

"I think you do."

I counted twenty-eight metal toys. I walked over to count the various action figures on a different shelf.

"What about these?" I picked up a GI Joe.

"Sit, Paris."

"And these?" I picked up a red figurine. "Power Rangers, huh?" I snorted. "I remember that show when I was little. Alice loved it."

"Paris."

I picked up another toy without looking at it.

"Paris."

And another.

"Paris."

Yet again.

I didn't notice Carmichael had stood until he took the toy from my hand. He pointed to the chair. "Sit."

"I'm not a dog."

"No, you're not. But you're here to talk."

I went back to my seat.

"Now answer my question. Where does the anger come from?"

I leaned forward. I leaned back. The cotton shirt I wore turned into sandpaper. I pulled at the collar, trying to loosen it. "Nowhere."

"Anger strong enough to make you stab a boy over twenty times has to have a source."

"Then I don't remember."

"I think you do. I think you know exactly why you're angry."

"I. Don't. Remember."

Dr. Carmichael raised an eyebrow. "All right. Then tell me about the painting."

I stared at my feet.

"If you're not going to tell me where the anger comes from, then I want you to tell me about the painting."

"It's a painting."

"That you had to paint, right then. Why?"

"I felt like it."

"What I saw yesterday was not a man who felt like painting. It was a man who didn't have the choice not to. I want to know why."

"And I told you I don't know."

"We talk about the anger or the painting, Paris, your choice."

"There's nothing to talk about."

"The anger or the painting."

"I don't have an answer." I plucked at the hair on the side of my head.

"The anger or the painting. Tell me."

"I don't know."

"The anger or the painting. Decide."

I pressed my palms against the stabbing bolt piercing my temples. "And I told you I don't know."

"Either the anger or the painting."

"For God's sake, stop before you wake it up." I slapped my hand over my mouth.

Dr. Carmichael knelt in front of me. "Wake what up?"

The shaking started in my knees and ran to my shoulders. Dr. Carmichael held my wrist. There were short black hairs pinched between my fingers.

"Tell me what you're afraid of."

I leaned closer and so did he. "The monster." The words rolled from my lips on a trembling breath.

"Where did it come from?"

"The well. I think." His sandalwood cologne battled with the memory of wet earth.

"Why is it in the well?"

My bottom lip trembled. I had to bite it to make it stop. "I can't tell you."

"Yes, you can."

I shook my head.

"Yes, you can." There were flecks of brown in the gray of his eyes. "Whatever you say is between you and me." And a scar over the bridge of his nose. "No one will ever know unless you tell me it's okay to tell them."

I shook my head again. "I can't. I can't tell."

"Why not?"

"It's a secret."

"Paris. I want to help you. You know that, right?"

I nodded.

"Then you have to trust me to do what's right for you. And right now, what's right is for you to tell me the secret."

"Why?"

"Because I think it's why you're angry. I think it's why there's a monster. And I think it's why you paint."

It was there, my confession. The truth to my lie. It perched on my tongue waiting to be freed. All I had to do was open my mouth. Breathe the words. He was close enough he'd hear even the softest whisper. And maybe if I said it quietly enough, no one would ever know.

I tilted my head closer to his ear, and Dr. Carmichael shifted his weight to the left. Over his shoulder, on his chair, sat the white rabbit. Shoe button eyes watched me above a twitching nose.

"I need to go." I pulled, but he held on.

Dr. Carmichael glanced over his shoulder. "What are you looking at?"

"Nothing, goddamn it. Now leave me the fuck alone." The rabbit rose up on its hind legs to sniff the air. I shoved Dr. Carmichael back, and he hit the floor. I ran from his office and down the hall. Tiny paws padded against the floor at my heels. I didn't so much hear it, as I felt it.

There were a few other people in the art room. I shoved a woman out of my path to the roll of newsprint. There were pictures on the wall today. I snatched them off.

"Hey, those belong to people."

I whirled on the black man, and he recoiled. An old woman had the tray of paint. I took it.

"Paris." Carmichael came into the room.

I smeared a streak of blue on the paper. Then yellow. Then red. Then green.

Dr. Carmichael tried to grab my arm and earned a streak of orange across his face.

The white rabbit stared up at me from the floor. "I'm doing it as fast as I can."

Its eyes begged me to hurry.

"This is your mess."

"I'm sorry."

"Here, dig."

"The ground's too hard."

"You're useless, Paris, useless. C'mon."

"Where are we going?"

"Since you can't dig a proper hole, we'll have to do something else."

"What?"

"Be quiet and pick it up."

The white rabbit's head bobbed with the ragged motions of my hand as I drew line after line, cutting through the negative space until it was butchered and broken. I dove into the horizon, shadowed the depths, and fed light to the foreground.

Sweat dripped into my eyes and was lost to the tears. My heart raced until it bruised my ribs. I sucked in air as fast as I exhaled it, and I painted until the muscles in my arms melted. I couldn't quit. If I did, it would wake up.

As the newsprint filled, the tension boiling inside me dropped to a simmer, and the fear faded back into the shadows. I collapsed. Only my shoulder against the wall kept me from falling over.

From far away, someone said my name. A hand under my chin tilted up my face.

"Can you hear me?"

I squinted at the man in front of me, and the features of his face fell together. "Yeah."

"Can you stand?"

The lead in my veins made it impossible for me to get to my knees. Dr. Carmichael patted me on the shoulder. "Don't worry, Oscar will help you."

I didn't know who Oscar was. Dr. Carmichael took one of my arms and Oscar the other. His hands were bigger than Roy's. Together they pulled me to my feet. "Take Paris to his room. I'll be there in a minute."

Oscar led me to the door. "Wait." I struggled. "Wait, I have to see it."

"The painting?" His voice was deeper than Roy's too, but it didn't touch me in the same way.

"Yes." Oscar held me while I trudged up the courage to raise my gaze.

He was skin and bones lying among a cornucopia of food. He ate, but it fell out the hole in his throat. He pleaded for a meal, just one meal, just one glass of water. The people around him ignored his cries so he turned to me.

I looked away. "The Glutton."

"What?" Oscar said.

"The name of the painting. It's called The Glutton."

Oscar glanced back at the sheet of paint-covered newsprint hanging on the wall. "C'mon. Let's do what the doc said and get you back to your room."

At some point, I passed out and he carried me.

Chapter Thirteen

The phone in my room rang. I'd stared at the thing all day, willing it to do something even if all it did was melt into a puddle on the floor. Now that it had, I had to force myself to answer.

"Hello?" Roy said.

My exhale echoed over the receiver.

"Paris, are you there?"

God, his voice. It shimmied down my skin and settled between my legs. "Yes."

"Are you okay?"

My entire body ached for him. "I'm fine, just don't stop talking."

"What?"

I swallowed the taste of his cum on my tongue. "Talk to me. Tell me the weather forecast, anything."

"Are you sure you're okay?"

"Yes. Just don't stop talking. I need to hear your voice."

"Don't you think I want to hear your voice too?"

I smiled and wished he could see it. Because it wasn't fake, and he was the only one I let see my real ones.

"How are things going with the..."

"Therapy?"

"Yeah."

"I talk to him. That's what I'm supposed to do, right?"

"What about the meds? Are you taking them?"

"Yes."

"You're not spitting them out in the toilet?"

"I promise."

"Good. I want you to get better."

I did too. "What if... what if I can't?"

"Get better?"

"I'm a thousand pieces of broken colored glass. You throw something like that away. Doing anything else is a waste of time."

"It won't matter."

"Yes, it will."

"Tell me why?"

"Because..." *How could he ever love me if I couldn't be fixed?*

"Paris?"

I cleared my throat and scrubbed away the tear making an escape down my cheek. "I'm here."

"I'll still love you. Remember that."

"But you deserve...someone normal."

"I only want you."

I didn't bother to wipe away the second tear. "Thank you."

"For what?"

"Not giving up on me."

"Never."

"I miss you." I inhaled a watery breath.

"I miss you too."

"And I'm horny all the time."

"What did you just say?"

I laughed. "I said I'm horny. All I can think about is you, and then your clothes fall off."

Roy was the one who laughed this time. "I thought that only happens when you drink tequila?"

"The rules don't apply to you, I guess. They never apply to you." I hugged the phone closer, wishing for the warmth of his skin, the spice of his scent, the taste of his lips. "I'm never going to survive this."

He shushed me. "Of course, you will."

"It's only been a few days, and it feels like years. By the time thirty days is up, I'll be old and gray and crippled and..."

"You'll be fine."

"I'm not so sure."

"You have to." He sighed, and my heart skipped. "For me."

"Okay. I will. I promise." I hoped to God I would not let him down.

"Are you alone?"

"What? Why?"

"Are you alone?"

"Yeah, sure. I'm in my room. It's private."

"Shut the door."

"Wha—"

"Shut the door." He all but growled the command.

I carried the phone with me and did as Roy asked. "Why did you want me to shut the door?"

"Now get on the bed."

"Roy?"

"No questions. Just get on the bed. But strip, first."

"Are you trying to have phone sex with me?"

"Don't ruin the moment, or I'll hang up."

"Don't you dare." My cock stiffened before I could get back on the bed.

"Are you lying down?"

I stroked myself. "Yes."

"Get your hand off your dick." This time, he did growl, and I almost came from the sound.

"God." The heat of needing him rushed under my skin, and I panted.

"Don't worry, I'll get to that, but first, I want you to wet your fingers."

I stuck them in my mouth.

"Don't take them out yet. I want to hear you suck them. I want you to convince me it's my cock in your mouth."

I groaned.

"That's right, baby. All the way to the back of your throat, then back to your lips."

My fingers made a wet sound as I sucked them. The burn of desire condensed into a weight in my gut, making my balls ache. I undulated against the bed, and my weeping cock slapped my stomach. I could almost feel him. Stretching me, filling me. But my imagination would only get me so far. I whimpered around my fingers.

"Now," Roy said. "Pinch your nipples."

I dragged my fingers down my chin, leaving a wet line all the way to my chest.

"Hard. The way you like it."

The electric bite made my breath erupt. I twisted the tight bud of flesh until tears pooled in the corners of my eyes.

"That's it." He grunted. "I can see you now. Lips swollen, face flushed, how much you want me inside you painted on your beautiful face."

"Roy…"

"I'm not done with you yet."

"You've got your hand on your cock, don't you?"

"Yeah."

"I want to taste you. I want you to pull my hair and fuck my mouth. I want you to come, and I want to drink you down."

"You will. When I get my hands on you, you're going to do all those things and more."

"Can't…" A prickling sensation shot through me. "Wait." My jaw ached from the memory of his girth forcing my mouth wide.

"Now, tug your balls. Just like I do when I touch you there."

I did. Slowly pulling each of them until the barest spike of pain traveled to the center of my body. I gasped and scissored my legs, bunching the covers around my ankles.

"Tell me what it feels like," Roy said.

"Good."

"Not just good. I want to feel what you feel. Convince me it's my hand between your legs."

"Heavy. Both sacks are heavy and the skin like silk." God, I don't think I'd ever ached this badly for release. "Hairs are thinner here. When they're pulled, the flesh dimples." I plucked at a few and gasped. "Hurts and feels good." I took both balls in my palm and squeezed hard enough to make me cry out. "Oh God, that…"

"Feel, Paris. I want to know what it feels like."

I was out of words to describe the sensations or maybe my mind was too far gone. "Yellow and orange. Jagged lines broken, patterns with sharp edges, and detailed lines splitting the negative space." I slammed my head against the pillow. "Please don't make me wait."

"Soon." His inhale stuttered. "God, Paris, I can feel your mouth on me, your tongue and how you rake your teeth around the head of my dick."

I tugged my sacks harder. I would never come like this, and the urge already surpassed the waves of green and into blood red.

"Hand on your cock, Paris."

The skin to skin contact seared my flesh, and I bit back my yell.

"Stroke, hard, fast, and don't leave out a single detail."

"Bright red beside violent green. It..." I gasped. "It hurts to look at it, but the contrast is too beautiful to look away. Purple curls around white and silver covering my bones. I burn like crimson. The colors fill me. You fill me. Your hand on my cock, velvet and stone. God, I'm so hard, Roy. Grays divide the blues, and the blues divide the yellow. But it's breaking apart."

"Come for me, Paris."

A terrifying keen tore from my throat. My cock pulsed, and strings of cum stretched from my stomach to my neck.

From the other end of the line, Roy barked out in that deep guttural way, making me think of the rolling thunder only found in summer storms. He followed up with a soft moan and broken gasps.

I collapsed against the mattress.

"Feel better?"

I nodded and then remembered he wasn't there to see it. "Yeah."

"Good. Never forget, Paris. I love you."

"I won't." I was sure any moment I would float away.

"I have to go now. But I'll call you again soon."

The door to my room burst open, and two orderlies stopped dead in their tracks. Their gaze went from my face to my cock in my hand.

"Yeah," I said. "I gotta go too."

****

There was a Chinese woman in Dr. Carmichael's office when I arrived. She was petite, with simple features, but the air about her vibrated with streaks of violent oranges and yellows.

I'd never considered bringing a woman to my bed before. This lady actually put the thought in my mind.

"Paris, this is Carla Chang, she's your new advocate."

Mrs. Chang switched the clipboard to her other hand and offered it to me. I had the strangest compulsion to kiss the back. After all, wasn't that what you did in the presence of royalty? We shook, and I sat on the cushy chair. She sat in Carmichael's. He propped a hip on his desk.

"Do you know what an advocate is, Mr. Duvoe?"

"Just Paris, please. And no. Not really."

279

"An advocate is someone who will speak in court on your behalf to give the judge information that will help him make an informed decision."

"Sounds like a lawyer."

"No, sir. Nothing of the sort. Advocates are more often used in child abuse cases. But on occasion, we do take cases with Adult Protective Services, especially when the individual has been deemed incompetent by the state and the source of the abuse is believed to be the acting guardian."

Incompetent. I'd never taken into consideration Julia's guardianship was based on that word. It made sense, though. It also made me wonder if I was truly able to refute it.

"I'm not sure I can pay you. Julia controls the money."

She smiled. Her features might have been simple, but like her presence, her smile was blinding. "Don't worry. I'm a volunteer. As for your money, securing what is yours is my second priority."

"What's your first?"

"Making sure you're safe."

I believed her too. I could honestly see this woman dropkicking Julia in the street. I stared at my worn-out boat shoes because I didn't know what to say. All this sudden concern for my well-being was kind of scary.

"If you don't mind, I'd like to ask you a few questions."

I nodded. "Sure."

"Has your sister ever hit you?"

"Only when I say the word vagina."

Mrs. Chang raised her eyebrows.

"Yes. Sometimes."

"And from what I understand, she forces you to have sex with other men for money."

I held Dr. Carmichael's gaze when I said, "I enjoy sex. A lot."

"But she makes you go home with certain people."

"If you're asking me if she puts a gun to my head, no."

"So you can refuse if you want to?"

I crossed my arms and bounced my leg.

"Paris?" She tried to catch my gaze.

I looked away.

"Does Julia give you drugs?"

"Sometimes."

"What kind?"

"X, uppers, downers, I don't know."

"And does the money from your estate all come from your paintings?"

"Just some. My mother had a list of stocks, bonds, and land when she died. I never got to see what all was there."

"Why not?"

I gave her a crooked smile. "Like you said, incompetent."

"What can you tell me about your estate?"

"My mother died, she left it to me, Julia holds the checkbook. Not much else to tell you other than that."

"Did everything transfer directly to you after your mother's death or after your father's?"

"I think it went directly to me." I shrugged. "Why?"

Mrs. Chang cast a look in Carmichael's direction.

"Is that bad?" I said.

She shook her head. "Usually when a married person dies, control of the estate goes to the spouse. Do you know why she left it to you, and just you?"

"No."

She scribbled on her clipboard. "Do you know what banks you have accounts at?"

I scrubbed a hand over my face. She must have read something in my expression because she smiled and said, "I take that as a no. How old were you when Julia retained guardianship?"

"Ten, I think."

"After your father died?"

"Yeah."

"When did she gain guardianship over you as an adult?"

"Not sure. Eighteen, I guess."

"So she's always had control."

"Yeah."

Her pen scratched across the paper. "Who did the competency evaluation presented to the court?"

I looked at Carmichael and he said, "That would be the doctor who deemed you unfit to have appropriate judgment in concerns to your well-being."

"Dr. Mason, I guess."

"Has he always been your doctor?"

"Yeah."

"Have you ever seen anyone else?"

"No."

"Who's your family doctor?"

"I haven't seen anyone else since Harrison died."

A wrinkle creased the space above her nose while she made a few more notes. "Does your other sister have access to your accounts?"

"I'm not sure. I know she does the shopping. She buys my clothes, takes them to the cleaners. I think we're probably the only people who have a housekeeper that never gets to do anything." Not that I'd blame her. Julia probably paid her pennies on the hour.

"And what about you, Paris?" She laid the clipboard in her lap. "What is it you want?"

Her powerful gaze struck me head-on, and all I could do was blink. "I'm sorry I don't think I understand."

"I'm going to be acting as your advocate, so I need to know what you want."

"I still don't…" I looked at Carmichael, then Mrs. Chang. The reality of what she asked hit me full force.

What did *I* want?

It was a simple question, but I'd never thought about it because no one had ever cared before. Not even me.

And now that someone had, I didn't have a fucking clue.

I laughed. I kept laughing. They stared at me while I sat there braying like a donkey. Then the laughter faded into silent crying. I fought every surge of tears and every watery breath, but it wouldn't stop.

I slid from the sofa onto the floor, and I cried until my eyes were swollen shut, my throat burned, and my skin was on fire. I cried every tear my body could possibly make, and then I cried some more.

I have no idea how long I lay there, smearing tears and snot all over Dr. Carmichael's rug. But after a while, the solitude of the room settled around me and I was alone with Dr. Carmichael sitting beside me.

"It's all right."

"I know." I could hardly understand myself. I lay there while he rubbed the knots bunching around my spine while trying to remember how my arms and legs worked.

"Do you need help?"

"No." I rolled on my side and wound up sitting with my back against the sofa.

"Here you go." He put a wad of tissue in my hand. "Feel better?"

"I'm not sure." I mopped my face.

He handed me more. "I would think after a cry like that you would."

"Are you sure that's what that was?" I blew my nose, and my ears popped.

"In my expert opinion, yes."

I laughed, and it made my ribs hurt. "I've cried, maybe more lately than ever, but never like that."

"It's good to cry, even like that."

We sat there, me trying to breathe, him examining the cuticles of his fingernails. Shiny, smooth and clean. He either liked a good manicure, or my chewed paint-stained nails were that bad.

"Where's Mrs. Chang?" I was actually worried to see her gone.

"She wanted to give you some space. She'll come back later in the week, and you two can talk again."

"About what?"

"That's up to you."

"What would I talk to her about?"

"Don't you have any questions?"

I scraped my thumbnail against a fleck of blue stuck in the crease of my palm. "Not really."

"Well, maybe by the time she gets back, you will."

A doctor was paged over the intercom, and laughter from the hallway was muffled by the closed door.

It took me a while to find my courage to ask, "I'm fucked up, aren't I? I mean, I know I am, but it's worse than I ever thought, isn't it?"

Dr. Carmichael exhaled a measured breath and hung his arms over his knees. "Yes, you're very sick."

Something inside me dropped. I think it was the grain of hope I had left. I never imagined something so small and fragile could weigh so much.

"But it doesn't mean you can't live a productive, happy life."

"If I keep crying like that, my body is just going to quit on me."

He smiled, and the crow's feet around his eyes deepened. "It's good you're crying. It means your emotions are working and you're trying to heal."

"It hurts."

"I know."

"I don't think I'm strong enough."

"Oh, Paris," he laughed. "You're incredibly strong."

I folded my legs just like him and laid my forehead on my knees. Every other breath I took rattled. I meant it when I told him I didn't think I was strong enough. The only reason I'd lasted this long was because of Roy.

He said he would call soon. Did that mean a day, two days, a week?

His growl reverberated through my body, and his voice moved across my skin.

"Come for me, Paris."

"What are you smiling about?"

I sniffled. "You don't want to know."

"Sure, I do. That's why I'm here. You tell me what's on your mind, and I listen."

"No, I'm pretty sure you don't want to know."

"Try me."

"I was thinking about Roy's dick in my ass and how he does this little jerk that nails me right in the pros--"

He held up a hand. "Not funny."

"You asked."

"I did." He shook his head.

"So now what?"

He nodded at the clock on the wall. "We still have thirty minutes."

"More talking?"

"Easier than crying."

284

"I tried to tell you what was on my mind once already, and you didn't appreciate it."

"I think there are far more interesting things to talk about than your sex life." He pulled the floppy hippo from the arm of the couch, and hugged the stuffed animal to his stomach.

I could just imagine someone's grandmother stitching together the chubby little hippo, then giving it to some kid to keep them company at night.

"You want to hold him for a while?" Dr. Carmichael opened his arms in offering.

"Him?"

"Sure. His name is Buford."

"You've got to be kidding me." I had no idea why, but I took the damn thing. Its fat legs thumped my arm when I shook it. Buford made his way to my lap, and I sat cross-legged holding him in much the same way Dr. Carmichael had.

I petted Buford's crinkled pelt, and the fluttering left behind in my chest slowed.

"Does wonders, doesn't it?"

I wiggled Buford's weighted front legs. "Yeah."

"You sound surprised."

"Who thinks about holding a stuffed animal to make you feel better?"

"Children."

I plucked at one of Buford's ears. There was a thread hanging loose where a stitch had let go. "I think the rules change when you're not a kid anymore."

"Why is that?"

I shrugged.

"When you were young, what did you hold?"

It was dark in my room, but the TV was on downstairs and they were laughing.

"Paris?"

"A pillow."

"Pillows are good."

I huddled in the corner.

"What kinds of things made you want to hold a pillow?"

Dishes clanked in the sink. "I don't know."

285

"Were you sad, or lonely, or—"

"Scared." *The carpet was thick on the stairs so they didn't creak, but I always knew when he was there.*

"What scared you?"

I don't know how I knew. "Harrison."

"And why were you afraid of your father?"

He'd stand there for what seemed like hours with his hand on the doorknob. "I'm not sure."

"Did he hit you?"

"No. He just watched me." *I always turned off the nightlight because I was convinced if he couldn't see me, he'd forget I was ever there.*

"And what were you doing when he watched you?"

I barricaded the door with toys. "Eating, playing, running." *When I was older, I used the chair from my desk.*

"Do you think he watched you because he was worried about you?"

By the time I was in the second grade, I used my drafting table. "No."

"Then why do you think he watched you?"

Sleep became a luxury I couldn't afford. "He was starving."

"What do you mean?"

I quit getting up to go to the bathroom. A few times, I urinated out the window but was afraid of getting caught so I snuck an empty bottle into my room and would empty it in the morning before I left for school and after he'd gone to work.

"I don't know."

"Then why would you say he was hungry?"

"I don't think I knew he was. Not then."

"Did he say something to make you think that?"

He didn't have to. His eyes said everything his mouth didn't. I crushed the stuffed animal against my chest.

"Can we talk about something else?" I left Buford on the floor and climbed back into the chair. I draped my legs over the arm and nestled my back against the other. "You need a couch. This chair is too cramped. All head doctors are supposed to have a couch. You have toys, and you need a couch. I'm sure there's something Freudian about that."

"What would you rather we talk about?"

I shrugged.

Carmichael moved to his chair. "All right. Tell me about the painting you did the other day. You called it The Glutton. Why?"

"No clue."

"I don't believe that."

"Not my problem."

"I can't help you unless you talk to me."

I threw my arm over my face. "Why does it matter what I called the painting? It's not like you could understand anyhow. No one sees the pictures. They can't."

"But Roy can."

I dropped my arm back into my lap.

"He told me about the showing at the gallery and the things he saw in your paintings."

There were pockmarks in the tile ceiling. I played connect the dots in my head.

"Some of the things he described to me are disturbing. Are all your paintings like that?"

"No."

"The one your sister sold. What was it?"

"I don't want to talk about that, either."

"It had to be important."

"It doesn't matter. It's gone."

"You sell a lot of your paintings. Why was that one so special?"

"What time is it?"

"Paris."

"Has to be close to lunch. I'm hungry."

"It's ten thirty."

"Feels later."

"Tell me about the painting your sister sold."

"There's nothing to tell."

He cocked his mouth to the side and drummed his fingers on the arm of his chair. "Okay. Fine. Then tell me about Harrison."

"There's nothing to tell you about him either."

"It's either Harrison or the painting, you choose."

I straightened up and wound up with my boxers crowding my ass crack. I wiggled, trying to get them to move.

"Paris?"

"Fine." I rubbed my face. "What do you want to know?"

"Tell me about the day he killed himself."

The blood on his hands looked black under the bare light bulb. The metal cage vibrated. Round and round the rabbit went. Eyes wild and screaming as it smashed into the sides.

"It rained." *Somewhere between the shed and the woods, the sky spit icy droplets that sucked the heat from the day. My clothes, the leaves, the mud, it all stuck to my body.* "It was cold." *There was no blood on my hands. There should have been. Like the rabbit's feet, my palms should have been raw.*

The rabbit was dead. Alice was going to be so heartbroken.

"What about the rabbit?"

I jerked my head up? "Huh?"

"You said the rabbit. What about it?"

I'd spoken aloud? What else had I said? "Nothing."

"It was something. You went somewhere. You saw something."

I shook my head.

"The rabbit."

"No."

"I want to know about the rabbit."

Oh God. My heart gave one sluggish beat after the other.

"Is that what the painting was about? The one your sister sold?"

"No. That was a happy moment. A good thing the…"

"The rabbit wasn't?"

"No."

"Did Harrison kill the rabbit?"

I needed to shut up. I tried to, but the words kept coming. "It died because it was scared to death by what it saw."

"And what did it see?"

"Something Harrison did."

"And what did he do?"

"I…" Earth sucked a sloppy wet kiss against the monster's mottled skin.

288

"What did he do, Paris?"

A jagged pain dug at the inside of my skull with wicked claws. *"You breathe a word of this, Paris, so help me..."*

I jerked myself out of the chair. Carmichael followed me and blocked the door. "Get out of my way. I'm done."

"I can't help you unless you open a line of communication with me."

I tried to shove past him, and he held my arm. "Let go."

Carmichael searched my face, then released my arm. "Fine."

"I'll see you tomorrow."

"You do that."

I opened the door.

"And by the way," Carmichael said. "The craft studio is off limits to you from here on out."

I laughed. "Like you can stop me."

"I can. This is my facility. I can't make you talk, but I can take away the privileges I give you."

No paint. No way to escape. No way to quiet the noise in my head.

"Fine. I guess I'll see myself to the exit." Fuck him. He could keep his art supplies. I had better ones at my apartment.

"You aren't authorized to leave."

"I checked myself in."

"You did. But I'm the one who decides whether or not you're well enough to leave."

I balled up my fists. "You bastard."

"It's for your own good."

"My own good? I agreed to be here so I could escape a tyrannical bitch, not be trapped by you."

"Julia doesn't have your best interests at heart."

"And you do? You don't even know me." I pounded a hand against my chest. "You know nothing about me."

"Only because you won't let me. I know you want to tell me things. I know you want to tell the world. It's why you paint."

"I paint because I like it."

"Some, yes. But what I've seen you do here, you don't do it for pleasure. You do it out of fear." He took a step closer. "I want to know what you're so afraid of. What's your secret, Paris? Is it the rabbit? Or something else?"

It was right there churning in my gut, boiling a path up my throat, filling my mouth. I wanted to puke it all up on the polished gray floor. All over my thrift store shoes and Carmichael's penny loafers.

I wanted to be free of the darkness. I wanted the beast exorcised from my soul.

"Paris."

"I…"

He cupped my face. "Tell me. Tell me about the rabbit. Tell me about The Glutton. Tell me anything."

"I can't." Tears cut cool lines down my burning cheeks.

"You can."

I shook my head. "No. You don't understand."

"Then help me understand."

I leaned closer and so did he. "It knows." I whispered.

"It?"

"The rabbit."

"What does it know?"

"It saw. It saw everything."

"What did it see?"

"The truth."

"And what was the truth, Paris?" He begged me with his eyes to let him bear this burden for me. And I was so tired. What would it be like to sleep? To really sleep? Without the drugs, the alcohol? Just the silence found in a world without my terrible sin?

The rabbit sat on Carmichael's desk.

"Paris?"

It watched me, and I watched it.

Carmichael followed my gaze. "What are you looking at?"

The rabbit bobbed its head, and its pink nose crinkled as it sniffed the air.

"Tell me what you see."

Its right ear twitched and then the left.

"Let it out, Paris."

The rabbit hopped to Carmichael's chair, disappearing from my line of sight. I craned my neck, trying to keep my eye on it. It hopped into the doorway from behind the wall.

The rabbit pawed its face.

I tried to pull out of Carmichael's grip, but he held on. "I have to go."

"Where?"

"The art room."

"Why?"

"It's coming."

"The monster?"

"Yes. Yes."

"And you need to paint?"

"Yes."

"Because when you paint it goes away."

"Yes, yes...please..."

"And what happens if you don't paint?"

"It will come out of here." I put a hand on my chest. "It will be angry, and then the only way to escape will be down the rabbit hole."

"The rabbit lives there?"

"The white rabbit. I'll have to follow it down the hole, or the monster will kill me."

"Why does it want to kill you?"

"Because it's angry. It's so angry."

"Tell me why it's angry."

My lip trembled, and tears ran down my cheeks, soaking the front of my shirt.

"Tell me, Paris. Why is the monster angry?"

"Because..."

"Because why?"

I shook my head. "Please, I have to paint. Just let me paint."

"So it will go away?"

"Yes."

But he wasn't going to let me. His determination slid through his gray eyes and consumed any pity he felt for me. I didn't care if he pitied me or not. I just needed him to understand why he had to get out of my way.

"I want to see it."

He had no idea what he was asking. "No."

"I'm not afraid of it."

I tried to twist away, and he pinned me to the wall. "You don't understand. You can't. No. Don't let it. Don't…" If it took getting on my knees and begging, I would do it.

"Show it to me."

Beside me, the white rabbit stood on its hind legs and cocked its head.

Fear erupted from my chest on the back of a scream. I shoved Carmichael back and ran down the hall. When I reached the art room, the door wouldn't open. There was a clear view of the roll of paper sitting next to the shelves through the window. A brand new crate of paints was on the floor beside it.

"Paris…" Carmichael and two orderlies approached from the end of the hall.

The white rabbit rubbed against my ankle, and I drove my fist through the glass. A shower of fragments hit the ground, but the metal weave inside kept it from giving way. I clawed at the wire, tearing my fingernails and cutting fiery lines into my skin. The edge came loose, and I was able to get my hand through the hole and undo the lock.

Powerful arms wrapped around me.

The monster stirred.

"No, please, you can't."

Its eyes opened.

"You have to let me paint."

"I just want to help you." Carmichael tried to make me look at him. I snapped my teeth, just missing the tips of his fingers.

"Goddamn you, you'll wake it up."

The white rabbit had a smear of crimson across its side. It kicked up its rear legs and bounded down the hall.

"No, please. I don't want to go with you." But it was too late.

The monster rose out of its pit. Decay and filth sloughed off its mottled flesh. A stinking cloud of sour milk and rotten cabbage followed.

It took a step, and even the earth trembled in fear.

"I'm sorry."

Yellow eyes regarded me with no empathy. I was a coward.

"Please, I was scared."

I'd let it suffer, and now I would feel its wrath. I was a liar. "Stop. Please, oh, please stop."

The monster dug its fingers into my chest and cracked me open. Then it spilled out of me and into the world.

****

Strength is the only thing I remembered clearly. It shot me into a high as addictive as any drug or sex with Roy.

With every pump of my heart, the rage inside me grew until it swept away pain, mercy, and my conscience. Until it filled me, overflowed, and contaminated everything around me.

The orderly tightened his grip, but he had me around my ribs, leaving my arms free. I shoved my elbow into his nose and slammed my foot back into his knee. The second man tackled me, and we hit the floor. I head-butted him in the face. He let me go. The tread on my shoes lost traction when I hit a smear of blood.

Caught in the fury, I could only panic. Clawing at the wire and slamming into the door over and over, unable to remember how to open it or even what it was. I only knew the barrier was in my way and I had to get through it.

Then it was gone.

Dr. Carmichael said my name, but I was trapped inside the monster's belly. Swallowed whole, I would remain there until it shit me out.

Brushes, crayons, and poorly drawn still-lifes shredded under my hands. I threw aside the chairs and tables in my way.

The monster had nothing but its anger and hate for me. It screamed. It bit. It destroyed everything in its path.

Another group of orderlies descended and took me to the floor. My limbs were restrained, my body pinned. I sank my teeth into one man's shoulder and nearly bit through a second man's thumb.

The monster had gone rabid. I twisted in their grip until my joints popped and my bones strained. I screamed when they wouldn't let go. I screamed until the air would no longer fill my lungs.

They carried me, frothing and struggling, into an empty room.

"You fucking little whore." *I shrank away.* "Look what you've made me do." *The boy with no name lay with his hand out. Reaching for me. Begging me.* "Everything was fine until you came along." *But I was too afraid.* "Dirty, filthy boy. It's all your fault." *The rabbit watched me with the same dead gaze as the boy.* "All of it."

293

Harrison was right. It was my fault.

All of it.

A pinprick set me on fire and a tide of smoke, rendered the monster deaf, dumb, and blind.

Chapter Fourteen

Dr. Carmichael called to me from far away, but I was in the bottom of the rabbit hole. Dirt pillowed my head, and I alternated from warm to cold.

Carmichael continued to call.

The white rabbit hunkered down near my face, and we lay there nose to nose. I scratched the rabbit behind the ears with my left hand because my right one wouldn't work.

Dr. Carmichael kept calling my name.

I think I might have stayed there, but if I did, I couldn't fulfill the promise I'd made to Roy. I missed him so much. The warmth of his body, his touch. Down in the darkness, I would never have it again.

That was the only reason I got to my feet and began the long climb up the tangled roots and back to the surface.

"How do you feel?" Carmichael shined a light in one eye, then the other.

I tried to move, but a shock of lightning shot through my shoulder.

"Be still. You strained your radial."

My tailbone hurt too.

The room was bare of everything except the bed I was on and a sink and toilet stuck in the corner like pieces of forgotten furniture.

"Paris. I'm going to ask you some questions, and I want you to answer them as best as you can. What year were you born?"

"Nineteen eighty-six."

"How many sisters do you have?"

"Two"

"What's my name?"

"Cunt face."

He frowned. "That was uncalled for."

"You deserve it."

He patted my arm. "You scared me back there."

"I warned you."

"You did. But I'm glad I got to see." He took a syringe from his pocket, and I pulled away. "It will help with the pain."

"I don't do needles. Snort it, smoke it, pop it, yeah. But no needles."

"This only comes in an injection."

"Then I don't want it."

"Please."

A wash of dull aches in my shoulder promised high tide very soon. My resolve wilted. "Fine."

Carmichael lifted the edge of my hospital gown. The pinprick was short lived. He capped the needle and dropped it back into his pocket.

"Do you mind telling me where I am?" I said.

"The isolation ward."

"Looks more like a prison cell." I glanced over at the toilet.

"I wasn't sure what I'd be facing when you woke up." He leaned forward and studied my face. "Tell me what happened."

"You're the doctor. How about you tell me?"

"All right." He sat on the edge of the bed. "I haven't had enough time to think about what I saw to feel confident in a complete diagnosis, but I'm pretty sure what you experienced was an episode due to borderline personality disorder."

I laughed. "Great, so now I'm Sybil?"

"Not hardly. Sybil had multiple personality. What you display is completely different. It's why you rage."

"So give me a pill and send me home."

"It's not that simple."

"Then how do you fix it?"

"It can't be fixed in the truest sense of the word, but it can be managed. However, your situation is complicated because I believe you may be suffering from Post-Traumatic Stress Disorder, and bipolar, which would also be attributed to the mood swings and the psychosis."

"So I'm fucked?"

"No. Not at all. That can be managed as well. But I don't think anything will truly help you until you deal with whatever it is you're hiding."

He wanted me to face the monster. To walk into its filth and look into its eyes. Carmichael had no idea what he was asking. "I can't."

"You don't have a choice."

"Why can't I go back to my life? I was fine."

"No. You were self-medicating by keeping yourself high. And I think that has reached its limits. Think, how many times have you raged in your life that you know of?"

"I'm not sure."

"Oh, I think you do. In fact, I'd be willing to bet you've only done this once, maybe twice before. You said the first time you did this was when the cat was killed. Something about that cat dying set you off. But either way, you haven't done it very often, and now in a little over two weeks, you've done it at least twice."

"But when I started painting the ugly things I saw, they stopped."

"They stopped because you've stayed drunk or high. The drugs Dr. Mason has been giving you are not meant to be used to treat bi-polar because they can aggravate the cycling of mania to depression."

"You think he's been keeping me sick?"

"I think if he'd been treating you properly, you wouldn't be facing another psychotic episode. I think because of what he's been giving you, for whatever the reason he's been giving it to you, you have reached your limit.

"These episodes are only going to grow more frequent and more violent. You're already a danger to yourself and others."

My chest tightened. "So you're going to keep me here forever?"

"I told you when you first came here I want you to get better. That means facing some things you don't want to. If you don't, you will eventually hurt someone. Maybe even kill them. There is a very good chance that someone could be Roy."

"Just let me paint. When I paint, it goes away."

"It doesn't. I promise. You're telling a story in those paintings you create, but no one can understand what you're saying but you."

"Roy understands."

"That may be, but he's not enough. I think you know that. I think every brushstroke you put to canvas is a cry for help. This secret you're hiding is eating you alive." He stood.

"Can I go back to my room?"

"No."

"How long will you keep me here?"

"Until you're ready to work with me and tell me what's made you so angry."

"What if I don't know?"

"Oh, you know." He headed to the door. I sat up to go after him, but my feet and legs floated beyond my control. "Until you talk to me, there will be no paints, no TV, no private bathroom. No privileges of any kind."

"Roy is supposed to call."

"I'll keep him informed about what's going on."

"You won't let me talk to him?"

"No, I won't."

"Please don't do this."

"I'm sorry it has to be this way. And know that when you're ready to talk, I'll listen."

The sound of the door closing echoed a death knell through the room. I crawled out of the bed, but the drugs had stripped the connection between my brain and body. My legs buckled, and I tried to catch myself with my hands. My one arm was in the sling, and the other was about as effective as a rubber band. I collapsed and had just enough time to roll to the side before my face smashed into the ground.

I inched my way across the floor. Half the time, I wasn't even sure if I actually made any progress.

When I got to the door, I jiggled the knob. Locked. And the only window was a long narrow strip covered with mesh. I'd been a fool to come here. Dr. Carmichael would never let me leave. Roy would call, and Dr. Carmichael would give him some excuse. How many times would he believe it before he gave up?

A sob broke out of my chest.

I had to find some way to tell Roy what was happening. He'd help me. He wouldn't let them lock me up like this. He understood the paintings. He saw why I had to create them.

I just needed a phone.

Even if I could get back to my room, I wouldn't be able to dial out. I needed access to an outside line. The only place I'd find something like that was Carmichael's office or the nurse's station.

But first, I had to get out.

****

After four days in lockdown, a few orderlies escorted me to a tiled room for a bath. To keep the sling dry, there was only a few inches of water in the tub.

The poor nursing assistant assigned to me couldn't have been a week on the job. I must have been the talk of the mental ward with the way he jumped if I so much as breathed hard.

After he dropped the soap for the tenth time, I took the sponge out of his hand. "Please let me. I'd like to get this over with before the water frosts over."

"Sorry."

I lathered up the sponge. "How long have you been here?"

The bar slipped out of my hold two times, and then three. As soon as I picked it back up, it shot out of my hand and landed on the floor.

The nursing assistant retrieved it for me. "Two weeks."

I scrubbed my bad shoulder, my chest, and my legs. I couldn't reach my other arm. "Here." I gave back the sponge. "Do you mind?"

His hand shook as he brushed the sponge over my skin.

"You're going to have to scrub harder than that."

"Sorry, I just didn't want to hurt you."

"Why, because you think I'll hurt you back?"

He looked away.

"Jesus, what kind of shit do they talk about around here?"

"You broke a man's nose."

"So?"

"Fractured another orderly's skull."

"Worse happens in a bar fight."

"Yeah, but both of them outweigh you by a hundred pounds each."

"Lightweights. Should have seen what I did to the lion, tiger, and bear."

He stopped washing.

"It's a joke." I slapped at the water. "I feel like a kid."

"Just trying to keep the sling dry."

"Second time I've had a hurt arm." I examined the sling through the plastic bag wrapped around it.

"How did it happen the first time?"

"I slipped down the steps." With some help from Julia.

"Sorry to hear that." The nursing assistant put the sponge aside. "Stand up please."

I grabbed the handrail to pull myself up only to lose my grip and slop water out over his shoes.

"Fucking soap." I rubbed my thumb and finger together. Like the colors that formed one of my paintings, the feel of that soap formed a plan.

"Here, I'll rinse you off."

"Actually…I'd like to wash some more."

"You're clean."

"Not clean enough. I've been sitting in that room for days with only toilet paper and a sink. I'd like another going over."

"Mr. Duvoe, I promise you, you're clean." He smiled at me. I didn't smile back. "I really need to get you back to your room."

"I really need another bath."

"Sir."

I held out my hand. "Give me the fucking soap."

He handed it over.

"Help me stand."

"But—" I glared, and he pulled me up.

This was completely insane. But considering where I was, why not go with the flow? I scrubbed the soap over my body until I was coated in an oily white film the consistency of melted butter.

"Here, do my other arm."

"Shouldn't you sit—"

"Shut up and lather me up." He did, losing his grip on the soap twice. When I was head to knees in slime, I said, "Towel."

He picked it up. "Shouldn't you rinse?"

"Put it on the floor."

"Please—"

"Put the damn towel on the floor before I test the thickness of your skull."

He threw the towel down. I stepped out and scrubbed my feet on it until they were dry.

"Mr. Duvoe, you really should get back in the—"

"Open the door." I would have done it myself, but my hands were coated in soap.

"Sir?"

I turned on him, and he shrank back, tripping over the stool he'd been sitting on and landed on his ass. Water soaked through his blue scrubs, turning them dark around his thighs.

I almost laughed. "Open the door."

He scrambled to his feet.

"Please, Mr. Duvoe..."

I drew my lips back over my teeth.

The nurse's aide made a mad dash out of the room to get away.

One of the meatheads looked inside, and that's when I rushed him. He made a grab but lost his hold. Another tried to wrap me in a hug, and I dropped to my knees, shooting out of his grip like the bar of soap. The third one didn't get the chance to try for me. He stepped down on a streak of bubbles, lost his balance, and slammed into the wall.

My feet slid for a moment but it was only water. I got traction and ran down the hall. The nurse's station was just ahead. I'd never get past them and into the main wing. But I didn't need to get past. I just needed to get inside. I yanked the lever on a fire alarm mounted to the wall, and an electronic wail sent the nurses into a frenzy.

One of the women opened the door while the other one called out on the radio. At a full run, I dropped into a slide, heading right for the opening. My bad shoulder caught the corner of the doorjamb, and everything grayed out. I fought against the rise of nausea and blurred senses. If I passed out, I'd never get out of this hell.

The nurse tried to block the doorway. I knocked her feet out from under her, and she came down on top of me. She threw herself to the side and scurried out the door. I jammed my foot in the opening and slithered inside.

The door shut, and I slumped against it. The second nurse stood in the corner. She held up her hand as if to ward me off. I grabbed a chair to pull myself up and couldn't find traction.

"You can go," I said. She kept staring. "Get the fuck out of here."

She ran for the door.

"Slow down, or you'll..."

Just as she yanked open the door, she slipped. Her scream was muffled by the thick Plexiglas. The office door couldn't be opened

301

from the outside without a key, but there was a dead bolt on the inside so I engaged it. I guess it was a safety measure in case one of the patients acquired a card. Escape by soap probably never crossed their minds.

I wiggled across the room on my ass to keep from meeting the same fate as the fleeing nurse. When I got to the desk, I pulled down the phone and dialed Roy's cell. After a half dozen rings, it went to voice mail. I hung up and dialed again.

There was a click. "Roy?"

"Paris?"

"Listen, I don't have much time."

"Dr. Carmichael said he had you on lockdown."

"He does. Did. Just listen. I need you to come get me. He won't let me out."

"You hurt three people."

"He's the one who wouldn't let me paint. Please, Roy. I gotta get out of here."

"He's trying to help you."

I clenched the receiver. "Whatever he's told you isn't true."

"So you didn't hurt anyone?"

"Yes. No. I mean… It was an accident. Please, Roy, I need you to come get me."

"I'm sorry." He sighed. "I can't do that."

"What?"

"I can't come get you."

"Can't or won't?"

"Won't."

"You said you cared about me." My throat tightened.

"I do."

"Then help me."

"I am helping you."

"Helping me means getting me out of this shit hole."

"Dr. Carmichael wants you to get better."

"He doesn't want me better."

"Yes, he does."

"Then why won't he let me paint? Huh? Tell me. Why won't the son of a bitch let me paint?"

"It's for the best."

Fists pounded on the Plexiglas. Carmichael stared down at me with a hard expression.

I gave him my back and curled over the receiver. "Roy, if you really care about me, if you love me even the smallest amount, please, please help me. I have to paint. I have to get this out of me. You've seen it. You know how ugly it is."

"Yeah, I've seen it. That's why I know you need this. And because I love you, I'm not going to come get you out."

I hissed through gritted teeth. "You bastard."

"Paris…"

"You fucking bastard."

"Please, I don't want you to be angry."

"Angry? They don't even make a word for what I am. You set me up. All of you set me up. Are you trying to kill me? Is that what you want?"

"You know it isn't."

Dr. Carmichael knocked on the window. "Paris, don't make me have to cut the lock."

"What's going on?" Roy said.

"Nothing."

"Where is Dr. Carmichael? I'd like to talk to him."

"He's busy."

"Paris…"

"Go fuck yourself, Roy."

"You don't mean that."

"Yeah, I do."

"You're upset. I can understand—"

"That's where you're wrong. I do mean it. Every word."

His breath shuddered.

"Are you crying, Roy? I hope you are. I hope you choke on your tears."

"I…"

"Fuck you. Fuck. You. Don't call. Don't come see me. Stay the hell out of my life. I don't need you. I don't want you." I slammed the receiver down. The plastic was so cold against my hand. The hate I wanted to feel toward Roy didn't happen. What filled me instead was fear. Roy had betrayed me. He'd left me here to rot. He never loved me. It was a lie. Everything was a lie.

303

Especially me.

Dr. Carmichael kept knocking on the glass. Saying something. I don't know what. I couldn't have heard him even if I wanted to. My world had become void. I existed nowhere. I was no one.

****

I stared at the pockmarked ceiling with no strength to move, no strength to eat or drink, no strength to breathe.

Yet I continued to live. My body as much of a Judas as Julia, Dr. Carmichael, and now Roy.

The rabbit sat on my chest and regarded me with soulful eyes.

"This is all your fault."

The rabbit washed its face.

"Everything. All of it. It's your fault."

It hunkered down, and its whiskers tickled my chin.

"I hate you." I rolled over, and it waited for me on my pillow. "You're a waste of air."

It stretched out beside me. It smelled of alfalfa, dust, and of years past.

I scratched the side of the rabbit's face with a finger. Its eyelids slid lower.

"I'm all alone. Really alone."

It shook its head, and its ears slapped against the back of my hand. The rabbit licked his paws.

"He wants me to tell him."

It stopped.

"But if I do, it will wake up the monster."

The rabbit hopped away, disappearing from sight. I rolled over to my other side, and it sat by the door.

"I can't leave, stupid."

It hopped a few steps.

"Just go away. I don't want you here either."

It cleaned its face.

I rolled to my back and shut my eyes. Patterns of color danced in the darkness, moving, forming shapes, and fluttering away.

A weight pressed down on my chest.

"I told you to leave."

The rabbit hunkered down until it resembled a loaf of bread.

"I don't know how to tell him without making any noise."

It leaned over me and cocked its head. My face reflected in its liquid eyes.

"I need to paint. If I don't..." I fondled its ears. "It's all I know." It nuzzled my palm. "No paint, remember?"

The rabbit sank its teeth into my thumb.

I shot upright, and it tumbled away. "Fucking bastard." I stuck my thumb into my mouth, but it wouldn't stop throbbing. When I took it out, the gash across the middle filled up and dripped from my nail. The bright red droplets made carnations on the hospital gown. Red. A beautiful color. It was one of my favorites and often dominated my works. Even the Blue Crucifixion was spiced with the hue.

The rabbit sat up on its hind legs over by the window. Light from the narrow window cut a swath across the wall. They kept the lights off at night, but there was enough from the street lamp outside for me to see.

"Yeah, okay."

I staggered to my feet.

I smeared a line of crimson across the field of white. In the shadows, it turned black. With no other colors, the secret would be forced to the surface for everyone to see.

"You're sure you want me to tell him what we saw?" Julia would be pissed. She'd lock me away. But Julia couldn't hurt me anymore, and I was already as locked away as a person could get.

The flow of blood trickled to nothing. The rabbit put its paw on my foot. It was right, we had nothing to lose.

"Fine."

Under the setting sun, everything bled orange and gold. He had to go home soon, and I didn't want him to leave. He held my hand, and we slipped into the darkness of the shed.

I turned on the light, and we stood there in the open space surrounded by tools and kept company by the rabbit in its hutch.

As a man, I wondered if a boy could fall in love. As a boy, I already knew the answer.

The boy kissed me. Or maybe I kissed him. Either way, our lips met, and his hand tightened in mine. It was only a few seconds, barely a moment. And then the door flew open.

I didn't recognize Harrison at first because his face had contorted into a mass of rage and his eyes belonged to an animal. No. Not an animal. Something else. Something evil and stinking of hell.

He came at me, and the boy pushed me to the side. I crawled on hands and knees behind the crate leaning against the workbench. I expected the boy to run, but he got in Harrison's way.

It only took one punch to send the boy to the ground. A dust cloud puffed up around him thick enough to coat my nostrils when I inhaled. The flurry of movement spooked the rabbit. Around and around, it fled what it could not escape.

Blood coated the boy's face, and black lines of dirt distorted his features. His gaze was dulled, but I know he saw me. A kick to his side sent him over. I didn't think Harrison came in with the intention of raping anyone. I think it just happened. Like some involuntary muscle movement. He just did it without really realizing it.

When it was over, he stared down at the boy with a look of horror on his face.

But it was done, and it could not be undone.

Tears cut clean streaks through the dirt on the boy's face. Pain made his skin pale, and there was nothing but fear in his eyes. He reached out to me. He was so close. I could have touched his hand. Instead, I withdrew deeper into the shadows.

Harrison grabbed a hammer off the workbench, but the claw caught the edge of the rabbit hutch and it toppled over.

I think the boy knew he was going to die. I think I knew too. I could have run to find help. I could have screamed for Harrison to stop. I could have at least comforted the boy.

Instead, I watched it happen in the very same way the rabbit watched me tell the secret that had boiled inside me for almost two decades.

I used layers of my blood for contrast and spit to thin and lighten. The sling on my arm became the palette where I tested the results. With every new droplet I lost, I brought to life the dirty secret I'd been made to carry.

With each stroke I left on the wall, the monster stirred. When my finger quit bleeding, the rabbit bit me again.

Like the colors had hidden the terrors, I created the lie to hide the truth. Both were too ugly to face, and at the same time, they couldn't be stopped. But I no longer had colors to conceal the nightmares.

My fingers bled for me, and my flesh tore. My heartbeat filled each digit, and more aching points covered one arm. The monster saw freedom, and it ran for it, clawing, biting, fighting its way out of the prison I'd built.

Walls crumbled, and doors gave way. I could only hope it would forgive me, and if it didn't, it'd kill me quickly and not let me suffer. Even though I deserved it.

The outside light stripped away the layers of mottled flesh, the hate filled eyes, the sharp teeth, and the claws. Left in place of the creature I feared was the boy who kissed me.

Just one soft kiss.

The barest touch of lips.

Because he loved me.

"*¿Cómo te llamas?*"

"*I don't understand.*"

He smiled. "*Name. You name.*"

"*Paris. What's yours?*"

"*Me llamo...*"

I only had to dig it out of the festering wound within the remnants of my mind.

"*Me llamo...*"

I saw his face. His eyes. The color of his skin. The mole close to his ear. How his lips quirked to the side just before he laughed. He smelled of cheap laundry soap, lavender, and the chocolate candy we'd shared.

Sweat burned my eyes, mixing with tears. The muscles in my arms begged for mercy. The colors in my mind screamed.

I fell.

I got up.

I fell.

I got up again.

I laid down the last mark, just as my door opened and the lights came on. When my knees folded, I didn't fight my way back up. It was done. I was done. There was nothing left to hide.

A nurse, an orderly, and Carmichael stood in the doorway. They stared with slack mouths and horror-filled eyes at the truth.

It wasn't over. I had to look. I had to name it.

I lifted my head.

A kiss. A dead rabbit. The father who'd sinned and the sister who helped protect him.

The boy.

He lay in the dirt pleading with his eyes. He was so scared. He was in so much pain. He was so alone.

Punched into the negative space and heavy shadows, forever connected by his heart, his mind, and his body, was the madman.

The Liar.

****

"Who is the boy in the picture you drew?" Carmichael sat across the table from me in a small break room. There were a couple of vending machines, a coffeemaker and a box of doughnuts.

I had no idea where he'd gotten the glass of orange juice he gave me. The kitchen was probably open, but I couldn't be sure.

The bandages on my fingers made it difficult to hold the glass.

"Paris?"

What was the question? I looked around for the rabbit. It wasn't there. That didn't bother me as much as the lack of colors. Without them, everything seemed pale and washed out.

"What did you give me?"

"Risperdal."

"What is that?"

"An antipsychotic."

I rubbed my fingers against the tabletop. Nothing. I pushed the table. Even the harsh metal scrape made no vivid bursts inside my mind.

"How am I going to paint without the color?"

"I'm sorry, but it was necessary."

"But I need it."

"Paris, you were hurting yourself."

"It was the rabbit's idea."

"There is no rabbit."

Not now. Had it gone to the same place as the colors?

"I need you to tell me the name of the boy in the painting."

308

I pressed my thumb against my first finger. A dull throb traveled up the digit and into the palm of my hands. Still nothing. I pressed harder.

Carmichael held my wrist. "Stop."

There was nothing but an empty void in my skull where my thoughts echoed. "I can't do this. I can't live without the color. Please, please I have to have it."

"When I know you're not going to hurt yourself, I'll take you off the drugs."

I tried to chew my thumbnail, but the gauze was in the way. I nodded. "Promise me."

"I promise." He scooted closer. "Tell me who the boy is in the painting."

"My lie. The rabbit's secret."

"What's his name?"

"I can't remember."

"How old were you?"

"Nine, ten." I rubbed my head. The edges of my words tasted funny. Like I was drunk but not drunk. There was no buzz with whatever Carmichael gave me, only numbness. I drank some of the juice but couldn't taste it. "I'm not sure."

"Where did this happen?"

"In the shed behind the house. It was at the bottom of the hill. The lake was just on the other side."

"So you lived there."

I nodded.

"Was he a classmate? Or a neighbor?"

The static in my mind spiked. "I think his mother was our neighbor's housekeeper. He was Hispanic. Everyone in the neighborhood was white. They were two dimensions, he was three. They were vanilla, and he was a colored sprinkle." I laughed.

"How did you meet him?"

"He came out of the woods between the houses."

"And where is that house located?"

"South Carolina."

"Do you still own it?"

"I don't know."

"And you can't remember his name?"

I shook my head. "I want to. I want to, but I can't." My throat tightened. "I should. After what Harrison did to him, I should. After what I did to him…"

"You were a child."

"I didn't tell Julia no."

"You were probably in shock."

I muffled a sob with the palm of my hand. "But I lied."

"About what?"

"When his mother asked me if I knew where he was, I told her I didn't know." I curled against the table. "I could have told her."

"Why didn't you?"

"Julia."

"She threatened you?"

No. She didn't threaten. She never threatened. She promised. And Julia always kept her promises. "Yes."

Dr. Carmichael reached across the table and held my hand. "It wasn't your fault."

"But wasn't it? It was supposed to be me. I was the one he was angry with. He came there for me but the boy…why can't I remember his name?"

"Trauma can do that."

"Maybe he's not even real. Maybe he's like the rabbit. Maybe he's just in my head."

"I don't think so." Carmichael gave me a sad smile.

"But what if he is? Are you going to keep me here?"

"I don't know." I picked at the bandages. Dr. Carmichael made me stop "But I think this may be why you're so angry."

"I don't feel very angry right now."

"I'm sure you don't."

"I don't even feel alive." Was I?

"You are. I promise."

I laid my head down on my arms. The table was cool against my cheek.

"What else can you remember about the boy?"

"I loved him." For a moment, I was falling. I jerked my head up. I rubbed my face. "Why am I so tired?"

"It's a side effect."

"No more. Whatever you gave me, no more please."

"I told you. As soon as I know you're not going to hurt yourself, I'll quit the injections."

I scanned the small room. Vending machines, a coffeemaker, a box of doughnuts on a counter. "Where are we?"

"You don't remember?"

"I'm not sure." My words tumbled through the darkness and piled up into a twisted mess. "Have I been here before?"

"Not till a little while ago."

The walls were blank. "Where is it?"

"What?"

"The Liar."

Carmichael leaned back in his chair. "You mean the picture you drew?"

"Yeah."

"It's back in the room you were in."

Then where was this? Two vending machines, a coffeemaker, and a box of doughnuts on the counter. The tabletop was white flecked with gold. The chairs were plastic.

There was a fridge in the corner. Where did it come from?

I picked up the plastic cup of orange juice, but it was empty. I licked my lips. There was only the burn of citrus.

"Would you like some more?"

I wasn't sure. I pushed the cup over to him. Carmichael got up and went to the fridge. Condiments clicked together when he opened the door.

Two vending machines, a box of doughnuts. My fingers were bandaged. My feet were bare.

"Paris?" He held the orange juice out to me.

I drank some, but other than a slight burn in the back of my throat, I didn't taste it. I drank some more just to make sure. I looked around. "Where are we?"

"Paris, I need you to think."

But there were no colors to hold my thoughts together.

"What else can you tell me about the boy?"

"Harrison killed him." I put a hand over my heart to make sure it was still beating. The bandages made it difficult for me to tell. I stared at them, wondering where they came from.

"Yes," Carmichael said. "I think he did."

"I saw him."

"You did."

"Why?"

"Why what?"

"Why did he kill him?"

"I don't know."

"Julia saw."

"Is that why she's in the painting?"

"What painting?" I looked around. "He cried."

"The boy?"

"No. Harrison. He sat down in the dirt and wept."

"And what happened after that?"

A bare light bulb swung overhead and spider webs tickled my cheek. I breathed through my nose because the dust made me want to cough. It caked my nostrils and made mud with the tears on my cheeks.

I wiped my face, but there was nothing on the bandages when I looked.

"The door opened." *I'd never realized how loud it squeaked before. In the shed, with Harrison crying, it was deafening.*

"Who opened it?"

"Julia came looking for Harrison. He was supposed to...I don't know. But she came looking for him and found him in the shed. She saw the boy."

"What did she do?"

"She took Harrison inside."

"What about you?"

"I was hiding, but she saw me." *The anger she seethed was the same as when she hit me.* "Why didn't she kill me?"

Carmichael dropped his gaze. "Tell me what happened next."

"The hammer was right there. She could have killed me."

"Paris?"

"She made me help her."

"Do what?"

"She put him on a tarp, and she made me help her drag him into the woods." *Grit packed my fingernails.* "There were too many roots."

"For what?"

"I couldn't get the hole deep enough. She got mad. She pushed me down."

"This is all your fault, Paris. You're nothing but a filthy whore. I saw the way you looked at Daddy. You made him do this."

"It wasn't your fault, Paris."

I looked around. The fridge kicked on. Small colored magnets held up notes. "What did you say?"

"I said it wasn't your fault."

"But I kissed him. I didn't want to help her. 'You're just like him.' That's what she said."

"The boy?"

I shook my head. "I think she meant someone else."

"Who do you think she was talking about?" Dr. Carmichael furrowed his brow.

I'd never thought to ask myself that question before. "I don't know."

"You don't remember?"

"No. I mean. I don't know."

He nodded like he'd expected the answer. "Do you remember where you helped Julia take the body?"

I curled my hands into fists and pressed them against my temple. "We dropped him into the rabbit hole."

"Get over here and help me move this, Paris."

I took one end of the thick piece of plywood, Julia took the other. The swollen wood left streaks of green and black on my fingers. As we lifted it, the middle sagged and water seeped from the wrinkles.

Pill bugs, earth worms, and black widow spiders scattered in the daylight.

Framed by the perfect square of bare earth was a hole. Concrete edged the sides. What hadn't crumbled was covered in moss.

"Get his feet."

I wrapped the tarp around his shoulders.

"What are you doing?"

"I don't want him to be cold."

"He's dead. He's not going to get cold. Now help me."

I tucked in the edges. Julia made an ugly sound and shoved me away. She grabbed the tarp and yanked it toward the edge. Gravity did

the rest. But he didn't come unwrapped so he'd stay warm at the
bottom of the well.

    "Get up."

    I wondered if I should go down there so he wouldn't be lonely.

    "Get up. Now." She kicked me in the hip.

    Julia's hair clung to her cheeks, and her mascara was
smeared. Sweat made her skin gleam and her cheeks glow. There was
blood on her dress.

    I promptly threw up all over her bare feet.

    "Where did she take you?"

    "Huh?"

    Carmichael held out another cup of orange juice.

    "Where did she take you after you dropped the body down the
well?"

    "To the bathroom." I sniffed the cup. "I don't like orange
juice."

    "You drank two glasses."

    I did? I sipped it. There was nothing to like or dislike.

    Carmichael pulled out his chair and sat in front of me. "Paris,
what happened after she took you into the bathroom?"

    "She left me."

    "That's all?"

    "She told me to take a bath."

    "Anything else?"

    "She got mad when I couldn't remember how to get my
clothes off."

    "Are you sure he doesn't remember the name of the boy?"

    Carmichael held up a hand. I turned to see who spoke. A white
man wearing blue jeans sat on a chair near the wall. A Chinese woman
in a purple suit beside him. Next to her, a black woman with long
braids.

    Where had they come from?

    "Who are you?"

    "This is Mark Moore, a private investigator who's a friend of
mine, and Mrs. Samson, your court appointed guardian. And Mrs.
Chang, your advocate. You met her almost two weeks ago."

    I looked at Carmichael. "How long have they been in here?"

    "The whole time."

I ran another survey of the room. Two vending machines, a coffeepot, a box of doughnuts, a refrigerator, and to my left, a flat screen mounted to the wall. The eyes of a confused man stared back at me from the dark glass.

"Where am I?"

"The break room."

"I've asked you that before."

"Yes, several times."

I held up my hands and wiggled my fingers. Gauze covered almost every inch of my hands. "The rabbit bit me."

"You bit yourself."

"The rabbit bit me so I could show you."

"Ask him."

"Not now, Mark," Carmichael said.

To Mark, I said, "Ask me what?"

He sat back a little. "Are you sure you don't remember the name of the boy your father killed?"

Did I? I worried the bandages on my thumb between my front teeth. How did they know about the boy? How did they know about Harrison killing him? I couldn't remember. Everything was muted. All twisted up. Inside out. Upside down.

Black and white.

There was no color, and I was falling apart.

Dr. Carmichael stood. "C'mon, I'll take you back to your room." He put his hands on my shoulders, and I held onto the table.

"What's wrong with me?"

"You're just upset."

This wasn't upset. I didn't know what it was, but I'd never felt anything like it. Or maybe I had and simply forgotten. "Please tell me what's wrong with me."

"You're medicated."

"Why?"

"You had a psychotic episode."

"What does that mean?"

"You were confused about what's real and not real. You hurt yourself. I had to medicate you until you calmed down." Carmichael urged me to stand up, but I refused. "Paris, I think you need to go back to your room."

"Not yet."

"Why not?"

I didn't have an answer.

"Please stand up."

I did.

"Now come with me."

I looked around the room. Two vending machines, a coffeepot, a box of doughnuts on the counter, a fridge, a TV, and three people I didn't know. Maybe they weren't real. I pretended not to see them just in case.

Dr. Carmichael led me down the hall and into a room that looked like it belonged in a hotel. "I've been here before."

"This is your room."

The phone on the end table sat under the lamp. "Roy."

"What about him?"

"Has he called yet?" Dr. Carmichael sat me on the edge of the bed, and I clung to his arm.

"Not yet."

"He's not going to, is he?"

"Why would you think that?"

"I got angry. I told him not to call. I told him I didn't want him to call."

"He'll call."

"What if he doesn't?" I stared at the phone. *Please ring. Please, please, ring.*

"Lie down and get some sleep."

"I can't. He might call. If I go to sleep, the nurses won't transfer the call back here."

"He knows he can't call after five anyhow."

"Are you sure he didn't call?"

"I'm sure."

"Will you check?" I twisted his shirtsleeve between my fingers.

He pried my grip loose. "I'll check."

I went back to staring at the phone. "But he won't, will he?"

"Yes, he will."

"I told him not to."

"I called him after you were sedated. I explained to him what happened. He knows you were upset."

"What did he say?"

"He said he would call in a few days to see if you were able to talk with him."

"But he didn't."

Carmichael glanced at the phone.

"I've been in that room for more than a few days. And he didn't call."

"If you like, I'll call him tomorrow to let him know you can talk."

"You'll tell him I'm sorry?" I scooted up on the bed. Carmichael covered me with a blanket.

"You can tell him yourself."

"Okay." I nodded. "I will. I'll tell him."

"Do you want me to have some dinner brought to you?"

"No. I'm going to sleep. Just make sure you don't forget to call him."

"I won't."

I curled around my pillow. Carmichael hovered at the door for a moment before leaving.

The white rabbit emerged from under the covers near my foot. It watched me from the other side of the bed.

There were still no colors. Just it. Just me.

The rabbit washed its face.

"Dr. Carmichael will call Roy and tell him."

It scratched its shoulder.

"Roy will call me, then I can tell him. God. I'm so sorry. I'm so sorry." I hugged the pillow, and it soaked up my tears. "But everything will be okay. I'll make sure it will be okay."

The rabbit blinked, and I trembled.

Small sobs butchered my breaths, and the muscles in my throat ached with the strain of holding everything in.

I watched the rabbit, and the rabbit watched me.

"He's not going to call, is he?" I whispered.

The rabbit shook out its ears and resumed cleaning its face.

****

Roy did not call.

Eating became a burden I didn't have the strength for, washing and changing my clothes, an impossible task. Even Dr. Carmichael's offer to let me paint couldn't coax me toward the light.

I lay on the floor next to my bed, staring at the tile ceiling thinking about nothing, because creating a stream of thought fed the pain in my heart.

The rabbit sat on my chest all plump and white. Was it sizing up the tastiness of my throat? Just in case, I tilted my head back, giving it full access.

Apparently, the rabbit preferred fingers.

Carmichael knocked on the doorjamb before entering my room. I don't know why he bothered. "Paris, we need to talk."

He didn't use his concerned doctor voice when he spoke. I counted the dimples in the ceiling.

"Your sister has requested a phone conference with you."

The white rabbit half-lidded its eyes.

"Your advocate spoke on your behalf to the judge, but since you've been given guardianship of yourself, the judge says it's up to you and you alone to decide whether or not you talk to her."

I turned my head to the right. Maybe the rabbit didn't like that cut of meat.

"I'm going to strongly advise you not to talk to her."

I guess the rabbit wasn't hungry.

"A call will be routed to your room in the next half-hour."

Why did Carmichael sound so nervous?

"You can choose to ignore the phone call."

My nose itched, but it was too far away for me to scratch it.

"Paris, I need you to pay attention and listen carefully to what I'm going to tell you." He knelt. "The judge made his decision a week ago. You're your own guardian now. You can tell her no. You can refuse anything she asks you. She cannot control your life anymore." He patted me on the shoulder. "Please let me know you heard me."

"I heard you."

He nodded. "I'll be in my office if you need me."

I stayed on the floor, and the rabbit remained on my chest. I had no intentions of answering the phone when it rang, but the rabbit sat up.

It rang again.

The rabbit leaned over me.

"What?"

Another ring.

It jumped off my chest.

"Was that a hint?"

The shadows under the bed swallowed him whole except for his fluffy white tail. Then it hopped, and it was gone too.

I could just let the phone ring. Carmichael said I didn't have to answer it. Maybe it was years of programming and doing what Julia said, or maybe I just wanted to stop the excruciating sound, but I forced myself to my knees. The cord dangled from the bedside table. I yanked the phone onto the floor. The receiver bounced off the side of the bed, the door on the table, and came to rest on the floor. I put it to my ear and lay back down.

"Paris?"

When Roy said my name, it filled me with warmth. When Julia said it, I became covered in a million biting ants.

"Yes."

"Oh thank God. I've been trying to get Carmichael to let me speak to you for weeks. He wouldn't. He got the courts involved. It's a big mess, Paris. Are you all right?"

Her fake concern turned the ants into wasps.

The rabbit came from under the bed and settled on my chest again. I scratched its ears.

"I'm fine."

"I want you to come home."

"I can't."

"Yes, you can. The lawyer said you can change doctors. All you have to do is request they send you to Dr. Mason's facility. I won't make you stay in that horrible place. I'll make sure Dr. Mason signs you out."

"Maybe I want to."

"What do you mean?"

I moved to a spot on the rabbit's shoulder. It kicked up a foot when I scratched.

"You only want me home so I can paint for you."

"That's not true. Alice has been beside herself."

319

That I believed. "Tell her I'm fine. She believes everything you say."

"That's not the point. You belong here. At home. Other people miss you too."

"People miss buying my works. They don't miss me." I closed my eyes. The rabbit stretched out on my chest. I ran my hand down its body in long languid strokes. "But it doesn't matter because I can't paint for them anymore."

A cold silence met me from the other end of the line. Julia was transforming. Shedding her concern and extending her claws. Becoming the daughter who helped her father hide his sin.

"What do you mean?"

"It's gone."

"What are you talking about?"

"I let the monster out, but it wasn't a monster, it was a boy. No more secrets, Julia. No more lies."

"You're not making any sense."

"I don't have to paint it anymore."

"Paint what?"

"The secret."

"Paris…"

"The rabbit helped me tell them."

"What the hell have they done to you?" Her words bit the air.

"Nothing, except believe me."

"Come home."

"Sell the apartment, take the money and move somewhere else. I'm going to stay here, then maybe rent a place on the East Side."

"That's a ghetto."

"They only stole my wallet, cell phone, and shoes."

The rabbit rested its head on its paws. Its dark eyes were closed, and its small mouth went slack. "Do you think rabbits dream?"

"What?"

"Rabbits. When they sleep. Do you think they dream?"

"Like I give a fuck."

"Ah, there you are. I wondered when the real you would make an appearance."

"You tell that crack doctor of yours to transfer you to Mason's facility. I am not giving up my life so you can play sick in the loony

320

bin. You will come home. You will paint. And you will attend every showing I book."

"How does it feel to not be able to touch me anymore? I can do what I want now. And you know what I want? To never paint those horrible pictures again. I like flowers. I think that's what I will paint. Or maybe trees and mountains."

Julia's breathing quickened, and with each exhale, there was a sharp squeak.

"Or maybe I won't paint at all." That wasn't true, but I knew if I didn't, it would be a stake right through her bank account.

"Yes, you will."

"No. No. I don't think so. I'm hanging up now. The rabbit is taking a nap, and I think I'll take one with it." I reached for the cradle.

I still had the receiver close enough to my ear to hear her say, "If you don't come home, I will make sure your boyfriend rots in jail."

My thoughts tripped, then reason took hold. "You can't just put someone in jail."

"I don't have to. He's already there."

I sat upright, and the rabbit tumbled away.

"That's right, little brother. Your boyfriend is in jail because he wouldn't tell me where you were. I even went to that shit hole of his and offered him money. When that didn't work, I filed abduction charges against him. He told the judge what happened, but he wouldn't tell him where you were even when he was ordered to."

"No."

"Did you know he's served time in prison before? Would be a shame if they were to search his apartment and find drugs? How many years do you think he'd get? I'm sure it will be a lot longer than three.

"Right now it's only contempt and his thirty days are up tomorrow. If you don't come home, I'll make sure the police get an anonymous tip. And they'll find more than enough to charge him with distribution."

She had me, and she knew it.

"I'll have Dr. Mason get the transfer papers ready and send a car in the morning." Julia hung up.

****

I cornered Carmichael in his office. "Did you know?"

321

He moved papers around on his desk.

"You did."

"He'll be out tomorrow."

"You knew, and you didn't tell me."

"It was for the best." He went back to reading the papers on his desk.

"You had no right."

"You weren't in any condition to handle the news. You still aren't."

"Yeah, well, because of you, Julia's going to make sure Roy goes back to prison."

A smile cocked his lips. "I know you're used to her controlling your life, but I promise you, Julia does not have the power you think she does. She just can't wave her hand and make him stay."

"She can if she puts drugs in his apartment and calls the cops. He has a felony on his record. They'll bury him."

The crow's feet around Carmichael's eyes tightened. "If she's threatening you, we need to call your advocate."

"No. You should have told me. You should have done something to protect Roy. You know what she's capable of. I told you what she's capable of."

"I'll call Mike. He'll make sure Roy will be okay."

"I can't take that chance."

"And it's out of your hands." He gestured to the chair. "Sit and we'll talk."

"I'm done talking. I want a transfer."

He folded his hands across his stomach. "And where do you plan on going?" The smirk on his face was nothing like Julia's because it wasn't cruel, but it was enough to remind me of her.

"To Ridgefield. Dr. Mason's facility."

"I'm sorry, Paris, but I can't allow that."

I walked over and planted my hands on the edge of his desk. "I may not be able to leave, but I know I have the right to choose where I want to receive treatment. You can't deny my request. I'm my own guardian, remember? If you want to keep your license, I suggest you transfer me."

"It will take time. I'll have to contact Ridgefield so they can draw up the admissions forms."

"They're already on their way. Sign them. Julia is sending a car for me in the morning."

"You can't go back to her." Dr. Carmichael pleaded with his eyes. "Mike is working on some leads. He'll get evidence and take it to the police. If she finds out they're going to press charges, she could become dangerous."

"She's already dangerous."

"More dangerous."

"Julia can't get any more dangerous."

"I know you think you know your sister, but I promise you, you don't."

"What are you talking about?"

He rubbed his forehead. "Sit. Please."

"I don't want to sit."

He opened his desk drawer and took out a folder. "This is a missing person's report."

"The boy?" Maybe his name was in there. Maybe I would finally know.

"No." Carmichael laid the folder on his desk. "This report was filed about four years before you were born."

I reached for the folder, but he didn't move his hand.

"Please sit."

It was the tone of his voice. I'm not sure how to describe it. Dark gray, with orange maybe.

I pushed the cushy chair closer to his desk and sat. I reached for the file again. He still didn't remove his hand.

"I didn't want to show you this yet."

"Why?"

"You're not ready to see it."

"Then why are you showing me now?"

"Because I need you to understand how important it is for you to stay here."

I tugged on the file. After a long moment, he lifted his hand. Now that the folder was mine, I wasn't sure I wanted to open it. "What's in it besides the report?" It was too thick to just be a few sheets of paper.

"A couple of newspaper articles. And a few photos from Goldleaf Middle School."

"Where is that?"

"Connecticut."

Julia and Alice had been born in Connecticut. I started to open the file. Carmichael stopped me. The war between his professionalism and his desperation played through his features. Apparently, desperation won, because he let go.

I opened the file.

The words of the police report turned to gibberish the moment I saw the picture. The boy was too thin, pale, with dark hair and eyes. I knew him. I knew him, but I didn't. Yet I'd stared at his face every time I looked in a mirror at the age of eight.

"His name was Andrew."

I traced the shape of his face with my finger. He even had a mole on his neck close to his collarbone.

Mine was on the right, his was on the left.

"He was a year younger than Julia."

There was another picture. He stood between Julia and Alice. She held his hand, and Julia looked like she was trying to convince herself no one else was there.

"The police report stated he'd disappeared on his way home from school. But there were inconsistencies in statements taken from Julia and Harrison's and the one taken from Alice."

"He's dead, isn't he?" Did he like to paint like me? What was his favorite food? Did he hide in the dark from Harrison like I had?

"They never found a body."

"But he's dead."

"Presumably, yes."

"What happened?"

Carmichael pursed his lips. I leafed through the pages. There was only the missing person's report and a few vague notes. An article in the paper gave a brief description with a plea for help. "Tell me what happened to him."

"They don't know exactly."

"What do they think happened?"

"Going by the inconsistencies between the statements, I believe Harrison killed him." But there was more. So much more.

"What else do you believe?"

Carmichael scrubbed a hand over his mouth. He aged a hundred years sitting there in front of me. "I was able to contact the school counselor working at Gold Leaf Middle School. She told me Andrew had begun to display behaviors associated with sexual abuse."

"Isn't it illegal for her to tell you stuff?"

"It is. But she's in her seventies and is no longer practicing. She blames herself for what happened—could have happened—to him and believes if she'd gone to the police with her suspicions he might still be alive."

"Why didn't she?"

Dr. Carmichael slumped in his chair. Another war played through his expression, but I had no idea what it could have been about until he said, "She had absolutely no evidence. Not even his word. The school was afraid of being sued, and the police didn't think a good upstanding family like the Duvoes was capable of such a thing."

I went back to looking through the folder. With the initial shock worn off, bits and pieces of the report trickled in. "He looked just like me."

In all honesty, he could have been my twin. My only comfort was knowing he'd been born years before Harrison met my mother.

"I know."

"Do you think that's why he hated me so much?"

"If I had to guess, I would say that's part of it."

There was another police report in the back. The picture of that boy was only similar in hair and eye color. "Who's this?" If it was another sibling, I was going to be sick. But he didn't look like Julia or Alice either.

"He lived next door to your father when he was young."

"What happened to him?" Because something had. It seemed everything the man touched wilted.

"He was found hanged in his basement."

I skimmed the report. There had been no evidence, but they'd questioned Harrison because he and the boy had been close. "Did he kill him too?"

"I don't know. I think he may have had something to do with it. I'm just not sure how much. But if Harrison did, I think that's where it all began."

A beginning belonged to a story. And one death meant it was more than a few pages. Two deaths meant it had more than enough pages for a novel. "How many?" I was grateful Carmichael knew exactly what I meant when I asked because I wasn't sure I had the courage to explain the question.

"Five, we think. Including your friend."

"You think?"

"The mother of one boy tripped and fell down a flight of stairs. She'd gone to the police. She claimed to have evidence. She named your father."

"They didn't arrest him?"

"The evidence was never found. And since she died..."

"He killed her too?"

Carmichael shook his head. "He was on a business trip."

A tremor began in my hand and traveled down my body. I swallowed once, twice... "Julia." Not a question, a fact.

"She was ten."

"But it was still her, wasn't it?"

"She was attending a sleepover with her daughters. But no one saw anything."

"But it was her."

"I'm inclined to believe it was."

Because pushing people downstairs was something she was good at. "How come no one put all this together before?" Here it was, decades later, and Carmichael connected the dots. Why couldn't the police?

"Your father traveled, and they moved around a lot."

"But there's a reason...there's a reason why you think it's him." I tapped the file. "Besides this..." Pictures, articles, and a couple of police reports. I wasn't a lawyer, but even this was piss poor evidence.

"Yes. There is."

"What?"

"I tracked down the parents of Harrison's first wife. They said they became suspicious of Harrison when they found out he'd lied about his background and was a maintenance worker at the firm he worked at, not sitting on board of directors like he claimed. They told their daughter, but she still wanted to marry him. When they protested, she cut ties with them for almost a decade. Then one day, she called them. She was very upset but wouldn't say why, but they had the feeling it had to do with Harrison. The next time they spoke to her, she said it had been a misunderstanding, but her mother said she sounded afraid.

"Kelly was diagnosed with cancer a few weeks later, and gone shortly after that. Harrison had her cremated before her parents were even aware she was sick."

"Why are you telling me this?"

"The doctor who signed her death certificate was Mason."

"But he's a psychiatrist."

"He's still a doctor. He's also Harrison's brother."

"They don't have the same last name."

"Different fathers. Mason didn't take on the last name of his mother's second husband. Because they were brothers he had a vested interest in keeping the real cause of death hidden."

Real cause? I shook my head because my voice had shriveled up.

"I was able to obtain a copy of the original pathology report and sent it to a friend of mine. He said there'd been no autopsy since she'd been diagnosed with cancer.

"He said the tests done support the diagnosis, but the blood values were also consistent with select types of poisoning."

"Julia." Again, not a question.

He nodded. "But she would have had help. While the chemicals are fairly common, it would take someone with a medical background to know which ones to combine. And at her age... Anyhow, I think her mother found out what really happened to Andrew, and to protect her father, she poisoned her."

"And..." I wadded up the folder in my fists.

"Your mother's pathology report is almost identical to that of Julia and Alice's mother."

The air thickened. I sucked in one breath after the other, but couldn't fill my lungs fast enough.

Carmichael knelt in front of me and cupped my face. My tears turned him into a watery haze. He urged me to put my head between my knees. Air trickled in. At some point, he pried the file from my hands. It must have torn because there were fragments on the floor in front of my feet.

"Breathe, Paris. You're safe here."

After what felt like forever, the vise around my ribs eased and the tingling receded from my lips. The first full breath of air rushed in a cool wave down my throat.

I nodded and sat up. "Ww—" I wiped the tears from my eyes. "Why would she do that? Why would he…"

"Mike did some research. Harrison inherited his first wife's estate, but he lived beyond his means and it wasn't long before the money was gone. I'm pretty sure he married your mother because she was wealthy. He would have inherited that estate too, only your mother rewrote her will before she died and it was all left to you. Upon your death, it would be passed on to charity. It's an unusual arrangement. Enough so it makes me think she knew. Or at least knew enough to think you might be in danger."

"Why didn't she leave him?"

"I don't know. I doubt we'll ever know. But it's not uncommon for people to stay with a spouse even when it's dangerous for them and their families. But she did stay and after she died, Harrison found out about the will.

"He couldn't get rid of you, Paris, and then every day, he had to look at the face of a boy he'd killed."

It must have been maddening. No wonder he came after me. Only instead of me who died, it was the boy whose name I couldn't remember.

Harrison might be gone, but there was still a killer in the mix.

"Sign the transfer papers."

Confusion marred Carmichael's features. "You don't have to do what she says. I told you you're safe."

"I know."

"Then why would you want me to sign the papers? Especially after everything else?"

"Because…" My nose ran. I wiped it on my sleeve. "I'm safe. But Roy isn't."

"Don't do this. Roy would not want you to do this. You go back there, and you could relapse."

I didn't care if I exploded. Because now I knew she wouldn't just ruin Roy. She'd kill him.

"The papers, sign them. I'll go pack."

****

The rabbit and I watched the Jaguar make a lap around the lot.

I'd expected Julia to send our private driver, but at the same time, seeing Mason didn't surprise me. To make this lie work, to send me back into the hell he'd help create, they would need as few witnesses as possible.

"Paris?" Carmichael came running up the hallway and into the waiting room. He flicked a look to the car pulling into the pickup area. The worry lines on his face turned into the hard mask of anger.

"You're not talking me out of this."

The argument played through his eyes, but he held out a card. His name, office number, and three more phone numbers had been penned across the margin in blue.

"Call me. If you change your mind or need anything."

I knew with every fiber of my being if I did this, Julia would sink her claws so deep I would never escape. Now that I knew the things she'd done, there was a chance I wouldn't even survive.

She might let me keep breathing, but I would drink, snort, and take the pills she gave me. I would paint for her, and she would keep the money to buy all her fancy things. She would pass me around as a bonus prize to those willing to spend top dollar.

She would kill me. It just wouldn't be the kind of dead where I needed to be buried.

The automatic doors hissed open, and Dr. Mason walked in dressed in a three-piece suit and Italian shoes. I was willing to bet his ensemble cost more than what Carmichael made in a month.

Dr. Mason pulled back his shoulders. "Are you ready?"

Carmichael stepped in front of me. I'm not sure if it was on purpose or if his protective instincts moved his feet.

Dr. Mason pulled his lips into a pseudo-smile. "If you don't mind, I'd like to collect my patient."

"What you're doing is unethical."

"Paris." Dr. Mason motioned toward the door.

"He needs treatment."

329

"And I will provide that for him."

"How? By doping him up on pain pills, speed, and barbiturates?"

"I'm not here to discuss my medical practices with you. I'm here to pick up my patient. Now move."

I put a hand on Carmichael's arm. His eyes were so sad. "It's not your fault." I took his hand and shook it. "Thank you for everything." I meant it, and I think he knew I did.

"Remember what I told you," His grip tightened over mine.

"I will." I opened my fingers one by one. Once I let go, once I turned away, once I got inside the car, everything would end for me.

I think he knew that too.

Dr. Mason led me out the door.

"Backseat." He went to the driver's side and got in.

The rabbit hopped up from the floorboard onto the seat next to me.

"No luggage?" He looked at me in the rearview mirror.

I shook my head. I didn't want to be reminded of what I'd lost by leaving. If I could have gone without the clothes on my back, I would have.

The rabbit tucked up next to my hip until it became a fuzzy white ball with a twitchy pink nose.

I petted its ears.

Dr. Mason watched my reflection. "What are you doing?"

"It likes to have its ears scratched."

"Excuse me?"

"The rabbit."

He started the car and concentrated on the road.

The remaining clouds from last night's rain broke apart overhead. Sunlight cut streaks of gold, severing shadows left by predawn. It set everything on fire. Reds, yellows, whites, and blues. There was just enough bite in the air for frost to form on the grass. The crystalized surface shattered the colors into a million points of light. The details were smeared as the car accelerated, but the hue could not be dulled.

At least the colors were back. Hopefully, Mason would let me keep them. I was sure he would. Julia wouldn't want to chance affecting my ability to paint.

Anything green and living receded as we entered the city. The mirrored windows of my apartment building reflected the world around it. But that's all it was. A reflection. Not real. Two dimensional. And easily destroyed by one thrown rock.

Dr. Mason dropped me off at the lobby. "I don't have to tell you to go directly upstairs, do I?"

"No." I'd learned my lesson. I would never talk out of turn again.

Mason rolled up his window.

The rabbit followed me to the elevator but stopped at the threshold. It stood up on its hind legs sniffing the air; ears back, eyes rolling as it examined the space.

"You've been in an elevator before."

It shook its head, and its ears flopped. The rabbit washed its face.

The door started to close, and I stopped it. "Come on. I don't have all day."

The rabbit cleaned between the toes of its back feet.

"If you don't get in here, I'm just going to go without you."

The rabbit licked its privates.

"Fine. Be an ass."

I let the door go.

"Wait." There was no way I couldn't know that voice, and for an insane moment, I thought it had come from the rabbit. Then Roy put a weathered hand between the doors, stopping them.

There was a fresh bruise on his face, and he had a half-healed split lip.

The rabbit followed Roy into the elevator.

"Paris?" Roy's eyebrows came down, and his eyes softened. The combination made his handsome face tragic.

I stumbled back into the corner. "Are you real?"

"Yes, I'm real."

"How do I know? You could be just like the rabbit." He had to be because no sane man would want to be around me after everything that had happened.

"Rabbit?"

The real question was, did I care whether he was here in my mind or in the flesh? Roy was real enough to hold his hand out to me asking for my touch, and that became all that mattered.

I cleared the space between us until we touched head to toe. He was warm against my body, solid under my hands. His breath tasted like coffee, but his tongue was all him.

I worked my mouth against his, and he dug his fingers into my hair. I couldn't stop. I was determined to suck out his soul.

The hard line of his cock pressed against me from behind his jeans.

Roy pegged me against the wall and held me there, searching my face, holding me, loving me.

"God, Paris." A tear slid down his cheek. "I missed you so much."

I touched his split lip. A fresh dot of blood stained my finger. "I'm sorry."

"For what?"

"She sent you to jail."

"It was my choice not to tell the judge what he wanted to know."

"But she was going to make sure you stayed."

"She can't do that."

Roy. Always the optimist.

"Julia was going to plant drugs in your apartment. She was going to set you up."

Some of the color drained from his cheeks.

I nodded. "You shouldn't be here. You need to get away from me." Especially now.

"Julia told me you were getting released today. She lied, didn't she?"

The lump in my throat threatened to choke me. "Yeah."

"If you still need treatment, then why did Carmichael discharge you?"

"I asked for a transfer to Dr. Mason's facility."

"Why?"

I dropped my gaze. The rabbit sat on Roy's boots, looking up at me. "If I don't paint for her, she will destroy you."

"What about you? You go back to her, and she will destroy you."

"I'm already broken."

The elevator dinged. I pushed in my floor before it reached the level it had been summoned to.

A moment later, the lift stopped and the doors opened. Oil and mineral spirits, fresh wood and gesso filled my lungs on a single breath. I had no idea how bad I'd missed my studio until I stood in the middle of it.

I ran a hand along the edge of a bench. I touched a jar of paintbrushes, the section of framing for an unfinished canvas, tubes of oils, my palette, a blank canvas on the table waiting to be filled.

Roy pressed himself against my back and brushed his lips against my neck.

"I'm never going to escape, am I?"

"You need to go back to the hospital."

"She owns me."

"She doesn't."

"Yes, she does." I'd been a fool to think I could ever be free.

"Only because you let her."

I suppose I did. In much the same way, I let her make me help her drag that boy into the woods and drop him down an old bored well. I let her do those things, and that made my sin all the more difficult to bear. Perhaps that's why I was here. It was my penance. My hell on earth for the terrible thing I'd done.

"Roy, will you do something for me?"

"Anything."

"Go home so she can't hurt you anymore. Move so she can't find you." *So I can't find you.*

"You don't mean that."

"I don't want to. I want you here with me. In my bed. In my arms. I want you tucked against my body, held. I want to be held."

His arms tightened.

"But if you stay, she'll hurt you."

"What if I say no?"

I dropped my chin to my chest.

"What if I think it's worth the risk?"

Then I would have to choose a way out so I could save him. "Take me upstairs. Make love to me. At least do that."

The rabbit didn't follow us. I wasn't even sure it left the elevator. Not that walls, doors, or distance would contain it.

Like Roy's love for me.

We stopped beside the bed, and I started to undress. Roy put his hand over mine. "Let me."

He trailed his fingers along my neck and swept his thumbs across my cheeks. A shiver danced down my body. Closer, the scent of him, something earthy with a cinnamon flavor, filled me when I inhaled.

He pressed his lips against my temple and pushed my coat off my shoulders.

Through the flannel, I followed the contours of his muscles. I wanted to think I knew every dip and valley, but I didn't.

I was going to change that.

Roy's fingertips burned a path along my ribs as he stripped me of my shirt. On the way up, he flicked one nipple, then the other. The sharp sting traveled from my pectorals to my balls.

"Roy, please."

"Please what?" He nipped my ear and licked his way to my throat.

"I need more."

"And I'll give it to you." He caressed my sides, my stomach, and I groaned. He stopped at the edge of my jeans. The fabric parted, and cool air kissed my cock.

Roy peeled away the rest of my clothes as he lowered me to the bed.

"You're beautiful." His hands followed his gaze down the length of my body.

"You always say that."

And he smiled at me in a way that said he knew I never got tired of hearing him.

He undressed.

As each piece of clothing fell away, my skin tightened and my heart skipped. Naked, Roy climbed over me, bearing the weight of his body on his arms. I spread my legs, and he chuckled.

"Not yet." He fed me a long, slow kiss. Stroking his tongue against mine, probing, exploring. The growl in his throat echoed in my chest. I arched high enough to slide our cocks together.

Against my lips, he whispered, "I love you, and I will never abandon you."

The tightness in my throat sent an ache to my heart. I cried in there so he wouldn't hear the screams.

The drawer thumped. Roy peppered a line of kisses down the path of hair running under my navel. The thunder of my heart made it impossible for me to hear the snick of the lubricant bottle.

He flicked his tongue across the end of my cock and followed it with a caress of his lips. Then wet heat engulfed me.

"Ah, God..." I was able to keep myself from thrusting my hips, but I couldn't stop myself from pawing at his head and pulling at his thick waves of dark curls. There wasn't enough for me to wrap my hands in, but I still tried.

Roy milked me in long, slow strokes. Every time he reached the tip, he'd press his tongue against the slit hard enough to make me think any moment he'd burrow inside. The electric threads shooting up my spine made me wish he could.

He pushed his lubricant-slicked fingers between my ass cheeks and made circles around my opening, coming closer with each lap until he pressed against the tight ring of muscle.

"More." I pulled my legs up and lifted my ass. Pressure made me gasp and was followed by a stretch and burn. He worked two of his thick fingers as deep as they would go. The minimal preparation left me aching with a sense of fullness. The slight discomfort quickly turned into a needful pleasure.

I rolled my hips in an attempt to ride his hand and fuck his mouth, but every time I thought I'd established a rhythm, Roy changed his pace.

Just as the burn in my ass stopped, he pushed in a third. I slammed my head against the pillow. "Please, oh please..." I abandoned my attempts to pull his hair in favor of clinging to the iron headboard. Any moment I would fly apart, and I didn't want to be lost as the rush of spiraling euphoria drowned me alive.

"Gonna come, Roy, don't, please...I... want..."

His fingers and mouth disappeared, and I howled in frustration. Roy recaptured my mouth, fucked me with his tongue, showing me exactly what he planned on doing to my body.

There was a moment of fumbling when he worked to keep his mouth on mine and guided his cock to my hole. I locked my ankles around his back just as he breached my opening. The ache returned in a rush of pleasure. I tightened my legs and raised my ass, forcing him to take me in one thrust. He stilled, and the muscles in his arms quivered with restraint.

The desire in his eyes was for me, a result of what I did to him. How I made him feel and how he felt about me. But it was the love that glowed brighter than the sun.

Roy pulled back and pushed forward, setting up an agonizing pace, making me beg him to never stop. I buried my face against his neck, and his ragged breathing filled my ears. We stayed like that. Him making long slow thrusts, me holding him.

No words needed to be spoken because we said everything to each other through touch, looks, small kisses, and desperate breaths. This was making love, not fucking. Just the silence of two bodies as one.

It felt like hours before I came, and when I did, I lost my soul to him.

****

I left Roy asleep in my bed and walked to the balcony. The wind cut hard lines through the ivy cultivated from large stone pots against the wall. Cold radiated through the glass windows on the door and into my palms.

The rabbit hopped up beside me, and we stared out the french doors together.

"I don't know what else to do."

The rabbit looked up at me.

"It's the only way I can protect him, from her." And there was no cost too high to keep Julia from hurting Roy.

I unlocked the door. The wind ate right through the cotton pajama bottoms I wore and parted the fur on the rabbit's shoulder. My toes were numb before I had a patio chair moved next to the wall. The wooden seat made a small protest under my weight.

My tears froze, and my muscles danced, but it was no longer about being cold. I just wanted this to be over. All of it. Julia. The drugs. The alcohol. The lies. I'd been clean for over a month while in Carmichael's care. Not just because I didn't have access to the drugs. I didn't want them. I didn't need them. I was safe.

336

And I wanted to be safe again. I wanted to be held, kissed, loved. I had all those things in that fleeting moment of my life, and that meant I could die happy.

The rabbit was already on the ledge, hunkered down against the wind, when I straddled the wall. Below me, cars dotted the road, and in neighboring apartments, lights blinked on. But it was still too early for the commuters. My apartment overlooked a densely wooded area of the park so there was little chance I'd hit anyone when I landed.

Another blast of cold swept over me, and my muscles constricted. The crushing pain felt too much like it had when I thought Roy abandoned me.

I leaned forward and so did the rabbit.

This would end it all, the pain, the worries, the fear.

The rabbit put its paw on my thigh. Sadness filled its large dark eyes.

"I have to."

Its small mouth churned, and it lifted its chin.

"It's my choice."

The rabbit put its other paw with the first.

"And it's my life. I can do what I want with it." Even toss it over the edge of a building.

The rabbit looked back at the doors. My reflection was captured on the glass and divided by the grilles. Sometimes, a section of me was alone on the perfect square; other times, I was accompanied by a sliver of sky, wall, and even the rabbit. The contrast defined the outline of my form, pushing lost details to the surface.

And it was me who gave depth to the world.

Sometimes, all it took was a swatch of color on a greater field to complement the surrounding pigments and balance one of my works. It was an affect difficult to see when standing close, but revealed if I stepped back and observed the entire canvas. Adding new colors built depth, and once in place, deleting even the most insignificant stroke destroyed the harmony created by the presence of so many hues and shadows.

If I wanted to change the direction of movement, it meant laying down new lines, altering the depth of shadows to make the colors pop, not obliterate what existed. Because even if those new brushstrokes covered everything, their success was built on the presence of those first layers even when those layers were a conglomeration of mistakes and muddied hues.

Like the canvas, if I wanted to make things better for Roy, it meant changing my perspective and facing the monster. Not the one born in my mind and fed by my lie, but the creature that made me help her drag a boy's body out to a well and drop him into the darkness.

The one who made me into a liar.

Her father raped a boy of his life, and she'd raped me of my sanity. Both times, I let it happen because I'd been alone. But I wasn't alone now.

With Roy, I had the chance to set things right. I could destroy the lie with the truth. I could tell the world what really happened. I could lay to rest the boy who kissed me.

"Won't be quick, rabbit. She'll bleed us. She'll break our bones. We will suffer."

The rabbit flicked his ears.

Roy was willing. Why couldn't I be?

I climbed down off the wall and scooted the chair back into its place. The rabbit followed me inside.

My studio. My paintings. A comfort and a curse. My ability to paint allowed me to keep some semblance of humanity intact inside my soul, and it shackled me to the nightmare I lived in.

I touched my lips. They weren't anywhere as soft as the boy's had been.

Somehow through all the bad things, that one memory remained bright and perfect and unsoiled. The only part of my past that had come away clean. The only thing Julia hadn't taken. Sure, she'd stolen the painting, but she couldn't take those few moments in time, when the sun broke through the leaves in bits of gold and red.

For the first time, I was not afraid of the anger inside me. I begged the boy who kissed me to give me his strength and courage. From out of the darkness, he held out his hand, and I took it.

Together, we would ruin her.

I picked up the wood knife lying on the bench near a supply of brushes and carried it to the shelves where I stored my works. Pieces that were sold or would sell. Millions of dollars in art.

I pulled out the first. Apathy: a man on his knees wrapped in thorny vines stripping him of his flesh. He cried out in pain, but the people surrounding him gave him their backs and ignored his pleas.

The canvas gave way to the blade with a soft pop. A slow hiss of parting fabric followed the knife as I dragged it downward.

The edges of the gaping hole were rough with thick layers of paint. Threads dangled from the cut but wouldn't unravel because they were glued in place by gesso.

I traced the folds of cotton fabric as it wrapped the frame. Building the canvases was often as important to me as painting the images. As a white void, they numbed me in much the same way the drugs and alcohol did.

Then they took on my nightmares so I could breathe. I promised myself I would never burden such perfection with that kind of ugliness again.

I raised my leg and slammed one of the slats against my knee. The sharp crack echoed off the walls. On the bench, the white rabbit startled and kicked its feet.

I snapped another rung, leaving the canvas a crumpled mess.

The next painting was The Blind Man. I broke the frame, and the jagged wood punched a hole through the canvas. Then I gripped the wound and spread the fabric.

It bled. Blacks, reds, dark sooty browns. It poured out over my fingers and smeared the floor.

A third one.

The Rapist.

Together, the boy and I shredded the painting's flesh and broke its bones with our hands. Together, we bled it out.

When the rack was empty, I went for the benches, shoving brushes and paints onto the floor. I stomped on the tubes of pigment until they smeared on the tiles and squished up between my toes.

I threw the jars of mineral spirits, and the glass burst with liquid pops. It wasn't enough, it would never be enough. I went for the raw supplies: rolls of canvas, unassembled frames.

I grabbed one of the lengths of wood only to have it snatched away.

Roy tossed it aside and wrapped an arm around my chest. "Stop. Just stop."

339

"Let me go." I twisted in Roy's grasp. Streaks of red and yellow smeared across his arms.

"For God's sake, Paris, stop."

"I have to do this." Couldn't he see it? Already, Julia's pain boiled within the chaos.

"No, you don't."

"I have to take back what's mine. I have to ruin what she's stolen. No more, Roy. I will not let her take from me ever again."

He turned me around. A smudge of green made a line on one of his cheeks. More paint was stamped across his chest.

"Please," I said.

"Doing this isn't going to fix things."

"I know. I don't want to fix it. I just want to hurt her, and this will hurt her. Then I can get away. I can live. I want to live. I want to be happy. I want a life. With you. Just you. I want peace. That's all I ever wanted."

Roy's gaze went from my face to the destruction I'd started on my studio. I burned with the need to finish this. To end the suffering I'd released into the world.

Roy held up my hands. Blood from the cuts mixed with oils, and bruises bloomed on my arms. My thighs throbbed with the promise of grand additions.

"I'll be right back..." Spots of paint tracked him up the steps to my room. He returned with our shoes. He knelt. "There's glass on the floor." Roy slipped the shoes on my feet before putting on his boots. He stood and cupped my face with his hands. His lips were so soft against mine. And the kiss wasn't born of a memory.

We destroyed everything.

Every canvas, painted, not painted, shelves, brushes, jars of turpentine and mineral oil. Thousands of dollars in tubes of paint were crushed on the floor with their insides smeared.

With Roy's help, I didn't even need the anger of the boy who kissed me. Through the destruction, Roy and I fucked each other with violence. Never touching, but moving until we gleamed with sweat, grunted like animals, and strained for release, both riding on the waves of chaos we churned.

When we were done, the studio swam in the remains of my hell and the beginning of Julia's.

I staggered through the mess on trembling legs. Roy led me to the couch. I had a second to think about how the paint on our bodies would ruin the leather, and then I decided I didn't care.

We collapsed. Me in his arms, heaving like there was no air to breathe. No matter how hard I tried, I couldn't pull my gaze off of the apocalypse.

It was beautiful.

The rabbit surveyed the ruined studio. Paint covered its feet, and there were several blotches on its side. Had it lain down at one point to watch us lose our minds?

Roy petted my head. "I want you to go back to the hospital."

"Under one condition."

"What?"

"You use my money to get a lawyer." Roy stayed quiet. "Julia will make good on her threat. She will try and frame you, and she'll succeed unless you have someone on your side."

"Do you have any suggestions?"

I laughed. "I don't even know where to go to pay the utilities."

He kissed my temple. "We'll figure it out."

"We." I sighed into shoulder. "I like that. All purple and gold."

"Sounds pretty."

"More like strong."

"That you are."

"I'm not."

"You are, Paris."

"Only because you're here to hold me up." I put my fingers over his lips. "It's the truth, so get used to it."

He cocked his mouth to the side. "We should get a shower."

"What time is it?"

"Almost nine."

"We need to get dressed and leave. Alice will be here at ten, and then Julia will be here shortly after. We can make any phone calls on the way back." To the hospital; with its drugs, nurses, doctors, and locked doors. It had hotel-style rooms and a crappy art studio with crappier paint.

I missed it already. Even the shitty newsprint.

I unwound myself from the sofa. Roy took my hand, and I pulled him to his feet. A dab of purple paint streaked his upper lip and another spot of blue on the edge of his nose. For some strange reason, the colors were perfect on him.

"C'mon." I tugged him in the direction of the stairs. We stopped when the elevator door opened.

Julia's presence filled the lift. She was a lot shorter than me and several pounds lighter, but in that moment, she seemed ten feet tall and half a ton.

It was the air around her. It danced with jagged points of red and black.

Stray locks of her perfect hair stuck out to the side, leaving a visual path of where she had run her hand through it over and over. Maybe even pulled. I'd never known Julia to pull her hair.

She wore a peach-colored pants suit but no makeup. It might have been washed away because her eyes were puffy like she'd been crying for hours.

There was a small caliber gun in her right hand.

Over the years, I'd seen Julia in all stages of anger, all temperatures of rage, but in that moment, there were no words to describe the venom boiling in her eyes. It should have terrified me.

She stopped at the edge of the foyer. Her gaze went from me to the destruction of the studio. Her expression remained the same, but I couldn't shake the feeling she was almost pleased with what she saw.

"I got a call this morning from the real estate agent managing one of the rental properties. Apparently, the people leasing the place woke up to a bunch of cops crawling over the yard." She brushed her hair away from her face, but it clung to her cheeks in sticky clumps. "What did you tell them, Paris? What lies have you started up?"

"No lies."

"Of course, it's lies. It's always lies. That's all you do is lie." Her voice spiked an octave with every word she spat until spit flecked her lips.

"What was his name?"

Her eyes widened a moment, then a sneer pulled her lips into a grotesque shape. "Juan, Julio, Pablo, pick one. It won't make a difference. He was nothing but a worthless immigrant. No one knows who he was, and no one cares."

"I do."

She adjusted her grip on the gun. "Like I said, no one cares."

"It's over, Julia. Everything. The lies. Not mine. Yours. They know everything."

"Fires burn hot, little brother. Fueled by flammables like turpentine, oils, and paints, they can burn really hot." She raised the gun and pulled the trigger. A line seared across my shoulder. The glass on the french doors shattered behind me.

Blood cut a beautiful crimson path down my arm. Roy pulled me to the side. She fired again. Fragments of brick pelted my cheek.

With the open floor plan, there was nowhere to hide. The rabbit darted around the partition and into the kitchen. I pushed Roy to follow, but another shot plugged the wall near my head. We scrambled back to the corner.

We would die. Julia would make sure of it. Then she would set the place on fire, and there would be nothing left. Maybe it would kill more than just us. Maybe it would burn down the whole building.

But she was incapable of caring.

The rabbit peeked around the corner of the cabinets and bobbed its head. Before I even had time to run, Julia fired off another shot.

Roy jerked and a bloody flower bloomed on the thigh of his boxers. He fell against the wall. With all the noise, it was no wonder no one heard the lift doors open or saw Alice walk in until she said, "Did you shoot Andrew too?"

There was a second of fear in Julia's eyes. Maybe even some shame. But it vanished so quickly I could have imagined it.

"I thought I told you to go shopping."

"I did."

"Then what are you doing here?"

"The store refused the bank cards. I called the bank, but they said that information was private."

"What are you talking about?"

"They said the accounts had been frozen, but they wouldn't tell me why."

Julia's anger blazed hotter. I was almost grateful she had a gun. Otherwise, she might have found a much slower way to kill us.

"So did you?" Alice stepped up beside Julia. So calm. So serene. And so very sad. How the hell could she look at Julia with anything but fear?

"Did I what?"

"Shoot Andrew?"

"He ran away."

"No, he didn't."

"Yes, he did. Now go home."

"That's not what Daddy said."

"What are you talking about?"

"The day Daddy died. The day you went into the woods with Paris."

"You're confused, Alice. Why would I go into the woods with Paris?"

"I don't know. I never asked. But I saw you."

"You were in classes all day."

"I forgot my notes, so I came home."

Julia looked at her sister. Really looked at her.

"I saw him in Paris's room. He was talking to Dr. Mason. He told him to come over. He had a gun. He told Dr. Mason, 'Little boys run away all the time, so what's one more bullet?'"

While Julia watched Alice, I pulled Roy behind the partition. Another shot rang out. It tore through the thin wall. There was a metallic clang, then one of the copper pots flew off the hook and landed in the floor.

The rabbit skittered in a circle. White framed the rich brown irises of its eyes.

"Tell me, Julia." I'd never heard Alice yell before. It was frightening. "Did you shoot Andrew?"

"He's gone. It doesn't matter."

"It does. To me, it does." A sob butchered Alice's words.

I squeezed Roy's arm. Sweat beaded his forehead. He gripped his thigh, but the blood welled up between his fingers.

The rabbit paused at the other end of the wall, then dashed across the space.

I leaned forward. The rabbit stopped halfway to the elevator and looked back at us.

"Okay." I nodded. "Okay, we'll try."

"Try what?" Roy gave me a questioning look.

I shook my head. There was no time to explain the rabbit. Hell, there was no time for me to even understand it.

"Go home, Alice."

"I need to know."

"Why?"

I was almost to my feet when Alice said, "Because if you shot him, then I killed Daddy for no reason."

The silence was momentary but absolute.

Julia said, "What are you talking about?"

"He laid the gun down on the bedside table and was looking through Paris's backpack. I picked it up while he was turned around. He asked me what I was doing. I asked him if he killed Andrew, and he wouldn't tell me. He told me to give him the gun. I wouldn't, and he yelled at me. Daddy never yelled at me. He tried to take it away. I thought he killed him, Julia. I thought he killed Andrew so I pulled the trigger."

"Daddy killed himself." Julia's razor sharp tone had dulled with muted grays. "The police said so. He put the gun in his mouth and pulled the trigger."

"I got really close. I wanted to look at him in the eye so I would know if he was lying. I wanted him to tell me the truth, but he just yelled and yelled, and yelled."

I put Roy's arm around my shoulder. He shook his head. I think he saw in my eyes I was not going to leave him, because he nodded and helped me stand him up.

"Just go home, we'll talk about this later."

"No."

That was another first. Alice never told Julia no.

"I didn't have a choice, all right. He knew Daddy was weak. Andrew tricked him. He made him... Andrew was going to ruin everything. His lies were going to put us out on the street."

I took the opportunity to make a run for the door.

If I could get to the foyer, there was enough of an alcove between it and the lift we'd be shielded. It didn't even occur to me that the elevator might take time to open. Not that it mattered.

The bullet punched me in the back. Roy tried to catch me, and we wound up in a heap on the floor.

Alice grabbed Julia's hands, and the second shot shattered a lamp on a side table. Glass fragments littered the floor in chips of white.

The rabbit slipped on the tile and crashed into the wall. It regained its balance, then scurried across the room and dove behind the sofa.

Julia shoved Alice into one of the workbenches and slipped on a smear of paint. Julia tried to counter her fall, but a shredded canvas tangled up in her fancy high heels.

She fell against a stool, it toppled over and both of them went to the floor.

There was a dull pop, then Julia lay there looking surprised. Alice rolled away. Blood gushed from the hole in her back. She got to her knees, reached for the edge of the table but collapsed.

Julia stared at the gun in her hand, then me. Her face turned a shade close to purple. "Look what you made me do!"

Alice dragged herself across the floor.

Julia stood.

"Look what you made me do, Paris." Tears streaked Julia's face. She raised the gun, then Alice said her name. She lowered the weapon.

"It hurts." Alice sobbed on the floor.

I wanted to go to her, but even if it was safe, I'm not sure I could have. The dull throb in my shoulder turned into a creeping numbness. I didn't even realize Roy was pulling me toward the elevator until the rug in the foyer bunched under my hip.

"Julia." Alice rolled onto her back. "Julia, I'm scared."

She knelt beside Alice. It was the first act of remorse I think I'd ever seen her commit.

Julia petted Alice's cheek. "It'll be okay. I'll call the doctor, and we'll make everything better."

It was a lie. I knew it was a lie. If she did, the police would come, and she would have no explanation.

Roy reached for the elevator button. It dinged, and Julia turned.

We were at the right height for a chest or headshot, not moving, and no more than fifty feet separated us. Even with bad aim, she wouldn't miss, and if she did, all she had to do was take a few steps. The elevator was only seconds away, but it would be long enough for her to clear the room and put the muzzle right to my head.

I think Roy knew too. He shielded me with his body as if he had some hope of stopping this. But he didn't. No matter how much he wanted it. No matter how much he was willing to sacrifice.

Roy's scent filled me, his warmth brought me comfort, and the vise of fear choking me fell away. I might die, but it would be in the arms of someone I loved.

A gift I'd never thought possible.

Alice screamed.

One high-pitched angry sound. It should have shattered glass. God knows it shattered all the colors in my mind. I don't know when she grabbed the canvas blade. Somewhere between where she lay and where she fell. Or maybe it was right there all along.

She shoved herself upright and drove it into the side of Julia's neck. The gun went off. The ringing sound in my ears swelled until it turned black. Until there was nothing left but the darkness.

"I love you." I could only hope Roy heard me before it was too late.

Chapter Fifteen

They say when you're about to die your life flashes before your eyes.

All I saw was the boy.

The sunlight split across the edges of falling leaves and made beautiful glowing threads as they turned.

His dark eyes watched me. Not with animosity or anger but with happiness.

Maybe even love.

I waited. Would he take me with him? With the way he looked at me, I was sure he wanted to.

He put his hand on his chest. "Lorenzo Martinez."

I put my hand on my chest. "Paris Duvoe."

Then Lorenzo pointed.

Roy stood with his hand out. Lorenzo nodded, and I took Roy's hand. After that, Lorenzo was gone.

I was afraid his name was only a figment of my imagination. Or maybe a hallucination, like the rabbit.

But it wasn't.

Lorenzo Martinez had been born on March 1st, 1985, a year before me. He and his mother had emigrated from Spain to join their father in the US. But he died six months after they arrived, and she had to take a job cleaning houses.

The track lighting forced the reds and yellows to the surface of the painting. They moved in fluid waves across the canvas, curling into wisps that trickled into blues and greens, broken by purple.

The rabbit perched its rump on my left foot.

"Comfortable?"

It cleaned its face.

I gave it a nudge, and it hopped a few feet and raised its head. Then without any warning, the rabbit darted around the partition the painting hung on.

I didn't know the woman wearing the gaudy pearl necklace, but she took me by my hand as if we were old friends.

"It's beautiful, Paris."

I smiled because it was beautiful.

"I didn't think anything could outdo your other paintings, but these…" She sighed. "I have no words."

Neither did I.

"Is it true?"

"What?" I sipped my champagne.

"You know, what they say about how you paint these."

I smiled around the edge of my glass. "What are they saying?"

The woman's cheeks reddened. She leaned closer. "They say you roll around on the canvas while you're…"

"While I'm what?"

The man with her said, "Danielle thinks you get those lovely shapes by having sex on a canvas smeared with paint."

I arched an eyebrow. "Really?"

She dropped her gaze.

The man shook his head. "I told you. You need to quit reading that gossip magazine." He pulled her away.

I'd gone to doing the initial layer in acrylic, then after it dried, adding the details in oil, but it could still be difficult to remove. Especially when you got it in some unreachable places like the crack of your ass.

I tilted my head. If I squinted, I could almost make out the shape of a hand and pair of knee prints. There were other less nameable shapes that might have been the heel or a cock. Who knows? I rarely paid much attention to what got rolled where.

What would Mrs. Gaudy Pearls say if she knew just how right she was? Better yet, what would her stuffy husband say?

"However you paint it, I think it's pretty." Alice held my hand. Every day I looked at her, I could hardly believe she was still here. But then I was amazed every day I was still here. I wouldn't be if Roy hadn't put himself between Julia and me.

By passing through his body, the bullet slowed enough that when it hit me in the chest it lodged in my sternum, never reaching my heart.

"How are you doing?" And Alice would know I meant in a way that didn't mean *today* but every second, minute, hour, day.

Her smile softened. "Good."

"And?"

"We talk. But he's easy to talk to."

Dr. Carmichael was easy to talk to. And when you couldn't talk, he would sit there and let you cry.

"Did you decide whether or not you're going to go see Alma?" Alice said.

"I don't know." I'd said the same thing when Alice asked me if I was going to talk to her on the phone.

I had no idea Carmichael had contacted Lorenzo's mother. He told me when she asked to speak with me.

It had taken me a week to shore up the courage. Twice, I backed out, and Carmichael had to apologize to her. He tricked me into it the third time. He had her on speakerphone when I went into his office. She said hello, and my knees folded.

At least I landed on the chair. After that, I was a captive audience.

She did most of the talking. Actually, she did all of the talking. I just sat there and listened while she told me she wasn't angry and never blamed me.

I'm not sure what was worse, the fear of being hated, or knowing I'd been loved by a total stranger who knew I'd suffered for loving her son and she'd been powerless to help me.

When she called the police with her concerns, they'd dismissed her complaint because she barely spoke English and couldn't give them her address because she feared they would deport her.

I'd never left her thoughts, though.

She told me how she'd kept a scrapbook with clippings from art magazines. It sat on a shelf next to a photo album with Lorenzo's pictures.

She wanted me to meet me for lunch. I still hadn't given her an answer. Listening to her talk was one thing. Seeing her face to face?

I wasn't sure I wouldn't completely fall apart.

I kissed Alice's knuckles. A man in a blue suit standing at the next painting over frowned at me.

"I think you have an admirer," I said.

She looked, and the man went back to staring at the painting. "His name is Matthew."

"You know him?"

She nodded. "He asked me out on a date last week."

"Did you go?"

Her smile faltered.

"You should go."

Alice squeezed my hand. "I don't think I'm ready. I don't think I'll ever be ready."

"Why not?"

"Because every time I even think about liking someone, I hear...I hear him saying that boys are dirty. I hear her too."

"So what if we are?"

"But you're not."

I shrugged. "We might be."

Alice bit her lip.

"But don't worry, we clean up pretty good."

Then she laughed. It was barely more than a giggle, but it was real. Like the happiness in her eyes when she looked at me. "So it will be all right? You won't mind?"

"Alice, the only thing I don't want is for you to be unhappy. If going out with Martin—"

"Matthew."

"My mistake." Accidentally on purpose, mistake. "If going out with him will make you happy, then go."

"I'll have to take a day off so I can get my hair done."

"Balancing the checkbook can wait a few days."

Alice laughed again, and her cheeks reddened. "It would only be a date. I wouldn't be gone for a few days."

"You might be surprised."

Matthew continued staring at us, but Alice hadn't noticed.

"I think he's jealous." I kissed her knuckles again, and his frown returned.

"Why, you're my brother?"

"Does he know that?"

"I don't know. He just moved here from California. This is the first showing he's ever been to."

"You know a lot about him."

"We talk some."

"Then go talk to him some more."

Alice gave me one of those unsure looks. I used to think they were about her, because Julia always called her fragile. After a few weeks out of the hospital, when the media swarmed, the police were at our doorstep every morning, the lawyers right behind them, I'd learned her worried gaze was for me.

Would I be all right?

"I'll be fine," I said.

"I don't want you to be by yourself."

"I won't."

"You have a date?"

I smiled. "Absolutely."

Alice kissed me on the cheek. "I'll go talk to him. Then I'll let you know when he wants to go out."

I turned her around and gave her a little shove. Matthew went back to staring at the painting again. Alice stopped beside him, they exchanged words, then he glanced my way. The tension in his expression disappeared. He held out his arm to Alice, and she took it.

I'd never imagined the demons Alice carried with her. She'd loved Andrew. As an older brother, he'd doted on her to no end. Then Julia took him away because he was going to tell what Harrison was doing.

It wasn't love that motivated her.

Their mother suspected Harrison of having something to do with Andrew's disappearance. Alice said Julia overheard her talking about filing for divorce. Julia refused to get stuck with the woman who told them no, the woman who expected them to do chores, and required respect.

Julia was not going to live her life under a tyrant.

Then a few days before their mother was scheduled to go to the lawyer, she got sick. Then sicker. In less than two weeks, she was dead.

We'd never know how Julia poisoned her: food, drink, or some other way. But the forensic pathologist who'd looked into the case for Carmichael, was sure that's exactly what happened.

Apparently, money motivated Julia at a very early age.

Even after her death, the lawyers were still digging up accounts Julia had hidden. She'd had years to skim money, and the amounts she'd acquired were astronomical. A funny thing, greed. She'd kept me around to fill her pockets until I became too much of a liability, then she'd taken out an insurance policy on my life.

A bonus, I guess, for her sisterly duties.

None of this would have happened if Harrison had gotten caught. But Dr. Mason had been the one to order their mother's blood work. He'd done the same for my mother.

Mason claimed he had no part in any of the killings, but he did help cover them up. He said his reasons were his own. It was unlikely he'd ever share what those reasons were, but the private detective, David, suspected it had something to do with the boy who'd hung himself.

Alice never knew any of those things, and she'd cried for days when she found out. Not because she was angry with Julia or even her father. She was angry at herself for ever believing Andrew had run away in the first place.

But everything would be all right. Maybe not today or tomorrow, but it would.

In truth, we'd be better than before. No more secrets. No more lies.

A husband and wife smiled at me. Beyond them was a small group of people. Farther over, a journalist from the local newspaper. Anna Joseph loved to take my picture.

Not for the paper, of course.

Next week her beautiful photography would be revealed to the public. The Lorenzo gallery wasn't large, but it was fast become the jumping off point for many new artists and attracting the attention of several artistic celebrities. Anna's first showing was to be hosted by Kristine Kline, author of the bestselling series Extraordinary Boy.

If Mrs. Gaudy Pearls came to the next showing, her question about my attire while I painted would be answered. Personally, I couldn't wait to see the reactions.

Serena Haus, my new agent, was sure my paintings would go up in value.

Whether they did or didn't made no difference to me. The only thing I cared about was creating beautiful colors.

"You look like you could use some company." The man who spoke was not cut by money or political interest, and the Armani he wore accented his wide shoulders, his narrow waist, and made his dark skin golden.

His deep chuckle vibrated down my body. Rich golds, earthy browns, and streaks of blazing green followed.

The rabbit regarded us with one dark eye.

"Actually, I'm waiting on someone."

"Really?" He moved closer. His rich scent was still spiced with sex and a hint of acrylic. "You sure he's going to show up?"

"Of course."

"So you have an evening planned?"

"He's taking me to dinner."

The man was slightly taller, but it was his presence that told me he was dangerous enough to kill me if he wanted. He rested his large hands on my hips and pressed his chest against my back. The thick line of his cock nestled against my ass.

"And where is he taking you?" His heated breath brushed the nape of my neck.

"A place."

"Just a place?"

"A café, actually."

"Sounds…boring."

"Maybe a little. But the company is good, and the cheesecake is to die for." I walked over to the painting a few partitions down and closer to the back of the gallery.

The man followed. "How about you ditch your date and come home with me instead?"

"And why would I do that?"

He stopped beside me.

One of the waiters came by and offered to take my empty glass. I thanked him, and he moved on.

The man herded me into an area of the gallery where the paintings ended and a luxurious curtain hid a door leading to the boiler room and storage area.

The rabbit hopped past me and burrowed under the edge of the curtain. Its body made a bump in the folds of blue.

I found myself cornered against the wall with the man's strong arms boxing me in.

He brushed his lips against my neck. The heat of his tongue traced a line to my ear.

I shuddered. "You never did tell me."

"What?"

"Why I should ditch my date and go home with you."

"Do I need a reason?"

"Yes."

He pushed his knee between my legs. I couldn't stop myself from grinding into his thigh.

"There's a room in the back. Come with me and let me convince you."

"To go home with you?"

His expensive slacks barely held back his rock hard cock. "Yes."

"What if he comes looking for me?" I buried my hands in his hair and tilted up my head.

"I take it he's the jealous type."

"Protective."

He growled, and I was sure I'd come in my pants.

"I'm willing to take the chance." He pushed aside the curtain. The door was right there, and of course, it was unlocked.

Harsh fluorescents replaced the track lighting. The door closed. Then there was a click of a lock. "Just in case," he said.

It was my turn to laugh. "I thought it was worth the risk."

"No need to make it easy on him."

The man shoved me against the wall and assaulted my mouth. His tongue fought with mine in a battle of dominance.

One I lost as soon as he had his hands on my cock. "Oh, God." I thrust into the tunnel of his fist.

"I'm going to fuck you."

"You sure you don't want me to fuck you instead?"

Fire ignited in his green eyes. "Not tonight. Tomorrow maybe."

"You sound awfully sure you'll wind up in my bed."

"You know I will." He spun me around. My pants landed in a puddle around my ankles.

A rustle of fabric was followed by the soft clink of a belt. Then the heated length of his cock was sliding between my legs.

"I could change my mind."

"You won't." He pushed his cold slick fingers between my ass cheeks and rubbed my hole.

"So sure that you brought lubricant with you?" I glanced back.

His cheeks reddened. "Actually, I forgot the lubricant."

"Then what are you using?" The cold turned into a pleasant burn.

The man in the Armani held up a tube of mint lip balm.

I bit my lip. "I hope that thing is full because you're going to need it."

"Brand new. Bought it in the gift shop." Another glob brought ice into the burn.

"Fuck that feels good."

"Is that your way of telling me I should use it more often?" He pushed a finger into my hole. I rode back against him.

"More." I needed him now.

"So eager."

"Please..."

"I thought you were worried about your boyfriend catching you."

"Finders keepers."

The man pushed in a second finger. Together, those thick digits were bigger than most men's cocks.

I shook a foot free from my slacks so I could widen my stance and take his cock so deep I wouldn't be able to breathe. "Now."

He thrust his fingers.

"Don't make me wait. Please don't make me—" The sudden emptiness wouldn't last because the man would never leave me unfulfilled.

The fat head of his cock breached my opening. With every inch, my breath shortened. By the time he stopped, that wonderful sense of fullness gripped me.

I tried to rock back, but he held me against the wall.

"Not yet." He pushed his hands under my shirt. A flick from his thumbs over my nipples sent an electric thrill to my cock. Then he found the scar near the center of my chest and traced it.

Most of the time, the skin there was numb, but at times like this, the nerves lit up. There was no pain, just the eternal reminder of the man who'd been willing to die for me.

He tightened his hold. "I love you so much."

Sometimes, the man in the Armani whispered those words in my ear when he thought I was asleep. And when he was asleep I would hold him, especially when the nightmares about my death gripped him.

I would tell him everything was all right, we were safe, I was alive, and with him for as long as he would keep me.

"I love you too." I turned my head enough to catch his mouth. His kiss was more methodical this time. Him exploring me, me tasting him.

Sometimes when I painted, that's all we'd do was kiss. Rolling back and forth on the canvas stretched across the studio floor. Wrapped in each other's arms.

Captured in each other's hearts.

Then while the paint was still damp, we'd cut up the canvas and stretch it over a frame. It would dry, and I would apply the pure colors only found in oils.

But the imprints of our bodies, ridges, valleys, faint lines and curves, perfect interruptions in the vast field of color, would remain.

He rocked back, pulling out enough to make me gasp, then slowly went deep again.

We also made love on those canvases. Sometimes, we'd even fall asleep. Even thinned with vegetable oil, the acrylic would dry enough we'd have to peel each other off.

The voids of color left behind were always speckled with lines where our flesh melded together. I surrounded those spaces with the brightest colors. I wanted them to stand out. To be unforgettable. Like the loss of those you love.

Like a mother.

A brother.

Or a boy who gave you your first kiss.

He fondled my cock with one hand and held my shoulder with the other. Braced against the wall, I was at his mercy. The slow movements of his hips quickened into short violent thrusts.

I locked my hands around the back of his head, forcing our bodies together. I claimed his mouth, and he drank my pleas from my lips.

Harder, faster. He thrust into me until sweat soaked my skin and my muscles ached with the need for release.

Small barks of pleasure rumbled in his chest, adding to the thrill of being possessed by him. But I didn't stay with the man in the Armani because I had no choice. I stayed because he set me free.

"Almost." He buried the word into my neck.

"Yes." I clenched around him as he fucked me harder.

He stroked my cock. The calluses on his hands intensified the friction. "Come for me, Paris."

His voice alone, the colors it created, was more than enough to push me over the edge.

My muscles tightened, and a prickling sensation spread across my skin. The crash of euphoria dragged a cry from my chest. I called to him. I pleaded with him. I howled that I loved him.

He jerked hard enough to shove me into the wall, and his cock pulsed inside me. I loved that feeling. The thickening of flesh, the rush of warmth, how he exhaled a sigh against my cheek as he sobered.

The man in the Armani cradled me close, for the longest time. Just us, there, in that narrow hallway, still inside me, reluctant to let go.

I held his hand, and he held mine. Blue and green outlined his cuticles. Mine were stained with orange and yellow.

"So." The word was nothing more than a breath against the shell of my ear. "Tell me about yourself."

I couldn't stop the grin. "What would you like to know?"

"We could start with your name."

"Maybe I don't want to tell you."

"Of course, you do."

"And why is that?"

"Because if you don't, I can't tell you mine."

"And who says I want to know?"

He peppered kisses down the column of my neck. "You will."

"I will?"

"Yes."

"And why is that?"

He pushed a cum-covered finger between my lips. "Because you'll want something to scream when I make you come again." He left a wet trail across my bottom lip to my chin.

"Paris…Duvoe." I turned my head enough to nip his jaw. "Yours?"

"Roy Callahan." He huffed a breath against my throat. "You are so beautiful."

"You always say that."

"I'll always mean it."

And he did.

358

About the Author
Born and bred in Georgia, I am a writer, artist, and general pain in the
ass.
Visit me on the web @ adriennewilder.com
And don't be shy. I love to hear from readers.

17043460R00203

Made in the USA
San Bernardino, CA
26 November 2014